CONTENTS

INTRODUCTION

It goes by many names: "The Crisis," "The Dark Years," "The Walking Plague," as well as newer and more "hip" titles such as "World War Z" or "Z War One." I personally dislike this last moniker as it implies an inevitable "Z War Two." For me, it will always be "The Zombie War," and while many may protest the scientific accuracy of the word *zombie*, they will be hard-pressed to discover a more globally accepted term for the creatures that almost caused our extinction. *Zombie* remains a devastating word, unrivaled in its power to conjure up so many memories or emotions, and it is these memories, and emotions, that are the subject of this book.

This record of the greatest conflict in human history owes its genesis to a much smaller, much more personal conflict between me and the chairperson of the United Nation's Postwar Commission Report. My initial work for the Commission could be described as nothing short of a labor of love. My travel stipend, my security access, my battery of translators, both human and electronic, as well as my small, but nearly priceless voice-activated transcription "pal" (the greatest gift the world's slowest typist could ask for), all spoke to the respect and value my work was afforded on this project. So, needless to say, it came as a shock when I found almost half of that work deleted from the report's final edition.

"It was all too intimate," the chairperson said during one of our many "animated" discussions. "Too many opinions, too many feelings. That's not what this report is about. We need clear facts and figures, unclouded by the human factor." Of course, she was right. The official report was a collection of cold, hard data, an objective "after-action report" that would allow future generations to study the events of that apocalyptic decade without being influenced by "the human factor." But isn't the human factor what connects us so deeply to our past? Will future generations care as much for chronologies and casualty statistics as they would for the personal accounts of individuals not so different from themselves? By excluding the human factor, aren't we risking the kind of personal detachment from a history that may, heaven forbid, lead us one day to repeat it? And in the end, isn't the human factor the only true difference between us and the enemy we now refer to as "the living dead"? I presented this argument, perhaps less professionally than was appropriate, to my "boss," who after my final exclamation of "we can't let these stories die" responded immediately with, "Then don't. Write a book. You've still got all your notes, and the legal freedom to use them. Who's stopping you from keeping these stories alive in the pages of your own (expletive deleted) book?"

Some critics will, no doubt, take issue with the concept of a personal history book so soon after the end of worldwide hostilities. After all, it has been only twelve years since VA Day was declared in the continental United States, and barely a decade since the last major world power celebrated its deliverance on "Victory in China Day." Given that most people consider VC Day to be the official end, then how can we have real perspective when, in the words of a UN colleague, "We've been at peace about as long as we were at war." This is a valid argument, and one that begs a response. In the case of this generation, those who have fought and suffered to win us this decade of peace, time is as much an enemy as it is an ally. Yes, the coming years will provide hindsight, adding greater wisdom to memories seen through the light of a matured, postwar world. But many of those memories may no longer exist, trapped in bodies and spirits too damaged or infirm to see the fruits of their victory harvested. It is no great secret that global life expectancy is a mere shadow of its former prewar figure. Malnutrition, pollution, the rise of previously eradicated ailments, even in the United States, with its resurgent economy and universal health care are the present reality; there simply are not enough resources to care for all the physical and psychological casualties. It is because of this enemy, the enemy of time, that I have forsaken the luxury of hindsight and published these survivors' accounts. Perhaps decades from now, someone will take up the task of recording the recollections of the much older, much wiser survivors. Perhaps I might even be one of them.

Although this is primarily a book of memories, it includes many of the details, technological, social, economic, and so on, found in the original Commission Report, as they are related to the stories of those voices featured in these pages. This is their book, not mine, and I have tried to maintain as invisible a presence as possible. Those questions included in the text are only there to illustrate those that might have been posed by readers. I have attempted to reserve judgment, or commentary of any kind, and if there is a human factor that should be removed, let it be my own.

WARNINGS

GREATER CHONGQING, THE UNITED FEDERATION OF CHINA

[At its prewar height, this region boasted a population of over thirty-five million people. Now, there are barely fifty thousand. Reconstruction funds have been slow to arrive in this part of the country, the government choosing to concentrate on the more densely populated coast. There is no central power grid, no running water besides the Yangtze River. But the streets are clear of rubble and the local "security council" has prevented any postwar outbreaks. The chairman of that council is Kwang Jingshu, a medical doctor who, despite his advanced age and wartime injuries, still manages to make house calls to all his patients.]

The first outbreak I saw was in a remote village that officially had no name. The residents called it "New Dachang," but this was more out of nostalgia than anything else. Their former home, "Old Dachang," had stood since the period of the Three Kingdoms, with farms and houses and even trees said to be centuries old. When the Three Gorges Dam was completed, and reservoir waters began to rise, much of Dachang had been disassembled, brick by brick, then rebuilt on higher ground. This New Dachang, however, was not a town anymore, but a "national historic museum." It must have been a heartbreaking irony for those poor peasants, to see their town saved but then only being able to visit it as a tourist. Maybe that is why some of them chose to name their newly constructed hamlet "New Dachang" to preserve some connection to their heritage, even if it was only in name. I personally didn't know that this other New Dachang existed, so you can imagine how confused I was when the call came in.

The hospital was quiet; it had been a slow night, even for the increasing number of drunk-driving accidents. Motorcycles were becoming very popular. We used to say that your Harley-Davidsons killed more young Chinese than all the GIs in the Korean War. That's why I was so grateful for a quiet shift. I was tired, my back and feet ached. I was on my way out to smoke a cigarette and watch the dawn when I heard my name being paged. The receptionist that night was new and couldn't quite understand the dialect. There had been an accident, or an illness. It was an emergency, that part was obvious, and could we please send help at once.

What could I say? The younger doctors, the kids who think medicine is just a way to pad their bank accounts, they certainly weren't going to go help some "nongmin" just for the sake of helping. I guess I'm still an old revolutionary at heart. "Our duty is to hold ourselves responsible to the people."[1] Those words still mean something to me . . . and I tried to remember that as my Deer[2] bounced and banged over dirt roads the government had promised but never quite gotten around to paving.

I had a devil of a time finding the place. Officially, it didn't exist and therefore wasn't on any map. I became lost several times and had to ask directions from locals who kept thinking I meant the museum town. I was in an impatient mood by the time I reached the small collection of hilltop

---

1. From "Quotations from Chairman Maozedong," originally from "The Situation and Our Policy After the Victory in the War of Resistance Against Japan," August 13, 1945.
2. A prewar automobile manufactured in the People's Republic.

homes. I remember thinking, *This had better be damned serious*. Once I saw their faces, I regretted my wish.

There were seven of them, all on cots, all barely conscious. The villagers had moved them into their new communal meeting hall. The walls and floor were bare cement. The air was cold and damp. *Of course they're sick*, I thought. I asked the villagers who had been taking care of these people. They said no one, it wasn't "safe." I noticed that the door had been locked from the outside. The villagers were clearly terrified. They cringed and whispered; some kept their distance and prayed. Their behavior made me angry, not at them, you understand, not as individuals, but what they represented about our country. After centuries of foreign oppression, exploitation, and humiliation, we were finally reclaiming our rightful place as humanity's middle kingdom. We were the world's richest and most dynamic superpower, masters of everything from outer space to cyber space. It was the dawn of what the world was finally acknowledging as "The Chinese Century" and yet so many of us still lived like these ignorant peasants, as stagnant and superstitious as the earliest Yangshao savages.

I was still lost in my grand, cultural criticism when I knelt to examine the first patient. She was running a high fever, forty degrees centigrade, and she was shivering violently. Barely coherent, she whimpered slightly when I tried to move her limbs. There was a wound in her right forearm, a bite mark. As I examined it more closely, I realized that it wasn't from an animal. The bite radius and teeth marks had to have come from a small, or possibly young, human being. Although I hypothesized this to be the source of the infection, the actual injury was surprisingly clean. I asked the villagers, again, who had been taking care of these people. Again, they told me no one. I knew this could not be true. The human mouth is packed with bacteria, even more so than the most unhygienic dog. If no one had cleaned this woman's wound, why wasn't it throbbing with infection?

I examined the six other patients. All showed similar symptoms, all had similar wounds on various parts of their bodies. I asked one man, the most lucid of the group, who or what had inflicted these injuries. He told me it had happened when they had tried to subdue "him."

"Who?" I asked.

I found "Patient Zero" behind the locked door of an abandoned house across town. He was twelve years old. His wrists and feet were bound with plastic packing twine. Although he'd rubbed off the skin around his bonds, there was no blood. There was also no blood on his other wounds, not on the gouges on his legs or arms, or from the large dry gap where his right big toe had been. He was writhing like an animal; a gag muffled his growls.

At first the villagers tried to hold me back. They warned me not to touch him, that he was "cursed." I shrugged them off and reached for my mask and gloves. The boy's skin was as cold and gray as the cement on which he lay. I could find neither his heartbeat nor his pulse. His eyes were wild, wide and sunken back in their sockets. They remained locked on me like a predatory beast. Throughout the examination he was inexplicably hostile, reaching for me with his bound hands and snapping at me through his gag.

His movements were so violent I had to call for two of the largest villagers to help me hold him down. Initially they wouldn't budge, cowering in the doorway like baby rabbits. I explained that there was no risk of infection if they used gloves and masks. When they shook their heads, I made it an order, even though I had no lawful authority to do so.

That was all it took. The two oxen knelt beside me. One held the boy's feet while the other grasped his hands. I tried to take a blood sample and instead extracted only brown, viscous matter. As I was withdrawing the needle, the boy began another bout of violent struggling.

One of my "orderlies," the one responsible for his arms, gave up trying to hold them and thought it might safer if he just braced them against the floor with his knees. But the boy jerked again and I heard his left arm snap. Jagged ends of both radius and ulna bones stabbed through his gray flesh. Although the boy didn't cry out, didn't even seem to notice, it was enough for both assistants to leap back and run from the room.

I instinctively retreated several paces myself. I am embarrassed to admit this; I have been a doctor for most of my adult life. I was trained and . . . you could even say "raised" by the People's Liberation Army. I've treated more than my share of combat injuries, faced my own death on more than one occasion, and now I was scared, truly scared, of this frail child.

The boy began to twist in my direction, his arm ripped completely free. Flesh and muscle tore from one another until there was nothing except the stump. His now free right arm, still tied to the severed left hand, dragged his body across the floor.

I hurried outside, locking the door behind me. I tried to compose myself, control my fear and shame. My voice still cracked as I asked the villagers how the boy had been infected. No one answered. I began to hear banging on the door, the boy's fist pounding weakly against the thin wood. It was all I could do not to jump at the sound. I prayed they would not notice the color draining from my face. I shouted, as much from fear as frustration, that I *had* to know what happened to this child.

A young woman came forward, maybe his mother. You could tell that she had been crying for days; her eyes were dry and deeply red. She admitted that it had happened when the boy and his father were "moon fishing," a term that describes diving for treasure among the sunken ruins of the Three Gorges Reservoir. With more than eleven hundred abandoned villages, towns, and even cities, there was always the hope of recovering something valuable. It was a very common practice in those days, and also very illegal. She explained that they weren't looting, that it was their own village, Old Dachang, and they were just trying to recover some heirlooms from the remaining houses that hadn't been moved. She repeated the point, and I had to interrupt her with promises not to inform the police. She finally explained that the boy came up crying with a bite mark on his foot. He didn't know what had happened, the water had been too dark and muddy. His father was never seen again.

I reached for my cell phone and dialed the number of Doctor Gu Wen Kuei, an old comrade from my army days who now worked at the Institute of Infectious Diseases at Chongqing University.[3] We exchanged pleasantries, discussing our health, our grandchildren; it was only proper. I then told him about the outbreak and listened as he made some joke about the

---

3. The Institute of Infectious and Parasitic Diseases of the First Affiliated Hospital, Chongqing Medical University.

hygiene habits of hillbillies. I tried to chuckle along but continued that I thought the incident might be significant. Almost reluctantly he asked me what the symptoms were. I told him everything: the bites, the fever, the boy, the arm . . . his face suddenly stiffened. His smile died.

He asked me to show him the infected. I went back into the meeting hall and waved the phone's camera over each of the patients. He asked me to move the camera closer to some of the wounds themselves. I did so and when I brought the screen back to my face, I saw that his video image had been cut.

"Stay where you are," he said, just a distant, removed voice now. "Take the names of all who have had contact with the infected. Restrain those already infected. If any have passed into coma, vacate the room and secure the exit." His voice was flat, robotic, as if he had rehearsed this speech or was reading from something. He asked me, "Are you armed?" "Why would I be?" I asked. He told me he would get back to me, all business again. He said he had to make a few calls and that I should expect "support" within several hours.

They were there in less than one, fifty men in large army Z-8A helicopters; all were wearing hazardous materials suits. They said they were from the Ministry of Health. I don't know who they thought they were kidding. With their bullying swagger, their intimidating arrogance, even these backwater bumpkins could recognize the Guoanbu.[4]

Their first priority was the meeting hall. The patients were carried out on stretchers, their limbs shackled, their mouths gagged. Next, they went for the boy. He came out in a body bag. His mother was wailing as she and the rest of the village were rounded up for "examinations." Their names were taken, their blood drawn. One by one they were stripped and photographed. The last one to be exposed was a withered old woman. She had a thin, crooked body, a face with a thousand lines and tiny feet that had to have been bound when she was a girl. She was shaking her bony fist at the

4. Guokia Anquan Bu: The prewar Ministry of State Security.

"doctors." "This is your punishment!" she shouted. "This is revenge for Fengdu!"

She was referring to the City of Ghosts, whose temples and shrines were dedicated to the underworld. Like Old Dachang, it had been an unlucky obstacle to China's next Great Leap Forward. It had been evacuated, then demolished, then almost entirely drowned. I've never been a superstitious person and I've never allowed myself to be hooked on the opiate of the people. I'm a doctor, a scientist. I believe only in what I can see and touch. I've never seen Fengdu as anything but a cheap, kitschy tourist trap. Of course this ancient crone's words had no effect on me, but her tone, her anger . . . she had witnessed enough calamity in her years upon the earth: the warlords, the Japanese, the insane nightmare of the Cultural Revolution . . . she knew that another storm was coming, even if she didn't have the education to understand it.

My colleague Dr. Kuei had understood all too well. He'd even risked his neck to warn me, to give me enough time to call and maybe alert a few others before the "Ministry of Health" arrived. It was something he had said . . . a phrase he hadn't used in a very long time, not since those "minor" border clashes with the Soviet Union. That was back in 1969. We had been in an earthen bunker on our side of the Ussuri, less than a kilometer downriver from Chen Bao. The Russians were preparing to retake the island, their massive artillery hammering our forces.

Gu and I had been trying to remove shrapnel from the belly of this soldier not much younger than us. The boy's lower intestines had been torn open, his blood and excrement were all over our gowns. Every seven seconds a round would land close by and we would have to bend over his body to shield the wound from falling earth, and every time we would be close enough to hear him whimper softly for his mother. There were other voices, too, rising from the pitch darkness just beyond the entrance to our bunker, desperate, angry voices that weren't supposed to be on our side of the river. We had two infantrymen stationed at the bunker's entrance. One of them shouted "Spetsnaz!" and started firing into the dark. We could hear other shots now as well, ours or theirs, we couldn't tell.

Another round hit and we bent over the dying boy. Gu's face was only a few centimeters from mine. There was sweat pouring down his forehead. Even in the dim light of one paraffin lantern, I could see that he was shaking and pale. He looked at the patient, then at the doorway, then at me, and suddenly he said, "Don't worry, everything's going to be all right." Now, this is a man who has never said a positive thing in his life. Gu was a worrier, a neurotic curmudgeon. If he had a headache, it was a brain tumor; if it looked like rain, this year's harvest was ruined. This was his way of controlling the situation, his lifelong strategy for always coming out ahead. Now, when reality looked more dire than any of his fatalistic predictions, he had no choice but to turn tail and charge in the opposite direction. "Don't worry, everything's going to be all right." For the first time everything turned out as he predicted. The Russians never crossed the river and we even managed to save our patient.

For years afterward I would tease him about what it took to pry out a little ray of sunshine, and he would always respond that it would take a hell of a lot worse to get him to do it again. Now we were old men, and something worse was about to happen. It was right after he asked me if I was armed. "No," I said, "why should I be?" There was a brief silence, I'm sure other ears were listening. "Don't worry," he said, "everything's going to be all right." That was when I realized that this was not an isolated outbreak. I ended the call and quickly placed another to my daughter in Guangzhou.

Her husband worked for China Telecom and spent at least one week of every month abroad. I told her it would be a good idea to accompany him the next time he left and that she should take my granddaughter and stay for as long as they could. I didn't have time to explain; my signal was jammed just as the first helicopter appeared. The last thing I managed to say to her was "Don't worry, everything's going to be all right."

[Kwang Jingshu was arrested by the MSS and incarcerated without formal charges. By the time he escaped, the outbreak had spread beyond China's borders.]

❦

LHASA, THE PEOPLE'S REPUBLIC OF TIBET

[The world's most populous city is still recovering from the re-
sults of last week's general election. The Social Democrats have
smashed the Llamist Party in a landslide victory and the streets
are still roaring with revelers. I meet Nury Televaldi at a
crowded sidewalk café. We have to shout over the euphoric din.]

Before the outbreak started, overland smuggling was never popular. To
arrange for the passports, the fake tour buses, the contacts and protection
on the other side all took a lot of money. Back then, the only two lucrative
routes were into Thailand or Myanmar. Where I used to live, in Kashi, the
only option was into the ex-Soviet republics. No one wanted to go there,
and that is why I wasn't initially a shetou.[1] I was an importer: raw opium,
uncut diamonds, girls, boys, whatever was valuable from those primitive
excuses for countries. The outbreak changed all that. Suddenly we were
besieged with offers, and not just from the liudong renkou,[2] but also, as you
say, from people on the up-and-up. I had urban professionals, private farmers, even low-level government officials. These were people who had a
lot to lose. They didn't care where they were going, they just needed to
get out.

Did you know what they were fleeing?

We'd heard the rumors. We'd even had an outbreak somewhere in Kashi.
The government had hushed it up pretty quickly. But we guessed, we knew
something was wrong.

---

1. Shetou: A "snake head," the smuggler of "renshe" or "human snake" of refugees.
2. Liudong renkou: China's "floating population" of homeless labor.

Didn't the government try to shut you down?

Officially they did. Penalties on smuggling were hardened; border check-points were strengthened. They even executed a few shetou, publicly, just to make an example. If you didn't know the true story, if you didn't know it from my end, you'd think it was an efficient crackdown.

You're saying it wasn't?

I'm saying I made a lot of people rich: border guards, bureaucrats, police, even the mayor. These were still good times for China, where the best way to honor Chairman Mao's memory was to see his face on as many hundred yuan notes as possible.

You were that successful.

Kashi was a boomtown. I think 90 percent, maybe more, of all westbound, overland traffic came through with even a little left over for air travel.

Air travel?

Just a little. I only dabbled in transporting renshe by air, a few cargo flights now and then to Kazakhstan or Russia. Small-time jobs. It wasn't like the east, where Guangdong or Jiangsu were getting thousands of people out every week.

Could you elaborate?

Air smuggling became big business in the eastern provinces. These were rich clients, the ones who could afford prebooked travel packages and first-class tourist visas. They would step off the plane at London or Rome, or even San Francisco, check into their hotels, go out for a day's sightseeing, and simply vanish into thin air. That was big money. I'd always wanted to break into air transport.

But what about infection? Wasn't there a risk of being discovered?

That was only later, after Flight 575. Initially there weren't too many infected taking these flights. If they did, they were in the very early stages. Air transport shetou were very careful. If you showed any signs of advanced infection, they wouldn't go near you. They were out to protect their business. The golden rule was, you couldn't fool foreign immigration officials until you fooled your shetou first. You had to look and act completely healthy, and even then, it was always a race against time. Before Flight 575, I heard this one story about a couple, a very well-to-do businessman and his wife. He had been bitten. Not a serious one, you understand, but one of the "slow burns," where all the major blood vessels are missed. I'm sure they thought there was a cure in the West, a lot of the infected did. Apparently, they reached their hotel room in Paris just as he began to collapse. His wife tried to call the doctor, but he forbade it. He was afraid they would be sent back. Instead, he ordered her to abandon him, to leave now before he lapsed into coma. I hear that she did, and after two days of groans and commotion, the hotel staff finally ignored the DO NOT DISTURB sign and broke into the room. I'm not sure if that is how the Paris outbreak started, though it would make sense.

You say they didn't call for a doctor, that they were afraid they'd be sent back, but then why try to find a cure in the West?

You really don't understand a refugee's heart, do you? These people were desperate. They were trapped between their infections and being rounded up and "treated" by their own government. If you had a loved one, a family member, a child, who was infected, and you thought there was a shred of hope in some other country, wouldn't you do everything in your power to get there? Wouldn't you want to believe there was hope?

You said that man's wife, along with the other renshe, vanished into thin air.

It has always been this way, even before the outbreaks. Some stay with family, some with friends. Many of the poorer ones had to work off their bao[3] to the local Chinese mafia. The majority of them simply melted into the host country's underbelly.

The low-income areas?

If that's what you want to call them. What better place to hide than among that part of society that no one else even wants to acknowledge. How else could so many outbreaks have started in so many First World ghettos?

It's been said that many shetou propagated the myth of a miracle cure in other countries.

Some.

Did you?

    [Pause.]

No.

    [Another pause.]

How did Flight 575 change air smuggling?

Restrictions were tightened, but only in certain countries. Airline shetou were careful but they were also resourceful. They used to have this saying, "every rich man's house has a servant's entrance."

What does that mean?

If western Europe has increased its security, go through eastern Europe. If the U.S. won't let you in, go through Mexico. I'm sure it helped make the

---

3. Bao: The debt many refugees incurred during their exodus.

rich white countries feel safer, even though they had infestations already bubbling within their borders. This is not my area of expertise, you remember, I was primarily land transport, and my target countries were in central Asia.

Were they easier to enter?

They practically begged us for the business. Those countries were in such economic shambles, their officials were so backward and corrupt, they actually helped us with the paperwork in exchange for a percentage of our fee. There were even shetou, or whatever they called them in their barbarian babble, who worked with us to get renshe across the old Soviet republics into countries like India or Russia, even Iran, although I never asked or wanted to know where any of the renshe were going. My job ended at the border. Just get their papers stamped, their vehicles tagged, pay the guards off, and take my cut.

Did you see many infected?

Not in the beginning. The blight worked too fast. It wasn't like air travel. It might take weeks to reach Kashi, and even the slowest of burns, I've been told, couldn't last longer than a few days. Infected clients usually reanimated somewhere on the road, where they would be recognized and collected by the local police. Later, as the infestations multiplied and the police became overwhelmed, I began to see a lot of infected on my route.

Were they dangerous?

Rarely. Their family usually had them bound and gagged. You'd see something moving in the back of a car, squirming softly under clothing or heavy blankets. You'd hear banging from a car's boot, or, later, from crates with airholes in the backs of vans. Airholes . . . they really didn't know what was happening to their loved ones.

Did you?

By then, yes, but I knew trying to explain it to them would be a hopeless cause. I just took their money and sent them on their way. I was lucky. I never had to deal with the problems of sea smuggling.

That was more difficult?

And dangerous. My associates from the coastal provinces were the ones who had to contend with the possibility of an infected breaking its bonds and contaminating the entire hold.

What did they do?

I've heard of various "solutions." Sometimes ships would pull up to a stretch of deserted coast—it didn't matter if it was the intended country, it could have been any coast—and "unload" the infected renshe onto the beach. I've heard of some captains making for an empty stretch of open sea and just tossing the whole writhing lot overboard. That might explain the early cases of swimmers and divers starting to disappear without a trace, or why you'd hear of people all around the world saying they saw them walking out of the surf. At least I never had to deal with that.

I did have one similar incident, the one that convinced me it was time to quit. There was this truck, a beat-up old jalopy. You could hear the moans from the trailer. A lot of fists were slamming against the aluminum. It was actually swaying back and forth. In the cab there was a very wealthy investment banker from Xi'an. He'd made a lot of money buying up American credit card debt. He had enough to pay for his entire extended family. The man's Armani suit was rumpled and torn. There were scratch marks down the side of his face, and his eyes had that frantic fire I was starting to see more of every day. The driver's eyes had a different look, the same one as me, the look that maybe money wasn't going to be much good for much longer. I slipped the man an extra fifty and wished him luck. That was all I could do.

Where was the truck headed?

Kyrgyzstan.

❧

METEORA, GREECE

[The monasteries are built into the steep, inaccessible rocks, some buildings sitting perched atop high, almost vertical columns. While originally an attractive refuge from the Ottoman Turks, it later proved just as secure from the living dead. Postwar staircases, mostly metal or wood, and all easily retractable, cater to the growing influx of both pilgrims and tourists. Meteora has become a popular destination for both groups in recent years. Some seek wisdom and spiritual enlightenment, some simply search for peace. Stanley MacDonald is one of the latter. A veteran of almost every campaign across the expanse of his native Canada, he first encountered the living dead during a different war, when the Third Battalion of Princess Patricia's Canadian Light Infantry was involved in drug interdiction operations in Kyrgyzstan.]

Please don't confuse us with the American "Alpha teams." This was long before their deployment, before "the Panic," before the Israeli self-quarantine . . . this was even before the first major public outbreak in Cape Town. This was just at the beginning of the spread, before anybody knew anything about what was coming. Our mission was strictly conventional, opium and hash, the primary export crop of terrorists around the world. That's all we'd ever encountered in that rocky wasteland. Traders and thugs and locally hired muscle. That's all we expected. That's all we were ready for.

The cave entrance was easy to find. We'd tracked it back from the blood trail leading to the caravan. Right away we knew something was wrong. There were no bodies. Rival tribes always left their victims laid out and mutilated as a warning to others. There was plenty of blood, blood and bits of brown rotting flesh, but the only corpses we found were the pack mules. They'd been brought down, not shot, by what looked like wild animals. Their bellies were torn out and large bite wounds covered their flesh. We guessed it had to be wild dogs. Packs of those damn things roamed the valleys, big and nasty as Arctic wolves.

What was most puzzling was the cargo, still in their saddlebags, or just scattered about the bodies. Now, even if this wasn't a territorial hit, even if it was a religious or tribal revenge killing, no one just abandons fifty kilos of prime, raw, Bad Brown,[1] or perfectly good assault rifles, or expensive personal trophies like watches, mini disc players, and GPS locaters.

The blood trail led up the mountain path from the massacre in the wadi. A lot of blood. Anyone who lost that much wouldn't be getting up again. Only somehow he did. He hadn't been treated. There were no other track marks. From what we could tell, this man had run, bled, fallen facedown— we still could see his bloody face-mark imprinted in the sand. Somehow, without suffocating, without bleeding to death, he'd lain there for some time, then just gotten up again and started walking. These new tracks were very different from the old. They were slower, closer together. His right foot was dragging, clearly why he'd lost his shoe, an old, worn-out Nike high-top. The drag marks were sprinkled with fluid. Not blood, not human, but droplets of hard, black, crusted ooze that none of us recognized. We followed these and the drag marks to the entrance of the cave.

There was no opening fire, no reception of any kind. We found the tunnel entrance unguarded and wide open. Immediately we began to see bodies, men killed by their own booby traps. They looked like they'd been trying . . . running . . . to get out.

Beyond them, in the first chamber, we saw our first evidence of a

1. Bad Brown: A nickname for the type of opium grown in the Badakhshan Province of Afghanistan.

one-sided firefight, one-sided because only one wall of the cavern was pockmarked by small arms. Opposite that wall were the shooters. They'd been torn apart. Their limbs, their bones, shredded and gnawed . . . some still clutching their weapons, one of those severed hands with an old Makarov still in the grip. The hand was missing a finger. I found it across the room, along with the body of another unarmed man who'd been hit over a hundred times. Several rounds had taken the top of his head off. The finger was still stuck between his teeth.

Every chamber told a similar story. We found smashed barricades, discarded weapons. We found more bodies, or pieces of them. Only the intact ones died from head shots. We found meat, chewed, pulped flesh bulging from their throats and stomachs. You could see by the blood trails, the footprints, the shell casings, and pockmarks that the entire battle had originated from the infirmary.

We discovered several cots, all bloody. At the end of the room we found a headless . . . I'm guessing, doctor, lying on the dirt floor next to a cot with soiled sheets and clothes and an old, left-footed, worn-out Nike high-top.

The last tunnel we checked had collapsed from the use of a booby-trapped demolition charge. A hand was sticking out of the limestone. It was still moving. I reacted from the gut, leaned forward, grabbed the hand, felt that grip. Like steel, almost crushed my fingers. I pulled back, tried to get away. It wouldn't let me go. I pulled harder, dug my feet in. First the arm came free, then the head, the torn face, wide eyes and gray lips, then the other hand, grabbing my arm and squeezing, then came the shoulders. I fell back, the thing's top half coming with me. The waist down was still jammed under the rocks, still connected to the upper torso by a line of entrails. It was still moving, still clawing me, trying to pull my arm into its mouth. I reached for my weapon.

The burst was angled upward, connecting just under and behind the chin and spraying its brains across the ceiling above us. I'd been the only one in the tunnel when it happened. I was the only witness . . .

[He pauses.]

"Exposure to unknown chemical agents." That's what they told me back in Edmonton, that or an adverse reaction to our own prophylactic medication. They threw in a healthy dose of PTSD[2] for good measure. I just needed rest, rest and long-term "evaluation" . . .

"Evaluation" . . . that's what happens when it's your own side. It's only "interrogation" when it's the enemy. They teach you how to resist the enemy, how to protect your mind and spirit. They don't teach you how to resist your own people, especially people who think they're trying to "help" you see "the truth." They didn't break me, I broke myself. I wanted to believe them and I wanted them to help me. I was a good soldier, well trained, experienced; I knew what I could do to my fellow human beings and what they could do to me. I thought I was ready for anything. [He looks out at the valley, his eyes unfocused.] Who in his right mind could have been ready for this?

❦

THE AMAZON RAIN FOREST, BRAZIL

[I arrive blindfolded, so as not to reveal my "hosts'" location. Outsiders call them the Yanomami, "The Fierce People," and it is unknown whether this supposedly warlike nature or the fact that their new village hangs suspended from the tallest trees was what allowed them to weather the crisis as well, if not better, than even the most industrialized nation. It is not clear whether Fernando Oliveira, the emaciated, drug-addicted white man "from the edge of the world," is their guest, mascot, or prisoner.]

I was still a doctor, that's what I told myself. Yes, I was rich, and getting richer all the time, but at least my success came from performing necessary

2. PTSD: Post-traumatic stress disorder.

medical procedures. I wasn't just slicing and dicing little teenage noses or sewing Sudanese "pintos" onto sheboy pop divas.[1] I was still a doctor, I was still helping people, and if it was so "immoral" to the self-righteous, hypocritical North, why did their citizens keep coming?

The package arrived from the airport an hour before the patient, packed in ice in a plastic picnic cooler. Hearts are extremely rare. Not like livers or skin tissue, and certainly not like kidneys, which, after the "presumed consent" law was passed, you could get from almost any hospital or morgue in the country.

Was it tested?

For what? In order to test for something, you have to know what you're looking for. We didn't know about Walking Plague then. We were concerned with conventional ailments—hepatitis or HIV/AIDS—and we didn't even have time to test for those.

Why is that?

Because the flight had already taken so long. Organs can't be kept on ice forever. We were already pushing our luck with this one.

Where had it come from?

China, most likely. My broker operated out of Macau. We trusted him. His record was solid. When he assured us that the package was "clean," I took him at his word; I had to. He knew the risks involved, so did I, so did the patient. Herr Muller, in addition to his conventional heart ailments, was cursed with the extremely rare genetic defect of dextrocardia with situs inversus. His organs lay in their exact opposite position; the liver was on the left side, the heart entryways on the right, and so on. You see the unique situation we were facing. We couldn't have just transplanted a conven-

---

1. It has been alleged that, before the war, the sexual organs of Sudanese men convicted of adultery were severed and sold on the world black market.

tional heart and turned it backward. It just doesn't work that way. We needed another fresh, healthy heart from a "donor" with exactly the same condition. Where else but China could we find that kind of luck?

It was luck?

[Smiles.] And "political expediency." I told my broker what I needed, gave him the specifics, and sure enough, three weeks later I received an e-mail simply titled "We have a match."

So you performed the operation.

I assisted, Doctor Silva performed the actual procedure. He was a prestigious heart surgeon who worked the top cases at the Hospital Israelita Albert Einstein in São Paulo. Arrogant bastard, even for a cardiologist. It killed my ego to have to work with . . . under . . . that prick, treating me like I was a first-year resident. But what was I going to do . . . Herr Muller needed a new heart and my beach house needed a new herbal Jacuzzi.

Herr Muller never came out of the anesthesia. As he lay in the recovery room, barely minutes after closing, his symptoms began to appear. His temperature, pulse rate, oxygen saturation . . . I was worried, and it must have tickled my more "experienced colleague." He told me that it was either a common reaction to the immunosuppressant medication, or the simple, expected complications of an overweight, unhealthy, sixty-seven-year-old man who'd just gone through one of the most traumatic procedures in modern medicine. I'm surprised he didn't pat me on the head, the prick. He told me to go home, take a shower, get some sleep, maybe call a girl or two, relax. He'd stay and watch him and call me if there was any change.

[Oliveira purses his lips angrily and chews another wad of the mysterious leaves at his side.]

And what was I supposed to think? Maybe it was the drugs, the OKT 3. Or maybe I was just being a worrier. This was my first heart transplant.

What did I know? Still . . . it bothered me so much that the last thing I wanted to do was sleep. So I did what any good doctor should do when his patient is suffering; I hit the town. I danced, I drank, I had salaciously indecent things done to me by who knows who or what. I wasn't even sure it was my phone vibrating the first couple of times. It must have been at least an hour before I finally picked up. Graziela, my receptionist, was in a real state. She told me that Herr Muller had slipped into a coma an hour before. I was in my car before she could finish the sentence. It was a thirty-minute drive back to the clinic, and I cursed both Silva and myself every second of the way. So I *did* have reason to be concerned! So I *was* right! Ego, you could say; even though to be right meant dire consequences for me as well, I still relished tarnishing the invincible Silva's reputation.

I arrived to find Graziela trying to comfort a hysterical Rosi, one of my nurses. The poor girl was inconsolable. I gave her a good one across the cheek—that calmed her down—and asked her what was going on. Why were there spots of blood on her uniform? Where was Doctor Silva? Why were some of the other patients out of their rooms, and what the hell was that goddamn banging noise? She told me that Herr Muller had flat-lined, suddenly, and unexpectedly. She explained that they had been trying to revive him when Herr Muller had opened his eyes and bitten Doctor Silva on the hand. The two of them struggled; Rosi tried to help but was almost bitten herself. She left Silva, ran from the room, and locked the door behind her.

I almost laughed. It was so ridiculous. Maybe Superman had slipped up, misdiagnosed him, if that was possible. Maybe he'd just risen from the bed, and, in a stupor, had tried to grab on to Doctor Silva to steady himself. There had to be a reasonable explanation . . . and yet, there was the blood on her uniform and the muffled noise from Herr Muller's room. I went back to the car for my gun, more so to calm Graziela and Rosi than for myself.

You carried a gun?

I lived in Rio. What do you think I carried, my "pinto"? I went back to Herr Muller's room, I knocked several times. I heard nothing. I whispered his and Silva's names. No one responded. I noticed blood seeping out from under the door. I entered and found it covering the floor. Silva was lying in the far corner, Muller crouching over him with his fat, pale, hairy back to me. I can't remember how I got his attention, whether I called his name, uttered a swear, or did anything at all but just stand there. Muller turned to me, bits of bloody meat falling from his open mouth. I saw that his steel sutures had been partially pried open and a thick, black, gelatinous fluid oozed through the incision. He got shakily to his feet, lumbering slowly toward me.

I raised my pistol, aiming at his new heart. It was a "Desert Eagle," Israeli, large and showy, which is why I'd chosen it. I'd never fired it before, thank God. I wasn't ready for the recoil. The round went wild, literally blowing his head off. Lucky, that's all, this lucky fool standing there with a smoking gun, and a stream of warm urine running down my leg. Now it was my turn to get slapped, several times by Graziela, before I came to my senses and telephoned the police.

Were you arrested?

Are you crazy? These were my partners, how do you think I was able to get my homegrown organs. How do you think I was able to take care of this mess? They're very good at that. They helped explain to my other patients that a homicidal maniac had broken into the clinic and killed both Herr Muller and Doctor Silva. They also made sure that none of the staff said anything to contradict that story.

What about the bodies?

They listed Silva as the victim of a probable "car jacking." I don't know where they put his body; maybe some ghetto side street in the City of God, a drug score gone bad just to give the story more credibility. I hope they just burned him, or buried him . . . deep.

Do you think he . . .

I don't know. His brain was intact when he died. If he wasn't in a body bag . . . if the ground was soft enough. How long would it have taken to dig out?

[He chews another leaf, offering me some. I decline.]

And Mister Muller?

No explanation, not to his widow, not to the Austrian embassy. Just another kidnapped tourist who'd been careless in a dangerous town. I don't know if Frau Muller ever believed that story, or if she ever tried to investigate further. She probably never realized how damn lucky she was.

Why was she lucky?

Are you serious? What if he hadn't reanimated in my clinic? What if he'd managed to make it all the way home?

Is that possible?

Of course it is! Think about it. Because the infection started in the heart, the virus had direct access to his circulatory system, so it probably reached his brain seconds after it was implanted. Now you take another organ, a liver or a kidney, or even a section of grafted skin. That's going to take a lot longer, especially if the virus is only present in small amounts.

But the donor . . .

Doesn't have to be fully reanimated. What if he's just newly infected? The organ may not be completely saturated. It might only have an infinitesimal trace. You put that organ in another body, it might take days, weeks, before it eventually works its way out into the bloodstream. By that point the patient might be well on the way to recovery, happy and healthy and living a regular life.

But whoever is removing the organ . . .

. . . may not know what he's dealing with. I didn't. These were the very early stages, when nobody knew anything yet. Even if they did know, like elements in the Chinese army . . . you want to talk about immoral . . . Years before the outbreak they'd been making millions on organs from executed political prisoners. You think something like a little virus is going to make them stop sucking that golden tit?

But how . . .

You remove the heart not long after the victim's died . . . maybe even while he's still alive . . . they used to do that, you know, remove living organs to ensure their freshness . . . pack it in ice, put it on a plane for Rio . . . China used to be the largest exporter of human organs on the world market. Who knows how many infected corneas, infected pituitary glands . . . Mother of God, who knows how many infected kidneys they pumped into the global market. And that's just the organs! You want to talk about the "donated" eggs from political prisoners, the sperm, the blood? You think immigration was the only way the infection swept the planet? Not all the initial outbreaks were Chinese nationals. Can you explain all those stories of people suddenly dying of unexplained causes, then reanimating without ever having been bitten? Why did so many outbreaks begin in hospitals? Illegal Chinese immigrants weren't going to hospitals. Do you know how many thousands of people got illegal organ transplants in those early years leading up to the Great Panic? Even if 10 percent of them were infected, even 1 percent . . .

Do you have any proof of this theory?

No . . . but that doesn't mean it didn't happen! When I think about how many transplants I performed, all those patients from Europe, the Arab world, even the self-righteous United States. Few of you Yankees asked where your new kidney or pancreas was coming from, be it a slum kid from the City of God or some unlucky student in a Chinese political prison. You didn't know, you didn't care. You just signed your traveler's checks, went under the knife, then went home to Miami or New York or wherever.

Did you ever try to track these patients down, warn them?

No, I didn't. I was trying to recover from a scandal, rebuild my reputation, my client base, my bank account. I wanted to forget what happened, not investigate it further. By the time I realized the danger, it was scratching at my front door.

❧

BRIDGETOWN HARBOR, BARBADOS, WEST INDIES FEDERATION

[I was told to expect a "tall ship," although the "sails" of IS *Imfingo* refer to the four vertical wind turbines rising from her sleek, trimaran hull. When coupled with banks of PEM, or proton exchange membrane, fuel cells, a technology that converts seawater into electricity, it is easy to see why the prefix "IS" stands for "Infinity Ship." Hailed as the undisputed future of maritime transport, it is still rare to see one sailing under anything but a government flag. The *Imfingo* is privately owned and operated. Jacob Nyathi is her captain.]

I was born about the same time as the new, postapartheid South Africa. In those euphoric days, the new government not only promised the democracy of "one man, one vote," but employment and housing to the entire country. My father thought that meant immediately. He didn't understand that these were long-term goals to be achieved after years— generations—of hard work. He thought that if we abandoned our tribal homeland and relocated to a city, there would be a brand-new house and high-paying jobs just sitting there waiting for us. My father was a simple man, a day laborer. I can't blame him for his lack of formal education, his dream of a better life for his family. And so we settled in Khayelitsha, one of the four main townships outside of Cape Town. It was a life of grinding, hopeless, humiliating poverty. It was my childhood.

The night it happened, I was walking home from the bus stop. It was around five A.M. and I'd just finished my shift waiting tables at the T.G.I. Friday's at Victoria Wharf. It had been a good night. The tips were big, and news from the Tri Nations was enough to make any South African feel ten feet tall. The Springboks were trouncing the All Blacks . . . again!

[He smiles with the memory.]

Maybe those thoughts were what distracted me at first, maybe it was simply being so knackered, but I felt my body instinctively react before I consciously heard the shots. Gunfire was not unusual, not in my neighborhood, not in those days. "One man, one gun," that was the slogan of my life in Khayelitsha. Like a combat veteran, you develop almost genetic survival skills. Mine were razor sharp. I crouched, tried to triangulate the sound, and at the same time look for the hardest surface to hide behind. Most of the homes were just makeshift shanties, wood scraps or corrugated tin, or just sheets of plastic fastened to barely standing beams. Fire ravaged these lean-tos at least once a year, and bullets could pass through them as easily as open air.

I sprinted and crouched behind a barbershop, which had been constructed from a car-sized shipping container. It wasn't perfect, but it would do for a few seconds, long enough to hole up and wait for the shooting to die down. Only it didn't. Pistols, shotguns, and that clatter you never forget, the kind that tells you someone has a Kalashnikov. This was lasting much too long to be just an ordinary gang row. Now there were screams, shouts. I began to smell smoke. I heard the stirrings of a crowd. I peeked out from around the corner. Dozens of people, most of them in their night-clothes, all shouting "Run! Get out of there! They're coming!" House lamps were lighting all around me, faces poking out of shanties. "What's going on here?" they asked. "Who's coming?" Those were the younger faces. The older ones, they just started running. They had a different kind of survival instinct, an instinct born in a time when they were slaves in their own country. In those days, everyone knew who "they" were, and if "they" were ever coming, all you could do was run and pray.

Did you run?

I couldn't. My family, my mother and two little sisters, lived only a few "doors" down from the Radio Zibonele station, exactly where the mob was fleeing from. I wasn't thinking. I was stupid. I should have doubled back around, found an alley or quiet street.

I tried to wade through the mob, pushing in the opposite direction. I thought I could stay along the sides of the shanties. I was knocked into one, into one of their plastic walls that wrapped around me as the whole structure collapsed. I was trapped, I couldn't breathe. Someone ran over me, smashed my head into the ground. I shook myself free, wriggled and rolled out into the street. I was still on my stomach when I saw them: ten or fifteen, silhouetted against the fires of the burning shanties. I couldn't see their faces, but I could hear them moaning. They were slouching steadily toward me with their arms raised.

I got to my feet, my head swam, my body ached all over. Instinctively I began to withdraw, backing into the "doorway" of the closest shack. Something grabbed me from behind, pulled at my collar, tore the fabric. I spun, ducked, and kicked hard. He was large, larger and heavier than me by a few kilos. Black fluid ran down the front of his white shirt. A knife protruded from his chest, jammed between the ribs and buried to the hilt. A scrap of my collar, which was clenched between his teeth, dropped as his lower jaw fell open. He growled, he lunged. I tried to dodge. He grabbed my wrist. I felt a crack, and pain shot up through my body. I dropped to my knees, tried to roll and maybe trip him up. My hand came up against a heavy cooking pot. I grabbed it and swung hard. It smashed into his face. I hit him again, and again, bashing his skull until the bone split open and the brains spilled out across my feet. He slumped over. I freed myself just as another one of them appeared in the entrance. This time the structure's flimsy nature worked to my advantage. I kicked the back wall open, slinking out and bringing the whole hut down in the process.

I ran, I didn't know where I was going. It was a nightmare of shacks and fire and grasping hands all racing past me. I ran through a shanty where a woman was hiding in the corner. Her two children were huddled against her, crying. "Come with me!" I said. "Please, come, we have to go!" I held out my hands, moved closer to her. She pulled her children back, brandishing a sharpened screwdriver. Her eyes were wide, scared. I could hear sounds behind me . . . smashing through shanties, knocking them over as they came. I switched from Xhosa to English. "Please," I begged, "you have to run!" I reached for her but she stabbed my hand. I left her there. I didn't know what else to do. She is still in my memory, when I sleep or maybe close my eyes sometimes. Sometimes she's my mother, and the crying children are my sisters.

I saw a bright light up ahead, shining between the cracks in the shanties. I ran as hard as I could. I tried to call to them. I was out of breath. I crashed through the wall of a shack and suddenly I was in open ground. The headlights were blinding. I felt something slam into my shoulder. I think I was out before I even hit the ground.

I came to in a bed at Groote Schuur Hospital. I'd never seen the inside of a recovery ward like this. It was so clean and white. I thought I might be dead. The medication, I'm sure, helped that feeling. I'd never tried any kind of drugs before, never even touched a drink of alcohol. I didn't want to end up like so many in my neighborhood, like my father. All my life I'd fought to stay clean, and now . . .

The morphine or whatever they had pumped into my veins was delicious. I didn't care about anything. I didn't care when they told me the police had shot me in the shoulder. I saw the man in the bed next to me frantically wheeled out as soon as his breathing stopped. I didn't even care when I overheard them talking about the outbreak of "rabies."

Who was talking about it?

I don't know. Like I said, I was as high as the stars. I just remember voices in the hallway outside my ward, loud voices angrily arguing. "That wasn't rabies!" one of them yelled. "Rabies doesn't do that to people!" Then . . . something else . . . then "well, what the hell do you suggest, we've got fifteen downstairs right here! Who knows how many more are still out there!" It's funny, I go over that conversation all the time in my head, what I should have thought, felt, done. It was a long time before I sobered up again, before I woke up and faced the nightmare.

❧

TEL AVIV, ISRAEL

[Jurgen Warmbrunn has a passion for Ethiopian food, which is our reason for meeting at a Falasha restaurant. With his bright pink skin, and white, unruly eyebrows that match his "Einstein" hair, he might be mistaken for a crazed scientist or college professor. He is neither. Although never acknowledging which Israeli intelligence service he was, and possibly still is, employed by, he openly admits that at one point he could be called "a spy."]

Most people don't believe something can happen until it already has. That's not stupidity or weakness, that's just human nature. I don't blame anyone for not believing. I don't claim to be any smarter or better than them. I guess what it really comes down to is the randomness of birth. I happened to be born into a group of people who live in constant fear of extinction. It's part of our identity, part of our mind-set, and it has taught us through horrific trial and error to always be on our guard.

The first warning I had of the plague was from our friends and customers over in Taiwan. They were complaining about our new software decryption program. Apparently it was failing to decode some e-mails from PRC sources, or at least decoding them so poorly that the text was unintelligible. I suspected the problem might not be in the software but in the translated messages themselves. The mainland Reds ... I guess they weren't really Reds anymore but ... what do you want from an old man? The Reds had a nasty habit of using too many different computers from too many different generations and countries.

Before I suggested this theory to Taipei, I thought it might be a good idea to review the scrambled messages myself. I was surprised to find that the characters themselves were perfectly decoded. But the text itself ... it all had to do with a new viral outbreak that first eliminated its victim, then reanimated his corpse into some kind of homicidal berzerker. Of course, I didn't believe this was true, especially because only a few weeks later the crisis in the Taiwan Strait began and any messages dealing with rampaging corpses abruptly ended. I suspected a second layer of encryption, a code within a code. That was pretty standard procedure, going back to the first days of human communication. Of course the Reds didn't mean actual dead bodies. It had to be a new weapon system or ultrasecret war plan. I let the matter drop, tried to forget about it. Still, as one of your great national heroes used to say: "My spider sense was tingling."

Not long afterward, at the reception for my daughter's wedding, I found myself speaking to one of my son-in-law's professors from Hebrew University. The man was a talker, and he'd had a little too much to drink. He was rambling about how his cousin was doing some kind of work in South Africa and had told him some stories about golems. You know about the Golem, the old legend about a rabbi who breathes life into an inanimate statue? Mary Shelley stole the idea for her book *Frankenstein*. I didn't say anything at first, just listened. The man went on blathering about how these golems weren't made from clay, nor were they docile and obedient. As soon as he mentioned reanimating human bodies, I asked for the man's number. It turns out he had been in Cape Town on one of those "Adrenaline Tours," shark feeding I think it was.

[He rolls his eyes.]

Apparently the shark had obliged him, right in the tuchus, which is why he had been recovering at Groote Schuur when the first victims from Khayelitsha township were brought in. He hadn't seen any of these cases firsthand, but the staff had told him enough stories to fill my old Dictaphone. I then presented his stories, along with those decrypted Chinese e-mails, to my superiors.

And this is where I directly benefited from the unique circumstances of our precarious security. In October of 1973, when the Arab sneak attack almost drove us into the Mediterranean, we had all the intelligence in front of us, all the warning signs, and we had simply "dropped the ball." We never considered the possibility of an all-out, coordinated, conventional assault from several nations, certainly not on our holiest of holidays. Call it stagnation, call it rigidity, call it an unforgivable herd mentality. Imagine a group of people all staring at writing on a wall, everyone congratulating one another on reading the words correctly. But behind that group is a mirror whose image shows the writing's true message. No one looks at the mirror. No one thinks it's necessary. Well, after almost allowing the Arabs to finish what Hitler started, we realized that not only was that mirror image necessary, but it must forever be our national policy. From 1973 onward, if nine intelligence analysts came to the same conclusion, it was the duty of the tenth to disagree. No matter how unlikely or far-fetched a possibility might be, one must always dig deeper. If a neighbor's nuclear power plant might be used to make weapons-grade plutonium, you dig; if a dictator was rumored to be building a cannon so big it could fire anthrax shells across whole countries, you dig; and if there was even the slightest chance that dead bodies were being reanimated as ravenous killing machines, you dig and dig until you stike the absolute truth.

And that is what I did, I dug. At first it wasn't easy. With China out of the picture . . . the Taiwan crisis put an end to any intelligence gathering . . . I was left with very few sources of information. A lot of it was chaff, especially on the Internet; zombies from space and Area 51 . . . what is your country's fetish for Area 51, anyway? After a while I started to uncover more useful data: cases of "rabies" similar to Cape Town . . . it wasn't called African rabies until later. I uncovered the psychological evaluations of some Canadian mountain troops recently returned from Kyrgyzstan. I found the blog records of a Brazilian nurse who told her friends all about the murder of a heart surgeon.

The majority of my information came from the World Health Organization. The UN is a bureaucratic masterpiece, so many nuggets of valuable data buried in mountains of unread reports. I found incidents all over the world, all of them dismissed with "plausible" explanations. These cases allowed me to piece together a cohesive mosaic of this new threat. The subjects in question were indeed dead, they were hostile, and they were undeniably spreading. I also made one very encouraging discovery: how to terminate their existence.

Going for the brain.

[He chuckles.] We talk about it today as if it is some feat of magic, like holy water or a silver bullet, but why wouldn't destruction of the brain be the only way to annihilate these creatures? Isn't it the only way to annihilate us as well?

You mean human beings?

[He nods.] Isn't that all we are? Just a brain kept alive by a complex and vulnerable machine we call the body? The brain cannot survive if just one part of the machine is destroyed or even deprived of such necessities as food or oxygen. That is the only measurable difference between us and "The Undead." Their brains do not require a support system to survive, so it is necessary to attack the organ itself. [His right hand, in the shape of a gun, rises to touch his temple.] A simple solution, but only if we recognized the problem! Given how quickly the plague was spreading, I thought it might be prudent to seek confirmation from foreign intelligence circles.

Paul Knight had been a friend of mine for a long time, going all the way back to Entebbe. The idea to use a double of Amin's black Mercedes, that was him. Paul had retired from government service right before his agency's "reforms" and gone to work for a private consulting firm in Bethesda, Maryland. When I visited him at his home, I was shocked to find that not only had he been working on the very same project, on his own time, of course, but that his file was almost as thick and heavy as mine. We sat up the whole night reading each other's findings. Neither of us spoke. I don't think we were even conscious of each other, the world around us, anything except the words before our eyes. We finished almost at the same time, just as the sky began to lighten in the east.

Paul turned the last page, then looked to me and said very matter-of-factly, "This is pretty bad, huh?" I nodded, so did he, then followed up with "So what are we going to do about it?"

And that is how the "Warmbrunn-Knight" report was written.

I wish people would stop calling it that. There were fifteen other names on that report: virologists, intelligence operatives, military analysts, journalists, even one UN observer who'd been monitoring the elections in Jakarta when the first outbreak hit Indonesia. Everyone was an expert in his or her field, everyone had come to their own similar conclusions before ever being contacted by us. Our report was just under a hundred pages long. It was concise, it was fully comprehensive, it was everything we thought we needed to make sure this outbreak never reached epidemic proportions. I know a lot of credit has been heaped upon the South African war plan, and deservedly so, but if more people had read our report and worked to make its recommendations a reality, then that plan would have never needed to exist.

But some people did read and follow your report. Your own government . . .

Barely, and just look at the cost.

❦

BETHLEHEM, PALESTINE

[With his rugged looks and polished charm, Saladin Kader could be a movie star. He is friendly but never obsequious, self-assured but never arrogant. He is a professor of urban planning at Khalil Gibran University, and, naturally, the love of all his female students. We sit under the statue of the university's namesake. Like everything else in one of the Middle East's most affluent cities, its polished bronze glitters in the sun.]

I was born and raised in Kuwait City. My family was one of the few "lucky" ones not to be expelled after 1991, after Arafat sided with Saddam, against the world. We weren't rich, but neither were we struggling. I was comfortable, even sheltered, you might say, and oh did it show in my actions.

I watched the Al Jazeera broadcast from behind the counter at the Starbucks where I worked every day after school. It was the afternoon rush hour and the place was packed. You should have heard the uproar, the jeers and catcalls. I'm sure our noise level matched that on the floor of the General Assembly.

Of course we thought it was a Zionist lie, who didn't? When the Israeli ambassador announced to the UN General Assembly that his country was enacting a policy of "voluntary quarantine," what was I supposed to think? Was I supposed to really believe his crazy story that African rabies was actually some new plague that transformed dead bodies into bloodthirsty cannibals? How can you possibly believe that kind of foolishness, especially when it comes from your most hated enemy?

I didn't even hear the second part of that fat bastard's speech, the part about offering asylum, no questions asked, to any foreign-born Jew, any foreigner of Israeli-born parents, any Palestinian living in the formerly occupied territories, and any Palestinian whose family had once lived within the borders of Israel. The last part applied to my family, refugees from the '67 War of Zionist aggression. At the heeding of the PLO leadership, we had fled our village believing we could return as soon as our Egyptian and Syrian brothers had swept the Jews into the sea. I had never been to Israel, or what was about to be absorbed into the new state of Unified Palestine,

What did you think was behind the Israeli ruse?

Here's what I thought: The Zionists have just been driven out of the occupied territories, they say they left voluntarily, just like Lebanon, and most
recently the Gaza Strip, but really, just like before, we knew we'd driven
them out. They know that the next and final blow would destroy that illegal atrocity they call a country, and to prepare for that final blow, they're
attempting to recruit both foreign Jews as cannon fodder and . . . *and*—I
thought I was so clever for figuring this part out—kidnapping as many
Palestinians as they could to act as human shields! I had all the answers.
Who doesn't at seventeen?

My father wasn't quite convinced of my ingenious geopolitical insights.
He was a janitor at Amiri Hospital. He'd been on duty the night it had its
first major African rabies outbreak. He hadn't personally seen the bodies
rise from their slabs or the carnage of panicked patients and security
guards, but he'd witnessed enough of the aftermath to convince him that
staying in Kuwait was suicidal. He'd made up his mind to leave the same
day Israel made their declaration.

That must have been difficult to hear.

It was blasphemy! I tried to make him see reason, to convince him with my
adolescent logic. I'd show the images from Al Jazeera, the images coming
out of the new West Bank state of Palestine; the celebrations, the demonstrations. Anyone with eyes could see total liberation was at hand. The Israelis had withdrawn from all the occupied territory and were actually
preparing to evacuate Al Quds, what they call Jerusalem! All the factional
fighting, the violence between our various resistance organizations, I knew
that would die down once we unified for the final blow against the Jews.
Couldn't my father see this? Couldn't he understand that, in a few years, a
few months, we *would* be returning to our homeland, this time as libera-
tors, not as refugees.

How was your argument resolved?

"Resolved," what a pleasant euphemism. It was "resolved" after the second
outbreak, the larger one at Al Jahrah. My father had just quit his job,
cleared out our bank account, such as it was . . . our bags were packed . . .

our e-tickets confirmed. The TV was blaring in the background, riot police storming the front entrance of a house. You couldn't see what they were shooting at inside. The official report blamed the violence on "pro-Western extremists." My father and I were arguing, as always. He tried to convince me of what he'd seen at the hospital, that by the time our leaders acknowledged the danger, it would be too late for any of us.

I, of course, scoffed at his timid ignorance, at his willingness to abandon "The Struggle." What else could I expect from a man who'd spent his whole life scrubbing toilets in a country that treated our people only slightly better than its Filipino guest workers. He'd lost his perspective, his self-respect. The Zionists were offering the hollow promise of a better life, and he was jumping at it like a dog with scraps.

My father tried, with all the patience he could muster, to make me see that he had no more love for Israel than the most militant Al Aqsa martyr, but they seemed to be the only country actively preparing for the coming storm, certainly the only one that would so freely shelter and protect our family.

I laughed in his face. Then I dropped the bomb: I told him that I'd already found a website for the Children of Yassin[1] and was waiting for an e-mail from a recruiter supposedly operating right in Kuwait City. I told my father to go and be the yehud's whore if he wanted, but the next time we'd meet was when I would be rescuing him from an internment camp. I was quite proud of those words, I thought they sounded very heroic. I glared in his face, stood from the table, and made my final pronouncement: "Surely the vilest of beasts in Allah's sight are those who disbelieve!"[2]

The dinner table suddenly became very silent. My mother looked down, my sisters looked at each other. All you could hear was the TV, the frantic words of the on-site reporter telling everyone to remain calm. My father was not a large man. By that time, I think I was even bigger than him. He

1. Children of Yassin: A youth-based terrorist organization named for the late Sheikh Yassin. Under strict recruitment codes, all martyrs could be no older than eighteen.
2. "Sure the vilest of beasts in Allah's sight are those who disbelieve, then they would not believe." From the Holy Koran, part 8, Section 55.

was also not an angry man; I don't think he ever raised his voice. I saw something in his eyes, something I didn't recognize, and then suddenly he was on me, a lightning whirlwind that threw me up against the wall, slapped me so hard my left ear rang. "You WILL go!" he shouted as he grabbed my shoulders and repeatedly slammed me against the cheap drywall. "I am your father! You WILL OBEY ME!" His next slap sent my vision flashing white. "YOU WILL LEAVE WITH THIS FAMILY OR YOU WILL NOT LEAVE THIS ROOM ALIVE!" More grabbing and shoving, shouting and slapping. I didn't understand where this man had come from, this lion who'd replaced my docile, frail excuse for a parent. A lion protecting his cubs. He knew that fear was the only weapon he had left to save my life and if I didn't fear the threat of the plague, then dammit, I was going to fear him!

Did it work?

[Laughs.] Some martyr I turned out to be, I think I cried all the way to Cairo.

Cairo?

There were no direct flights to Israel from Kuwait, not even from Egypt once the Arab League imposed its travel restrictions. We had to fly from Kuwait to Cairo, then take a bus across the Sinai Desert to the crossing at Taba.

As we approached the border, I saw the Wall for the first time. It was still unfinished, naked steel beams rising above the concrete foundation. I'd known about the infamous "security fence"—what citizen of the Arab world didn't—but I'd always been led to believe that it only surrounded the West Bank and Gaza Strip. Out here, in the middle of this barren desert, it only confirmed my theory that the Israelis were expecting an attack along their entire border. *Good,* I thought. *The Egyptians have finally rediscovered their balls.*

At Taba, we were taken off the bus and told to walk, single file, past cages that held very large and fierce-looking dogs. We went one at a time.

A border guard, this skinny black African—I didn't know there were black Jews[3]—would hold out his hand. "Wait there!" he said in barely recognizable Arabic. Then, "you go, come!" The man before me was old. He had a long white beard and supported himself on a cane. As he passed the dogs, they went wild, howling and snarling, biting and charging at the confines of their cages. Instantly, two large chaps in civilian clothing were at the old man's side, speaking something in his ear and escorting him away. I could see the man was injured. His dishdasha was torn at the hip and stained with brown blood. These men were certainly no doctors, however, and the black, unmarked van they escorted him to was certainly no ambulance. *Bastards*, I thought, as the old man's family wailed after him. *Weeding out the ones too sick and old to be of any use to them*. Then it was our turn to walk the gauntlet of dogs. They didn't bark at me, nor the rest of my family. I think one of them even wagged its tail as my sister held out her hand. The next man after us, however . . . again came the barks and growls, again came the nondescript civilians. I turned to look at him and was surprised to see a white man, American maybe, or Canadian . . . no, he had to be American, his English was too loud. "C'mon, I'm fine!" He shouted and struggled. "C'mon, man, what the fuck?" He was well dressed, a suit and tie, matching luggage that was tossed aside as he began to fight with the Israelis. "Dude, c'mon, get the fuck off me! I'm one'a you! C'mon!" The buttons on his shirt ripped open, revealing a bloodstained bandage wrapped tightly around his stomach. He was still kicking and screaming as they dragged him into the back of the van. I didn't understand it. Why these people? Clearly, it wasn't just about being an Arab, or even about being wounded. I saw several refugees with severe injuries pass through without molestation from the guards. They were all escorted to waiting ambulances, real ambulances, not the black vans. I knew it had something to do with the dogs. Were they screening for rabies? That made the most sense to me, and it continued to be my theory during our internment outside Yeroham.

3. By this point, the Israeli government had completed operation "Moses II," which transported the last of the Ethiopian "Falasha" into Israel.

The resettlement camp?

Resettlement and quarantine. At that time, I just saw it as a prison. It was exactly what I'd expected to happen to us: the tents, the overcrowding, the guards, barbed wire, and the seething, baking Negev Desert sun. We felt like prisoners, we *were* prisoners, and although I would have never had the courage to say to my father "I told you so," he could see it clearly in my sour face.

What I didn't expect was the physical examinations; every day, from an army of medical personnel. Blood, skin, hair, saliva, even urine and feces[4] . . . it was exhausting, mortifying. The only thing that made it bearable, and probably what prevented an all-out riot among some of the Muslim detainees, was that most of the doctors and nurses doing the examinations were themselves Palestinian. The doctor who examined my mother and sisters was a woman, an American woman from a place called Jersey City. The man who examined us was from Jabaliya in Gaza and had himself been a detainee only a few months before. He kept telling us, "You made the right decision to come here. You'll see. I know it's hard, but you'll see it was the only way." He told us it was all true, everything the Israelis had said. I still couldn't bring myself to believe him, even though a growing part of me wanted to.

We stayed at Yeroham for three weeks, until our papers were processed and our medical examinations finally cleared. You know, the whole time they barely even glanced at our passports. My father had done all this work to make sure our official documents were in order. I don't think they even cared. Unless the Israeli Defense Force or the police wanted you for some previous "unkosher" activities, all that mattered was your clean bill of health.

The Ministry of Social Affairs provided us with vouchers for subsidized housing, free schooling, and a job for my father at a salary that would support the entire family. *This is too good to be true*, I thought as we boarded the bus for Tel Aviv. *The hammer is going to fall anytime now.*

---

4. At the time, it was unsure whether the virus could survive in solid waste outside of the human body.

It did once we entered the city of Beer Sheeba. I was asleep, I didn't hear the shots or see the driver's windscreen shatter. I jerked awake as I felt the bus swerve out of control. We crashed into the side of a building. People screamed, glass and blood were everywhere. My family was close to the emergency exit. My father kicked the door open and pushed us out into the street.

There was shooting, from the windows, doorways. I could see that it was soldiers versus civilians, civilians with guns or homemade bombs. *This is it!* I thought. My heart felt like it was going to burst! *This liberation has started!* Before I could do anything, run out to join my comrades in battle, someone had me by my shirt and was pulling me through the doorway of a Starbucks.

I was thrown on the floor next to my family, my sisters were crying as my mother tried to crawl on top of them. My father had a bullet wound in the shoulder. An IDF soldier shoved me on the ground, keeping my face away from the window. My blood was boiling; I started looking for something I could use as a weapon, maybe a large shard of glass to ram through the yehud's throat.

Suddenly a door at the back of the Starbucks swung open, the soldier turned in its direction and fired. A bloody corpse hit the floor right beside us, a grenade rolled out of his twitching hand. The soldier grabbed the bomb and tried to hurl it into the street. It exploded in midair. His body shielded us from the blast. He tumbled back over the corpse of my slain Arab brother. Only he wasn't an Arab at all. As my tears dried I noticed that he wore payess and a yarmulke and bloody tzitzit snaked out from his damp, shredded trousers. This man was a Jew, the armed rebels out in the street were Jews! The battle raging all around us wasn't an uprising by Palestinian insurgents, but the opening shots of the Israeli Civil War.

In your opinion, what do you believe was the cause of that war?

I think there were many causes. I know the repatriation of Palestinians was unpopular, so was the general pullout from the West Bank. I'm sure the Strategic Hamlet Resettlement Program must have inflamed more than its share of hearts. A lot of Israelis had to watch their houses bulldozed in order to make way for those fortified, self-sufficient residential compounds. Al Quds, I believe . . . that was the final straw. The Coalition Government decided that it was the one major weak point, too large to control and a hole that led right into the heart of Israel. They not only evacuated the city, but the entire Nablus to Hebron corridor as well. They believed that rebuilding a shorter wall along the 1967 demarcation line was the only way to ensure physical security, no matter what backlash might occur from their own religious right. I learned all this much later, you understand, as well as the fact that the only reason the IDF eventually triumphed was because the majority of the rebels came from the ranks of the Ultra-Orthodox and therefore most had never served in the armed forces. Did you know that? I didn't. I realized I practically didn't know anything about these people I'd hated my entire life. Everything I thought was true went up in smoke that day, supplanted by the face of our real enemy.

I was running with my family into the back of an Israeli tank,[5] when one of those unmarked vans came around the corner. A handheld rocket slammed right into its engine. The van catapulted into the air, crashed upside down, and exploded into a brilliant orange fireball. I still had a few steps to go before reaching the doors of the tank, just enough time to see the whole event unfold. Figures were climbing out of the burning wreckage, slow-moving torches whose clothes and skin were covered in burning petrol. The soldiers around us began firing at the figures. I could see little pops in their chests where the bullets were passing harmlessly through. The squad leader next to me shouted "B'rosh! Yoreh B'rosh!" and the soldiers adjusted their aim. The figures' . . . the creatures' heads exploded. The petrol was just burning out as they hit the ground, these charred black, headless corpses. Suddenly I understood what my father had been trying to warn me about, what the Israelis had been trying to warn the rest of the world about! What I couldn't understand was why the rest of the world wasn't listening.

---

5. Unlike most country's main battle tanks, the Israeli "Merkava" contains rear hatches for troop deployment.

BLAME

LANGLEY, VIRGINIA, USA

[The office of the director of the Central Intelligence Agency
could belong to a business executive or doctor or an everyday,
small-town high school principal. There are the usual collection
of reference books on the shelf, degrees and photos on the wall,
and, on his desk, an autographed baseball from Cincinnati Reds
catcher Johnny Bench. Bob Archer, my host, can see by my face
that I was expecting something different. I suspect that is why
he chose to conduct our interview here.]

When you think about the CIA, you probably imagine two of our most
popular and enduring myths. The first is that our mission is to search the
globe for any conceivable threat to the United States, and the second is
that we have the power to perform the first. This myth is the by-product of
an organization, which, by its very nature, must exist and operate in secrecy. Secrecy is a vacuum and nothing fills a vacuum like paranoid speculation. "Hey, did you hear who killed so and so, I hear it was the CIA. Hey,

what about that coup in El Banana Republico, must have been the CIA. Hey, be careful looking at that website, you know who keeps a record of every website anyone's ever looked at ever, the CIA!" This is the image most people had of us before the war, and it's an image we were more than happy to encourage. We wanted bad guys to suspect us, to fear us and maybe think twice before trying to harm any of our citizens. This was the advantage of our image as some kind of omniscient octopus. The only disadvantage was that our own people believed in that image as well, so whenever anything, anywhere occurred without any warning, where do you think the finger was pointed: "Hey, how did that crazy country get those nukes? Where was the CIA? How come all those people were murdered by that fanatic? Where was the CIA? How come, when the dead began coming back to life, we didn't know about it until they were breaking through our living room windows? Where the hell was the goddamn CIA!?!"

The truth was, neither the Central Intelligence Agency nor any of the other official and unofficial U.S. intelligence organizations have ever been some kind of all-seeing, all-knowing, global illuminati. For starters, we never had that kind of funding. Even during the blank check days of the cold war, it's just not physically possible to have eyes and ears in every back room, cave, alley, brothel, bunker, office, home, car, and rice paddy across the entire planet. Don't get me wrong, I'm not saying we were impotent, and maybe we can take credit for some of the things our fans, and our critics, have suspected us of over the years. But if you add up all the crackpot conspiracy theories from Pearl Harbor[1] to the day before the Great Panic, then you'd have an organization not only more powerful than the United States, but the united efforts of the entire human race.

We're not some shadow superpower with ancient secrets and alien technology. We have very real limitations and extremely finite assets, so why would we waste those assets chasing down each and every potential threat? That goes to the second myth of what an intelligence organization really does. We can't just spread ourselves thin looking for, and hoping to stumble

1. The CIA, originally the OSS, was not created until June 1942, six months after the Japanese attack on Pearl Harbor.

on, new and possible dangers. Instead, we've always had to identify and focus on those that are already clear and present. If your Soviet neighbor is trying to set fire to your house, you can't be worrying about the Arab down the block. If suddenly it's the Arab in your backyard, you can't be worrying about the People's Republic of China, and if one day the ChiComs show up at your front door with an eviction notice in one hand and a Molotov cocktail in the other, then the last thing you're going to do is look over his shoulder for a walking corpse.

But didn't the plague originate in China?

It did, as well as did one of the greatest single Maskirovkas in the history of modern espionage.

I'm sorry?

It was deception, a fake out. The PRC knew they were already our number-one surveillance target. They knew they could never hide the existence of their nationwide "Health and Safety" sweeps. They realized that the best way to mask what they were doing was to hide it in plain sight. Instead of lying about the sweeps themselves, they just lied about what they were sweeping for.

The dissident crackdown?

Bigger, the whole Taiwan Strait incident: the victory of the Taiwan National Independence Party, the assassination of the PRC defense minister, the buildup, the war threats, the demonstrations and subsequent crackdowns were all engineered by the Ministry of State Security and all of it was to divert the world's eye from the real danger growing within China. And it worked! Every shred of intel we had on the PRC, the sudden disappearances, the mass executions, the curfews, the reserve call-ups— everything could easily be explained as standard ChiCom procedure. In fact, it worked so well, we were so convinced that World War III was about to break out in the Taiwan Strait, that we diverted other intel assets from countries where undead outbreaks were just starting to unfold.

The Chinese were that good.

And we were that bad. It wasn't the Agency's finest hour. We were still reeling from the purges . . .

You mean the reforms?

No, I mean the purges, because that's what they were. When Joe Stalin either shot or imprisoned his best military commanders, he wasn't doing half as much damage to his national security as what that administration did to us with their "reforms." The last brushfire war was a debacle and guess who took the fall. We'd been ordered to justify a political agenda, then when that agenda became a political liability, those who'd originally given the order now stood back with the crowd and pointed the finger at us. "Who told us we should go to war in the first place? Who mixed us up in all this mess? The CIA!" We couldn't defend ourselves without violating national security. We had to just sit there and take it. And what was the result? Brain drain. Why stick around and be the victim of a political witch hunt when you could escape to the private sector: a fatter paycheck, decent hours, and maybe, just maybe, a little respect and appreciation by the people you work for. We lost a lot of good men and women, a lot of experience, initiative, and priceless analytical reasoning. All we were left with were the dregs, a bunch of brownnosing, myopic eunuchs.

But that couldn't have been everyone.

No, of course not. There were some of us who stayed because we actually believed in what we were doing. We weren't in this for money or working conditions, or even the occasional pat on the back. We were in this because we wanted to serve our country. We wanted to keep our people safe. But even with ideals like that there comes a point when you have to realize that the sum of all your blood, sweat, and tears will ultimately amount to zero.

So you knew what was really happening.

No . . . no . . . I couldn't. There was no way to confirm . . .

But you had suspicions.

I had . . . doubts.

Could you be more specific?

No, I'm sorry. But I can say that I broached the subject a number of times to my coworkers.

What happened?

The answer was always the same, "Your funeral."

And was it?

[Nods.] I spoke to . . . someone in a position of authority . . . just a five-minute meeting, expressing some concerns. He thanked me for coming in and told me he'd look into it right away. The next day I received transfer orders: Buenos Aires, effective immediately.

Did you ever hear of the Warmbrunn-Knight report?

Sure now, but back then . . . the copy that was originally hand delivered by Paul Knight himself, the one marked "Eyes Only" for the director . . . it was found at the bottom of the desk of a clerk in the San Antonio field office of the FBI, three years after the Great Panic. It turned out to be academic because right after I was transferred, Israel went public with its statement of "Voluntary Quarantine." Suddenly the time for advanced warning was over. The facts were out; it was now a question of who would believe them.

❧

VAALAJARVI, FINLAND

[It is spring, "hunting season." As the weather warms, and the bodies of frozen zombies begin to reanimate, elements of the UN N-For (Northern Force) have arrived for their annual "Sweep and Clear." Every year the undead's numbers dwindle. At current trends, this area is expected to be completely "Secure" within a decade. Travis D'Ambrosia, Supreme Allied Commander, Europe, is here to personally oversee operations. There is a softness to the general's voice, a sadness. Throughout our interview, he struggles to maintain eye contact.]

I won't deny mistakes were made. I won't deny we could have been better prepared. I'll be the first one to admit that we let the American people down. I just want the American people to know why.

"What if the Israelis are right?" Those were the first words out of the chairman's mouth the morning after Israel's UN declaration. "I'm not saying they are," he made sure to stress that point, "I'm just saying, what if?" He wanted candid, not canned, opinions. He was that type of man, the chairman of the Joint Chiefs. He kept the conversation "hypothetical," indulging in the fantasy that this was just some intellectual exercise. After all, if the rest of the world wasn't ready to believe something so outrageous, why should the men and women in this room?

We kept up with the charade as long as we could, speaking with a smile or punctuating with a joke . . . I'm not sure when the transition happened. It was so subtle, I don't think anyone even noticed, but suddenly you had a room full of military professionals, each one with decades of combat experience and more academic training than the average civilian brain surgeon, and all of us speaking openly, and honestly, about the possible threat of walking corpses. It was like . . . a dam breaking; the taboo was shattered, and the truth just started flooding out. It was . . . liberating.

So you had had your own private suspicions?

For months before the Israeli declaration; so had the chairman. Everyone in that room had heard something, or suspected something.

Had any of you read the Warmbrunn-Knight report?

No, none of us. I had heard the name, but had no idea about its content. I actually got my hands on a copy about two years after the Great Panic. Most of its military measures were almost line for line in step with our own.

Your own what?

Our proposal to the White House. We outlined a fully comprehensive program, not only to eliminate the threat within the United States, but to roll back and contain it throughout the entire world.

What happened?

The White House loved Phase One. It was cheap, fast, and if executed properly, 100 percent covert. Phase One involved the insertion of Special Forces units into infested areas. Their orders were to investigate, isolate, and eliminate.

Eliminate?

With extreme prejudice.

Those were the Alpha teams?

Yes, sir, and they were extremely successful. Even though their battle record is sealed for the next 140 years, I can say that it remains one of the most outstanding moments in the history of America's elite warriors.

So what went wrong?

Nothing, with Phase One, but the Alpha teams were only supposed to be a stopgap measure. Their mission was never to extinguish the threat, only delay it long enough to buy time for Phase Two.

But Phase Two was never completed.

Never even begun, and herein lies the reason why the American military was caught so shamefully unprepared.

Phase Two required a massive national undertaking, the likes of which hadn't been seen since the darkest days of the Second World War. That kind of effort requires Herculean amounts of both national treasure and national support, both of which, by that point, were nonexistent. The American people had just been through a very long and bloody conflict. They were tired. They'd had enough. Like the 1970s, the pendulum was swinging from a militant stance to a very resentful one.

In totalitarian regimes—communism, fascism, religious fundamental-ism—popular support is a given. You can start wars, you can prolong them, you can put anyone in uniform for any length of time without ever having to worry about the slightest political backlash. In a democracy, the polar opposite is true. Public support must be husbanded as a finite national re-source. It must be spent wisely, sparingly, and with the greatest return on your investment. America is especially sensitive to war weariness, and nothing brings on a backlash like the perception of defeat. I say "percep-tion" because America is a very all-or-nothing society. We like the big win, the touchdown, the knockout in the first round. We like to know, and for everyone else to know, that our victory wasn't only uncontested, it was positively devastating. If not . . . well . . . look at where we were before the Panic. We didn't lose the last brushfire conflict, far from it. We actually accomplished a very difficult task with very few resources and under extremely unfavorable circumstances. We won, but the public didn't see it that way because it wasn't the blitzkrieg smackdown that our national spirit demanded. Too much time had gone by, too much money had been spent, too many lives had been lost or irrevocably damaged. We'd not only squandered all our public support, we were deeply in the red.

Think about just the dollar value of Phase Two. Do you know the price tag of putting just one American citizen in uniform? And I don't just mean the time that he's actively in that uniform: the training, the equipment, the food, the housing, the transport, the medical care. I'm talking about the long-term dollar value that the country, the American taxpayer, has to shell out to that person for the rest of their natural life. This is a crushing financial burden, and in those days we barely had enough funding to maintain what we had.

Even if the coffers hadn't been empty, if we'd had all the money to make all the uniforms we needed to implement Phase Two, who do you think we could have conned into filling them? This goes to the heart of America's war weariness. As if the "traditional" horrors weren't bad enough—the dead, the disfigured, the psychologically destroyed—now you had a whole new breed of difficulties, "The Betrayed." We were a volunteer army, and look what happened to our volunteers. How many stories do you remember about some soldier who had his term of service extended, or some ex-reservist who, after ten years of civilian life, suddenly found himself recalled into active duty? How many weekend warriors lost their jobs or houses? How many came back to ruined lives, or, worse, didn't come back at all? Americans are an honest people, we expect a fair deal. I know that a lot of other cultures used to think that was naïve and even childish, but it's one of our most sacred principles. To see Uncle Sam going back on his word, revoking people's private lives, revoking their *freedom* . . .

After Vietnam, when I was a young platoon leader in West Germany, we'd had to institute an incentives program just to keep our soldiers from going AWOL. After this last war, no amount of incentives could fill our

depleted ranks, no payment bonuses or term reductions, or online recruit-
ing tools disguised as civilian video games.[1] This generation had had
enough, and that's why when the undead began to devour our country, we
were almost too weak and vulnerable to stop them.

I'm not blaming the civilian leadership and I'm not suggesting that we
in uniform should be anything but beholden to them. This is our system
and it's the best in the world. But it must be protected, and defended, and
it must never again be so abused.

❧

VOSTOK STATION: ANTARCTICA

[In prewar times, this outpost was considered the most remote
on Earth. Situated near the planet's southern geomagnetic pole,
atop the four-kilometer ice crust of Lake Vostok, temperatures
here have been recorded at a world record negative eighty-nine
degrees Celsius, with the highs rarely reaching above negative
twenty-two. This extreme cold, and the fact that overland transport takes over a month to reach the station, were what made
Vostok so attractive to Breckinridge "Breck" Scott.

We meet in "The Dome," the reinforced, geodesic greenhouse
that draws power from the station's geothermal plant. These and
many other improvements were implemented by Mister Scott
when he leased the station from the Russian government. He has
not left it since the Great Panic.]

Do you understand economics? I mean big-time, prewar, global capital-
ism. Do you get how it worked? I don't, and anyone who says they do is full

---

1. Before the war, an online "shooter game" known as "America's Army" was made available, free of charge, by the U.S. government to the general public, some have alleged, to
   entice new recruits.

of shit. There are no rules, no scientific absolutes. You win, you lose, it's a total crapshoot. The only rule that ever made sense to me I learned from a history, not an economics, professor at Wharton. "Fear," he used to say, "fear is the most valuable commodity in the universe." That blew me away. "Turn on the TV," he'd say. "What are you seeing? People selling their products? No. People selling the fear of you having to live without their products." Fuckin' A, was he right. Fear of aging, fear of loneliness, fear of poverty, fear of failure. Fear is the most basic emotion we have. Fear is primal. Fear sells. That was my mantra. "Fear sells."

When I first heard about the outbreaks, back when it was still called African rabies, I saw the opportunity of a lifetime. I'll never forget that first report, the Cape Town outbreak, only ten minutes of actual reporting then a full hour of speculating about what would happen if the virus ever made it to America. God bless the news. I hit speed dial thirty seconds later.

I met with some of my nearest and dearest. They'd all seen the same report. I was the first one to come up with a workable pitch: a vaccine, a real vaccine for rabies. Thank God there is no cure for rabies. A cure would make people buy it only if they thought they were infected. But a vaccine! That's preventative! People will keep taking that as long as they're afraid it's out there!

We had plenty of contacts in the biomed industry, with plenty more up on the Hill and Penn Ave. We could have a working proto in less than a month and a proposal written up within a couple of days. By the eighteenth hole, it was handshakes all around.

What about the FDA?

Please, are you serious? Back then the FDA was one of the most under-funded, mismanaged organizations in the country. I think they were still high-fiving over getting Red No. 2[1] out of M&Ms. Plus, this was one of the most business-friendly administrations in American history. J. P. Morgan

---

1. Myth; although red M&Ms were removed from 1976 to 1985, they did not use Red Dye No. 2.

and John D. Rockefeller were getting wood from beyond the grave for this guy in the White House. His staff didn't even bother to read our cost assessment report. I think they were already looking for a magic bullet. They railroaded it through the FDA in two months. Remember the speech the prez made before Congress, how it had been tested in Europe for some time and the only thing holding it up was our own "bloated bureaucracy"? Remember the whole thing about "people don't need big government, they need big protection, and they need it big-time!" Jesus Christmas, I think half the country creamed their pants at that. How high did his approval rating go that night, 60 percent, 70? I just know that it jacked our IPO 389 percent on the first day! Suck on that, Baidu dot-com!

And you didn't know if it would work?

We knew it would work against rabies, and that's what they said it was, right, just some weird strain of jungle rabies.

Who said that?

You know, "they," like, the UN or the . . . somebody. That's what everyone ended up calling it, right, "African rabies."

Was it ever tested on an actual victim?

Why? People used to take flu shots all the time, never knowing if it was for the right strain. Why was this any different?

But the damage . . .

Who thought it was going to go that far? You know how many disease scares there used to be. Jesus, you'd think the Black Death was sweeping the globe every three months or so . . . ebola, SARS, avian flu. You know how many people made money on those scares? Shit, I made my first million on useless antiradiation pills during the dirty bomb scares.

But if someone discovered . . .

Discovered what? We never lied, you understand? They told us it was rabies, so we made a vaccine for rabies. We said it had been tested in Europe, and the drugs it was based on had been tested in Europe. Technically, we never lied. Technically, we never did anything wrong.

But if someone discovered that it wasn't rabies . . .

Who was going to blow the whistle? The medical profession? We made sure it was a prescription drug so doctors stood just as much to lose as us. Who else? The FDA who let it pass? The congressmen who all voted for its acceptance? The surgeon general? The White House? This was a win-win situation! Everyone got to be heroes, everyone got to make money. Six months after Phalanx hit the market, you started getting all these cheaper, knockoff brands, all solid sellers as well as the other ancillary stuff like home air purifiers.

But the virus wasn't airborne.

It didn't matter! It still had the same brand name! "From the Makers of . . ." All I had to say was "May Prevent *Some* Viral Infections." That was it! Now I understand why it used to be illegal to shout fire in a crowded theater. People weren't going to say "Hey, I don't smell smoke, is there really a fire," no, they say "Holy shit, there's a fire! RUN!" [Laughs.] I made money on home purifiers, car purifiers; my biggest seller was this little doodad you wore around your neck when you got on a plane! I don't know if it even filtered ragweed, but it sold.

Things got so good, I started setting up these dummy companies, you know, with plans to build manufacturing facilities all over the country. The shares from these dumbos sold almost as much as the real stuff. It wasn't even the idea of safety anymore, it was the idea of the idea of safety! Remember when we started to get our first cases here in the States, that guy in Florida who said he'd been bitten but survived because he was taking Phalanx? OH! [He stands, mimes the act of frantic fornication.] God freakin' bless that dumbass, whoever he was.

But that wasn't because of Phalanx. Your drug didn't protect people at all.

It protected them from their fears. That's all I was selling. Hell, because of Phalanx, the biomed sector started to recover, which, in turn, jump-started the stock market, which then gave the impression of a recovery, which then restored consumer confidence to stimulate an actual recovery! Phalanx hands down ended the recession! I . . . I ended the recession!

And then? When the outbreaks became more serious, and the press finally reported that there was no wonder drug?

Pre-fucking-cisely! That's the alpha cunt who should be shot, what's her name, who first broke that story! Look what she did! Pulled the fuckin' rug right out from under us all! She caused the spiral! She caused the Great Panic!

And you take no personal responsibility?

For what? For making a little fuckin' cash . . . well, not a little [giggles]. All I did was what any of us are ever supposed to do. I chased my dream, and I got my slice. You wanna blame someone, blame whoever first called it rabies, or who knew it wasn't rabies and gave us the green light anyway. Shit, you wanna blame someone, why not start with all the sheep who forked over their greenbacks without bothering to do a little responsible research. I never held a gun to their heads. They made the choice themselves. They're the bad guys, not me. I never directly hurt anybody, and if anybody was too stupid to get themselves hurt, boo-fuckin-hoo. Of course . . .

If there's a hell . . . [giggles as he talks] . . . I don't want to think about how many of those dumb shits might be waiting for me. I just hope they don't want a refund.

❧

AMARILLO, TEXAS, USA

[Grover Carlson works as a fuel collector for the town's experimental bioconversion plant. The fuel he collects is dung. I follow the former White House chief of staff as he pushes his wheelbarrow across the pie-laden pastures.]

Of course we got our copy of the Knight-WarnJews report, what do you think we are, the CIA? We read it three months before the Israelis went public. Before the Pentagon started making noise, it was my job to personally brief the president, who in turn even devoted an entire meeting to discussing its message.

Which was?

Drop everything, focus all our efforts, typical alarmist crap. We got dozens of these reports a week, every administration did, all of them claiming that their particular boogeyman was "the greatest threat to human existence." C'mon! Can you imagine what America would have been like if the federal government slammed on the brakes every time some paranoid crackpot cried "wolf" or "global warming" or "living dead"? Please. What we did, what every president since Washington has done, was provide a measured, appropriate response, in direct relation to a realistic threat assessment.

And that was the Alpha teams.

Among others things. Given how low a priority the national security adviser thought this was, I think we actually gave it some pretty healthy table

time. We produced an educational video for state and local law enforcement about what to do in case of an outbreak. The Department of Health
and Human Services had a page on its website for how citizens should respond to infected family members. And hey, what about pushing Phalanx
right through the FDA?

But Phalanx didn't work.

Yeah, and do you know how long it would have taken to invent one that
did? Look how much time and money had been put into cancer research,
or AIDS. Do you want to be the man who tells the American people that
he's diverting funds from either one of those for some new disease that
most people haven't even heard of? Look at what we've put into research
during and after the war, and we *still* don't have a cure or a vaccine. We
knew Phalanx was a placebo, and we were grateful for it. It calmed people
down and let us do our job.

What, you would have rather we told people the truth? That it wasn't a
new strain of rabies but a mysterious uber-plague that reanimated the
dead? Can you imagine the panic that would have happened: the protest,
the riots, the billions in damage to private property? Can you imagine all
those wet-pants senators who would have brought the government to a
standstill so they could railroad some high-profile and ultimately useless
"Zombie Protection Act" through Congress? Can you imagine the damage
it would have done to that administration's political capital? We're talking
about an election year, and a damn hard, uphill fight. We were the "cleanup
crew," the unlucky bastards who had to mop up all the shit left by the last
administration, and believe me, the previous eight years had piled up one
tall mountain of shit! The only reason we squeaked back into power was
because our new propped-up patsy kept promising a "return to peace and
prosperity." The American people wouldn't have settled for anything less.
They thought they'd been through some pretty tough times already, and it
would have been political suicide to tell them that the toughest ones were
actually up ahead.

So you never really tried to solve the problem.

Oh, c'mon. Can you ever "solve" poverty? Can you ever "solve" crime? Can you ever "solve" disease, unemployment, war, or any other societal herpes? Hell no. All you can hope for is to make them manageable enough to allow people to get on with their lives. That's not cynicism, that's maturity. You can't stop the rain. All you can do is just build a roof that you hope won't leak, or at least won't leak on the people who are gonna vote for you.

What does that mean?

C'mon . . .

Seriously. What does that mean?

Fine, whatever, "Mister Smith goes to motherfuckin' Washington," it means that, in politics, you focus on the needs of your power base. Keep them happy, and they keep you in office.

Is that why certain outbreaks were neglected?

Jesus, you make it sound like we just forgot about them.

Did local law enforcement request additional support from the federal government?

When have cops *not* asked for more men, better gear, more training hours, or "community outreach program funds"? Those pussies are almost as bad as soldiers, always whining about never having "what they need," but do they have to risk their jobs by raising taxes? Do they have to explain to Suburban Peter why they're fleecing him for Ghetto Paul?

You weren't worried about public disclosure?

From who?

The press, the media.

The "media"? You mean those networks that are owned by some of the largest corporations in the world, corporations that would have taken a nosedive if another panic hit the stock market? That media?

So you never actually instigated a cover-up?

We didn't have to; they covered it up themselves. They had as much, or more, to lose than we did. And besides, they'd already gotten their stories the year before when the first cases were reported in America. Then winter came, Phalanx hit the shelves, cases dropped. Maybe they "dissuaded" a few younger crusading reporters, but, in reality, the whole thing was pretty much old news after a few months. It had become "manageable." People were learning to live with it and they were already hungry for something different. Big news is big business, and you gotta stay fresh if you want to stay successful.

But there were alternative media outlets.

Oh sure, and you know who listens to them? Pansy, overeducated know-it-alls, and you know who listens to them? Nobody! Who's going to care about some PBS-NPR fringe minority that's out of touch with the mainstream? The more those elitist eggheads shouted "The Dead Are Walking," the more most real Americans tuned them out.

So, let me see if I understand your position.

The administration's position.

The administration's position, which is that you gave this problem the amount of attention that you thought it deserved.

Right.

Given that at any time, government always has a lot on its plate, and especially at this time because another public scare was the last thing the American people wanted.

Yep.

So you figured that the threat was small enough to be "managed" by both the Alpha teams abroad and some additional law enforcement training at home.

You got it.

Even though you'd received warnings to the contrary, that it could never just be woven into the fabric of public life and that it actually was a global catastrophe in the making.

[Mister Carlson pauses, shoots me an angry look, then heaves a shovelful of "fuel" into his cart.]

Grow up.

❖

TROY, MONTANA, USA

[This neighborhood is, according to the brochure, the "New Community" for the "New America." Based on the Israeli "Masada" model, it is clear just from first glance that this neighborhood was built with one goal in mind. The houses all rest on stilts, so high as to afford each a perfect view over the twenty-foot-high, reinforced concrete wall. Each house is accessed by a retractable staircase and can connect to its neighbor by a similarly retractable walkway. The solar cell roofs, the shielded wells, the gardens, lookout towers, and thick, sliding, steel-reinforced gate have all served to make Troy an instant success with its inhabitants, so much so that its developer has already received seven more orders across the continental United States. Troy's developer, chief architect, and first mayor is Mary Jo Miller.]

Oh yeah, I was worried, I was worried about my car payments and Tim's business loan. I was worried about that widening crack in the pool and the new nonchlorinated filter that still left an algae film. I was worried about our portfolio, even though my e-broker assured me this was just first-time investor jitters and that it was much more profitable than a standard 401(k). Aiden needed a math tutor, Jenna needed just the right Jamie Lynn Spears cleats for soccer camp. Tim's parents were thinking of coming to stay with us for Christmas. My brother was back in rehab. Finley had worms, one of the fish had some kind of fungus growing out of its left eye. These were just some of my worries. I had more than enough to keep me busy.

Did you watch the news?

Yeah, for about five minutes every day: local headlines, sports, celebrity gossip. Why would I want to get depressed by watching TV? I could do that just by stepping on the scale every morning.

What about other sources? Radio?

Morning drive time? That was my Zen hour. After the kids were dropped off, I'd listen to [name withheld for legal reasons]. His jokes helped me get through the day.

What about the Internet?

What about it? For me, it was shopping; for Jenna, it was homework; for Tim, it was . . . stuff he kept swearing he'd never look at again. The only news I ever saw was what popped up on my AOL welcome page.

At work, there must have been some discussion . . .

Oh yeah, at first. It was kinda scary, kinda weird, "you know I hear it's not really rabies" and stuff like that. But then that first winter things died down, remember, and anyway, it was a lot more fun to rehash last night's episode of *Celebrity Fat Camp* or totally bitch out whoever wasn't in the break room at that moment.

One time, around March or April, I came into work and found Mrs. Ruiz clearing out her desk. I thought she was being downsized or maybe outsourced, you know, something I considered a real threat. She explained that it was "them," that's how she always referred to it, "them" or "everything that's happening." She said that her family'd already sold their house and were buying a cabin up near Fort Yukon, Alaska. I thought that was the stupidest thing I'd ever heard, especially from someone like Inez. She wasn't one of the ignorant ones, she was a "clean" Mexican. I'm sorry to use that term, but that was how I thought back then, that was who I was.

Did your husband ever show any concern?

No, but the kids did, not verbally, or consciously, I think. Jenna started getting into fights. Aiden wouldn't go to sleep unless we left the lights on. Little things like that. I don't think they were exposed to any more information than Tim, or I, but maybe they didn't have the adult distractions to shut it out.

How did you and your husband respond?

Zoloft and Ritalin SR for Aiden, and Adderall XR for Jenna. It did the trick for a while. The only thing that pissed me off was that our insurance didn't cover it because the kids were already on Phalanx.

How long had they been on Phalanx?

Since it became available. We were all on Phalanx, "Piece of Phalanx, Peace of Mind." That was our way of being prepared . . . and Tim buying a gun. He kept promising to take me to the range to learn how to shoot. "Sunday," he'd always say, "we're goin' this Sunday." I knew he was full of it. Sundays were reserved for his mistress, that eighteen-footer, twin-engine bitch he seemed to sink all his love into. I didn't really care. We had our pills, and at least he knew how to use the Glock. It was part of life, like smoke alarms or airbags. Maybe you think about it once in a while, it was always just . . . "just in case." And besides, really, there was already so much out there to worry about, every month, it seemed, a new nail-biter. How can you keep track of all of it? How do you know which one is really real?

How did you know?

It had just gotten dark. The game was on. Tim was in the BarcaLounger with a Corona. Aiden was on the floor playing with his Ultimate Soldiers. Jenna was in her room doing homework. I was unloading the Maytag so I didn't hear Finley barking. Well, maybe I did, but I never gave it any thought. Our house was in the community's last row, right at the foot of the hills. We lived in a quiet, just developed part of North County near San Diego. There was always a rabbit, sometimes a deer, running across the lawn, so Finley was always throwing some kind of a shit fit. I think I glanced at the Post-it to get him one of those citronella bark collars. I'm not sure when the other dogs started barking, or when I heard the car alarm down the street. It was when I heard something that sounded like a gunshot that I went into the den. Tim hadn't heard anything. He had the volume jacked up too high. I kept telling him he had to get his hearing checked, you just don't spend your twenties in a speed metal band without . . . [sighs]. Aiden'd heard something. He asked me what it was. I was about to say I didn't know when I saw his eyes go wide. He was looking past me, at the glass sliding door that led to the backyard. I turned just in time to see it shatter.

It was about five foot ten, slumped, narrow shoulders with this puffy, wagging belly. It wasn't wearing a shirt and its mottled gray flesh was all torn and pockmarked. It smelled like the beach, like rotten kelp and salt-water. Aiden jumped up and ran behind me. Tim was out of the chair, standing between us and that thing. In a split second, it was like all the lies fell away. Tim looked frantically around the room for a weapon just as it grabbed him by the shirt. They fell on the carpet, wrestling. He shouted for us to get in the bedroom, for me to get the gun. We were in the hallway when I heard Jenna scream. I ran to her room, threw open the door. An-other one, big, I'd say six and a half feet with giant shoulders and bulging arms. The window was broken and it had Jenna by the hair. She was screaming "Mommymommymommy!"

What did you do?

I . . . I'm not totally sure. When I try to remember, everything goes by too fast. I had it by the neck. It pulled Jenna toward its open mouth. I squeezed hard . . . pulled . . . The kids say I tore the thing's head off, just ripped it right out with all the flesh and muscle and whatever else hanging in tat-ters. I don't think that's possible. Maybe with all your adrenaline pump-ing . . . I think the kids just have built it up in their memories over the years, making me into SheHulk or something. I know I freed Jenna. I remem-ber that, and just a second later, Tim came in the room, with this thick, black goo all over his shirt. He had the gun in one hand and Finley's leash in the other. He threw me the car keys and told me to get the kids in the Suburban. He ran into the backyard as we headed for the garage. I heard his gun go off as I started the engine.

THE GREAT PANIC

[Gavin Blaire pilots one of the D-17 combat dirigibles that make
up the core of America's Civil Air Patrol. It is a task well suited
to him. In civilian life, he piloted a Fujifilm blimp.]

It stretched to the horizon: sedans, trucks, buses, RVs, anything that
could drive. I saw tractors, I saw a cement mixer. Seriously, I even saw a
flatbed with nothing but a giant sign on it, a billboard advertising a "Gentlemen's Club." People were sitting on top of it. People were riding on top
of everything, on roofs, in between luggage racks. It reminded me of some
old picture of trains in India with people hanging on them like monkeys.

All kinds of crap lined the road—suitcases, boxes, even pieces of expensive furniture. I saw a grand piano, I'm not kidding, just smashed like it was
thrown off the top of a truck. There were also a lot of abandoned cars.
Some had been pushed over, some were stripped, some looked burned out.
I saw a lot of people on foot, walking across the plains or alongside the
road. Some were knocking on windows, holding up all kinds of stuff. A few

women were exposing themselves. They must have been looking to trade, probably gas. They couldn't have been looking for rides, they were moving faster than cars. It wouldn't make sense, but . . . [shrugs].

Back down the road, about thirty miles, traffic was moving a little better. You'd think the mood would be calmer. It wasn't. People were flashing their lights, bumping the cars in front of them, getting out and throwing down. I saw a few people lying by the side of the road, barely moving or not at all. People were running past them, carrying stuff, carrying children, or just running, all in the same direction of the traffic. A few miles later, I saw why.

Those creatures were swarming among the cars. Drivers on the outer lanes tried to veer off the road, sticking in the mud, trapping the inner lanes. People couldn't open their doors. The cars were too tightly packed. I saw those things reach in open windows, pulling people out or pulling themselves in. A lot of drivers were trapped inside. Their doors were shut and, I'm assuming, locked. Their windows were rolled up, it was safety tempered glass. The dead couldn't get in, but the living couldn't get out. I saw a few people panic, try to shoot through their windshields, destroying the only protection they had. Stupid. They might have bought themselves a few hours in there, maybe even a chance to escape. Maybe there was no escape, just a quicker end. There was a horse trailer, hitched to a pickup in the center lane. It was rocking crazily back and forth. The horses were still inside.

The swarm continued among the cars, literally eating its way up the stalled lines, all those poor bastards just trying to get away. And that's what haunts me most about it, they weren't headed anywhere. This was the I-80, a strip of highway between Lincoln and North Platte. Both places were heavily infested, as well as all those little towns in between. What did they think they were doing? Who organized this exodus? Did anyone? Did people see a line of cars and join them without asking? I tried to imagine what it must have been like, stuck bumper to bumper, crying kids, barking dog, knowing what was coming just a few miles back, and hoping, praying that someone up ahead knows where he's going.

You ever hear about that experiment an American journalist did in Moscow in the 1970s? He just lined up at some building, nothing special about it, just a random door. Sure enough, someone got in line behind him, then a couple more, and before you knew it, they were backed up around the block. No one asked what the line was for. They just assumed it was worth it. I can't say if that story was true. Maybe it's an urban legend, or a cold war myth. Who knows?

❧

ALANG, INDIA

[I stand on the shore with Ajay Shah, looking out at the rusting wrecks of once-proud ships. Since the government does not possess the funds to remove them and because both time and the elements have made their steel next to useless, they remain silent memorials to the carnage this beach once witnessed.]

They tell me what happened here was not unusual, all around our world where the ocean meets the land, people trying desperately to board whatever floated for a chance of survival at sea.

I didn't know what Alang was, even though I'd lived my entire life in nearby Bhavnagar. I was an office manager, a "zippy," white-collar professional from the day I left university. The only time I'd ever worked with my hands was to punch a keyboard, and not even that since all our software went voice recognition. I knew Alang was a shipyard, that's why I tried to make for it in the first place. I'd expected to find a construction site cranking out hull after hull to carry us all to safety. I had no idea that it was just the opposite. Alang didn't build ships, it killed them. Before the war, it was the largest breakers yard in the world. Vessels from all nations were bought by Indian scrap-iron companies, run up on this beach, stripped, cut, and disassembled until not the smallest bolt remained. The several dozen vessels I saw were not fully loaded, fully functional ships, but naked hulks lining up to die.

There were no dry docks, no slipways. Alang was not so much a yard as a long stretch of sand. Standard procedure was to ram the ships up onto the shore, stranding them like beached whales. I thought my only hope was the half dozen new arrivals that still remained anchored offshore, the ones with skeleton crews and, I hoped, a little bit of fuel left in their bunkers. One of these ships, the *Veronique Delmas*, was trying to pull one of her beached sisters out to sea. Ropes and chains were haphazardly lashed to the stern of the APL *Tulip*, a Singapore container ship that had already been partially gutted. I arrived just as the *Delmas* fired up her engines. I could see the white water churning as she strained against the lines. I could hear some of the weaker ropes snap like gunshots.

The stronger chains though . . . they held out longer than the hull. Beaching the *Tulip* must have badly fractured her keel. When the *Delmas* began to pull, I heard this horrible groan, this creaking screech of metal. The *Tulip* literally split in two, the bow remaining on shore while the stern was pulled out to sea.

There was nothing anyone could do, the *Delmas* was already at flank speed, dragging the *Tulip*'s stern out into deep water where it rolled over and sank within seconds. There must have been at least a thousand people aboard, packing every cabin and passageway and square inch of open deck space. Their cries were muffled by the thunder of escaping air.

Why didn't the refugees just wait aboard the beached ships, pull up the ladders, make them inaccessible?

You speak with rational hindsight. You weren't there that night. The yard was crammed right up to the shoreline, this mad dash of humanity backlit by inland fires. Hundreds were trying to swim out to the ships. The surf was choked with those who didn't make it.

Dozens of little boats were going back and forth, shuttling people from shore to ships. "Give me your money," some of them would say, "everything you have, then I'll take you."

Money was still worth something?

Money, or food, or anything they considered valuable. I saw one ship's crew that only wanted women, young women. I saw another that would only take light-skinned refugees. The bastards were shining their torches in people's faces, trying to root out darkies like me. I even saw one captain, standing on the deck of his ship's launch, waving a gun and shouting "No scheduled castes, we won't take untouchables!" Untouchables? Castes? Who the hell still thinks like that? And this is the crazy part, some older people actually got out of the queue! Can you believe that?

I'm just highlighting the most extreme negative examples, you understand. For every one profiteer, or repulsive psychopath, there were ten good and decent people whose karma was still untainted. A lot of fishermen and small boat owners who could have simply escaped with their families chose to put themselves in danger by continuing to return to shore. When you think about what they were risking: being murdered for their boats, or just marooned on the beach, or else attacked from beneath by so many underwater ghouls . . .

There were quite a few. Many infected refugees had tried to swim for the ships and then reanimated after they drowned. It was low tide, just deep enough for a man to drown, but shallow enough for a standing ghoul to reach up for prey. You saw many swimmers suddenly vanish below the surface, or boats capsize with their passengers dragged under. And still rescuers continued to return to shore, or even jumped from ships to save people in the water.

That was how I was saved. I was one of those who tried to swim. The ships looked much closer than they actually were. I was a strong swimmer, but after walking from Bhavnagar, after fighting for my life for most of that day, I barely had enough strength to float on my back. By the time I reached my intended salvation, there wasn't enough air in my lungs to call for help. There was no gangway. The smooth side towered over me. I banged on the steel, shouting up with the last bit of breath I had.

Just as I slipped below the surface, I felt a powerful arm wrap around my chest. *This is it*, I thought; any second, I thought I would feel teeth dig into my flesh. Instead of pulling me down, the arm hauled me back up to the surface. I ended up aboard the *Sir Wilfred Grenfell*, an ex-Canadian Coast Guard cutter. I tried to talk, to apologize for not having any money, to explain that I could work for my passage, do anything they needed. The crewman just smiled. "Hold on," he said to me, "we're about to get under way." I could feel the deck vibrate then lurch as we moved.

That was the worst part, watching the other ships we passed. Some of the onboard infected refugees had begun to reanimate. Some vessels were floating slaughterhouses, others just burned at anchor. People were leaping into the sea. Many who sank beneath the surface never reappeared.

❧

TOPEKA, KANSAS, USA

[Sharon could be considered beautiful by almost any standard— with long red hair, sparkling green eyes, and the body of a dancer or a prewar supermodel. She also has the mind of a four-year-old girl.

We are at the Rothman Rehabilitation Home for Feral Children. Doctor Roberta Kelner, Sharon's caseworker, describes her condition as "lucky." "At least she has language skills, a cohesive thought process," she explains. "It's rudimentary, but at least it's fully functional." Doctor Kelner is eager for the interview, but Doctor Sommers, Rothman's program director, is not. Funding has always been spotty for this program, and the present administration is threatening to close it down altogether.

Sharon is shy at first. She will not shake my hand and seldom makes eye contact. Although Sharon was found in the ruins of Wichita, there is no way of knowing where her story originally occurred.]

We were in church, Mommy and me. Daddy told us that he would come find us. Daddy had to go do something. We had to wait for him in church.

Everybody was there. They all had stuff. They had cereal, and water, and juice, and sleeping bags and flashlights and . . . [she mimes a rifle]. Mrs. Randolph had one. She wasn't supposed to. They were dangerous. She told me they were dangerous. She was Ashley's mommy. Ashley was my friend. I asked her where was Ashley. She started to cry. Mommy told me not to ask her about Ashley and told Mrs. Randolph that she was sorry. Mrs. Randolph was dirty, she had red and brown on her dress. She was fat. She had big, soft arms.

There were other kids, Jill and Abbie, and other kids. Mrs. McGraw was watching them. They had crayons. They were coloring on the wall. Mommy told me to go play with them. She told me it was okay. She said Pastor Dan said it was okay.

Pastor Dan was there, he was trying to make people listen to him. "Please everyone . . ." [she mimics a deep, low voice] "please stay calm, the 'thor-ties' are coming, just stay calm and wait for the 'thorties.' " No one was lis-tening to him. Everyone was talking, nobody was sitting. People were trying to talk on their things [mimes holding a cell phone], they were angry at their things, throwing them, and saying bad words. I felt bad for Pastor Dan. [She mimics the sound of a siren.] Outside. [She does it again, start-ing soft, then growing, then fading out again multiple times.]

Mommy was talking to Mrs. Cormode and other mommies. They were fighting. Mommy was getting mad. Mrs. Cormode kept saying [in an angry drawl], "Well what if? What else can you do?" Mommy was shaking her head. Mrs. Cormode was talking with her hands. I didn't like Mrs. Cor-mode. She was Pastor Dan's wife. She was bossy and mean.

Somebody yelled . . . "Here they come!" Mommy came and picked me up. They took our bench and put it next to the door. They put all the benches next to the door. "Quick!" "Jam the door!" [She mimics several different voices.] "I need a hammer!" "Nails!" "They're in the parking lot!" "They're coming this way!" [She turns to Doctor Kelner.] Can I?

[Doctor Sommers looks unsure. Doctor Kelner smiles and nods. I later learn that the room is soundproofed for this reason.]

[Sharon mimics the moan of a zombie. It is undoubtedly the most realistic I have ever heard. Clearly, by their discomfort, Sommers and Kelner agree.]

They were coming. They came bigger. [Again she moans. Then follows up by pounding her right fist on the table.] They wanted to come in. [Her blows are powerful, mechanical.] People screamed. Mommy hugged me tight. "It's okay." [Her voice softens as she begins to stroke her own hair.] "I won't let them get you. Shhhh. . . ."

[Now she bangs both fists on the table, her strikes becoming more chaotic as if to simulate multiple ghouls.] "Brace the door!" "Hold it! Hold it!" [She simulates the sound of shattering glass.] The windows broke, the windows in the front next to the door. The lights got black. Grown-ups got scared. They screamed.

[Her voice returns to her mother's.] "Shhhh . . . baby. I won't let them get you." [Her hands go from her hair to her face, gently stroking her forehead and cheeks. Sharon gives Kelner a questioning look. Kelner nods. Sharon's voice suddenly simulates the sound of something large breaking, a deep phlegm-filled rumble from the bottom of her throat.] "They're coming in! Shoot 'em, shoot 'em!" [She makes the sound of gunfire then . . .] "I won't let them get you, I won't let them get you." [Sharon suddenly looks away, over my shoulder to something that isn't there.] "The children! Don't let them get the children!" That was Mrs. Cormode. "Save the children! Save the children!" [Sharon makes more gunshots. She balls her hands into a large double fist, bringing it down hard on an invisible form.] Now the kids started crying. [She simulates stabbing, punching, striking with objects.] Abbie cried hard. Mrs. Cormode picked her up. [She mimes lifting something, or someone, up and swinging them against the wall.] And then Abbie stopped. [She goes back to stroking her own face, her mother's voice has become harder.] "Shhh . . . it's okay, baby, it's okay . . ." [Her hands move down from her face to her throat, tightening into a strangling grip.] "I won't let them get you. I WON'T LET THEM GET YOU!"

[Sharon begins to gasp for air.]

[Doctor Sommers makes a move to stop her. Doctor Kelner puts up a hand. Sharon suddenly ceases, throwing her arms out to the sound of a gunshot.]

Warm and wet, salty in my mouth, stinging my eyes. Arms picked me up and carried me. [She gets up from the table, mimicking a motion close to a football.] Carried me into the parking lot. "Run, Sharon, don't stop!" [This is a different voice now, not her mother's.] "Just run, run-run-run!" They pulled her away from me. Her arms let me go. They were big, soft arms.

❦

KHUZHIR, OLKHON ISLAND, LAKE BAIKAL, THE HOLY RUSSIAN EMPIRE

[The room is bare except for a table, two chairs, and a large wall mirror, which is almost sure to be one-way glass. I sit across from my subject, writing on the pad provided for me (my transcriber has been forbidden for "security reasons"). Maria Zhuganova's face is worn, her hair is graying, her body strains the seams of the fraying uniform she insists on wearing for this interview. Technically we are alone, although I sense watching eyes behind the room's one-way glass.]

We didn't know that there was a Great Panic. We were completely isolated. About a month before it began, about the same time as that American newswoman broke the story, our camp was placed on indefinite communication blackout. All the televisions were removed from the barracks, all the personal radios and cell phones, too. I had one of those cheap disposable types with five prepaid minutes. It was all my parents could afford. I was supposed to use it to call them on my birthday, my first birthday away from home.

We were stationed in North Ossetia, Alania, one of our wild southern republics. Our official duty was "peacekeeping," preventing ethnic strife between the Ossetia and Ingush minorities. Our rotation was up about the same time they cut us off from the world. A matter of "state security" they called it.

Who were "they"?

Everyone: our officers, the Military Police, even a plain-clothed civilian who just seemed to appear one day out of nowhere. He was a mean little bastard, with a thin, rat face. That's what we called him: "Rat Face."

Did you ever try to find out who he was?

What, me personally? Never. Neither did anyone else. Oh, we griped; soldiers always gripe. But there also wasn't time for any serious complaints. Right after the blackout was put into effect, we were placed on full combat alert. Up until then it had been easy duty—lazy, monotonous, and broken only by the occasional mountain stroll. Now we were in those mountains for days at a time with full battle dress and ammo. We were in every village, every house. We questioned every peasant and traveler and . . . I don't know . . . goat that crossed our path.

Questioned them? For what?

I didn't know. "Is everyone in your family present?" "Has anyone gone missing?" "Has anyone been attacked by a rabid animal or man?" That was the part that confused me the mosti Rabid? I understood the animal part, but man? There were a lot of physical inspections, too, stripping these people to their bare skin while the medics searched every inch of their bodies for . . . something . . . we weren't told what.

It didn't make sense, nothing did. We once found a whole cache of weapons, 74s, a few older 47s, plenty of ammo, probably bought from some corrupt opportunist right in our battalion. We didn't know who the weapons belonged to; drug runners, or the local gangsters, maybe even those supposed "Reprisal Squads" that were the reason for our deployment in the first place. And what did we do? We left it all. That little civilian, "Rat Face," he had a private meeting with some of the village elders. I don't know what was discussed, but I can tell you that they looked scared half to death: crossing themselves, praying silently.

We didn't understand. We were confused, angry. We didn't understand what the hell we were doing out there. We had this one old veteran in our platoon, Baburin. He'd fought in Afghanistan and twice in Chechnya. It was rumored that during Yeltsin's crackdown, his BMP[1] was the first to fire on the Duma. We used to like to listen to his stories. He was always good-natured, always drunk . . . when he thought he could get away with it. He changed after the incident with the weapons. He stopped smiling, there were no more stories. I don't think he ever touched a drop after that, and when he spoke to you, which was rare, the only thing he ever said was, "This isn't good. Something's going to happen." Whenever I tried to ask him about it, he would just shrug and walk away. Morale was pretty low after that. People were tense, suspicious. Rat Face was always there, in the shadows, listening, watching, whispering into the ears of our officers.

He was with us the day we swept a little no-name town, this primitive hamlet at what looked like the edge of the world. We'd executed our standard searches and interrogations. We were just about to pack it in. Suddenly this child, this little girl came running down the only road in town. She was crying, obviously terrified. She was chattering to her parents . . . I wish I could have taken the time to learn their language . . . and pointing across the field. There was a tiny figure, another little girl, staggering across the mud toward us. Lieutenant Tikhonov raised his binoculars and I watched his face lose its color. Rat Face came up next to him, gave a look through his own glasses, then whispered something in the lieutenant's ear. Petrenko, platoon sharpshooter, was ordered to raise his weapon and center the girl in his sights. He did. "Do you have her?" "I have her." "Shoot."

---

1. The BMP is an armored personnel carrier invented and used by Soviet, and now Russian, military forces.

That's how it went, I think. I remember there was a pause. Petrenko looked up at the lieutenant and asked him to repeat the order. "You heard me," he said angrily. I was farther away than Petrenko and even I'd heard him. "I said eliminate the target, now!" I could see the tip of his rifle was shaking. He was a skinny little runt, not the bravest or the strongest, but suddenly he lowered his weapon and said he wouldn't do it. Just like that. "No, sir." It felt like the sun froze in the sky. No one knew what to do, especially Lieutenant Tikhonov. Everyone was looking at one another, then we were all looking out at the field.

Rat Face was walking out there, slowly, almost casually. The little girl was now close enough so we could see her face. Her eyes were wide, locked on Rat Face. Her arms were raised, and I could just make out this high-pitched, rasping moan. He met her halfway across the field. It was over before most of us realized what had happened. In one smooth motion, Rat Face pulled a pistol from underneath his coat, shot her right between the eyes, then turned around and sauntered back toward us. A woman, probably the little girl's mother, exploded into sobs. She fell to her knees, spitting and cursing at us. Rat Face didn't seem to care or even notice. He just whispered something to Lieutenant Tikhonov, then remounted the BMP as if he was hailing a Moscow taxicab.

That night . . . lying awake in my bunk, I tried not to think about what had happened. I tried not to think about the fact that the MPs had taken Petrenko away, or that our weapons had been locked in the armory. I knew I should have felt bad for the child, angry, even vengeful toward Rat Face, and maybe even a little bit guilty because I didn't lift a finger to stop it. I knew those were the kinds of emotions I should have been feeling; at that point the only thing I could feel was fear. I kept thinking about what Baburin had said, that something bad was going to happen. I just wanted to go home, see my parents. What if there'd been some horrible terrorist attack? What if it was a war? My family lived in Bikin, almost within sight of the Chinese border. I needed to speak to them, to make sure they were okay. I worried so much that I started throwing up, so much so that they checked me into the infirmary. That's why I missed the patrol that day, that's why I was still on bed rest when they came back the following afternoon.

I was in my bunk, rereading an outdated copy of *Semnadstat*.[2] I heard a commotion, vehicle engines, voices. A crowd was already assembled on the parade ground. I pushed my way through and saw Arkady standing in the center of the mob. Arkady was the heavy machine gunner from my squad, a big bear of a man. We were friends because he kept the other men away from me, if you understand what I mean. He said I reminded him of his sister. [Smiles sadly.] I liked him.

There was someone crawling at his feet. It looked like an old woman, but there was a burlap hood over her head and a chain leash wrapped around her neck. Her dress was torn and the skin of her legs had been scraped clean off. There was no blood, just this black pus. Arkady was well into a loud, angry speech. "No more lies! No more orders to shoot civilians on sight! And that's why I put the little zhopoliz down . . ."

I looked for Lieutenant Tikhonov but I couldn't see him anywhere. I got a ball of ice in my stomach.

". . . because I wanted you all to see!" Arkady lifted the chain, pulling the old babushka up by her throat. He grabbed the hood and ripped it off. Her face was gray, just like the rest of her, her eyes were wide and fierce. She snarled like a wolf and tried to grab Arkady. He wrapped one powerful hand around her throat, holding her at arm's length.

"I want you all to see why we are here!" He grabbed the knife from his belt and plunged it into the woman's heart. I gasped, we all did. It was buried up to the hilt and she continued to squirm and growl. "You see!" he shouted, stabbing her several more times. "You see! This is what they're not telling us! This is what they have us breaking our backs to find!" You could see heads start to nod, a few grunts of agreement. Arkady continued, "What if these things are everywhere? What if they're back home, with our families right now!" He was trying to make eye contact with as many of us as possible. He wasn't paying enough attention to the old woman. His grip loosened, she pulled free and bit him on the hand. Arkady roared. His fist caved in the old woman's face. She fell to his feet, writhing and gurgling

2. *Semnadstat* was a Russian magazine aimed at teenage girls. It's title, *17*, was illegally copied from an American publication of the same name.

that black goo. He finished the job with his boot. We all heard her skull crack.

Blood was trickling down the gouge in Arkady's fist. He shook it at the sky, screaming as the veins in his neck began to bulge. "We want to go home!" he bellowed. "We want to protect our families!" Others in the crowd began to pick it up. "Yes! We want to protect our families! This is a free country! This is a democracy! You can't keep us in prison!" I was shouting, too, chanting with the rest. That old woman, the creature that could take a knife in the heart without dying . . . what if they were back home? What if they were threatening our loved ones . . . my parents? All the fear, all the doubt, every tangled, negative emotion all fused into rage. "We want to go home! We want to go home!" Chanting, chanting, and then . . . A round cracked past my ear and Arkady's left eye imploded. I don't remember running, or inhaling the tear gas. I don't remember when the Spetznaz commandos appeared, but suddenly they were all around us, beating us down, shackling us together, one of them stepping on my chest so hard I thought I was going to die right then and there.

Was that the Decimation?

No, that was the beginning. We weren't the first army unit to rebel. It had actually started about the time the MPs first closed down the base. About the time we staged our little "demonstration," the government had decided how to restore order.

[She straightens her uniform, composes herself before speaking.]

To "decimate" . . . I used to think it meant just to wipe out, cause horrible damage, destroy . . . it actually means to kill by a percentage of ten, one out of every ten must die . . . and that's exactly what they did to us.

The Spetznaz had us assemble on the parade ground, full dress uniform no less. Our new commanding officer gave a speech about duty and responsibility, about our sworn oath to protect the motherland, and how we

had betrayed that oath with our selfish treachery and individual cow-
ardice. I'd never heard words like that before. "Duty?" "Responsibility?"
Russia, my Russia, was nothing but an apolitical mess. We lived in chaos
and corruption, we were just trying to get through the day. Even the army
was no bastion of patriotism; it was a place to learn a trade, get food and a
bed, and maybe even a little money to send home when the government
decided it was convenient to pay its soldiers. "Oath to protect the motherland?" Those weren't the words of my generation. That was what you'd
hear from old Great Patriotic War veterans, the kind of broken, demented
geezers who used to besiege Red Square with their tattered Soviet banners
and their rows and rows of medals pinned to their faded, moth-eaten uniforms. Duty to the motherland was a joke. But I wasn't laughing. I knew
the executions were coming. The armed men surrounding us, the men in
the guard towers, I was ready, every muscle in my body was tensing for the
shot. And then I heard those words . . .

"You spoiled children think democracy is a God-given right. You expect
it, you demand it! Well, now you're going to get your chance to practice it."

His exact words, stamped behind my eyelids for the rest of my life.

What did he mean?

We would be the ones to decide who would be punished. Broken up into
groups of ten, we would have to vote on which one of us was going to be
executed. And then we . . . the soldiers, we would be the ones to personally murder our friends. They rolled these little pushcarts past us. I can still
hear their creaking wheels. They were full of stones, about the size of your
hand, sharp and heavy. Some cried out, pleaded with us, begged like children. Some, like Baburin, simply knelt there silently, on this knees, staring
right into my face as I brought the rock down into his.

[She sighs softly, glancing over her shoulder at the one-way glass.]

Brilliance. Sheer fucking brilliance. Conventional executions might
have reinforced discipline, might have restored order from the top down,

but by making us all accomplices, they held us together not just by fear, but by guilt as well. We could have said no, could have refused and been shot ourselves, but we didn't. We went right along with it. We all made a conscious choice and because that choice carried such a high price, I don't think anyone ever wanted to make another one again. We relinquished our freedom that day, and we were more than happy to see it go. From that moment on we lived in true freedom, the freedom to point to someone else and say "They told me to do it! It's their fault, not mine." The freedom, God help us, to say "I was only following orders."

BRIDGETOWN, BARBADOS, WEST INDIES FEDERATION

[Trevor's Bar personifies the "Wild West Indies," or, more specifically, each island's "Special Economic Zone." This is not a place most people would associate with the order and tranquility of postwar Caribbean life. It is not meant to be. Fenced off from the rest of the island and catering to a culture of chaotic violence and debauchery, the Special Economic Zones are engineered specifically to separate "off-islanders" from their money. My discomfort seems to please T. Sean Collins. The giant Texan slides a shot of "kill-devil" rum in my direction, then swings his massive, boot-clad feet onto the table.]

They haven't come up with a name for what I used to do. Not a real one, not yet. "Independent contractor" sounds like I should be layin' drywall and smearin' plaster. "Private security" sounds like some dumbass mall guard. "Mercenary" is the closest, I guess, but at the same time, about as far from the real me as you could have gotten. A mercenary sounds like some crazed-out 'Nam vet, all tats and handlestache, humpin' in some Third World cesspool 'cause he can't hack it back in the real world. That wasn't me at all. Yeah, I was a vet, and yeah, I used my training for cash . . . funny thing about the army, they always promise to teach you "marketable skills," but they never mention that, by far, there's nothing more marketable than knowing how to kill some people while keeping others from being killed.

Maybe I was a mercenary, but you'd never know it to look at me. I was clean-cut, nice car, nice house, even a housekeeper who came in once a week. I had plenty of friends, marriage prospects, and my handicap at the country club was almost as good as the pros. Most importantly, I worked for a company no different from any other before the war. There was no cloak and dagger, no back rooms and midnight envelopes. I had vacation days and sick days, full medical and a sweet dental package. I paid my taxes, too much; I paid into my IRA. I could have worked overseas; Lord knows there was plenty of demand, but after seeing what my buddies went through in the last brushfire, I said, screw it, let me guard some fat CEO or worthless, dumb celebrity. And that's where I found myself when the Panic hit.

You don't mind if I don't mention any names, 'kay? Some of these people are still alive, or their estates are still active, and . . . can you believe, they're still threatening to sue. After all that's gone down? Okay, so I can't name names or places, but figure it's an island . . . a big island . . . a *long* island, right next to Manhattan. Can't sue me for that, right?

My client, I'm not sure what he really did. Something in entertainment, or high finance. Beats me. I think he might have even been one of the senior shareholders in my firm. Whatever, he had bucks, lived in this amazing pad by the beach.

Our client liked to know people who were known by all. His plan was to provide safety for those who could raise his image during and after the war, playing Moses to the scared and famous. And you know what, they fell for it. The actors, and singers, and rappers and pro athletes, and just the professional faces, like the ones you see on talk shows or reality shows, or even that little rich, spoiled, tired-looking whore who was famous for just being a rich, spoiled, tired-looking whore.

There was that record mogul guy with the big 'ole diamond earrings. He had this tricked-out AK with a grenade launcher. He loved to talk about how it was an exact replica of the one from *Scarface*. I didn't have the heart to tell him that Señor Montana had used a sixteen A-1.

There was the political comedy guy, you know, the one with the show. He was snorting blow between the air bags of this teeny Thai stripper while spewing about how what was happening wasn't just about the living versus the dead, it would send shock waves through every facet of our society: social, economic, political, even environmental. He said that, subconsciously, everyone already knew the truth during the "Great Denial," and that's why they wigged out so hard when the story was finally broken. It all actually kinda made sense, until he started spewing about high fructose corn syrup and the feminization of America.

Crazy, I know, but you kinda expected those people to be there, at least I did. What I didn't expect was all their "people." Every one of them, no matter who they were or what they did, had to have, at least, I don't know how many stylists and publicists and personal assistants. Some of them, I think, were pretty cool, just doing it for the money, or because they figured they'd be safe there. Young people just trying to get a leg up. Can't fault them for that. Some of the others though . . . real pricks all high on the smell of their own piss. Just rude and pushy and ordering everyone else around. One guy sticks out in my mind, only because he wore this baseball cap that read "Get It Done!" I think he was the chief handler of the fat fuck who won that talent show. That guy must have had fourteen people around him! I remember thinking at first that it would be impossible to take care of all these people, but after my initial tour of the premises, I realized our boss had planned for everything.

He'd transformed his home into a survivalists' wet dream. He had enough dehydrated food to keep an army fed for years, as well as an endless supply of water from a desalinizer that ran right out into the ocean. He had wind turbines, solar panels, and backup generators with giant fuel tanks buried right under the courtyard. He had enough security measures to hold off the living dead forever: high walls, motion sensors, and weapons, oh the weapons. Yeah, our boss had really done his homework, but what he was most proud of was the fact that every room in the house was wired for a simultaneous webcast that went out all over the world 24/7. This was the real reason for having all his "closest" and "best" friends over. He didn't just want to ride out the storm in comfort and luxury, he wanted everyone to *know* he'd done it. That was the celebrity angle, his way of ensuring high-profile exposure.

Not only did you have a webcam in almost every room, but there was all the usual press you'd find on the Oscar's red carpet. I honestly never knew how big an industry entertainment journalism was. There had to be dozens of them there from all these magazines and TV shows. "How are you feeling?" I heard that a lot. "How are you holding up?" "What do you think is going to happen?" and I swear I even heard someone ask "What are you wearing?"

For me, the most surreal moment was standing in the kitchen with some of the staff and other bodyguards, all of us watching the news that was showing, guess what, us! The cameras were literally in the other room, pointed at some of the "stars" as they sat on the couch watching another news channel. The feed was live from New York's Upper East Side; the dead were coming right up Third Avenue, people were taking them on hand to hand, hammers and pipes, the manager of a Modell's Sporting Goods was handing out all his baseball bats and shouting "Get 'em in the head!" There was this one guy on rollerblades. He had a hockey stick in his hand, a big 'ole meat cleaver bolted to the blade. He was doing an easy thirty, at that speed he might have taken a neck or two. The camera saw the whole thing, the rotted arm that shot out of the sewer drain right in front of him, the poor guy back flipping into the air, coming down hard on his face, then being dragged, screaming, by his ponytail into the drain. At that moment the camera in our living room swung back to catch the reactions of the watching celebs. There were a few gasps, some honest, some staged. I remember thinking I had less respect for the ones who tried to fake some tears than I did for the little spoiled whore who called the rollerblading guy a "dumbass." Hey, at least she was being honest. I remember I was standing next to this guy, Sergei, a miserable, sad-faced, hulking motherfucker. His stories about growing up in Russia convinced me that not all Third World cesspools had to be tropical. It was when the camera was catching the reactions of the beautiful people that he mumbled something to himself in Russian. The only word I could make out was "Romanovs" and I was about to ask him what he meant when we all heard the alarm go off.

Something had triggered the pressure sensors we'd placed several miles around the wall. They were sensitive enough to detect just one zombie, now they were going crazy. Our radios were squawking: "Contact, contact, southwest corner . . . shit, there's hundreds of them!" It was a damn big house, it took me a few minutes to get to my firing position. I didn't understand why the lookout was so nervous. So what if there were a couple hundred. They'd never get over the wall. Then I heard him shout "They're running! Holy fuckin' shit, they're fast!" Fast zombies, that turned my gut. If they could run, they could climb, if they could climb, maybe they could think, and if they could think . . . now I was scared. I remember our boss's friends were all raiding the armory, racing around like extras in an '80s action flick by the time I made the third-floor guestroom window.

I flipped the safety off my weapon and flipped the guards off my sight. It was one of the newest Gen's, a fusion of light amplification and thermal imaging. I didn't need the second part because Gs gave off no body heat. So when I saw the searing, bright green signatures of several hundred runners, my throat tightened. Those weren't living dead.

"There it is!" I heard them shout. "That's the house on the news!" They were carrying ladders, guns, babies. A couple of them had these heavy satchels strapped to their backs. They were booking it for the front gate, big tough steel that was supposed to stop a thousand ghouls. The explosion tore them right off their hinges, sent them flipping into the house like giant ninja stars. "Fire!" the boss was screaming into the radio. "Knock 'em down! Kill 'em! Shootshootshoot!"

The "attackers," for lack of a better label, stampeded for the house. The courtyard was full of parked vehicles, sports cars and Hummers, and even a monster truck belonging to some NFL cat. Freakin fireballs, all of them, blowing over on their sides or just burning in place, this thick oily smoke from their tires blinding and choking everyone. All you could hear was gunfire, ours and theirs, and not just our private security team. Any big shot who wasn't crapping his pants either had it in his head to be a hero, or felt he had to protect his rep in front of his peeps. A lot of them demanded that their entourage protect them. Some did, these poor twenty-year-old personal assistants who'd never fired a gun in their lives. They didn't last very long. But then there were also the peons who turned and joined the attackers. I saw this one real queeny hairdresser stab an actress in the mouth with a letter opener, and, ironically, I watched Mister "Get It Done" try to wrestle a grenade away from the talent show guy before it went off in their hands.

It was bedlam, exactly what you thought the end of the world was supposed to look like. Part of the house was burning, blood everywhere, bodies or bits of them spewed over all that expensive stuff. I met the whore's rat dog as we were both heading for the back door. He looked at me, I looked at him. If it'd been a conversation, it probably woulda gone like, "What about your master?" "What about yours?" "Fuck 'em." That was the attitude among a lot of the hired guns, the reason I hadn't fired a shot all night. We'd been paid to protect rich people from zombies, not against other not-so-rich people who just wanted a safe place to hide. You could hear them shouting as they charged in through the front door. Not "grab the booze" or "rape the bitches"; it was "put out the fire!" and "get the women and kids upstairs!"

I stepped over Mister Political Comedy Guy on my way out to the beach. He and this chick, this leathery old blonde who I thought was supposed to be his political enemy, were goin' at it like there was no tomorrow, and, hey, maybe for them, there wasn't. I made it out to the sand, found a surfboard, probably worth more than the house I grew up in, and started paddling for the lights on the horizon. There were a lot of boats on the water that night, a lot of people gettin' outta Dodge. I hoped one of them might give me a ride as far as New York Harbor. Hopefully I could bribe them with a pair of diamond earrings.

[He finishes his shot of rum and signals for another.]

Sometimes I ask myself, why didn't they all just shut the fuck up, you know? Not just my boss, but all of those pampered parasites. They had the means to stay way outta harm's way, so why didn't they use it; go to Antarctica or Greenland or just stay where they were but stay the hell outta the public eye? But then again, maybe they couldn't, like a switch you just can't turn off. Maybe it's what made them who they were in the first place. But what the hell do I know?

[The waiter arrives with another shot and T. Sean flicks a silver rand coin to him.]

"If you got it, flaunt it."

❦

ICE CITY, GREENLAND

[From the surface, all that is visible are the funnels, the massive, carefully sculpted wind catchers that continue to bring fresh, albeit cold, air to the three-hundred-kilometer maze below. Few of the quarter million people who once inhabited this hand-carved marvel of engineering have remained. Some stay to encourage the small but growing tourist trade. Some are here as custodians, living on the pension that goes with UNESCO's renewed World Heritage Program. Some, like Ahmed Farahnakian, formerly Major Farahnakian of the Iranian Revolution Guards Corps Air Force, have nowhere else to go.]

India and Pakistan. Like North and South Korea or NATO and the old Warsaw Pact. If two sides were going to use nuclear weapons against each other, it had to be India and Pakistan. Everyone knew it, everyone expected it, and that is exactly why it didn't happen. Because the danger was so omnipresent, all the machinery had been put in place over the years to avoid it. The hotline between the two capitals was in place, ambassadors were on a first-name basis, and generals, politicians, and everyone involved in the process was trained to make sure the day they all feared never came. No one could have imagined—I certainly didn't—that events would unfold as they did.

The infection hadn't hit us as hard as some other countries. Our land was very mountainous. Transportation was difficult. Our population was relatively small; given the size of our country and when you consider that many of our cities could be easily isolated by a proportionately large military, it is not difficult to see how optimistic our leadership was.

The problem was refugees, millions of them from the east, millions! Streaming across Baluchistan, throwing our plans into disarray. So many areas were already infected, great swarms slouching toward our cities. Our border guards were overwhelmed, entire outposts buried under waves of ghouls. There was no way to close the border and at the same time deal with our own outbreaks.

We demanded that the Pakistanis get control of their people. They assured us they were doing all they could. We knew they were lying.

The majority of refugees came from India, just passing through Pakistan in an attempt to reach someplace safe. Those in Islamabad were quite willing to let them go. Better to pass the problem along to another nation than have to deal with it themselves. Perhaps if we could have combined our forces, coordinated a joint operation at some appropriately defensible location. I know the plans were on the table. Pakistan's south central mountains: the Pab, the Kirthar, the Central Brahui range. We could have stopped any number of refugees, or living dead. Our plan was refused. Some paranoid military attaché at their embassy told us outright that any foreign troops on their soil would be seen as a declaration of war. I don't know if their president ever saw our proposal; our leaders never spoke to him directly. You see what I mean about India and Pakistan. We didn't have their relationship. The diplomatic machinery was not in place. For all we know this little shit-eating colonel informed his government that we were attempting to annex their western provinces!

But what could we do? Every day hundreds of thousands of people crossed our border, and of those perhaps tens of thousands were infected! We had to take decisive action. We had to protect ourselves!

There is a road that runs between our two countries. It is small by your standards, not even paved in most places, but it was the main southern artery in Baluchistan. To cut it at just one place, the Ketch River Bridge, would have effectively sealed off 60 percent of all refugee traffic. I flew the mission myself, at night with a heavy escort. You didn't need image intensifiers. You could see the headlights from miles away, a long, thin white trail in the darkness. I could even see small-arms flashes. The area was heavily infested. I targeted the bridge's center foundation, which would be the hardest part to repair. The bombs separated cleanly. They were high-explosive, conventional ordnance, just enough to do the job. American aircraft, from when we used to be your allies of convenience, used to destroy a bridge built with American aid for the same purpose. The irony was not lost on the high command. Personally, I could have cared less. As soon as I felt my Phantom lighten, I hit my burners, waited for my observer plane's report, and prayed with all my might that the Pakistanis wouldn't retaliate.

Of course my prayers went unanswered. Three hours later their garrison at Qila Safed shot up our border station. I know now that our president and Ayatollah were willing to stand down. We'd gotten what we wanted, they'd gotten their revenge. Tit for tat, let it go. But who was going to tell the other side? Their embassy in Tehran had destroyed its codes and radios. That sonofabitching colonel had shot himself rather than betray any "state secrets." We had no hotline, no diplomatic channels. We didn't know how to contact the Pakistani leadership. We didn't even know if there was any leadership left. It was such a mess, confusion turning to anger, anger turning on our neighbors. Every hour the conflict escalated. Border clashes, air strikes. It happened so fast, just three days of conventional warfare, neither side having any clear objective, just panicked rage.

[He shrugs.]

We created a beast, a nuclear monster that neither side could tame . . . Tehran, Islamabad, Qom, Lahore, Bandar Abbas, Ormara, Emam Khomeyni, Faisalabad. No one knows how many died in the blasts or would die when the radiation clouds began to spread over our countries, over India, Southeast Asia, the Pacific, over America.

No one thought it could happen, not between us. For God's sake, they helped us build our nuclear program from the ground up! They supplied the materials, the technology, the third party brokering with North Korea and Russian renegades . . . we wouldn't have been a nuclear power if it wasn't for our fraternal Muslim brothers. No one would have expected it, but then again, no one would have expected the dead to rise, now would they? Only one could have foreseen this, and I don't believe in him anymore.

❧

DENVER, COLORADO, USA

[My train is late. The western drawbridge is being tested. Todd Wainio doesn't seem to mind waiting for me at the platform. We shake hands under the station's mural of *Victory*, easily the most recognizable image of the American experience in World War Z. Originally taken from a photograph, it depicts a squad of soldiers standing on the New Jersey side of the Hudson River, their backs turned to us as they watch dawn break over Manhattan. My host looks very small and frail next to these towering, two-dimensional icons. Like most men of his generation, Todd Wainio is old before his time. With an expanding paunch, receding, graying hair, and three, deep, parallel scars down the side of his right cheek, it would be difficult to guess that this former U.S. Army infantryman is still, at least chronologically, at the beginning of his life.]

The sky was red that day. All the smoke, the crap that'd been filling the air all summer. It put everything in an amber red light, like looking at the world through hell-colored glasses. That's how I first saw Yonkers, this little, depressed, rust-collar burb just north of New York City. I don't think anybody ever heard of it. I sure as hell hadn't, and now it's up there with, like, Pearl Harbor . . . no, not Pearl . . . that was a surprise attack. This was more like Little Bighorn, where we . . . well . . . at least the people in charge, *they* knew what was up, or they should have. The point is, it wasn't a surprise, the war . . . or emergency, or whatever you want to call it . . . it was already on. It had been, what, three months since everyone jumped on the panic train.

You remember what it was like, people just freaking out . . . boarding up their houses, stealing food, guns, shooting everything that moved. They probably killed more people, the Rambos and the runaway fires, and the traffic accidents and just the . . . the whole shit storm that we now call "the Great Panic"; I think that killed more people at first than Zack.

I guess I can see why the powers that be thought that one big stand-up battle was such a good idea. They wanted to show the people that they were still in charge, get them to calm the hell down so they could deal with the real problem. I get it, and because they needed a propaganda smack-down, I ended up in Yonkers.

It actually wasn't the worst place to make a stand. Part of the town sat right in this little valley, and right over the west hills you had the Hudson River. The Saw Mill River Parkway ran right through the center of our main line of defense and the refugees streaming down the freeway were leading the dead right to us. It was a natural choke point, and it was a good idea . . . the only good idea that day.

[Todd reaches for another "Q," the homegrown, American variety cigarette so named for its one-quarter tobacco content.]

Why didn't they put us on the roofs? They had a shopping center, a couple of garages, big buildings with nice flat tops. They could have put a whole company right above the A&P. We could have seen the whole valley, *and* we would have been completely safe from attack. There was this apartment building, about twenty stories, I think . . . each floor had a commanding view of the freeway. Why wasn't there a rifle team in each window?

You know where they put us? Right down on the ground, right behind sandbags or in fighting holes. We wasted so much time, so much energy preparing these elaborate firing positions. Good "cover and concealment," they told us. Cover and concealment? "Cover" means physical protection, conventional protection, from small arms and artillery or air-dropped ordnance. That sound like the enemy we were about to go up against? Was Zack now calling in air strikes and fire missions? And why the hell were we worried about concealment when the whole point of the battle was to get Zack to come directly at us! So backasswards! All of it!

I'm sure whoever was in charge must have been one of the last of the Fulda Fucktards, you know, those generals who spent their nard-drop years training to defend West Germany from Ivan. Tight-assed, narrow-minded . . . probably pissed off from so many years of brushfire war. He must have been an FF because everything we did freakin' stunk of Cold War Static Defense. You know they even tried to dig fighting holes for the tanks? The engineers blasted them right out of the A&P parking lot.

You had tanks?

Dude, we had everything: tanks, Bradleys, Humvees armed with everything from fifty cals to these new Vasilek heavy mortars. At least those *might* have been useful. We had Avenger Humvee mounted Stinger surface-to-air missile sets, we had this AVLB portable bridge layer system, perfect for the three-inch-deep creek that ran by the freeway. We had a bunch of XM5 electronic warfare vehicles all crammed with radar and jamming gear and . . . and . . . oh yeah, and we even had a whole FOL, Family of Latrines, just plopped right there in the middle of everything. Why, when the water pressure was still on and toilets were still flushing in every building and house in the neighborhood? So much we didn't need! So much shit that only blocked traffic and looked pretty, and that's what I think they were really there for, just to look pretty.

For the press.

Hell yeah, there must have been at least one reporter for every two or three uniforms![1] On foot and in vans, I don't know how many news choppers must have been circling . . . you'd think with so many they'd spare a few to try and rescue people from Manhattan . . . hell yeah, I think it was all for the press, show them our big green killpower . . . or tan . . . some were just back from the desert, they hadn't even been repainted yet. So much of it was for show, not just the vehicles but us as well. They had us in MOPP 4, dude, Mission Oriented Protective Posture, big bulky suits and masks that are supposed to protect you from a radioactive or biochem environment.

Could your superiors have believed the undead virus was airborne?

If that's true, why didn't they protect the reporters? Why didn't our "superiors" wear them, or anyone else immediately behind the line. They were cool and comfortable in their BDUs while we sweated under layers of rubber, charcoal, and thick, heavy body armor. And what genius thought to put us in body armor anyway? Because the press reamed 'em for not having enough in the last war? Why the hell do you need a helmet when you're fighting a living corpse? They're the ones who need the helmets, not us! And then you've got the Net Rigs . . . the Land Warrior combat integration system. It was this whole personal electronics suite that allowed each one of us to link up with each other and the higher-ups to link up with us. Through your eyepiece you could download maps, GPS data, real-time satellite recon. You could find your exact position on a battlefield, your buddies' positions, the bad guys . . . you could actually look through the video camera on your weapon, or anyone else's, to see what's over a hedge or around a corner. Land Warrior allowed every soldier to have the information of an entire command post, and let the command post control those soldiers as a single unit. "Netrocentric," that's what I kept hearing

1. Although this is an exaggeration, prewar records have shown Yonkers to have the largest press-to-military ratio than any other battlefield in history.

from the officers in front of the cameras. "Netrocentric" and "hyperwar." Cool terms, but they didn't mean shit when you're trying to dig a fighting hole with MOPP gear and body armor, and Land Warrior and standard combat load, and all of it on the hottest day in what was one of the hottest summers on record. I can't believe I was still standing when Zack began to show up.

It was just a trickle at first, ones and twos staggering between the abandoned cars that jammed the deserted freeway. At least the refugees had been evacuated. Okay, that was another thing they did right. Picking a choke point and clearing the civilians, great job. Everything else . . .

Zack started entering the first kill zone, the one designated for the MLRS. I didn't hear the rockets launch, my hood muffled the noise, but I saw them streak toward the target. I saw them arch on their way down, as their casings broke away to reveal all those little bomblets on plastic streamers. They're about the size of a hand grenade, antipersonnel with a limited antiarmor capacity. They scattered amongst the Gs, detonating once they hit the road or an abandoned car. Their gas tanks went up in like little volcanoes, geysers of fire and debris that added to the "steel rain." I got to be honest, it was a rush, dudes were cheering in their mikes, me too, watching ghouls start to tumble. I'd say there were maybe thirty, maybe forty or fifty, zombies spread out all across this half mile stretch of freeway. The opening bombardment took out at least three-quarters of them.

Only three-quarters.

[Todd finishes his cigarette in one long, angry drag. Immediately, he reaches for another.]

Yep, and that's what should have made us worry right then and there. "Steel rain" hit each and every single one of them, shredded their insides; organs and flesh were scattered all over the damn place, dropping from their bodies as they came toward us . . . but head shots . . . you're trying to destroy the brain, not the body, and as long as they got a working thinker and some mobility . . . some were still walking, others too thrashed to stand were crawling. Yeah, we should have worried, but there wasn't time.

The trickle was now turning into a stream. More Gs, dozens now, thick among the burning cars. Funny thing about Zack . . . you always think he's gonna be dressed in his Sunday best. That's how the media portrayed them, right, especially in the beginning . . . Gs in business suits and dresses, like, a cross section of everyday America, only dead. That's not what they looked like at all. Most infected, the early infected, the ones who went in that first wave, they either died under treatment or at home in their own beds. Most were either in hospital gowns, or pajamas and nightshirts. Some were in sweats or their undies . . . or just naked, a lot of them completely buck bare. You could see their wounds, the dried marks on their bodies, the gouges that made you shiver even inside that sweltering gear.

The second "steel rain" didn't have half the impact of the first, no more gas tanks to catch, and now the more tightly packed Gs just happened to be shielding each other from a possible head wound. I wasn't scared, not yet. Maybe my wood was gone, but I was pretty sure it'd be back when Zack entered the Army's kill zone.

Again, I couldn't hear the Paladins, too far back up the hill, but I sure heard, and saw, their shells land. These were standard HE 155s, a high explosive core with a fragmentation case. They did even less damage than the rockets!

Why is that?

No balloon effect for one. When a bomb goes off close to you, it causes the liquid in your body to burst, literally, like a freakin' balloon. That doesn't happen with Zack, maybe because he carries less bodily fluid than us or because that fluid's more like a gel. I don't know. But it didn't do shit, neither did the SNT effect.

What is SNT?

Sudden Nerve Trauma, I think that's what you call it. It's another effect of close-in high explosives. The trauma is so great sometimes that your organs, your brain, all of it, just shuts down like God flickin' your life switch. Something to do with electrical impulses or whatnot. I don't know, I'm not a fuckin' doctor.

But that didn't happen.

Not once! I mean . . . don't get me wrong . . . it's not like Zack just skipped through the barrage unscathed. We saw bodies blown to shit, tossed into the air, ripped to pieces, even complete heads, live heads with eyes and jaws still moving, popping sky high like freakin' Cristal corks . . . we were taking them down, no doubt, but not as many or as fast as we needed to!

The stream was now like a river, a flood of bodies, slouching, moaning, stepping over their mangled bros as they rolled slowly and steadily toward us like a slow-motion wave.

The next kill zone was direct fire from the heavy arms, the tank's main 120s and Bradleys with their chain guns and FOTT missiles. The Humvees also began to open up, mortars and missiles and the Mark-19s, which are, like, machine guns, but firing grenades. The Comanches came whining in at what felt like inches above our heads with chains and Hellfires and Hydra rocket pods.

It was a fuckin' meat grinder, a wood chipper, organic matter clouding like sawdust above the horde.

Nothing can survive this, I was thinking, and for a little while, it looked like I was right . . . until the fire started to die.

Started to die?

Petering out, withering . . .

[For a second he is silent, and then, angrily, his eyes refocus.]

No one thought about it, *no one!* Don't pull my pud with stories about budget cuts and supply problems! The only thing in short supply was common fucking sense! Not one of those West Point, War College, medals-up-the-ass, four-star fart bags said, "Hey, we got plenty of fancy weapons, we got enough shit for them to shoot!?!" No one thought about how many rounds the artillery would need for sustained operations, how many rockets for the MLRS, how many canister shots . . . the tanks had these things called canister shots . . . basically a giant shotgun shell. They fired these little tungsten balls . . . not perfect you know, wasting like a hundred balls for every G, but fuck, dude, at least it was something! Each Abrams only had three, *three!* Three out of a total loadout of forty! The rest were standard HEAT or SABOT! Do you know what a "Silver Bullet," an armor-piercing, depleted-uranium dart is going to do to a group of walking corpses? Nothing! Do you know what it feels like to see a sixty-something-ton tank fire into a crowd with absolutely ass-all result! Three canister rounds! And what about flechettes? That's the weapon we always hear about these days, flechettes, these little steel spikes that turn any weapon into an instant scattergun. We talk about them like they're a new invention, but we had them as far back as, like, Korea. We had them for the Hydra rockets and the Mark-19s. Just imagine that, just one 19 firing three hundred and fifty rounds a minute, each round holding, like, a hundred[2] spikes! Maybe it wouldn't have turned the tide . . . but . . . Goddammit!

The fire was dying, Zack was still coming . . . and the fear . . . everyone was feeling it, in the orders from the squad leaders, in the actions of the men around me . . . That little voice in the back of your head that just keeps squeaking "Oh shit, oh shit."

We were the last line of defense, the afterthought when it came to firepower. We were supposed to pick off the random lucky G who happened to slip through the giant bitchslap of our heavier stuff. Maybe one in three of us was expected to fire his weapon, one in every ten was expected to score a kill.

They came by the thousands, spilling out over the freeway guardrails, down the side streets, around the houses, through them . . . so many of them, their moans so loud they echoed right through our hoods.

2. The standard, prewar 40-mm canister cartridge held 115 flechettes.

We flipped our safeties off, sighted our targets, the order came to fire . . . I was a SAW[3] gunner, a light machine gun that you're supposed to fire in short, controlled bursts about as long as it takes to say "Die motherfucker die." The initial burst was too low. I caught one square in the chest. I watched him fly backward, hit the asphalt, then get right back up again as if nothing had happened. Dude . . . when they get back up . . .

[The cigarette has burned down to his fingers. He drops and crushes it without noticing.]

I did my best to control my fire, and my sphincter. "Just go for the head," I kept telling myself. "Keep it together, just go for the head." And all the time my SAW's chattering "Die motherfucker die."

We could have stopped them, we should have, one guy with a rifle, that's all you need, right? Professional soldiers, trained marksmen . . . how could they get through? They still ask that, critics and armchair Pattons who weren't there. You think it's that simple? You think that after being "trained" to aim for the center mass your whole military career you can suddenly make an expert head shot every time? You think in that strait-jacket and suffocation hood it's easy to recharge a clip or clear a weapon jam? You think that after watching all the wonders of modern warfare fall flat on their high-tech hyper ass, that after already living through three months of the Great Panic and watching everything you knew as reality be eaten alive by an enemy that wasn't even supposed to exist that you're gonna keep a cool fucking head and a steady fucking trigger finger?

[He stabs that finger at me.]

Well, we did! We *still* managed to do our job and make Zack pay for every fuckin' inch! Maybe if we'd had more men, more ammo, maybe if we'd just been allowed to focus on our job . . .

---

3. SAW: A light machine gun, short for Squad Automatic Weapon.

[His finger curls back into his fist.]

Land Warrior, high-tech, high-priced, high-profile netro-fucking-centric Land Warrior. To see what was in front of our face was bad enough, but spybird uplinks were also showing how truly large the horde was. We might be facing thousands, but behind them were millions! Remember, we were taking on the bulk of New York City's infestation! This was only the head of one really long undead snake stretching all the way back to Times Fuckin' Square! We didn't need to see that. I didn't need to know that! That little scared voice wasn't so little anymore. "Oh shit, OH SHIT!" And suddenly it wasn't in my head anymore. It was in my earpiece. Every time some jerkoff couldn't control his mouth, Land Warrior made sure the rest of us heard it. "There's too many!" "We gotta get the fuck outta here!" Someone from another platoon, I didn't know his name, started hollering "I hit him in the head and he didn't die! They don't die when you shoot them in the head!" I'm sure he must have missed the brain, it can happen, a round just grazing the inside of the skull . . . maybe if he'd been calm and used his own brain, he would have realized that. Panic's even more infectious than the Z Germ and the wonders of Land Warrior allowed that germ to become airborne. "What?" "They don't die?" "Who said that?" "You shot it in the head?" "Holy crap! They're indestructible!" All over the net you could hear this, browning shorts across the info superhighway.

"Everyone pipe down!" someone shouted. "Hold the line! Stay off the net!" an older voice, you could tell, but suddenly it was drowned out in this scream and suddenly my eyepiece, and I'm sure everyone else's, was filled with the sight of blood spurting into a mouth of broken teeth. The sight was from a dude in the yard of a house behind the line. The owners must have left a few reanimated family members locked in when they bugged out. Maybe the shock from the explosions weakened the door or something, because they came bursting out, right into this poor bastard. His gun camera recorded the whole thing, fell right at the perfect angle. There were five of them, a man, a woman, three kids, they had him pinned on his back, the man was on his chest, the kids had him by the arms, trying to bite through his suit. The woman tore his mask off, you could see the terror in his face. I'll never forget his shriek as she bit off his chin and lower lip. "They're behind us!" someone was shouting. "They're coming out of the houses! The line's broken! They're everywhere!" Suddenly the image went dark, cut off from an external source, and the voice, the older voice, was back again . . . "Stay off the net!" he ordered, trying real hard to control his voice and then the link went dead.

I'm sure it must have taken more than a few seconds, it had to, even if they'd been hovering above our heads, but, it seemed like right after the communications line blacked out that the sky was suddenly screaming with JSFs.[4] I didn't see them release their ordnance. I was at the bottom of my hole cursing the army and God, and my own hands for not digging deeper. That ground shook, the sky went dark. Debris was everywhere, earth and ash and burning whatever flying above my head. I felt this weight slam between my shoulder blades, soft and heavy. I rolled over, it was a head and torso, all charred black and still smoking and still trying to bite! I kicked it away and scrambled out of my hole seconds after the last of the JSOW[5] fell.

I found myself staring into this cloud of black smoke where the horde had been. The freeway, the houses, everything was covered by this mid-night cloud. I vaguely remember other guys getting out of their holes, hatches opening on tanks and Bradleys, everyone just staring into the darkness. There was a quiet, a stillness that, in my mind, lasted for hours.

And then they came, right out of the smoke like a freakin' little kid's nightmare! Some were steaming, some were even still burning . . . some were walking, some crawling, some just dragging themselves along on their torn bellies . . . maybe one in twenty was still able to move, which left . . . shit . . . a couple thousand? And behind them, mixing with their ranks and pushing steadily toward us, the remaining million that the air strike hadn't even touched!

And that was when the line collapsed. I don't remember it all at once. I see these flashes: people running, grunts, reporters. I remember a newsman

4. JSF: Joint Strike Fighters.
5. JSOW: Joint Standoff Weapon.

with a big Yosemite Sam mustache trying to pull a Beretta from his vest be-fore three burning Gs pulled him down . . . I remember a dude forcing open the door of a news van, jumping in, throwing out a pretty blond re-porter, and trying to drive away before a tank crushed them both. Two news choppers crashed together, showering us with their own steel rain. One Comanche driver . . . brave, beautiful motherfucker . . . tried to turn his rotor into the oncoming Gs. The blade diced a path right down their mass before catching on a car and hurling him into the A&P. Shooting . . . crazy random shooting . . . I took a round in the sternum, in my armor's center plate. I felt like I'd run into a wall, even though I'd been standing still. It knocked me on my ass, I couldn't breathe, and just then some dumb-ass lobbed a flash bang right in front of me.

The world was white, my ears were ringing. I froze . . . hands were claw-ing me, grabbing my arms. I kicked and punched, I felt my crotch get warm and wet. I shouted but couldn't hear my own voice. More hands, stronger, were trying to haul me somewhere. Kicking, squirming, cursing, crying . . . suddenly a fist clocked me in the jaw. It didn't knock me out, but I was sud-denly relaxed. These were my buddies. Zack don't punch. They dragged me into the closest Bradley. My vision cleared just long enough to see the line of light vanish with the closing hatch.

[He reaches for another Q, then abruptly decides against it.]

I know "professional" historians like to talk about how Yonkers repre-sented a "catastrophic failure of the modern military apparatus," how it proved the old adage that armies perfect the art of fighting the last war just in time for the next one. Personally, I think that's a big 'ole sack of it. Sure, we were unprepared, our tools, our training, everything I just talked about, all one class-A, gold-standard clusterfuck, but the weapon that really failed wasn't something that rolled off an assembly line. It's as old as . . . I don't know, I guess as old as war. It's fear, dude, just fear and you don't have to be Sun freakin Tzu to know that real fighting isn't about killing or even hurt-ing the other guy, it's about scaring him enough to call it a day. Break their spirit, that's what every successful army goes for, from tribal face paint to the "blitzkrieg" to . . . what did we call the first round of Gulf War Two, "Shock and Awe"? Perfect name, "Shock and Awe"! But what if the enemy can't be shocked and awed? Not just won't, but biologically *can't!* That's what happened that day outside New York City, that's the failure that almost lost us the whole damn war. The fact that we couldn't shock and awe Zack boomeranged right back in our faces and actually allowed Zack to shock and awe us! They're not afraid! No matter what we do, no matter how many we kill, they will never, ever be afraid!

Yonkers was supposed to be the day we restored confidence to the American people, instead we practically told them to kiss their ass good-bye. If it wasn't for the Sou'frican Plan, I have no doubt, we'd all be slouching and moaning right now.

The last thing I remember was the Bradley being tossed like a Hot Wheels car. I don't know where the hit was, but I'm guessing it must have been close. I'm sure had I still been standing out there, exposed, I wouldn't be standing here today.

Have you ever seen the effects of a thermobaric weapon? Have you ever asked anyone with stars on their shoulders about them? I bet my ballsack you'll never get the full story. You'll hear about heat and pressure, the fireball that continues expanding, exploding, and literally crushing and burning everything in its path. Heat and pressure, that's what thermobaric means. Sounds nasty enough, right? What you won't hear about is the immediate aftereffect, the vacuum created when that fireball suddenly contracts. Anyone left alive will either have the air sucked right out of their lungs, or—and they'll *never* admit this to anyone—have their lungs ripped right out of their mouth. Obviously no one's going to live long enough to tell that kind of horror story, probably why the Pentagon's been so good at covering up the truth, but if you ever see a picture of a G, or even an example of a real walking specimen, and he's got both air bags and windpipe just dangling out from his lips, make sure you give him my number. I'm always up for meeting another veteran of Yonkers.

TURNING THE TIDE

[Xolelwa Azania greets me at his writing desk, inviting me to switch places with him so I can enjoy the cool ocean breeze from his window. He apologizes for the "mess" and insists on clearing the notes off his desk before we continue. Mister Azania is halfway through his third volume of *Rainbow Fist: South Africa at War*. This volume happens to be about the subject we are discussing, the turning point against the living dead, the moment when his country pulled itself back from the brink.]

Dispassionate, a rather mundane word to describe one of history's most controversial figures. Some revere him as a savior, some revile him as a monster, but if you ever met Paul Redeker, ever discussed his views of the world and the problems, or more importantly, the solutions to the problems that plague the world, probably the one word that would always cling to your impression of the man is *dispassionate*.

Paul always believed, well, perhaps not always, but at least in his adult life, that humanity's one fundamental flaw was emotion. He used to say that the heart should only exist to pump blood to the brain, that anything else was a waste of time and energy. His papers from university, all dealing with alternate "solutions" to historical, societal quandaries, were what first brought him to the attention of the apartheid government. Many psychobiographers have tried to label him a racist, but, in his own words, "racism is a regrettable by-product of irrational emotion." Others have argued that, in order for a racist to hate one group, he must at least love another. Redeker believed both love and hate to be irrelevant. To him, they were "impediments of the human condition," and, in his words again, "imagine what could be accomplished if the human race would only shed its humanity." Evil? Most would call it that, while others, particularly that small cadre in the center of Pretoria's power, believed it to be "an invaluable source of liberated intellect."

It was the early 1980s, a critical time for the apartheid government. The country was resting on a bed of nails. You had the ANC, you had the Inkatha Freedom Party, you even had extremist, right-wing elements of the Afrikaner population that would have liked nothing better than open revolt in order to bring about a complete racial showdown. On her border, South Africa faced nothing but hostile nations, and, in the case of Angola, a Soviet-backed, Cuban-spearheaded civil war. Add to this mixture a growing isolation from the Western democracies (which included a critical arms embargo) and it was no surprise that a last-ditch fight for survival was never far from Pretoria's mind.

This is why they enlisted the aid of Mister Redeker to revise the government's ultrasecret "Plan Orange." "Orange" had been in existence since the apartheid government first came to power in 1948. It was the doomsday scenario for the country's white minority, the plan to deal with an all-out uprising of its indigenous African population. Over the years it had been updated with the changing strategic outlook of the region. Every decade that situation grew more and more grim. With multiplying independence of her neighbor states, and multiplying voices for freedom from the majority of her own people, those in Pretoria realized that a full-blown confrontation might not just mean the end for the Afrikaner government, but the Afrikaners themselves.

This is where Redeker stepped in. His revised Plan Orange, appropriately completed in 1984, was the ultimate survival strategy for the Afrikaner people. No variable was ignored. Population figures, terrain, resources, logistics . . . Redeker not only updated the plan to include both Cuba's chemical weapons and his own country's nuclear option, but also, and this is what made "Orange Eighty-Four" so historic, the determination of which Afrikaners would be saved and which had to be sacrificed.

Sacrificed?

Redeker believed that to try to protect everyone would stretch the government's resources to the breaking point, thus dooming the entire population. He compared it to survivors from a sinking ship capsizing a lifeboat that simply did not have room for them all. Redeker had even gone so far as to calculate who should be "brought aboard." He included income, IQ, fertility, an entire checklist of "desirable qualities," including the subject's location to a potential crisis zone. "The first casualty of the conflict must be our own sentimentality" was the closing statement for his proposal, "for its survival will mean our destruction."

Orange Eighty-Four was a brilliant plan. It was clear, logical, efficient, and it made Paul Redeker one of the most hated men in South Africa. His first enemies were some of the more radical, fundamentalist Afrikaners, the racial ideologues and the ultrareligious. Later, after the fall of apartheid, his name began circulating among the general population. Of course he was invited to appear before the "Truth and Reconciliation" hearings, and, of course, he refused. "I won't pretend to have a heart simply to save my skin," he stated publicly, adding, "No matter what I do, I'm sure they will come for me anyway."

And they did, although it probably was not in the manner Redeker could have expected. It was during our Great Panic, which began several weeks before yours. Redeker was holed up in the Drakensberg cabin he had bought with the accumulated profits of a business consultant. He liked business, you know. "One goal, no soul," he used to say. He wasn't surprised when the door blew off its hinges and agents of the National Intelligence Agency rushed in. They confirmed his name, his identity, his past actions. They asked him point-blank if he had been the author of Orange Eighty-Four. He answered without emotion, naturally. He suspected, and accepted, this intrusion as a last-minute revenge killing; the world was going to hell anyway, why not take a few "apartheid devils" down first. What he could have never predicted was the sudden lowering of their firearms, and the removal of the gas masks of the NIA agents. They were of all colors: black, Asian, colored, and even a white man, a tall Afrikaner who stepped forward, and without giving his name or rank, asked abruptly . . . "You've got a plan for this, man. Don't you?"

Redeker had, indeed, been working on his own solution to the undead epidemic. What else could he do in this isolated hideaway? It had been an intellectual exercise; he never believed anyone would be left to read it. It had no name, as explained later "because names only exist to distinguish one from others," and, until that moment, there had been no other plan like his. Once again, Redeker had taken everything into account, not only the strategic situation of the country, but also the physiology, behavior, and "combat doctrine" of the living dead. While you can research the details of the "Redeker Plan" in any public library around the world, here are some of the fundamental keys:

First of all, there was no way to save everyone. The outbreak was too far gone. The armed forces had already been too badly weakened to effectively isolate the threat, and, spread so thinly throughout the country, they could only grow weaker with each passing day. Our forces had to be consolidated, withdrawn to a special "safe zone," which, hopefully, would be aided by some natural obstacle such as mountains, rivers, or even an offshore island. Once concentrated within this zone, the armed forces could eradicate the infestation within its borders, then use what resources were available to defend it against further onslaughts of the living dead. That was the first part of the plan and it made as much sense as any conventional military retreat.

The second part of the plan dealt with the evacuation of civilians, and this could not have been envisioned by anyone else but Redeker. In his mind, only a small fraction of the civilian population could be evacuated to the safe zone. These people would be saved not only to provide a labor pool for the eventual wartime economic restoration, but also to preserve the legitimacy and stability of the government, to prove to those already within the zone that their leaders were "looking out for them."

There was another reason for this partial evacuation, an eminently logical and insidiously dark reason that, many believe, will forever ensure Redeker the tallest pedestal in the pantheon of hell. Those who were left behind were to be herded into special isolated zones. They were to be "human bait," distracting the undead from following the retreating army to their safe zone. Redeker argued that these isolated, uninfected refugees must be kept alive, well defended and even resupplied, if possible, so as to keep the undead hordes firmly rooted to the spot. You see the genius, the sickness? Keeping people as prisoners because "every zombie besieging those survivors will be one less zombie throwing itself against our defenses." That was the moment when the Afrikaner agent looked up at Redeker, crossed himself, and said, "God help you, man." Another one said, "God help us all." That was the black one who appeared to be in charge of the operation. "Now let's get him out of here."

Within minutes they were on a helicopter for Kimberley, the very underground base where Redeker had first written Orange Eighty-Four. He was ushered into a meeting of the president's surviving cabinet, where his report was read aloud to the room. You should have heard the uproar, with no voice louder than the defense minister's. He was a Zulu, a ferocious man who'd rather be fighting in the streets than cowering in a bunker.

The vice president was more concerned about public relations. He didn't want to imagine what his backside would be worth if news of this plan ever leaked to the population.

The president looked almost personally insulted by Redeker. He physically grabbed the lapels of the safety and security minister and demanded why in hell he brought him this demented apartheid war criminal.

The minister stammered that he didn't understand why the president was so upset, especially when it was he who gave the order to find Redeker.

The president threw his hands in the air and shouted that he never gave such an order, and then, from somewhere in the room, a faint voice said, "I did."

He had been sitting against the back wall; now he stood, hunched over by age, and supported by canes, but with a spirit as strong and vital as it had ever been. The elder statesman, the father of our new democracy, the man whose birth name had been Rolihlahla, which some have translated simply into "Troublemaker." As he stood, all others sat, all others except Paul Redeker. The old man locked eyes on him, smiled with that warm squint so famous the world over, and said, "Molo, mhlobo wam." "Greetings, person of my region." He walked slowly over to Paul, turned to the governing body of South Africa, then lifted the pages from the Afrikaner's hand and said in a suddenly loud and youthful voice, "This plan will save our people." Then, gesturing to Paul, he said, "This *man* will save our people." And then came that moment, the one that historians will probably debate until the subject fades from memory. He embraced the white Afrikaner. To anyone else this was simply his signature bear hug, but to Paul Redeker . . . I know that the majority of psychobiographers continue to paint this man without a soul. That is the generally accepted notion. Paul Redeker: no feelings, no compassion, no heart. However, one of our most revered authors, Biko's old friend and biographer, postulates that Redeker was actually a deeply sensitive man, too sensitive, in fact, for life in apartheid South Africa. He insists that Redeker's lifelong jihad against emotion was the only way to protect his sanity from the hatred and brutality he witnessed on a daily basis. Not much is known about Redeker's childhood, whether he even had parents, or was raised by the state, whether he had friends or was ever loved in any way. Those who knew him from work were hard-pressed to remember witnessing any social interaction or even any physical act of warmth. The embrace by our nation's father, this genuine emotion piercing his impenetrable shell . . .

[Azania smiles sheepishly.]

Perhaps this is all too sentimental. For all we know he was a heartless monster, and the old man's embrace had absolutely no impact. But I can tell you that that was the last day anyone ever saw Paul Redeker. Even now, no one knows what really happened to him. That is when I stepped in, in those chaotic weeks when the Redeker Plan was implemented throughout the country. It took some convincing to say the least, but once I'd convinced them that I'd worked for many years with Paul Redeker, and, more importantly, I understood his way of thinking better than anyone left alive in South Africa, how could they refuse? I worked on the retreat, then afterward, during the consolidation months, and right up until the end of the war. At least they were appreciative of my services, why else would they grant me such luxurious accommodations? [Smiles.] Paul Redeker, an angel and a devil. Some hate him, some worship him. Me, I just pity him. If he still exists, somewhere out there, I sincerely hope he's found his peace.

[After a parting embrace from my guest, I am driven back to my ferry for the mainland. Security is tight as I sign out my entrance badge. The tall Afrikaner guard photographs me again. "Can't be too careful, man," he says, handing me the pen. "Lot of people out there want to send him to hell." I sign next to my name, under the heading of Robben Island Psychiatric Institution. NAME OF PATIENT YOU ARE VISITING: PAUL REDEKER.]

❦

ARMAGH, IRELAND

[While not a Catholic himself, Philip Adler has joined the throngs of visitors to the pope's wartime refuge. "My wife is Bavarian," he explains in the bar of our hotel. "She had to make the pilgrimage to Saint Patrick's Cathedral." This is his first time away from Germany since the end of the war. Our meeting is accidental. He does not object to my recorder.]

Hamburg was heavily infested. They were in the streets, in the buildings, pouring out of the Neuer Elbtunnel. We'd tried to blockade it with civilian vehicles, but they were squirming through any open space like bloated, bloody worms. Refugees were also all over. They'd come from as far away as Saxony, thinking they could escape by sea. The ships were long gone, the port was a mess. We had over a thousand trapped at the Reynolds Aluminiumwerk and at least triple that at the Eurokai terminal. No food, no clean water, just waiting to be rescued with the dead swarming outside, and I don't know how many infected inside.

The harbor was choked with corpses, but corpses that were still moving. We'd blasted them into the harbor with antiriot water cannons; it saved ammo and it helped to keep the streets clear. It was a good idea, until the pressure in the hydrants died. We'd lost our commanding officer two days earlier . . . freak accident. One of our men had shot a zombie that was almost on top of him. The bullet had gone right through the creature's head, taking bits of diseased brain tissue out the other end and into the colonel's shoulder. Insane, eh? He turned over sector command to me before dying. My first official duty was to put him down.

I'd set up our command post in the Renaissance Hotel. It was a decent location, good fields of fire with enough space to house our own unit and several hundred refugees. My men, those not involved in holding the barricades, were attempting to perform these conversions on similar buildings. With the roads blocked and trains inoperative, I thought it best to sequester as many civilians as possible. Help would be coming, it was just a question of when it would arrive.

I was about to organize a detail to scrounge for converted hand-to-hand weapons, we were running low on ammunition, when the order came to retreat. This was not unusual. Our unit had been steadily withdrawing since the first days of the Panic. What *was* unusual, though, was the rally point. Division was using map-grid coordinates, the first time since the trouble began. Up until then they had simply used civilian designations on an open channel; this was so refugees could know where to assemble. Now it was a coded transmission from a map we hadn't used since the end of the cold war. I had to check the coordinates three times to confirm. They put us at

Schafstedt, just north of the Nord-Ostsee Kanal. Might as well be fucking Denmark!

We were also under strict orders *not* to move the civilians. Even worse, we were ordered *not* to inform them of our departure! This didn't make any sense. They wanted us to pull back to Schleswig-Holstein but leave the refugees behind? They wanted us to just cut and run? There had to be some kind of mistake.

I asked for confirmation. I got it. I asked again. Maybe they got the map wrong, or had shifted codes without telling us. (It wouldn't be their first mistake.)

I suddenly found myself speaking to General Lang, commander of the entire Northern Front. His voice was shaking. I could hear it even over the shooting. He told me the orders were not a mistake, that I was to rally what was left of the Hamburg Garrison and proceed immediately north. This isn't happening, I told myself. Funny, eh? I could accept everything else that was happening, the fact that dead bodies were rising to consume the world, but this . . . following orders that would indirectly cause a mass murder.

Now, I am a good soldier, but I am also a West German. You understand the difference? In the East, they were told that they were not responsible for the atrocities of the Second World War, that as good communists, they were just as much victims of Hitler as anyone else. You understand why the skinheads and proto-fascists were mainly in the East? They did not feel the responsibility of the past, not like we did in the West. We were taught since birth to bear the burden of our grandfathers' shame. We were taught that, even if we wore a uniform, that our first sworn duty was to our conscience, no matter what the consequences. That is how I was raised, that is how I responded. I told Lang that I could not, in good conscience, obey this order, that I could not leave these people without protection. At this, he exploded. He told me that I *would* carry out my instructions or I, and, more importantly, my men, would be charged with treason and prosecuted with "Russian efficiency." *And this is what we've come to*, I thought. We'd all heard of what was happening in Russia . . . the mutinies, the crackdowns, the decimations. I looked around at all these boys, eighteen, nineteen years old, all tired and scared and fighting for their lives. I couldn't do that to them. I gave the order to withdraw.

How did they take it?

There were no complaints, at least, not to me. They fought a little amongst themselves. I pretended not to notice. They did their duty.

What about the civilians?

[Pause.] We got everything we deserved. "Where are you going?" they shouted from buildings. "Come back, you cowards!" I tried to answer. "No, we're coming back for you," I said. "We're coming back tomorrow with more men. Just stay where you are, we'll be back tomorrow." They didn't believe me. "Fucking liar!" I heard one woman shout. "You're letting my baby die!"

Most of them didn't try to follow, too worried about the zombies in the streets. A few brave souls grabbed on to our armored personnel carriers. They tried to force their way down the hatches. We knocked them off. We had to button up as the ones trapped in buildings started throwing things, lamps, furniture, down on us. One of my men was hit with a bucket filled with human waste. I heard a bullet clang off the hatch of my Marder.

On our way out of the city we passed the last of our new Rapid Reaction Stabilization Units. They had been badly mauled earlier in the week. I didn't know it at the time, but they were one of those units classified as expendable. They were detailed to cover our retreat, to prevent too many zombies, or refugees, from following us. They were ordered to hold to the end.

Their commander was standing through the cupola of his Leopard. I knew him. We'd served together as part of the NATO's IFOR in Bosnia. Maybe it is melodramatic to say he saved my life, but he did take a Serbian's bullet that I'm sure was meant for me. The last time I saw him was in a hospital in Sarajevo, joking about getting out of this madhouse those people called a country. Now here we were, passing on the shattered auto-bahn in the heart of our homeland. We locked eyes, traded salutes. I ducked back into the APC, and pretended to study my map so the driver wouldn't see my tears. "When we get back," I told myself, "I'm going to kill that son of a bitch."

General Lang.

I had it all planned. I would not look angry, not give him any reason to worry. I'd submit my report and apologize for my behavior. Maybe he'd want to give me some kind of pep talk, try to explain or justify our retreat. Good, I thought, I'd listen patiently, put him at ease. Then, when he rose to shake my hand, I'd draw my weapon and blow his Eastern brains against the map of what used to be our country. Maybe his whole staff would be there, all the other little stooges who were "just following orders." I'd get them all before they took me! It would be perfect. I wasn't going to just goose-step my way into hell like some good little Hitler Jugend. I'd show him, and everyone else, what it meant to be a real Deutsche Soldat.

But that's not what happened.

No. I did manage to make it into General Lang's office. We were the last unit across the canal. He'd waited for that. As soon as the report came in, he'd sat down at his desk, signed a few final orders, addressed and sealed a letter to his family, then put a bullet through his brain.

Bastard. I hate him even more now than I did on the road from Hamburg.

Why is that?

Because I now understand why we did what we did, the details of the Prochnow Plan.[1]

1. Germany's version of the Redeker Plan.

Wouldn't this revelation engender sympathy for him?

Are you kidding? That's exactly why I hate him! He knew that this was just the first step of a long war and we were going to need men like him to help win it. Fucking coward. Remember what I said about being beholden to your conscience? You can't blame anyone else, not the plan's architect, not your commanding officer, no one but yourself. You have to make your own choices and live every agonizing day with the consequences of those choices. He knew this. That's why he deserted us like we deserted those civilians. He saw the road ahead, a steep, treacherous mountain road. We'd all have to hike that road, each of us dragging the boulder of what we'd done behind us. He couldn't do it. He couldn't shoulder the weight.

YEVCHENKO VETERANS' SANATORIUM, ODESSA, UKRAINE

[The room is windowless. Dim, fluorescent bulbs illuminate the concrete walls and unwashed cots. The patients here mainly suffer from respiratory disorders, many made worse by the lack of any usable medication. There are no doctors here, and understaffed nurses and orderlies can do little to ease the suffering. At least the room is warm and dry, and for this country in the dead of winter, that is a luxury beyond measure. Bohdan Taras Kondratiuk sits upright on his cot at the end of the room. As a war hero he rates a hung sheet for privacy. He coughs into his handkerchief before speaking.]

Chaos. I don't know how else to describe it, a complete breakdown of organization, of order, of control. We'd just fought four brutal engagements: Luck, Rovno, Novograd, and Zhitomir. Goddamn Zhitomir. My men were exhausted, you understand. What they'd seen, what they'd had to do, and all the time pulling back, rearguard actions, running. Every day you heard about another town falling, another road closing, another unit overwhelmed.

Kiev was supposed to be safe, behind the lines. It was supposed to be the center of our new safety zone, well garrisoned, fully resupplied, quiet. And so what happens as soon as we arrive? Are my orders to rest and refit? Repair my vehicles, reconstitute my numbers, rehabilitate my wounded? No, of course not. Why should things be as they should be? They never have been before.

The safety zone was being shifted again, this time to the Crimea. The government had already moved . . . fled . . . to Sevastopol. Civil order had collapsed. Kiev was being fully evacuated. This was the task of the military, or what was left of it.

Our company was ordered to oversee the escape route at Patona Bridge. It was the first all electrically welded bridge in the world, and many foreigners used to compare its achievement to that of the Eiffel Tower. The city had planned a major restoration project, a dream to renew its former glory. But, like everything else in our country, that dream never came true. Even before the crisis, the bridge had been a nightmare of traffic jams. Now it was crammed with evacuees. The bridge was supposed to be closed to road traffic, but where were the barricades we were promised, the concrete and steel that would have made any forced entry impossible? Cars were everywhere, little Lags and old Zhigs, a few Mercedes, and a mammoth GAZ truck sitting right in the middle, just turned over on its side! We tried to move it, get a chain around the axle and pull it free with one of the tanks. Not a chance. What could we do?

We were an armored platoon, you understand. Tanks, not military police. We never saw any MPs. We were assured they would be there, but we never saw or heard from them, neither did any of the other "units" along any of the other bridges. To even call them "units" is a joke. These were just mobs of men in uniforms, clerks and cooks; anyone who happened to be attached to the military suddenly became in charge of traffic control.

None of us were set up for this, weren't trained for it, weren't equipped . . . Where was the riot gear they promised us, the shields, the armor, where was the water cannon? Our orders were to "process" all evacuees. You understand "process," to see if any of them had been tainted. But where were the goddamn sniffer dogs? How are you supposed to check for infection without dogs? What are you supposed to do, visually inspect each refugee? Yes! And yet, that is what we were told to do. [Shakes his head.] Did they really think that those terrified, frantic wretches, with death at their backs and safety—perceived safety—only meters away were going to form an orderly line and let us strip them naked to examine every centimeter of skin? Did they think men would just stand by while we examined their wives, their mothers, their little daughters? Can you imagine? And we actually tried to do it. What other alternative was there? They had to be separated if any of us were going to survive. What's the point of even trying to evacuate people if they're just going to bring the infection with them?

[Shakes his head, laughs bitterly.] It was a disaster! Some just refused, others tried to run by or even jump into the river. Fights broke out. Many of my men were beaten badly, three were stabbed, one was shot by a frightened grandfather with a rusty old Tokarev. I'm sure he was dead before hitting the water.

I wasn't there, you understand. I was on the radio trying to call for support! Help is coming, they kept saying, do not break, do not despair, help is coming.

Across the Dnieper, Kiev burned. Black pillars rose from the city center. We were downwind, the stench was terrible, the wood and rubber and stink of burning flesh. We didn't know how far they were now, maybe a kilometer, maybe less. Up on the hill, the fire had engulfed the monastery. Goddamn tragedy. With its high walls, its strategic location, we could have made a stand. Any first-year cadet could have turned it into an impregnable fortress—stocked the basements, sealed the gates, and mounted snipers in the towers. They could have covered the bridge for . . . fucking forever!

I thought I heard something, a sound from the other bank . . . that sound, you know, when they are all together, when they are close, that . . . even

over the shouts, the curses, the honking horns, the distant sniper fire, you
know that sound.

[He attempts to mimic their moan but collapses into uncontrolled
coughs. He holds his handkerchief up to his face. It comes away
bloody.]

That sound was what pulled me away from the radio. I looked over at
the city. Something caught my eye, something above the rooftops and
closing fast.

The jet streaked over us at treetop level. There were four of them,
Sukhoi 25 "Rooks," close, and low enough to identify by sight. *What the
hell*, I thought, *are they going to try to cover the bridge's approach? Maybe bomb
the area behind it?* It had worked at Rovno, at least for a few minutes. The
Rooks circled, as if confirming their targets, then banked low and came
straight at us! *Devil's mother*, I thought, *they are going to bomb the bridge!*
They'd given up on the evacuation and were going to kill everyone!

"Off the bridge!" I started shouting. "Everyone get off!" Panic shot
through the crowd. You could see it like a wave, like a current of electricity. People started screaming, trying to push forward, back, into one another. Dozens were jumping into the water with heavy clothes and shoes
that prevented them from swimming.

I was pulling people across, telling them to run. I saw the bombs released, thought maybe I could dive at the last moment, shield myself from
the blast. Then the parachutes opened, and I knew. In a split second, I was
up and dashing like a frightened rabbit. "Button up!" I screamed. "Button
up!" I leapt onto the nearest tank, slammed the hatch down, and ordered
the crew to check the seals! The tank was an obsolete T-72. We couldn't
know if the overpressure system still worked, hadn't tested it in years. All
we could do was hope and pray while cringing in our steel coffin. The gunner was sobbing, the driver was frozen, the commander, a junior sergeant
just twenty years old, was balled up on the floor, clutching the little cross
he had around his neck. I put my hand on the top of his head, assured him
we would be fine while keeping my eyes glued to the periscope.

RVX doesn't start out as a gas, you see. It starts out as rain: tiny, oily droplets that cling to whatever they contact. It enters through the pores, the eyes, the lungs. Depending on the dosage, the effects can be instantaneous. I could see the evacuees' limbs begin to tremble, arms falling to their sides as the agent worked its way through their central nervous system. They rubbed their eyes, fought to speak, move, breathe. I was glad I couldn't smell the contents of their undergarments, the sudden discharge of bladder and bowels.

Why would they do it? I couldn't understand. Didn't the high command know that chemical weapons had no effect on the undead? Didn't they learn anything from Zhitomir?

The first corpse to move was a woman, just a second or more before the others, a twitching hand groping across the back of a man who looked like he'd been trying to shield her. He slipped off as she rose on uncertain knees. Her face was mottled and webbed with blackened veins. I think she saw me, or our tank. Her jaw dropped, her arms rose. I could see the others coming to life, every fortieth or fiftieth person, everyone who had been bitten and had previously tried to conceal it.

And then I understood. Yes, they'd learned from Zhitomir, and now they found a better use for their cold war stockpiles. How do you effectively separate the infected from the others? How do you keep evacuees from spreading the infection behind the lines? That's one way.

They were starting to fully reanimate, regaining their footing, shuffling slowly across the bridge toward us. I called for the gunner. He could barely stutter a response. I kicked him in the back, barked the order to sight his targets! It took a few seconds but he settled his crosshairs on the first woman and squeezed the trigger. I held my ears as the Coax belched. The other tanks followed suit.

Twenty minutes later, it was over. I know I should have waited for orders, at least reported our status or the effects of the strike. I could see six more flights of Rooks streaking over, five heading for the other bridges, the last for the city center. I ordered our company to withdraw, to head southwest and just keep going. There were a lot of bodies around us, the ones who'd just made it over the bridge before the gas hit. They popped as we ran over them.

Have you been to the Great Patriotic War Museum Complex? It was one of the most impressive buildings in Kiev. The courtyard was filled with machines: tanks, guns, every class and size, from the Revolution to the modern day. Two tanks faced each other at the museum's entrance. They were decorated with colorful drawings now, and children were allowed to climb and play on them. There was an Iron Cross, a full meter in size, made from the hundreds of real Iron Crosses taken from dead Hitlerites. There was a mural, from floor to ceiling, showing a grand battle. Our soldiers were all connected, in a seething wave of strength and courage that crashed upon the Germans, that drove them from our homeland. So many symbols of our national defense and none more spectacular than the statue of the *Rodina Mat (Motherland)*. She was the tallest building in the city, a more than sixty-meter masterpiece of pure stainless steel. She was the last thing I saw in Kiev, her shield and sword held high in everlasting triumph, her cold, bright eyes looking down at us as we ran.

❦

SAND LAKES PROVINCIAL WILDERNESS PARK, MANITOBA, CANADA

[Jesika Hendricks gestures to the expanse of subarctic wasteland. The natural beauty has been replaced by wreckage: abandoned vehicles, debris, and human corpses remain partially frozen into the gray snow and ice. Originally from Waukesha, Wisconsin, the now naturalized Canadian is part of this region's Wilderness Restoration Project. Along with several hundred other volunteers, she has come here every summer since the end of official hostilities. Although WRP claims to have made substantial progress, none can claim to see any end in sight.]

I don't blame them, the government, the people who were supposed to protect us. Objectively, I guess I can understand. They couldn't have everyone following the army west behind the Rocky Mountains. How were they going to feed all of us, how were they going to screen us, and how could they ever hope to stop the armies of undead that almost certainly would have been following us? I can understand why they would want to divert as many refugees north as possible. What else could they do, stop us at the Rockies with armed troops, gas us like the Ukrainians? At least if we went north, we might have a chance. Once the temperature dropped and the undead froze, some us might be able to survive. That was happening all around the rest of the world, people fleeing north hoping to stay alive until winter came. No, I don't blame them for wanting to divert us, I can forgive that. But the irresponsible way they did it, the lack of vital information that would have helped so many to stay alive . . . that I can never forgive.

It was August, two weeks after Yonkers and just three days after the government had started withdrawing west. We hadn't had too many outbreaks in our neighborhood. I'd only seen one, a collection of six feeding on a homeless man. The cops had put them down quickly. It happened three blocks from our house and that was when my father decided to leave.

We were in the living room; my father was learning how to load his new rifle while Mom finished nailing up the windows. You couldn't find a channel with anything *but* zombie news, either live images, or recorded footage from Yonkers. Looking back, I still can't believe how unprofessional the news media was. So much spin, so few hard facts. All those digestible sound bites from an army of "experts" all contradicting one another, all trying to seem more "shocking" and "in depth" than the last one. It was all so confusing, nobody seemed to know what to do. The only thing any of them could agree on was that all private citizens should "go north." Because the living dead freeze solid, extreme cold is our only hope. That's all we heard. No more instructions on *where* to head north, what to bring with us, how to survive, just that damn catchphrase you'd hear from every talking head, or just crawling over and over across the bottom of the TV. "Go north. Go north. Go north."

"That's it," Dad said, "we're getting out of here tonight and heading north." He tried to sound determined, slapping his rifle. He'd never touched a gun in his life. He was a gentleman in the most literal sense—he was a gentle man. Short, bald, a pudgy face that turned red when he laughed, he was the king of the bad jokes and cheesy one-liners. He always had something for you, a compliment or a smile, or a little extension to my allowance that Mom wasn't supposed to know about. He was the good cop in the family, he left all the big decisions to Mom.

Now Mom tried to argue, tried to make him see reason. We lived above the snowline, we had all we needed. Why trek into the unknown when we could just stock up on supplies, continue to fortify the house, and just wait until the first fall frost? Dad wouldn't hear it. We could be dead by the fall, we could be dead by next week! He was so caught up in the Great Panic. He told us it would be like an extended camping trip. We'd live on moose-burgers and wild berry desserts. He promised to teach me how to fish and asked me what I wanted to name my pet rabbit when I caught it. He'd lived in Waukesha his whole life. He'd never been camping.

[She shows me something in the ice, a collection of cracked DVDs.]

This is what people brought with them: hair dryers, GameCubes, laptops by the dozen. I don't think they were stupid enough to think they could use them. Maybe some did. I think most people were just afraid of losing them, that they'd come home after six months and find their homes looted. We actually thought we were packing sensibly. Warm clothes, cooking utensils, things from the medicine cabinet, and all the canned food we could carry. It looked like enough food for a couple of years. We finished half of it on the way up. That didn't bother me. It was like an adventure, the trek north.

All those stories you hear about the clogged roads and violence, that wasn't us. We were in the first wave. The only people ahead of us were the Canadians, and most of them were already long gone. There was still a lot of traffic on the road, more cars than I'd ever seen, but it all moved pretty quickly, and only really snarled in places like roadside towns or parks.

Parks?

Parks, designated campgrounds, any place where people thought they'd gone far enough. Dad used to look down on those people, calling them shortsighted and irrational. He said that we were still way too close to population centers and the only way to really make it was to head as far north as we could. Mom would always argue that it wasn't their fault, that most of them had simply run out of gas. "And whose fault is that," Dad would say. We had a lot of spare gas cans on the roof of the minivan. Dad had been stocking up since the first days of the Panic. We'd pass a lot of traffic snarls around roadside gas stations, most of which already had these giant signs outside that said NO MORE GAS. Dad drove by them really fast. He drove fast by a lot of things, the stalled cars that needed a jump, or hitchhikers who needed a ride. There were a lot of those, in some cases, walking in lines by the side of the road, looking like the way you think refugees are supposed to look. Every now and then a car would stop to pick up a couple, and suddenly everyone wanted a ride. "See what they got themselves into?" That was Dad.

We did pick up one woman, walking by herself and pulling one of those wheeled airline bags. She looked pretty harmless, all alone in the rain. That's probably why Mom made Dad stop to pick her up. Her name was Patty, she was from Winnipeg. She didn't tell us how she got out here and we didn't ask. She was really grateful and tried to give my parents all the money she had. Mom wouldn't let her and promised to take her as far as we were going. She started crying, thanking us. I was proud of my parents for doing the right thing, until she sneezed and brought up a handkerchief to blow her nose. Her left hand had been in her pocket since we picked her up. We could see that it was wrapped in a cloth and had a dark stain that looked like blood. She saw that we saw and suddenly looked nervous. She told us not to worry and that she'd just cut it by accident. Dad looked at Mom, and they both got very quiet. They wouldn't look at me, they didn't say anything. That night I woke up when I heard the passenger door slam shut. I didn't think it was anything unusual. We were always stopping for bathroom breaks. They always woke me up just in case I had to go, but this time I didn't know what had happened until the minivan was already moving. I looked around for Patty, but she was gone. I asked my parents what had happened and they told me she'd asked them to drop her off. I looked behind us and thought I could just make her out, this little spec getting smaller each second. I thought she looked like she was running after us, but I was so tired and confused I couldn't be sure. I probably just didn't want to know. I shut a lot out during that drive north.

Like what?

Like the other "hitchhikers," the ones who didn't run. There weren't a lot, remember, we're talking about the first wave. We encountered half a dozen at most, wandering down the middle of the road, raising their arms when we got close. Dad would weave around them and Mom would tell me to get my head down. I never saw them too close. I had my face against the seat and my eyes shut. I didn't want to see them. I just kept thinking about mooseburgers and wild berries. It was like heading to the Promised Land. I knew once we headed far enough north, everything would be all right.

For a little while it was. We had this great campsite right on the shore of a lake, not too many people around, but just enough to make us feel "safe," you know, if any of the dead showed up. Everyone was real friendly, this big, collective vibe of relief. It was kind of like a party at first. There were these big cookouts every night, people all throwing in what they'd hunted or fished, mostly fished. Some guys would throw dynamite in the lake and there'd be this huge bang and all these fish would come floating to the surface. I'll never forget those sounds, the explosions or the chainsaws as people cut down trees, or the music of car radios and instruments families had brought. We all sang around the campfires at night, these giant bonfires of logs stacked up on one another.

That was when we still had trees, before the second and third waves starting showing up, when people were down to burning leaves and stumps, then finally whatever they could get their hands on. The smell of plastic and rubber got really bad, in your mouth, in your hair. By that time the fish were all gone, and anything left for people to hunt. No one seemed to worry. Everyone was counting on winter freezing the dead.

But once the dead were frozen, how were you going to survive the winter?

Good question. I don't think most people thought that far ahead. Maybe they figured that the "authorities" would come rescue us or that they could just pack up and head home. I'm sure a lot of people didn't think about any-thing except the day in front of them, just grateful that they were finally safe and confident that things would work themselves out. "We'll all be home before you know it," people would say. "It'll all be over by Christmas."

[She draws my attention to another object in the ice, a Sponge-Bob SquarePants sleeping bag. It is small, and stained brown.]

What do you think this is rated to, a heated bedroom at a sleepover party? Okay, maybe they couldn't get a proper bag—camping stores were always the first bought out or knocked off—but you can't believe how ig-norant some of these people were. A lot of them were from Sunbelt states, some as far away as southern Mexico. You'd see people getting into their sleeping bags with their boots on, not realizing that it was cutting off their circulation. You'd see them drinking to get warm, not realizing it was actu-ally lowering their temperature by releasing more body heat. You'd see them wearing these big heavy coats with nothing but a T-shirt underneath. They'd do something physical, overheat, take off the coat. Their bodies'd be coated in sweat, a lot of cotton cloth holding in the moisture. The breeze'd come up . . . a lot of people got sick that first September. Cold and flu. They gave it to the rest of us.

In the beginning everyone was friendly. We cooperated. We traded or even bought what we needed from other families. Money was still worth something. Everyone thought the banks would be reopening soon. When-ever Mom and Dad would go looking for food, they'd always leave me with a neighbor. I had this little survival radio, the kind you cranked for power, so we could listen to the news every night. It was all stories of the pullout, army units leaving people stranded. We'd listen with our road map of the United States, pointing to the cities and towns where the reports were coming from. I'd sit on Dad's lap. "See," he'd say, "they didn't get out in time. They weren't smart like us." He'd try to force a smile. For a little while, I thought he was right.

But after the first month, when the food started running out, and the days got colder and darker, people started getting mean. There were no more communal fires, no more cookouts or singing. The camp became a mess, nobody picking up their trash anymore. A couple times I stepped in human shit. Nobody was even bothering to bury it.

I wasn't left alone with neighbors anymore, my parents didn't trust anyone. Things got dangerous, you'd see a lot of fights. I saw two women wrestling over a fur coat, tore it right down the middle. I saw one guy catching another guy trying to steal some stuff out of his car and beat his head in with a tire iron. A lot of it took place at night, scuffling and shouts. Every now and then you'd hear a gunshot, and somebody crying. One time we heard someone moving outside the makeshift tent we'd draped over the minivan. Mom told me to put my head down and cover my ears. Dad went outside. Through my hands I heard shouts. Dad's gun went off. Someone screamed. Dad came back in, his face was white. I never asked him what happened.

The only time anyone ever came together was when one of the dead showed up. These were the ones who'd followed the third wave, coming alone or in small packs. It happened every couple of days. Someone would sound an alarm and everyone would rally to take them out. And then, as soon as it was over, we'd all turn on each other again.

When it got cold enough to freeze the lake, when the last of the dead stopped showing up, a lot of people thought it was safe enough to try to walk home.

Walk? Not drive?

No more gas. They'd used it all up for cooking fuel or just to keep their car heaters running. Every day there'd be these groups of half-starved, ragged wretches, all loaded down with all this useless stuff they'd brought with them, all with this look of desperate hope on their faces.

"Where do they think they're going?" Dad would say. "Don't they know that it hasn't gotten cold enough farther south? Don't they know what's still waiting for them back there?" He was convinced that if we just held out long enough, sooner or later things would get better. That was in October, when I still looked like a human being.

[We come upon a collection of bones, too many to count. They lie in a pit, half covered in ice.]

I was a pretty heavy kid. I never played sports, I lived on fast food and snacks. I was only a little bit thinner when we arrived in August. By November, I was like a skeleton. Mom and Dad didn't look much better. Dad's tummy was gone, Mom had these narrow cheekbones. They were fighting a lot, fighting about everything. That scared me more than anything. They'd never raised their voices at home. They were school-teachers, "progressives." There might have been a tense, quiet dinner every now and then, but nothing like this. They went for each other every chance they had. One time, around Thanksgiving . . . I couldn't get out of my sleeping bag. My belly was swollen and I had these sores on my mouth and nose. There was this smell coming from the neighbor's RV. They were cooking something, meat, it smelled really good. Mom and Dad were outside arguing. Mom said "it" was the only way. I didn't know what "it" was. She said "it" wasn't "that bad" because the neighbors, not us, had been the ones to actually "do it." Dad said that we weren't going to stoop to that level and that Mom should be ashamed of herself. Mom really laid into Dad, screeching that it was all his fault that we were here, that I was dying. Mom told him that a real man would know what to do. She called him a wimp and said he wanted us to die so then he could run away and live like the "faggot" she always knew he was. Dad told her to shut the fuck up. Dad *never* swore. I heard something, a crack from outside. Mom came back in, holding a clump of snow over her right eye. Dad followed her. He didn't say anything. He had this look on his face

I'd never seen before, like he was a different person. He grabbed my survival radio, the one people'd try to buy . . . or steal, for a long time, and went back out toward the RV. He came back ten minutes later, without the radio but with a big bucket of this steaming hot stew. It was so good! Mom told me not to eat too fast. She fed me in little spoonfuls. She looked relieved. She was crying a little. Dad still had that look. The look I had myself in a few months, when Mom and Dad both got sick and I had to feed them.

[I kneel to examine the bone pile. They have all been broken, the marrow extracted.]

Winter really hit us in early December. The snow was over our heads, literally, mountains of it, thick and gray from the pollution. The camp got silent. No more fights, no more shooting. By Christmas Day there was plenty of food.

[She holds up what looks like a miniature femur. It has been scraped clean by a knife.]

They say eleven million people died that winter, and that's just in North America. That doesn't count the other places: Greenland, Iceland, Scandinavia. I don't want to think about Siberia, all those refugees from southern China, the ones from Japan who'd never been outside a city, and all those poor people from India. That was the first Gray Winter, when the filth in the sky started changing the weather. They say that a part of that filth, I don't know how much, was ash from human remains.

[She plants a marker above the pit.]

It took a lot of time, but eventually the sun did come out, the weather began to warm, the snow finally began to melt. By mid-July, spring was finally here, and so were the living dead.

[One of the other team members calls us over. A zombie is half buried, frozen from the waist down in the ice. The head, arms, and upper torso are very much alive, thrashing and moaning, and trying to claw toward us.]

Why do they come back after freezing? All human cells contain water, right? And when that water freezes, it expands and bursts the cell walls. That's why you can't just freeze people in suspended animation, so then why does it work for the living dead?

[The zombie makes one great lunge in our direction; its frozen lower torso begins to snap. Jesika raises her weapon, a long iron crowbar, and casually smashes the creature's skull.]

❧

UDAIPUR LAKE PALACE, LAKE PICHOLA, RAJASTHAN, INDIA

[Completely covering its foundation of Jagniwas Island, this idyllic, almost fairy-tale structure was once a maharaja's residence, then a luxury hotel, then a haven to several hundred refugees, until an outbreak of cholera killed them all. Under the direction of Project Manager Sardar Khan, the hotel, like the lake and surrounding city, is finally beginning to return to life. During his recollections, Mister Khan sounds less like a battle-hardened, highly educated civilian engineer, and more like a young, frightened lance corporal who once found himself on a chaotic mountain road.]

I remember the monkeys, hundreds of them, climbing and skittering among the vehicles, even over the tops of people's heads. I'd watched them as far back as Chandigarh, leaping from roofs and balconies as the living dead filled the street. I remember them scattering, chattering, scrambling straight up telephone poles to escape the zombies' grasping arms. Some didn't even wait to be attacked; they knew. And now they were here, on this narrow, twisting Himalayan goat track. They called it a road, but even in peacetime it had been a notorious death trap. Thousands of refugees were streaming past, or climbing over the stalled and abandoned vehicles. People were still trying to struggle with suitcases, boxes; one man was stubbornly holding on to the monitor for a desktop PC. A monkey landed on his head, trying to use it as a stepping-stone, but the man was too close to the edge and the two of them went tumbling over the side. It seemed like every second someone would lose their footing. There were just too many people. The road didn't even have a guardrail. I saw a whole bus go over, I don't even know how, it wasn't even moving. Passengers were climbing out of the windows because the doors of the bus had been jammed by foot traffic. One woman was halfway out the window when the bus tipped over. Something was in her arms, something clutched tightly to her. I tell myself that it wasn't moving, or crying, that it was just a bundle of clothes. No one within arm's reach tried to help her. No one even looked, they just kept streaming by. Sometimes when I dream about that moment, I can't tell the difference between them and the monkeys.

I wasn't supposed to be there, I wasn't even a combat engineer. I was with the BRO[1]; my job was to build roads, not blow them up. I'd just been wandering through the assembly area at Shimla, trying to find what remained of my unit, when this engineer, Sergeant Mukherjee, grabbed me by the arm and said, "You, soldier, you know how to drive?"

I think I stammered something to the affirmative, and suddenly he was shoving me into the driver's side of a jeep while he jumped in next to me with some kind of radiolike device on his lap. "Get back to the pass! Go! Go!" I took off down the road, screeching and skidding and trying desperately to explain that I was actually a steamroller driver, and not even fully qualified at that. Mukherjee didn't hear me. He was too busy fiddling with

---

1. BRO: The Border Roads Organization.

the device on his lap. "The charges are already set," he explained. "All we have to do is wait for the order!"

"What charges?" I asked. "What order?"

"To blow the pass, you arse head!" he yelled, motioning to what I now recognized as a detonator on his lap. "How the hell else are we going to stop them?"

I knew, vaguely, that our retreat into the Himalayas had something to do with some kind of master plan, and that part of that plan meant closing all the mountain passes to the living dead. I never dreamed, however, that I would be such a vital participant! For the sake of civil conversation, I will not repeat my profane reaction to Mukherjee, nor Mukherjee's equally profane reaction when we arrived at the pass and found it still full of refugees.

"It's supposed to be clear!" he shouted. "No more refugees!"

We noticed a soldier from the Rashtriya Rifles, the outfit that was supposed to be securing the road's mountain entrance, come running past the jeep. Mukherjee jumped out and grabbed the man. "What the hell is this?" he asked; he was a big man, tough and angry. "You were supposed to keep the road clear." The other man was just as angry, just as scared. "You want to shoot your grandmother, go ahead!" He shoved the sergeant aside and kept going.

Mukherjee keyed his radio and reported that the road was still highly active. A voice came back to him, a high-pitched, frantic younger voice of an officer screaming that his orders were to blow the road no matter how many people were on it. Mukherjee responded angrily that he had to wait till it was clear. If we blew it now, not only would we be sending dozens of people hurtling to their deaths, but we would be trapping thousands on the other side. The voice shot back that the road would *never* be clear, that the only thing behind those people was a raging swarm of God knows how many million zombies. Mukherjee answered that he would blow it when the zombies got here, and not a second before. He wasn't about to commit murder no matter what some pissant lieutenant . . .

But then Mukherjee stopped in midsentence and looked at something over my head. I whipped around, and suddenly found myself staring into the face of General Raj-Singh! I don't know where he came from, why he was there . . . to this day no one believes me, not that he wasn't there, but that *I* was. I was inches away from him, from the Tiger of Delhi! I've heard that people tend to view those they respect as appearing physically taller than they actually are. In my mind, he appears as a virtual giant. Even with his torn uniform, his bloody turban, the patch on his right eye and the bandage on his nose (one of his men had smashed him in the face to get him on the last chopper out of Gandhi Park). General Raj-Singh . . .

[Khan takes a deep breath, his chest filling with pride.]

"Gentlemen," he began . . . he called us "Gentlemen" and explained, very carefully, that the road had to be destroyed immediately. The air force, what was left of it, had its own orders concerning the closure of all mountain passes. At this moment, a single Shamsher fighter bomber was already on station above our position. If we found ourselves unable, or unwilling, to accomplish our mission, then the Jaguar's pilot was ordered to execute "Shiva's Wrath." "Do you know what that means?" Raj-Singh asked. Maybe he thought I was too young to understand, or maybe he must have guessed, somehow, that I was Muslim, but even if I'd known absolutely nothing about the Hindu deity of destruction, everyone in uniform had heard rumors about the "secret" code name for the use of thermonuclear weapons.

Wouldn't that have destroyed the pass?

Yes, and half the mountain as well! Instead of a narrow choke point hemmed in by sheer cliff walls, you would have had little more than a massive, gently sloping ramp. The whole point of destroying these roads was to create a barrier inaccessible to the living dead, and now some ignorant air force general with an atomic erection was going to give them the perfect entrance right into the safe zone!

Mukherjee gulped, not sure of what to do, until the Tiger held out his hand for the detonator. Ever the hero, he was now willing to accept the burden of mass murderer. The sergeant handed it over, close to tears. General Raj-Singh thanked him, thanked us both, whispered a prayer, then pressed his thumbs down on the firing buttons. Nothing happened, he tried again, no response. He checked the batteries, all the connections, and tried a third time. Nothing. The problem wasn't the detonator. Something had gone wrong with the charges that were buried half a kilometer down the road, set right in the middle of the refugees.

This is the end, I thought, *we're all going to die*. All I could think of was getting out of there, far enough away to maybe avoid the nuclear blast. I still feel guilty about those thoughts, caring only for myself in a moment like that.

Thank God for General Raj-Singh. He reacted . . . exactly how you would expect a living legend to react. He ordered us to get out of here, save ourselves and get to Shimla, then turned and ran right into crowd. Mukherjee and I looked at each other, without much hesitation, I'm happy to say, and took off after him.

Now we wanted to be heroes, too, to protect our general and shield him from the crowd. What a joke. We never even saw him once the masses enveloped us like a raging river. I was pushed and shoved from all directions. I don't know when I was punched in the eye. I shouted that I needed to get past, that this was army business. No one listened. I fired several shots in the air. No one noticed. I considered actually firing into the crowd. I was becoming as desperate as them. Out of the corner of my eye I saw Mukherjee go tumbling over the side with another man still fighting for his rifle. I turned to tell General Raj-Singh but couldn't find him in the crowd. I called his name, tried to spot him above the other heads. I climbed onto the roof of a microbus, trying to get my bearings. Then the wind came up; it brought the stink and moan whipping through the valley. In front of me, about half a kilometer ahead, the crowd began running. I strained my eyes . . . squinted. The dead were coming. Slow and deliberate, and just as tightly packed as the refugees they were devouring.

The microbus shook and I fell. First I was floating on a sea of human bodies, then suddenly I was beneath them, shoes and bare feet trampling on my flesh. I felt my ribs crack, I coughed and tasted blood. I pulled myself under the microbus. My body was aching, burning. I couldn't speak. I could barely see. I heard the sound of the approaching zombies. I guessed that they couldn't be more than two hundred meters away. I swore I wouldn't die like the others, all those victims torn to pieces, that cow I saw struggling and bleeding on the banks of the Satluj River in Rupnagar. I fumbled for my sidearm, my hand wouldn't work. I cursed and cried. I thought I'd be religious at that point, but I was just so scared and angry I started beating my head against the underside of the van. I thought if I hit it hard enough I could bash in my own skull. Suddenly there was a deafening roar and the ground rose up underneath me. A wave of screams and moans mixed with this powerful blast of pressurized dust. My face slammed into the machinery above, knocking me cold.

The first thing I remember when I came to was a very faint sound. At first I thought it was water. It sounded like a fast drip . . . tap-tap-tap, like that. The tap became clearer, and I suddenly became aware of two other sounds, the crackle of my radio . . . how that wasn't smashed I'll never know . . . and the ever-present howling of the living dead. I crawled out from under the microbus. At least my legs were still working well enough to stand. I realized that I was alone, no refugees, no General Raj-Singh. I was standing among a collection of discarded personal belongings in the middle of a deserted mountain path. In front of me was a charred cliff wall. Beyond it was the other side of the severed road.

That's where the moan was coming from. The living dead were still coming for me. With eyes front and arms outstretched, they were falling in droves off the shattered edge. That was the tapping sound: their bodies smashing on the valley floor far below.

The Tiger must have set the demolition charges off by hand. I guessed he must have reached them the same time as the living dead. I hope they didn't get their teeth in him first. I hope he's pleased with his statue that now stands over a modern, four-lane mountain freeway. I wasn't thinking about his sacrifice at that moment. I wasn't even sure if any of this was real. Staring silently at this undead waterfall, listening to my radio report from the other units:

"Vikasnagar: Secure."

"Bilaspur: Secure."

"Jawala Mukhi: Secure."

"All passes report secure: Over!"

Am I dreaming, I thought, *am I insane?*

The monkey didn't help matters any. He was sitting on top of the microbus, just watching the undead plunge to their end. His face appeared so serene, so intelligent, as if he truly understood the situation. I almost wanted him to turn to me and say, "This is the turning point of the war! We've finally stopped them! We're finally safe!" But instead his little penis popped out and he peed in my face.

HOME FRONT USA

TAOS, NEW MEXICO

[Arthur Sinclair, Junior, is the picture of an old-world patrician: tall, lean, with close-cropped white hair and an affected Harvard accent. He speaks into the ether, rarely making eye contact or pausing for questions. During the war, Mister Sinclair was director of the U.S. government's newly formed DeStRes, or Department of Strategic Resources.]

I don't know who first thought of the acronym "DeStRes" or if they consciously knew how much it sounded like "distress," but it certainly could not have been more appropriate. Establishing a defensive line at the Rocky Mountains might have created a theoretical "safe zone," but in reality that zone consisted mainly of rubble and refugees. There was starvation, disease, homelessness in the millions. Industry was in shambles, transportation and trade had evaporated, and all of this was compounded by the living dead both assaulting the Rocky Line and festering within our safe zone. We had to get our people on their feet again—clothed, fed, housed, and back to work—otherwise this supposed safe zone was only forestalling the inevitable. That was why the DeStRes was created, and, as you can imagine, I had to do a lot of on-the-job training.

Those first months, I can't tell you how much information I had to cram into this withered old cortex; the briefings, the inspection tours . . . when I did sleep, it was with a book under my pillow, each night a new one, from Henry J. Kaiser to Vo Nguyen Giap. I needed every idea, every word, every ounce of knowledge and wisdom to help me fuse a fractured land-scape into the modern American war machine. If my father had been alive, he probably would have laughed at my frustration. He'd been a staunch New Dealer, working closely with FDR as comptroller of New York State. He used methods that were almost Marxist in nature, the kind of collectivization that would make Ayn Rand leap from her grave and join the ranks of the living dead. I'd always rejected the lessons he'd tried to impart, running as far away as Wall Street to shut them out. Now I was wracking my brains to remember them. One thing those New Dealers did better than any generation in American history was find and harvest the right tools and talent.

Tools and talent?

A term my son had heard once in a movie. I found it described our recon-struction efforts rather well. "Talent" describes the potential workforce, its level of skilled labor, and how that labor could be utilized effectively. To be perfectly candid, our supply of talent was at a critical low. Ours was a postindustrial or service-based economy, so complex and highly specialized that each individual could only function within the confines of its narrow, compartmentalized structure. You should have seen some of the "careers" listed on our first employment census; everyone was some version of an "executive," a "representative," an "analyst," or a "consultant," all perfectly suited to the prewar world, but all totally inadequate for the present crisis. We needed carpenters, masons, machinists, gunsmiths. We had those people, to be sure, but not nearly as many as were necessary. The first labor survey stated clearly that over 65 percent of the present civilian workforce were classified F-6, possessing no valued vocation. We required a massive job retraining program. In short, we needed to get a lot of white collars dirty.

It was slow going. Air traffic was nonexistent, roads and rail lines were a shambles, and fuel, good Lord, you couldn't find a tank of gas between Blaine, Washington, and Imperial Beach, California. Add to this the fact that prewar America not only had a commuter-based infrastructure, but that such a method also allowed for severe levels of economic segregation. You would have entire suburban neighborhoods of upper-middle-class professionals, none of whom had possessed even the basic know-how to replace a cracked window. Those with that knowledge lived in their own blue-collar "ghettos," an hour away in prewar auto traffic, which translated to at least a full day on foot. Make no mistake, bipedal locomotion was how most people traveled in the beginning.

Solving this problem—no, challenge, there are no problems—was the refugee camps. There were hundreds of them, some parking-lot small, some spreading for miles, scattered across the mountains and coast, all requiring government assistance, all acute drains on rapidly diminishing resources. At the top of my list, before I tackled any other challenge, these camps had to be emptied. Anyone F-6 but physically able became unskilled labor: clearing rubble, harvesting crops, digging graves. A lot of graves needed to be dug. Anyone A-1, those with war-appropriate skills, became part of our CSSP, or Community Self-Sufficiency Program. A mixed group of instructors would be tasked with infusing these sedentary, overeducated, desk-bound, cubicle mice with the knowledge necessary to make it on their own.

It was an instant success. Within three months you saw a marked drop in requests for government aid. I can't stress how vital this was to victory. It allowed us to transition from a zero-sum, survival-based economy, into full-blown war production. This was the National Reeducation Act, the organic outgrowth of the CSSP. I'd say it was the largest jobs training program since the Second World War, and easily the most radical in our history.

You've mentioned, on occasion, the problems faced by the NRA . . .

I was getting to that. The president gave me the kind of power I needed to meet any physical or logistical challenge. Unfortunately, what neither he nor anyone on Earth could give me was the power to change the way people thought. As I explained, America was a segregated workforce, and in many cases, that segregation contained a cultural element. A great many of our instructors were first-generation immigrants. These were the people who knew how to take care of themselves, how to survive on very little and work with what they had. These were the people who tended small gardens in their backyards, who repaired their own homes, who kept their appliances running for as long as mechanically possible. It was crucial that these people teach the rest of us to break from our comfortable, disposable consumer lifestyle even though their labor had allowed us to maintain that lifestyle in the first place.

Yes, there was racism, but there was also classism. You're a high-powered corporate attorney. You've spent most of your life reviewing contracts, brokering deals, talking on the phone. That's what you're good at, that's what made you rich and what allowed you to hire a plumber to fix your toilet, which allowed you to keep talking on the phone. The more work you do, the more money you make, the more peons you hire to free you up to make more money. That's the way the world works. But one day it doesn't. No one needs a contract reviewed or a deal brokered. What it does need is toilets fixed. And suddenly that peon is your teacher, maybe even your boss. For some, this was scarier than the living dead.

Once, on a fact-finding tour through LA, I sat in the back of a reeducation lecture. The trainees had all held lofty positions in the entertainment industry, a mélange of agents, managers, "creative executives," whatever the hell that means. I can understand their resistance, their arrogance. Before the war, entertainment had been the most valued export of the United States. Now they were being trained as custodians for a munitions plant in Bakersfield, California. One woman, a casting director, exploded. How dare they degrade her like this! She had an MFA in Conceptual Theater, she had cast the top three grossing sitcoms in the last five seasons and she made more in a week than her instructor could dream of in several life-times! She kept addressing that instructor by her first name. "Magda," she kept saying, "Magda, enough already. Magda, please." At first I thought this woman was just being rude, degrading the instructor by refusing to use her title. I found out later that Mrs. Magda Antonova used to be this woman's cleaning lady. Yes, it was very hard for some, but a lot of them later admit-ted that they got more emotional satisfaction from their new jobs than anything closely resembling their old ones.

I met one gentleman on a coastal ferry from Portland to Seattle. He had worked in the licensing department for an advertising agency, specifically in charge of procuring the rights to classic rock songs for television com-mercials. Now he was a chimney sweep. Given that most homes in Seattle had lost their central heat and the winters were now longer and colder, he was seldom idle. "I help keep my neighbors warm," he said proudly. I know it sounds a little too Norman Rockwell, but I hear stories like that all the time. "You see those shoes, I made them," "That sweater, that's my sheep's wool," "Like the corn? My garden." That was the upshot of a more local-ized system. It gave people the opportunity to see the fruits of their labor, it gave them a sense of individual pride to know they were making a clear, concrete contribution to victory, and it gave me a wonderful feeling that I was part of that. I needed that feeling. It kept me sane for the other part of my job.

So much for "talent." "Tools" are the weapons of war, and the industrial and logistical means by which those weapons are constructed.

[He swivels in his chair, motioning to a picture above his desk. I lean closer and see that it's not a picture but a framed label.]

Ingredients:

molasses from the United States

anise from Spain

licorice from France

vanilla (bourbon) from Madagascar

cinnamon from Sri Lanka

cloves from Indonesia

wintergreen from China

pimento berry oil from Jamaica

balsam oil from Peru

And that's just for a bottle of peacetime root beer. We're not even talking about something like a desktop PC, or a nuclear-powered aircraft carrier.

Ask anyone how the Allies won the Second World War. Those with very little knowledge might answer that it was our numbers or generalship. Those without any knowledge might point to techno-marvels like radar or the atom bomb. [Scowls.] Anyone with the most rudimentary understanding of that conflict will give you three real reasons: first, the ability to manufacture more materiel: more bullets, beans, and bandages than the enemy; second, the natural resources available to manufacture that materiel; and third, the logistical means to not only transport those resources to the factories, but also to transport the finished products out to the front lines. The Allies had the resources, industry, and logistics of an entire planet. The Axis, on the other hand, had to depend on what scant assets they could scrape up within their borders. This time we were the Axis. The living dead controlled most of the world's landmass, while American war production depended on what could be harvested within the limits of the western states specifically. Forget raw materials from safe zones overseas; our merchant fleet was crammed to the decks with refugees while fuel shortages had dry-docked most of our navy.

We had some advantages. California's agricultural base could at least erase the problem of starvation, if it could be restructured. The citrus growers didn't go quietly, neither did the ranchers. The beef barons who controlled so much prime potential farmland were the worst. Did you ever hear of Don Hill? Ever see the movie Roy Elliot did on him? It was when the infestation hit the San Joaquin Valley, the dead swarming over his fences, attacking his cattle, tearing them apart like African driver ants. And there he was in the middle of it all, shooting and hollering like Gregory Peck in *Duel in the Sun*. I dealt with him openly and honestly. As with everyone else, I gave him the choice. I reminded him that winter was coming and there were still a lot of very hungry people out there. I warned him that when the hordes of starving refugees showed up to finish what the living dead started, he'd have no government protection whatsoever. Hill was a brave, stubborn bastard, but he wasn't an idiot. He agreed to surrender his land and herd only on the condition that his and everyone else's breeding stock remained untouched. We shook on that.

Tender, juicy steaks—can you think of a better icon of our prewar artificial standard of living? And yet it was that standard that ended up being our second great advantage. The only way to supplement our resource base was recycling. This was nothing new. The Israelis had started when they sealed their borders and since then each nation had adopted it to one degree or another. None of their stockpiles, however, could even compare to what we had at our disposal. Think about what life was like in the prewar America. Even those considered middle class enjoyed, or took for granted, a level of material comfort unheard of by any other nation at any other time in human history. The clothing, the kitchenware, the electronics, the automobiles, just in the Los Angeles basin alone, outnumbered the prewar population by three to one. The cars poured in by the millions, every house, every neighborhood. We had an entire industry of over a hundred thousand employees working three shifts, seven days a week: collecting, cataloging, disassembling, storing, and shipping parts and pieces to factories all over the coast. There was a little trouble, like with the cattle ranchers, people not wanting to turn over their Hummers or vintage Italian midlife crisis mobiles. Funny, no gas to run them but they still hung on anyway. It didn't bother me too much. They were a pleasure to deal with compared to the military establishment.

Of all my adversaries, easily the most tenacious were the ones in uniform. I never had direct control over any of their R&D, they were free to green light whatever they wanted. But given that almost all their programs were farmed out to civilian contractors and that those contractors depended on resources controlled by DeStRes, I had de facto control. "You *cannot* mothball our Stealth bombers," they would yell. "Who the Blank do you think you are to cancel our production of tanks?" At first I tried to reason with them: "The M-1 Abrams has a jet engine. Where are you going to find that kind of fuel? Why do you need Stealth aircraft against an enemy that doesn't have radar?" I tried to make them see that given what we had to work with, as opposed to what we were facing, we simply had to get the largest return on our investment or, in their language, the most bang for our buck. They were insufferable, with their all-hours phone calls, or just showing up at my office unannounced. I guess I can't really blame them, not after how we all treated them after the last brushfire war, and certainly not after almost having their asses handed to them at Yonkers. They were teetering on the edge of total collapse, and a lot of them just needed somewhere to vent.

[He grins confidently.]

I started my career trading on the floor of the NYSE, so I can yell as hard and long as any professional drill sergeant. After each "meeting," I'd expect the call, the one I'd been both dreading and hoping for: "Mister Sinclair, this is the president, I just want to thank you for your service and we'll no longer be requiring . . ." [Chuckles.] It never came. My guess is no one else wanted the job.

[His smile fades.]

I'm not saying that I didn't make mistakes. I know I was too anal about the air force's D-Corps. I didn't understand their safety protocols or what dirigibles could really accomplish in undead warfare. All I knew was that with our negligible helium supply, the only cost-effective lift gas was hydrogen and no way was I going to waste lives and resources on a fleet of modern-day Hindenburgs. I also had to be persuaded, by the president, no less, to reopen the experimental cold fusion project at Livermore. He argued that even though a breakthrough was, at best, still decades away, "planning for the future lets our people know there will be one." I was too conservative with some projects, and with others I was far too liberal.

Project Yellow Jacket—I still kick myself when I think about that one. These Silicon Valley eggheads, all of them geniuses in their own field, convinced me that they had a "wonder weapon" that could win the war, theoretically, within forty-eight hours of deployment. They could build micro missiles, millions of them, about the size of a .22 rimfire bullet, that could be scattered from transport aircraft, then guided by satellites to the brain of every zombie in North America. Sounds amazing, right? It did to me.

[He grumbles to himself.]

When I think of what we poured down that hole, what we could have produced instead . . . ahhh . . . no point in dwelling on it now.

I could have gone head-to-head against the military for the duration of the war, but I'm grateful, in the end, that I didn't have to. When Travis D'Ambrosia became chairman of the Joint Chiefs, he not only invented the resource-to-kill ratio, but developed a comprehensive strategy to employ it. I always listened to him when he told me a certain weapons system was vital. I trusted his opinion in matters like the new Battle Dress Uniform or the Standard Infantry Rifle.

What was so amazing to see was how the culture of RKR began to take hold among the rank and file. You'd hear soldiers talking on the street, in bars, on the train; "Why have X, when for the same price you could have ten Ys, which could kill a hundred times as many Zs." Soldiers even began coming up with ideas on their own, inventing more cost-effective tools than we could have envisioned. I think they enjoyed it—improvising, adapting, outthinking us bureaucrats. The marines surprised me the most. I'd always bought into the myth of the stupid jarhead, the knuckle-dragging, locked-jaw, testosterone-driven Neanderthal. I never knew that because the Corps always has to procure its assets through the navy, and because admirals are never going to get too fired up about land warfare, that improvisation has had to be one of their most treasured virtues.

[Sinclair points above my head to the opposite wall. On it hangs a heavy steel rod ending in what looks like a fusion of shovel and double-bladed battle-axe. Its official designation is the Standard Infantry Entrenchment Tool, although, to most, it is known as either the "Lobotomizer," or simply, the "Lobo."]

The leathernecks came up with that one, using nothing but the steel of re-cycled cars. We made twenty-three million during the war.

[He smiles with pride.]

And they're still making them today.

❧

BURLINGTON, VERMONT

[Winter has come later this season, as it has every year since the end of the war. Snow blankets the house and surrounding farm-land and frosts the trees that shade the dirt track by the river. Everything about this scene is peaceful, except for the man with me. He insists on calling himself "the Whacko," because "every-one else calls me that, why shouldn't you?" His stride is fast and purposeful, the cane given to him by his doctor (and wife) serves only to stab at the air.]

To be honest, I wasn't surprised to be nominated for vice president. Everyone knew a coalition party was inevitable. I'd been a rising star, at least until I "self-destructed." That's what they said about me, right? All the cowards and hypocrites who'd rather die than see a real man express his passion. So what if I wasn't the world's best politician? I said what I felt, and I wasn't afraid to say it loud and clear. That's one of the main reasons I was the logical choice for copilot. We made a great team; he was the light, I was the heat. Different parties, different personalities, and, let's not kid ourselves, different skin colors as well. I knew I wasn't the first choice. I know who my party secretly wanted. But America wasn't ready to go that far, as stupid, ignorant, and infuriatingly Neolithic as it sounds. They'd rather have a screaming radical for a VP than another one of "those people." So I wasn't surprised at my nomination. I was surprised at everything else.

You mean the elections?

Elections? Honolulu was still a madhouse; soldiers, congressmen, refugees, all bumping into one another trying to find something to eat or a place to sleep or just to find out what the hell was going on. And that was paradise next to the mainland. The Rocky Line was just being established; everything west of it was a war zone. Why go through all the trouble of elections when you could have Congress simply vote for extended emergency powers? The attorney general had tried it when he was mayor of New York, almost got away with it, too. I explained to the president that we didn't have the energy or resources to do anything but fight for our very existence.

What did he say?

Well, let's just say he convinced me otherwise.

Can you elaborate?

I could, but I don't want to mangle his words. The old neurons aren't firing like they used to.

Please try.

You'll fact-check with his library?

I promise.

Well . . . we were in his temporary office, the "presidential suite" of a hotel. He'd just been sworn in on Air Force Two. His old boss was sedated in the suite next to us. From the window you could see the chaos on the streets, the ships at sea lining up to dock, the planes coming in every thirty seconds and ground crew pushing them off the runway once they landed to make room for new ones. I was pointing to them, shouting and gesturing with the passion I'm most famous for. "We need a stable government, fast!" I kept saying. "Elections are great in principle but this is no time for high ideals."

The president was cool, a lot cooler than me. Maybe it was all that military training . . . he said to me, "This is the *only* time for high ideals because those ideals are all that we have. We aren't just fighting for our physical survival, but for the survival of our civilization. We don't have the luxury of old-world pillars. We don't have a common heritage, we don't have a millennia of history. All we have are the dreams and promises that bind us together. All we have . . . [struggling to remember] . . . all we have is what we want to be." You see what he was saying. Our country only exists because people believed in it, and if it wasn't strong enough to protect us from this crisis, then what future could it ever hope to have? He knew that America wanted a Caesar, but to be one would mean the end of America. They say great times make great men. I don't buy it. I saw a lot of weakness, a lot of filth. People who should have risen to the challenge and either couldn't or wouldn't. Greed, fear, stupidity, and hate. I saw it before the war, I see it today. My boss was a great man. We were damn lucky to have him.

The business of elections really set the tone for his entire administration. So many of his proposals looked crazy at first glance, but once you peeled back the first layer, you realized that underneath there existed a core of irrefutable logic. Take the new punishment laws, those really set me off. Putting people in stocks? Whipping them in town squares!?! What was this, Old Salem, the Taliban's Afghanistan? It sounded barbaric, un-

American, until you really thought about the options. What were you going to do with thieves and looters, put them in prison? Who would that help? Who could afford to divert able-bodied citizens to feed, clothe, and guard other able-bodied citizens? More importantly, why remove the punished from society when they could serve as such a valuable deterrent? Yes, there was the fear of pain—the lash, the cane—but all of that paled when compared to public humiliation. People were terrified of having their crimes exposed. At a time when everyone was pulling together, helping each other out, working to protect and take care of one another, the worst thing you could do to someone was to march them up into the public square with a giant poster reading "I Stole My Neighbor's Firewood." Shame's a powerful weapon, but it depended on everyone else doing the right thing. No one is above the law, and seeing a senator given fifteen lashes for his involvement in war profiteering did more to curb crime than a cop on every street corner. Yes, there were the work gangs, but those were the recidivists, those who'd been given chances time and time again. I remember the attorney general suggesting that we dump as many of them into the infested zones as possible, rid ourselves of the drain and potential hazard of their continued presence. Both the president and I opposed this proposition; my objections were ethical, his were practical. We were still talking about American soil, infested yes, but, hopefully one day to be liberated. "The last thing we needed," he said "was to come up against one of these ex-cons as The New Grand Warlord of Duluth." I thought he was joking, but later, as I saw the exact thing happen in other countries, as some exiled criminals rose to command their own isolated, and in some cases, powerful fiefdoms, I realized we'd dodged one hell of a speeding bullet. The work gangs were always an issue for us, politically, socially, even economically, but what other choice did we have for those who just refused to play nice with others?

You did use the death penalty.

Only in extreme cases: sedition, sabotage, attempted political secession. Zombies weren't the only enemies, at least not in the beginning.

The Fundies?

We had our share of religious fundamentalists, what country didn't? Many of them believed that we were, in some way, interfering with God's will.

[He chuckles.]

I'm sorry, I've gotta learn to be more sensitive, but for cryin' out loud, you really think the supreme creator of the infinite multiverse is going to have his plans unraveled by a few Arizona National Guardsmen?

[He waves the thought away.]

They got a lot more press than they should have, all because that nut-bird tried to kill the president. In reality, they were much more a danger to themselves, all those mass suicides, the "mercy" child killings in Medford . . . terrible business, same with the "Greenies," the leftie version of the Fundies. They believed that since the living dead only consumed animals, but not plants, it was the will of the "Divine Goddess" to favor flora over fauna. They made a little trouble, dumping herbicide in a town's water supply, booby-trapping trees so loggers couldn't use them for war production. That kind of ecoterrorism eats up headlines but didn't really threaten our national security. The Rebs, on the other hand: armed, organized political secessionists. That was easily our most tangible danger. It was also the only time I ever saw the president worried. He wouldn't let on, not with that dignified, diplomatic veneer. In public, he treated it as just another "issue," like food rationing or road repair. He'd say in private . . . "They must be eliminated swiftly, decisively, and by any means necessary." Of course, he was only talking about those within the western safe zone. These diehard renegades either had some beef with the government's wartime policy or had already planned to secede years before and were just using the crisis as their excuse. These were the "enemies of our country," the domestic ones anyone swearing to defend our country mentions in his or her oath. We didn't have to think twice about an appropriate response to them. But the secessionists east of the Rockies, in some of the besieged, isolated zones . . . that's when it got "complicated."

Why is that?

Because, as the saying went, "We didn't leave America. America left us." There's a lot of truth to that. We deserted those people. Yes, we left some Special Forces volunteers, tried to supply them by sea and air, but from a purely moral standing, these people were truly abandoned. I couldn't blame them for wanting to go their own way, nobody could. That's why when we began to reclaim lost territory, we allowed every secessionist enclave a chance for peaceful reintegration.

But there was violence.

I still have nightmares, places like Bolivar, and the Black Hills. I never see the actual images, not the violence, or the aftermath. I always see my boss, this towering, powerful, vital man getting sicker and weaker each time. He'd survived so much, shouldered such a crushing burden. You know, he never tried to find out what had happened to his relatives in Jamaica? Never even asked. He was so fiercely focused on the fate of our nation, so determined to preserve the dream that created it. I don't know if great times make great men, but I know they can kill them.

❧

WENATCHEE, WASHINGTON

[Joe Muhammad's smile is as broad as his shoulders. While his day job is as the owner of the town's bicycle repair shop, his spare time is spent sculpting molten metal into exquisite works

of art. He is, no doubt, most famous for the bronze statue on the
mall in Washington, D.C., the Neighborhood Security Memorial of
two standing citizens, and one seated in a wheelchair.]

The recruiter was clearly nervous. She tried to talk me out of it. Had I
spoken to the NRA representative first? Did I know about all the other essential war work? I didn't understand at first; I already had a job at the recycling plant. That was the point of Neighborhood Security Teams, right?
It was a part-time, volunteer service for when you were home from work. I
tried explaining this to her. Maybe there was something I wasn't getting.
As she tried some other half-hearted, half-assed excuses, I saw her eyes
flick to my chair.

[Joe is disabled.]

Can you believe that? Here we were with mass extinction knocking on
the door, and she's trying to be politically correct? I laughed. I laughed
right in her face. What, did she think I just showed up without knowing
what was expected of me? Didn't this dumb bitch read her own security
manual? Well, I'd read it. The whole point of the NST program was to patrol your own neighborhood, walking, or, in my case, rolling down the
sidewalk, stopping to check each house. If, for some reason, you had to go
inside, at least two members were always supposed to wait out in the street.
[Motions to himself.] Hell-o! And what did she think we were facing anyway? It's not like we had to chase them over fences and across backyards.
They came to us. And if and when they did so, let's just say, for the sake of
argument, there was more than we could handle? Shit, if I couldn't roll
myself faster than a walking zombie, how could I have lasted this long? I
stated my case very clearly and calmly, and I even challenged her to present a scenario in which my physical state could be an impediment. She
couldn't. There was some mumbling about having to check with her CO,
maybe I could come back tomorrow. I refused, told her she could call her

CO, and his CO and everyone right up to the Bear[1] himself, but I wasn't moving until I got my orange vest. I yelled so loud everyone in the room could hear. All eyes turned to me, then to her. That did it. I got my vest and was out of there faster than anyone else that day.

Like I said, Neighborhood Security literally means patrolling the neighborhood. It's a quasi-military outfit; we attended lectures and training courses. There were designated leaders and fixed regulations, but you never had to salute or call people "sir" or shit like that. Armament was pretty nonregulation as well. Mostly hand-to-hand jobs—hatchets, bats, a few crowbars and machetes—we didn't have Lobos yet. At least three people in your team had to have guns. I carried an AMT Lightning, this little semiauto .22-caliber carbine. It had no kick so I could shoot without having to lock down my wheels. Good gun, especially when ammo became standardized and reloads were still available.

Teams changed depending on your schedule. It was pretty chaotic back then, DeStRes reorganizing everything. Night shift was always tough. You forget how dark the night really is without streetlights. There were barely any houselights, too. People went to bed pretty early back then, usually when it got dark, so except for a few candles or if someone had a license for a generator, like if they were doing essential war work from home, the houses were pitch-black. You didn't even have the moon or the stars anymore, too much crap in the atmosphere. We patrolled with flashlights, basic civilian store-bought models; we still had batteries then, with red cellophane on the end to protect our night vision. We'd stop at each house, knock, ask whoever was on watch if everything was okay. The early months were a little unnerving because of the resettlement program. So many people were coming out of the camps that each day you might get at least a dozen new neighbors, or even housemates.

I never realized how good we had it before the war, tucked away in my little Stepford suburbistan. Did I really need a three-thousand-square-foot house, three bedrooms, two baths, a kitchen, living room, den, and home

1. "The Bear" was the Gulf War I nickname for the commandant of the NST program.

office? I'd lived alone for years and suddenly I had a family from Alabama, six of them, just show up at my door one day with a letter from the Department of Housing. It's unnerving at first, but you get used to it quickly. I didn't mind the Shannons, that was the family's name. We got along pretty well, and I always slept better with someone standing watch. That was one of the new rules for people at home. Someone had to be the designated night watchman. We had all their names on a list to make sure they weren't squatters and looters. We'd check their ID, their face, ask them if everything was all quiet. They usually said yes, or maybe reported some noise we'd have to check out. By the second year, when the refugees stopped coming and everyone got to know each other, we didn't bother with lists and IDs anymore. Everything was calmer then. That first year, when the cops were still re-forming and the safe zones weren't completely pacified . . .

[Shivers for dramatic effect.]

There were still a lot of deserted houses, shot up or broken into or just abandoned with the doors left wide open. We'd put police tape across all doorways and windows. If any of them were found snapped, that could mean a zombie was in the house. That happened a couple of times. I'd wait outside, rifle ready. Sometimes you'd hear shouts, sometimes shots. Sometimes, you'd just hear a moan, scuffling, then one of your teammates would come out with a bloody hand weapon and a severed head. I had to put a few down myself. Sometimes, when the team was inside, and I was watching the street, I'd hear a noise, a shuffling, a rasping, something dragging itself through the bushes. I'd hit it with the light, call for backup, then take it down.

One time I almost got tagged. We were clearing a two-story job: four bed, four bath, partially collapsed from where someone had driven a Jeep Liberty through the living room window. My partner asked if it was cool to take a powder break. I let her go behind the bushes. My bad. I was too distracted, too concerned with what was going on inside the house. I didn't notice what was behind me. Suddenly there was this tug on my chair. I tried to turn, but something had the right wheel. I twisted, brought my light around. It was a "dragger," the kind that's lost its legs. It snarled up at me from the asphalt, trying to climb over the wheel. The chair saved my life. It gave me the second and a half I needed to bring my carbine around. If I'd been standing, it might have grabbed my ankle, maybe even taken a chunk. That was the last time I slacked off at my job.

Zombies weren't the only problem we had to deal with back then. There were looters, not so much hardened criminals as just people who needed stuff to survive. Same with squatters; both cases usually ended well. We'd just invite them home, give them what they needed, take care of them until the housing folks could step in.

There were some real looters, though, professional bad guys. That was the only time I got hurt.

[He pulls down his shirt, exposing a circular scar the size of a prewar dime.]

Nine millimeter, right through the shoulder. My team chased him out of the house. I ordered him to halt. That was the only time I ever killed someone, thank God. When the new laws came in, conventional crime pretty much dried up altogether.

Then there were the ferals, you know, the homeless kids who'd lost their parents. We'd find them curled up in basements, in closets, under beds. A lot of them had walked from as far away as back east. They were in bad shape, all malnourished and sickly. A lot of times they'd run. Those were the only times I felt bad, you know, that I couldn't chase them. Someone else would go, a lot of times they'd catch up, but not always.

The biggest problem were quislings.

Quislings?

Yeah, you know, the people that went nutballs and started acting like zombies.

Could you elaborate?

Well, I'm not a shrink, so I don't know all the tech terms.

That's all right.

Well, as I understand it, there's a type of person who just can't deal with a fight-or-die situation. They're always drawn to what they're afraid of. Instead of resisting it, they want to please it, join it, try to be like it. I guess that happens in kidnap situations, you know, like a Patty Hearst/ Stockholm Syndrome–type, or, like in regular war, when people who are invaded sign up for the enemy's army. Collaborators, sometimes even more die-hard than the people they're trying to mimic, like those French fascists who were some of Hitler's last troops. Maybe that's why we call them quislings, like it's a French word or something.[2]

But you couldn't do it in this war. You couldn't just throw up your hands and say, "Hey, don't kill me, I'm on your side." There was no gray area in this fight, no in between. I guess some people just couldn't accept that. It put them right over the edge. They started moving like zombies, sounding like them, even attacking and trying to eat other people. That's how we found our first one. He was a male adult, midthirties. Dirty, dazed, shuffling down the sidewalk. We thought he was just in Z-shock, until he bit one of our guys in the arm. That was a horrible few seconds. I dropped the Q with a head shot then turned to check on my buddy. He was crumpled on the curb, swearing, crying, staring at the gash in his forearm. This was a death sentence and he knew it. He was ready to do himself until we discovered that the guy I shot had bright red blood pouring from his head. When we checked his flesh we found he was still warm! You should have seen our buddy lose it. It's not every day you get a reprieve from the big governor in the sky. Ironically, he almost died anyway. The bastard had so much bacteria in his mouth that it caused a near fatal staph infection.

2. Vidkun Abraham Lauritz Jonsson Quisling: The Nazi-installed president of Norway during World War II.

We thought maybe we stumbled onto some new discovery but it turned out it'd been happening for a while. The CDC was just about to go public. They even sent an expert up from Oakland to brief us on what to do if we encountered more of them. It blew our minds. Did you know that quislings were the reason some people used to think they were immune? They were also the reason all those bullshit wonder drugs got so much hype. Think about it. Someone's on Phalanx, gets bit but survives. What else is he going to think? He probably wouldn't know there was even such a thing as quislings. They're just as hostile as regular zombies and in some cases even more dangerous.

How so?

Well, for one thing, they didn't freeze. I mean, yeah, they would if they were exposed over time, but in moderate cold, if they'd gone under while wearing warm clothes, they'd be fine. They also got stronger from the people they ate. Not like zombies. They could maintain over time.

But you could kill them more easily.

Yes and no. You didn't have to hit them in head; you could take out the lungs, the heart, hit them anywhere, and eventually they'd bleed to death. But if you didn't stop them with one shot, they'd just keep coming until they died.

They don't feel pain?

Hell no. It's that whole mind-over-matter thing, being so focused you're able to suppress relays to the brain and all that. You should really talk to an expert.

Please continue.

Okay, well, that's why we could never talk them down. There was nothing left to talk to. These people were zombies, maybe not physically, but mentally you could not tell the difference. Even physically it might be hard, if they were dirty enough, bloody enough, diseased enough. Zombies don't really smell that bad, not individually and not if they're fresh. How do you tell one of these from a mimic with a whopping dose of gangrene? You couldn't. It's not like the military would let us have sniffer dogs or anything. You had to use the eye test.

Ghouls don't blink, I don't know why. Maybe because they use their senses equally, their brains don't value sight as much. Maybe because they don't have as much bodily fluid they can't keep using it to coat the eyes. Who knows, but they don't blink and quislings do. That's how you spotted them; back up a few paces, and wait a few seconds. Darkness was easier, you just shone a beam in their faces. If they didn't blink, you took them down.

And if they did?

Well, our orders were to capture quislings if possible, and use deadly force only in self-defense. It sounded crazy, still does, but we rounded up a few, hog-tied them, turned them over to police or National Guard. I'm not sure what they did with them. I've heard stories about Walla Walla, you know, the prison where hundreds of them were fed and clothed and even medically cared for. [His eyes flick to the ceiling.]

You don't agree.

Hey, I'm not going there. You want to open that can of worms, read the papers. Every year some lawyer or priest or politician tries to stoke that fire for whatever side best suits them. Personally, I don't care. I don't have any feelings toward them one way or the other. I think the saddest thing about them is that they gave up so much and in the end lost anyway.

Why is that?

'Cause even though we can't tell the difference between them, the real zombies can. Remember early in the war, when everybody was trying to work on a way to turn the living dead against one another? There was all this "documented proof" about infighting—eyewitness accounts and even footage of one zombie attacking another. Stupid. It was zombies attacking quislings, but you never would have known that to look at it. Quislings don't scream. They just lie there, not even trying to fight, writhing in that slow, robotic way, eaten alive by the very creatures they're trying to be.

❦

MALIBU, CALIFORNIA

[I don't need a photograph to recognize Roy Elliot. We meet for coffee on the restored Malibu Pier Fortress. Those around us also instantly recognize him, but, unlike prewar days, keep a respectful distance.]

ADS, that was my enemy: Asymptomatic Demise Syndrome, or, Apocalyptic Despair Syndrome, depending on who you were talking to. Whatever the label, it killed as many people in those early stalemate months as hunger, disease, interhuman violence, or the living dead. No one understood what was happening at first. We'd stabilized the Rockies, we'd sanitized the safe zones, and still we were losing upwards of a hundred or so people a day. It wasn't suicide, we had plenty of those. No, this was different. Some people had minimal wounds or easily treatable ailments; some were in perfect health. They would simply go to sleep one night and not wake up the next morning. The problem was psychological, a case of just giving up, not wanting to see tomorrow because you knew it could only bring more suffering. Losing faith, the will to endure, it happens in all wars. It happens in peacetime, too, just not on this scale. It was helplessness, or at least, the perception of helplessness. I understood that feeling. I directed movies all my adult life. They called me the boy genius, the wunderkind who couldn't fail, even though I'd done so often.

Suddenly I was a nobody, an F-6. The world was going to hell and all my vaunted talents were powerless to stop it. When I heard about ADS, the government was trying to keep it quiet—I had to find out from a contact at Cedars-Sinai. When I heard about it, something snapped. Like the time I made my first Super 8 short and screened it for my parents. This I can do, I realized. This enemy I can fight!

And the rest is history.

[Laughs.] I wish. I went straight to the government, they turned me down.

Really? I would think, given your career . . .

What career? They wanted soldiers and farmers, real jobs, remember? It was like "Hey, sorry, no dice, but can I get your autograph?" Now, I'm not the surrendering type. When I believe in my ability to do something, there is no such word as no. I explained to the DeStRes rep that it wouldn't cost Uncle Sam a dime. I'd use my own equipment, my own people, all I'd need from them was access to the military. "Let me show the people what you're doing to stop this," I told him. "Let me give them something to believe in." Again, I was refused. The military had more important missions right now than "posing for the camera."

Did you go over his head?

To who? There were no boats to Hawaii and Sinclair was racing up and down the West Coast. Anybody in any position to help was either physically unavailable or far too distracted with more "important" matters.

Couldn't you have become a freelance journalist, gotten a government press pass?

It would have taken too long. Most mass media was either knocked out or federalized. What was left had to rebroadcast public safety announcements, to make sure anyone just tuning in would know what to do. Everything was still such a mess. We barely had passable roads, let alone the bureaucracy to give me full-time journalist status. It might have taken months. Months, with a hundred dying every day. I couldn't wait. I had to do something immediately. I took a DV cam, some spare batteries, and a solar-powered charger. My oldest son came with me as my sound man and "first AD." We traveled on the road for one week, just the two of us on mountain bikes, looking for stories. We didn't have to go far.

Just outside of Greater Los Angeles, in a town called Claremont, are five colleges—Pomona, Pitzer, Scripps, Harvey Mudd, and Claremont Mckenna. At the start of the Great Panic, when everyone else was running, literally, for the hills, three hundred students chose to make a stand. They turned the Women's College at Scripps into something resembling a medieval city. They got their supplies from the other campuses; their weapons were a mix of landscaping tools and ROTC practice rifles. They planted gardens, dug wells, fortified an already existing wall. While the mountains burned behind them, and the surrounding suburbs descended into violence, those three hundred kids held off ten thousand zombies! Ten thousand, over the course of four months, until the Inland Empire could finally be pacified.[1] We were lucky to get there just at the tail end, just in time to see the last of the undead fall, as cheering students and soldiers linked up under the oversized, homemade Old Glory fluttering from the Pomona bell tower. What a story! Ninety-six hours of raw footage in the can. I would have liked to have gone longer, but time was critical. One hundred a day lost, remember.

We had to get this one out there as soon as possible. I brought the footage back to my house, cut it together in my edit bay. My wife did the narration. We made fourteen copies, all on different formats, and screened them that Saturday night at different camps and shelters all over LA. I called it *Victory at Avalon: The Battle of the Five Colleges*.

The name, *Avalon*, comes from some stock footage one of the students

---

1. California's Inland Empire was one of the last zones to be declared secure.

had shot during the siege. It was the night before their last, worst attack, when a fresh horde from the east was clearly visible on the horizon. The kids were hard at work—sharpening weapons, reinforcing defenses, standing guard on the walls and towers. A song came floating across the campus from the loudspeaker that played constant music to keep morale up. A Scripps student, with a voice like an angel, was singing the Roxy Music song. It was such a beautiful rendition, and such a contrast with the raging storm about to hit. I laid it over my "preparing for battle" montage. I still get choked up when I hear it.

How did it play with the audience?

It bombed! Not just the scene, but the whole movie; at least, that's what I thought. I'd expected a more immediate reaction. Cheering, applause. I would never have admitted this to anyone, even to myself, but I had this egotistical fantasy of people coming up to me afterward, tears in their eyes, grabbing my hands, thanking me for showing them the light at the end of the tunnel. They didn't even look at me. I stood by the doorway like some conquering hero. They just filed past silently with their eyes on their shoes. I went home that night thinking, "Oh well, it was a nice idea, maybe the potato farm in MacArthur Park can use another hand."

What happened?

Two weeks went by. I got a real job, helping to reopen the road at Topanga Canyon. Then one day a man rode up to my house. Just came in on horseback as if out of an old Cecil B. De Mille western. He was a psychiatrist from the county health facility in Santa Barbara. They'd heard about the success of my movie and asked if I had any extra copies.

Success?

That's what I said. As it turns out, the very night after *Avalon* made its "debut," ADS cases dropped in LA by a whole 5 percent! At first they thought it might just be a statistical anomaly, until a further study revealed that the decline was drastically noticeable only among communities where the movie was shown!

And no one told you?

No one. [Laughs.] Not the military, not the municipal authorities, not even the people who ran the shelters where it was continuing to be screened without my knowledge. I don't care. The point is it worked. It made a difference, and it gave me a job for the rest of the war. I got a few volunteers together, as much of my old crew as I could find. That kid who shot the Claremont stock footage, Malcolm Van Ryzin, yes, that Malcolm,[2] he became my DP.[3] We commandeered an abandoned dubbing house in West Hollywood and started cranking them out by the hundreds. We'd put them on every train, every caravan, every coastal ferry heading north. It took a while to get responses. But when they came . . .

[He smiles, holds his hands up in thanks.]

Ten percent drop throughout the entire western safe zone. I was already on the road by then, shooting more stories. *Anacapa* was already wrapped, and we were halfway through *Mission District*. By the time *Dos Palmos* hit screens, and ADS was down 23 percent . . . only then did the government finally take an interest in me.

Additional resources?

[Laughs.] No. I'd never asked for help and they sure weren't going to give it. But I did finally get access to the military and that opened up a whole new world.

2. Malcolm Van Ryzin: One of the most successful cinematographers in Hollywood.
3. DP: Director of Photography.

Is that when you made Fire of the Gods?

[Nods.] The army had two functioning laser weapons programs: Zeus and MTHEL. Zeus was originally designed for munitions clearing, zapping land mines and unexploded bombs. It was small and light enough to be mounted in a specialized Humvee. The gunner sighted a target through a coaxial camera in the turret. He placed the aim point on the intended surface, then fired a pulse beam through the same optical aperture. Is that too technical?

Not at all.

I'm sorry. I became extremely immersed in the project. The beam was a weaponized version of solid-state, industrial lasers, the kind used to cut steel in factories. It could either burn through a bomb's outer casing or heat it to a point that detonated the explosive package. The same principle worked for zombies. On higher settings it punched right through their foreheads. On lower settings, it literally boiled their brain till it exploded through the ears, nose, and eyes. The footage we shot was dazzling, but Zeus was a popgun next to MTHEL.

The acronym stands for Mobile Tactical High Energy Laser, codesigned by the United States and Israel to take out small incoming projectiles. When Israel declared self-quarantine, and when so many terrorist groups were lobbing mortar rounds and rockets across the security wall, MTHEL was what knocked them down. About the size and shape of a World War II searchlight, it was, in fact, a deuterium fluoride laser, much more powerful than the solid state on Zeus. The effects were devastating. It blasted flesh from bones that then heated white before shattering into dust. When played at regular speed, it was magnificent, but at slo-mo . . . fire of the gods.

Is it true that the number of ADS cases were halved a month after the movie's release?

I think that might be an overstatement, but people were lined up on their off-hours. Some saw it every night. The poster campaign showed a close-up of a zombie being atomized. The image was lifted right from a frame in the movie, the one classic shot when the morning fog actually allowed you to see the beam. The caption underneath read simply "Next." It single-handedly saved the program.

Your program.

No, Zeus and MTHEL.

They were in jeopardy?

MTHEL was due to close a month after shooting. Zeus had already been chopped. We had to beg, borrow, and steal, literally, to get it reactivated just for our cameras. DeStRes had deemed both as a gross waste of resources.

Were they?

Inexcusably so. The "M" in MTHEL's "Mobile" really meant a convoy of specialized vehicles, all of which were delicate, none truly all-terrain and each one completely dependent on the other. MTHEL also required both tremendous power and copious amounts of highly unstable, highly toxic chemicals for the lasering process.

Zeus was a little more economical. It was easier to cool, easier to maintain, and because it was Humvee-mounted, it could go anywhere it was needed. The problem was, why would it be needed? Even on high power, the gunner still had to hold a beam in place, on a moving target, mind you, for several seconds. A good sharpshooter could get the job done in half the time with twice the kills. That erased the potential for rapid fire, which was exactly what you needed in swarm attacks. In fact, both units had a squad of riflemen permanently assigned to them, people protecting a machine that is designed to protect people.

They were that bad?

Not for their original role. MTHEL kept Israel safe from terrorist bombardment, and Zeus actually came out of retirement to clear unexploded ordnance during the army's advance. As purpose-built weapons, they were outstanding. As zombie killers, they were hopeless duds.

So why did you film them?

Because Americans worship technology. It's an inherent trait in the national zeitgeist. Whether we realize it or not, even the most indefatigable Luddite can't deny our country's technoprowess. We split the atom, we reached the moon, we've filled every household and business with more gadgets and gizmos than early sci-fi writers could have ever dreamed of. I don't know if that's a good thing, I'm in no place to judge. But I do know that just like all those ex-atheists in foxholes, most Americans were still praying for the God of science to save them.

But it didn't.

But it didn't matter. The movie was such a hit that I was asked to do a whole series. I called it "Wonder Weapons," seven films on our military's cutting-edge technology, none of which made any strategic difference, but all of which were psychological war winners.

Isn't that . . .

A lie? It's okay. You can say it. Yes, they were lies and sometimes that's not a bad thing. Lies are neither bad nor good. Like a fire they can either keep you warm or burn you to death, depending on how they're used. The lies our government told us before the war, the ones that were supposed to keep us happy and blind, those were the ones that burned, because they prevented us from doing what had to be done. However, by the time I made *Avalon,* everyone was already doing everything they could possibly do to survive. The lies of the past were long gone and now the truth was everywhere, shambling down their streets, crashing through their doors, clawing at their throats. The truth was that no matter what we did, chances were most of us, if not all of us, were never going to see the future. The truth was that we were standing at what might be the twilight of our species and that truth was freezing a hundred people to death every night. They needed something to keep them warm. And so I lied, and so did the president, and every doctor and priest, every platoon leader and every parent. "We're going to be okay." That was our message. That was the message of every other filmmaker during the war. Did you ever hear of *The Hero City?*

Of course.

Great film, right? Marty made it over the course of the Siege. Just him, shooting on whatever medium he could get his hands on. What a masterpiece: the courage, the determination, the strength, dignity, kindness, and honor. It really makes you believe in the human race. It's better than anything I've ever done. You should see it.

I have.

Which version?

I'm sorry?

Which version did you see?

I wasn't aware . . .

That there were two? You need to do some homework, young man. Marty made both a wartime and postwar version of *The Hero City.* The version you saw, it was ninety minutes?

I think.

Did it show the dark side of the heroes in *The Hero City?* Did it show the violence and the betrayal, the cruelty, the depravity, the bottomless evil in some of those "heroes' " hearts? No, of course not. Why would it? That was our reality and it's what drove so many people to get snuggled in bed, blow out their candles, and take their last breath. Marty chose, instead, to show the other side, the one that gets people out of bed the next morning, makes them scratch and scrape and fight for their lives because someone is telling them that they're going to be okay. There's a word for that kind of lie. Hope.

❧

PARNELL AIR NATIONAL GUARD BASE, TENNESSEE

[Gavin Blaire escorts me to the office of his squadron commander, Colonel Christina Eliopolis. As much a legend for her temper as for her outstanding war record, it is difficult to see how so much intensity can be compacted into her diminutive, almost childlike frame. Her long black bangs and delicate facial features only reinforce the picture of eternal youth. Then she removes her sunglasses, and I see the fire behind her eyes.]

I was a Raptor driver, the FA-22. It was, hands down, the best air superiority platform ever built. It could outfly and outfight God and all his angels. It was a monument to American technical prowess . . . and in this war, that prowess counted for shit.

That must have been frustrating.

Frustrating? Do you know what it feels like to suddenly be told that the one goal you've worked toward your whole life, that you've sacrificed and suffered for, that's pushed you beyond limits you never knew you had is now considered "strategically invalid"?

Would you say this was a common feeling?

Let me put it this way; the Russian army wasn't the only service to be decimated by their own government. The Armed Forces Reconstruction Act basically neutered the air force. Some DeStRes "experts" had determined that our resource-to-kill ratio, our RKR, was the most lopsided of all the branches.

Could you give me some example?

How about the JSOW, the Joint Standoff Weapon? It was a gravity bomb, guided by GPS and Inertial Nav, that could be released from as far as forty miles away. The baseline version carried one hundred and forty BLU-97B submunitions, and each bomblet carried a shaped charge against armored targets, a fragmented case against infantry, and a zirconium ring to set the entire kill zone ablaze. It had been considered a triumph, until Yonkers.[1] Now we were told that the price of one JSOW kit—the materials, manpower, time, and energy, not to mention the fuel and ground maintenance needed for the delivery aircraft—could pay for a platoon of infantry pukes who could smoke a thousand times as many Gs. Not enough bang for our buck, like so many of our former crown jewels. They went through us like an industrial laser. The B-2 Spirits, gone; the B-1 Lancers, gone; even the old BUFFs, the B-52 Big Ugly Fat Fellows, gone. Throw in the Eagles, the Falcons, the Tomcats, Hornets, JSFs, and Raptors, and you have more combat aircraft lost to the stroke of a pen than to all the SAMs, Flak, and enemy fighters in history.[2] At least the assets weren't scrapped, thank God, just mothballed in warehouses or that big desert graveyard at AMARC.[3] "Long-term investment," they called it. That's the one thing

---

1. Joint Standoff Weapons were used in concert with a variety of other air-launched ordnance at Yonkers.
2. A slight exaggeration. The amount of combat aircraft "grounded" during World War Z does not equal those lost during World War II.
3. AMARC: Aerospace Maintenance and Regeneration Center outside of Tucson, Arizona.

you can always depend on; as we're fighting one war, we're always preparing for the next one. Our airlift capacity, at least the organization, was almost left intact.

Almost?

The Globemasters had to go, so did anything else powered by a "gas guzzling" jet. That left us with prop-powered aircraft. I went from flying the closest thing to an X-Wing fighter, to the next best thing to a U-Haul.

Was that the main mission of the air force?

Airborne resupply was our primary objective, the only one that really counted anymore.

[She points to a yellowed map on the wall.]

The base commander let me keep it, after what happened to me.

[The map is of the wartime continental United States. All land west of the Rockies is shadowed a light gray. Amongst this gray are a variety of colored circles.]

Islands in the Sea of Zack. Green denotes active military facilities. Some of them had been converted into refugee centers. Some were still contributing to the war effort. Some were well defended but had no strategic impact.

The Red Zones were labeled "Offensively Viable": factories, mines, power plants. The army'd left custodial teams during the big pullback. Their job was to guard and maintain these facilities for a time when, if, we could add them to the overall war effort. The Blue Zones were civilian areas where people had managed to make a stand, carve out a little piece of real estate, and figure some way to live within its boundaries. All these zones were in need of resupply and that's what the "Continental Airlift" was all about.

It was a massive operation, not just in terms of aircraft and fuel, but organization as well. Remaining in contact with all these islands, processing their demands, coordinating with DeStRes, then trying to procure and prioritize all the materiel for each drop made it the statistically largest undertaking in air force history.

We tried to stay away from consumables, things like food and medicine that required regular deliveries. These were classified as DDs, dependency drops, and they got a backseat to SSDs, self-sustaining drops, like tools, spare parts, and tools to make spare parts. "They don't need fish," Sinclair used to say, "they need fishing poles." Still, every autumn, we dropped a lot of fish, and wheat, and salt, and dried vegetables and baby formula . . . Winters were hard. Remember how long they used to be? Helping people to help themselves is great in theory, but you still gotta keep 'em alive.

Sometimes you had to drop in people, specialists like doctors or engineers, people with the kind of training you just can't get from a how-to manual. The Blue Zones got a lot of Special Forces instructors, not only to teach them how better to defend themselves, but to prepare them for the day they might have to go on the offensive. I have a lot of respect for those guys. Most of them knew it was for the duration; a lot of the Blue Zones didn't have airstrips, so they had to parachute in without any hope of pickup. Not all those Blue Zones remained secure. Some were eventually overrun. The people we dropped in knew the risks they were taking. A lotta heart, all of them.

That goes for the pilots as well.

Hey, I'm not minimizing our risks at all. Every day we had to fly over hundreds, in some cases thousands, of miles of infested territory. That's why we had Purple Zones. [She refers to the last color on the map. The purple circles are few and far between.] We set these up as refuel and repair facilities. A lot of the aircraft didn't have the range to reach remote drop zones on the East Coast if in-flight refueling assets weren't available. They helped reduce the number of ships and crews lost en route. They brought our fleet survivability up to 92 percent. Unfortunately, I was part of the other eight.

I'll never be sure what exactly brought us down: mechanical malfunction or metal fatigue combined with weather. It might have been the contents of our payload, mislabeled or mishandled. That happened a lot more than anyone wanted to think about. Sometimes if hazardous materials weren't packaged properly, or, God forbid, some shit-for-brains QC inspector let his people assemble their detonators *before* crating them for travel . . . that happened to a buddy of mine, just a routine flight from Palmdale to Vandenberg, not even across an infested area. Two hundred Type 38 detonators, all fully assembled with their power cells accidentally running, all set to blow on the same freq as our radio.

[She snaps her fingers.]

That could have been us. We were on a hop from Phoenix to the Blue Zone outside Tallahassee, Florida. It was late October, almost full winter back then. Honolulu was trying to squeeze out just a few more drops before the weather socked us in till March. It was our ninth haul that week. We were all on "tweeks," these little blue stims that kept you going without hampering your reflexes or judgment. I guess they worked well enough, but they made me have to piss my kidneys out every twenty minutes. My crew, the "guys," used to give me a lot of grief, you know, girls always having to go. I know they weren't really putting the hate on, but I still tried to hold it as long as I could.

After two hours of banging around in some seriously heavy turbulence, I finally broke down and turned the stick over to my copilot. I'd just zipped up when suddenly there was this massive jolt like God had just drop-kicked our tail . . . and suddenly our nose was dipping. The head on our C-130 wasn't even really a toilet, just a portable chempot with a heavy, plastic shower curtain. That's probably what ended up saving my life. If I'd been trapped in a real compartment, maybe knocked out or unable to reach the latch . . . Suddenly there was this screech, this overpowering blast of high-pressure air and I was sucked out right through the rear of the aircraft, right past where the tail should have been.

I was spiraling, out of control. I could just make out my ship, this gray mass shrinking and smoking on its way down. I straightened myself out, hit my chute. I was still in a daze, my head swimming, trying to catch my breath. I fumbled for my radio and started hollering for my crew to punch out. I didn't get an answer. All I could see was one other chute, the only other one that made it out.

That was the worst moment, right there, just hanging helplessly. I could see the other chute, above and north of me by about three and a half clicks. I looked for the others. I tried my radio again, but wasn't able to get a signal. I figured it had been damaged during my "exit." I tried to get my bearings, somewhere over southern Louisiana, a swampy wilderness that seemed to have no end. I wasn't sure exactly, my brain was still misfiring. At least I had sense enough to check the bare essentials. I could move my legs, my arms, I wasn't in pain or bleeding externally. I checked to make sure my survival kit was intact, still strapped to my thigh, and that my weapon, my Meg,[4] was still jamming me in the ribs.

Did the air force prepare you for situations like these?

We all had to pass the Willow Creek Escape and Evade program in the Klamath Mountains in California. It even had a few real Gs in there with us, tagged and tracked and placed at specific marks to give us the "real feel." It's a lot like what they teach you in the civilian manual: movement, stealth, how to take out Zack before he can howl your position. We all "made it," lived, I mean, although a couple of pilots washed out on a

4. Meg: The pilot's nickname for their standard issue .22 automatic pistol. It is suspected that the appearance of the weapon, its extended suppressor, folding stock, and telescopic sight, give it the appearance of the old Hasbro Transformers toy "Megatron." This fact has yet to be confirmed.

Section Eight. I guess they just couldn't hack the real feel. That never bothered me, being alone in hostile territory. That was standard operating procedure for me.

Always?

You wanna talk about being alone in a hostile environment, try my four years at Colorado Springs.

But there were other women . . .

Other cadets, other competitors who happen to have the same genitalia. Trust me, when the pressure kicked in, sisterhood punched out. No, it was me, only me. Self-contained, self-reliant, and always, unquestionably self-assured. That's the only thing that got me through four years of Academy hell, and it was the only thing I could count on as I hit the mud in the middle of G country.

I unclasped my chute—they teach you not to waste time concealing it—and headed in the direction of the other chute. It took me a couple hours, splashing through this cold slime that numbed everything below my knees. I wasn't thinking clearly, my head was still spinning. No excuse, I know, but that's why I didn't notice that the birds had suddenly beat it in the opposite direction. I did hear the scream though, faint and far away. I could see the chute tangled in the trees. I started running, another no-no, making all that noise without stopping to listen for Zack. I couldn't see anything, just all these naked gray branches until they were right on top of me. If it wasn't for Rollins, my copilot, I'm sure I'da been a goner.

I found him dangling from his harness, dead, twitching. His flight suit had been torn open[5] and his entrails were hanging . . . draped over five of them as they fed in this cloud of red-brown water. One of them had managed to get its neck entangled in a section of small intestine. Every time it

5. At this point in the war, the new battle dress uniforms (BDUs) were not in mass production.

moved it would jerk Rollins, ringing him like a fucking bell. They didn't notice me at all. Close enough to touch and they didn't even look.

At least I had the brains to snap on my suppressor. I didn't have to waste a whole clip, another fuckup. I was so angry I almost started kicking their corpses. I was so ashamed, so blinded by self-hate . . .

Self-hate?

I screwed the pooch! My ship, my crew . . .

But it was an accident. It wasn't your fault.

How do you know that? You weren't there. Shit, I wasn't even there. I don't know what happened. I wasn't doing my job. I was squatting over a bucket like a goddamn girl!

I found myself burning up, mentally. Fucking weakling, I told myself, fucking loser. I started to spiral, not just hating myself, but hating myself for hating myself. Does that make any sense? I'm sure I might have just stayed there, shaking and helpless and waiting for Zack.

But then my radio started squawking. "Hello? Hello? Is anyone out there? Anyone punch outta that wreck?" It was a woman's voice, clearly civilian by her language and tone.

I answered immediately, identified myself, and demanded that she respond in kind. She told me she was a skywatcher, and her handle was "Mets Fan," or just "Mets" for short. The Skywatch system was this ad hoc network of isolated ham radio operators. They were supposed to report on downed aircrews and do what they could to help with their rescue. It wasn't the most efficient system, mainly because there were so few, but it looked like today was my lucky day. She told me that she had seen the smoke and falling wreckage of my Herc' and even though she was probably less than a day's walk from my position, her cabin was heavily surrounded. Before I could say anything she told me not to worry, that she'd already reported my position to search and rescue, and the best thing to do was to get to open ground where I could rendezvous for pickup.

I reached for my GPS but it had been torn from my suit when I was sucked out of my ship. I had a backup survival map, but it was so big, so un-specific, and my hump took me over so many states that it was practically just a map of the U.S. . . . my head was still clouded with anger and doubt. I told her I didn't know my position, didn't know where to go . . .

She laughed. "You mean you've never made this run before? You don't have every inch of it committed to memory? You didn't see where you were as you were hanging by the silk?" She was so sure of me, trying to get me to think instead of just spoon-feeding me the answers. I realized that I did know this area well, that I *had* flown over it at least twenty times in the last three months, and that I had to be somewhere in the Atchafalaya basin. "Think," she told me, "what did you see from your chute? Were there any rivers, any roads?" At first, all I could remember were the trees, the endless gray landscape with no distinguishable features, and then gradually, as my brain cleared, I remembered seeing both rivers and a road. I checked on the map and realized that directly north of me was the I-10 freeway. Mets told me that was the best place for an S&R pickup. She told me it shouldn't take any longer than a day or two at best if I got a move on and stopped burning daylight.

As I was about to leave, she stopped me and asked if there was anything I'd forgotten to do. I remember that moment clearly. I turned back to Rollins. He was just starting to open his eyes again. I felt like I should say something, apologize, maybe, then I put a round through his forehead.

Mets told me not to blame myself, and no matter what, not to let it distract me from the job I had to do. She said, "Stay alive, stay alive and do your job." Then she added, "And stop using up your weekend minutes."

She was talking about battery power—she didn't miss a trick—so I signed off and started moving north across the swamp. My brain was now on full burner, all my lessons from the Creek came rolling back. I stepped, I halted, I listened. I stuck to dry ground where I could, and I made sure to pace myself very carefully. I had to swim a couple times, that really made me nervous. Twice I swear I could feel a hand just brush against my leg. Once, I found a road, small, barely two lanes and in horrible disrepair.

Still, it was better than trudging through the mud. I reported to Mets what I'd found and asked if it would take me right to the freeway. She warned me to stay off it and every other road that crisscrossed the basin. "Roads mean cars," she said, "and cars mean Gs." She was talking about any bitten human drivers who died of their wounds while still behind the wheel and, because a ghoul doesn't have the IQ points to open a door or unbuckle a seatbelt, would be doomed to spend the rest of their existence trapped in their cars.

I asked her what the danger of that was. Since they couldn't get out, and as long as I didn't let them reach through an open window to grab me, what did it matter how many "abandoned" cars I passed along the road. Mets reminded me that a trapped G was still able to moan and therefore still able to call for others. Now I was really confused. If I was going to waste so much time ducking a few back roads with a couple Zack-filled cars, why was I heading for a freeway that was sure to be jammed with them?

She said, "You'll be up above the swamp. How are more zombies gonna get to you?" Because it was built several stories above the swamp, this section of the I-10 was the safest place in the whole basin. I confessed I hadn't thought of that. She laughed and said, "Don't worry, honey. I have. Stick with me and I'll get you home."

And I did. I stayed away from anything even resembling a road and stuck to as pure a wilderness track as I could. I say "pure" but the truth was you couldn't avoid all signs of humanity or what could have been humanity a long time ago. There were shoes, clothes, bits of garbage, and tattered suitcases and hiking gear. I saw a lot of bones on the patches of raised mud. I couldn't tell if they were human or animal. One time I found this rib cage; I'm guessing it was a gator, a big one. I didn't want to think about how many Gs it took to bring that bastard down.

The first G I saw was small, probably a kid, I couldn't tell. Its face was eaten off, the skin, nose, eyes, lips, even the hair and ears . . . not completely gone, but partially hanging or stuck in patches to the exposed skull. Maybe there were more wounds, I couldn't tell. It was stuck inside one of those long civilian hiker's packs, stuffed in there tight with the drawstring pulled right up around its neck. The shoulder straps had gotten tangled on the roots of a tree, it was splashing around, half submerged. Its brain must have been intact, and even some of the muscle fibers connecting the jaw. That jaw started snapping as I approached. I don't know how it knew I was there, maybe some of the nasal cavity was still intact, maybe the ear canal.

It couldn't moan, its throat had been too badly mangled, but the splashing might have attracted attention, so I put it out of its misery, if it really was miserable, and tried not to think about it. That was another thing they taught us at Willow Creek: don't write their eulogy, don't try to imagine who they used to be, how they came to be here, how they came to be this. I know, who doesn't do that, right? Who doesn't look at one of those things and just naturally start to wonder? It's like reading the last page of a book . . . your imagination just naturally spinning. And that's when you get distracted, get sloppy, let your guard down and end up leaving someone else to wonder what happened to you. I tried to put her, it, out of my mind. Instead, I found myself wondering why it had been the only one I'd seen.

That was a practical survival question, not just idle musings, so I got on the radio and asked Mets if there was something I was missing here, if maybe there was some area I should be careful to avoid. She reminded me that this area was, for the most part, depopulated because the Blue Zones of Baton Rouge and Lafayette were pulling most of the Gs in either direction. That was bittersweet comfort, being right between two of the heaviest clusters for miles. She laughed, again . . . "Don't worry about it, you'll be fine."

I saw something up ahead, a lump that was almost a thicket, but too boxy and shining in places. I reported it to·Mets. She warned me not to go near it, keep on going and keep my eyes on the prize. I was feeling pretty good by this point, a little of the old me coming back.

As I got closer, I could see that it was a vehicle, a Lexus Hybrid SUV. It was covered in mud and moss and sitting in the water up to its doors. I could see that the rear windows were blocked with survival gear: tent, sleeping bag, cooking utensils, hunting rifle with boxes and boxes of shells, all new, some still in their plastic. I came around the driver's side window and caught the glint of a .357. It was still clutched in the driver's brown, shriveled hand. He was still sitting upright, looking straight ahead. There was light coming through the side of his skull. He was badly decomposed, at least a year, maybe more. He wore survival khakis, the kind you'd order from one of those upscale, hunting/safari catalogs. They were still clean and crisp, the only blood was from the head wound. I couldn't see any other wound, no bites, nothing. That hit me hard, a lot harder than the little faceless kid. This guy had had everything he needed to survive, everything except the will. I know that's supposition. Maybe there was a wound I couldn't see, hidden by his clothes or the advanced decomposition. But I knew it, leaning there with my face against the glass, looking at this monument to how easy it was to give up.

I stood there for a moment, long enough for Mets to ask me what was happening. I told her what I was seeing, and without pause, she told me to keep on going.

I started to argue. I thought I should at least search the vehicle, see if there was anything I needed. She asked me, sternly, if there was anything I needed, not wanted. I thought about it, admitted there wasn't. His gear was plentiful, but it was civilian, big and bulky; the food needed cooking, the weapons weren't silenced. My survival kit was pretty thorough, and, if for some reason I didn't find a helo waiting at the I-10, I could always use this as an emergency supply cache.

I brought up the idea of maybe using the SUV itself. Mets asked if I had a tow truck and some jumper cables. Almost like a kid, I answered no. She asked, "Then what's keeping you?" or something like that, pushing me to get a move on. I told her to just wait a minute, I leaned my head against the driver's side window, I sighed and felt beat again, drained. Mets got on my ass, pushing me. I snapped back for her to shut the fuck up, I just needed a minute, a couple seconds to . . . I don't know what.

I must have kept my thumb on the "transmit" button for a few seconds too long, because Mets suddenly asked, "What was that?" "What?" I asked. She'd heard something, something on my end.

She'd heard it before you?

I guess so, because in another second, once I'd cleared my head and opened my ears, I began to hear it too. The moan . . . loud and close, followed by the splashing of feet.

I looked up, through the car's window, the hole in the dead man's skull, and the window on the other side, and that's when I saw the first one. I spun around and saw five more coming at me from all directions. And behind them were another ten, fifteen. I took a shot at the first one, the round went wild.

Mets started squawking at me, demanding a contact report. I gave her a head count and she told me to stay cool, don't try to run, just stay put and follow what I'd learned at Willow Creek. I started to ask how she knew about Willow Creek when she shouted for me to shut up and fight.

I climbed to the top of the SUV—you're supposed to look for the closest physical defense—and started to measure ranges. I lined up my first target, took a deep breath, and dropped him. To be a fighter jock is to be able to make decisions as fast as your electrochemical impulses can carry them. I'd lost that nanosecond timing when I hit the mud, now it was back. I was calm, I was focused, all the doubt and weakness were gone. The whole engagement felt like ten hours, but I guess in reality, it was more like ten minutes. Sixty-one in total, a nice thick ring of submerged corpses. I took my time, checked my remaining ammo and waited for the next wave to come. None did.

It was another twenty minutes before Mets asked me for an update. I gave her a body count and she told me to remind her never to piss me off. I laughed, the first time since I'd hit the mud. I felt good again, strong and confident. Mets warned me that all these distractions had erased any chance of making it to the I-10 before nightfall, and that I should probably start thinking about where I was gonna catch my forty.

I got as far away from the SUV as I could before the sky started to darken and found a decent enough perch in the branches of a tall tree. My kit had this standard-issue microfiber hammock; great invention, light and strong and with clasps to keep you from rolling out. That part was also supposed to help calm you down, help you get to sleep faster . . . yeah, right! It didn't matter that I'd already been up for close to forty-eight hours, that I'd tried all the breathing exercises they taught us at the Creek, or that I even slipped two of my Baby-Ls.[6] You're only supposed to take one, but I figured that was for lightweight wussies. I was me again, remember, I could handle it, and hey, I needed to sleep.

I asked her, since there was nothing else to do, or think about, if it was okay to talk about her. Who was she, really? How'd she end up in this isolated cabin in the middle of Cajun country? She didn't sound Cajun, she didn't even have a southern accent. And how did she know so much about pilot training without ever going through it herself? I was starting to get my suspicions, starting to piece together a rough outline of who she really was.

Mets told me, again, that there would be plenty of time later for an episode of The View. Right now I needed my sleep, and to check in with her at dawn. I felt the Ls kick in between "check" and "in." I was out by "dawn."

I slept hard. The sky was already light by the time I opened my eyes. I'd been dreaming about, what else, Zack. His moans were still echoing in my ears when I woke up. And then I looked down and realized they weren't dreams. There must have been at least a hundred of them surrounding the tree. They were all reaching excitedly, all trying to climb over each other to get up to me. At least they couldn't ramp up, the ground wasn't solid enough. I didn't have the ammo to take all of them out, and since a firefight might also buy time for more to show up, I decided it was best to pack up my gear and execute my escape plan.

You had planned for this?

Not really planned, but they'd trained us for situations like this. It's a lot like jumping from an aircraft: pick your approximate landing zone, tuck and roll, keep loose, and get up as quick as you can. The goal is to put some serious distance between you and your attackers. You take off running,

6. "Baby-Ls": Officially a pain reliever but used by many military personnel as a sleep aid.

jogging, or even "speed walking"; yes, they actually told us to consider this as a low-impact alternative. The point is to get far enough way to give you time to plan your next move. According to my map, the I-10 was close enough for me to make a run for it, be spotted by a rescue chopper, and be lifted off before these stink bags would ever catch up. I got on the radio, reported my situation to Mets, and told her to signal S&R for an immediate pickup. She told me to be careful. I crouched, I jumped, and cracked my ankle on a submerged rock.

I hit the water, facedown. Its chill was the only thing that kept me from blacking out from the pain. I came up spluttering, choking, and the first thing I saw was the whole swarm coming at me. Mets must have known something was up by the fact that I didn't report my safe landing. Maybe she asked me what had happened, although I don't remember. I just remember her yelling at me to get up and run. I tried putting weight on my ankle, but lightning shot up through my leg and spine. It could bear the weight, but . . . I screamed so loud, I'm sure she heard me through her cabin's window. "Get out of there," she was yelling . . . "GO!" I started limping, splashing away with upwards of a hundred Gs on my ass. It must have been comical, this frantic race of cripples.

Mets yelled, "If you can stand on it, you can run on it! It's not a weight-bearing bone! You can do this!"

"But it hurts!" I actually said that, with tears running down my face, with Zack behind me howling for his lunch. I reached the freeway, looming above the swamp like the ruins of a Roman aqueduct. Mets had been right about its relative safety. Only neither of us had counted on my injury or my undead tail. There was no immediate entrance so I had to limp to one of the small, adjoining roads that Mets had originally warned me to avoid. I could see why as I began to get close. Wrecked and rusting cars were piled up by the hundreds and every tenth one had at least one G locked inside. They saw me and started to moan, the sound carried for miles in every direction.

Mets shouted, "Don't worry about that now! Just get on the on-ramp and watch the fucking grabbers!"

Grabbers?

The ones reaching through broken windows. On the open road, I at least had a chance of dodging them, but on the on-ramp, you're hemmed in on either side. That was the worst part, by far, those few minutes trying to get up onto the freeway. I had to go in between the cars; my ankle wouldn't let me get on top of them. These rotting hands would reach out for me, grabbing my flight suit or my wrist. Every head shot cost me seconds that I didn't have. The steep incline was already slowing me down. My ankle was throbbing, my lungs were aching, and the swarm was now gaining on me fast. If it hadn't been for Mets . . .

She was shouting at me the whole time. "Move your ass, you fuckin' bitch!" She was getting pretty raw by then. "Don't you dare quit . . . don't you DARE crap out on me!" She never let up, never gave me an inch. "What are you, some weak little victim?" At that point I thought I was. I knew I could never make it. The exhaustion, the pain, more than anything, I think, the anger at fucking up so badly. I actually considered turning my pistol around, wanting to punish myself for . . . you know. And then Mets really hit me. She roared, "What are you, your fucking mother!?!"

That did it. I hauled ass right up onto the interstate.

I reported to Mets that I'd made it, then asked, "Now what the fuck do I do?"

Her voice suddenly got very soft. She told me to look up. A black dot was heading at me from out of the morning sun. It was following the freeway and grew very quickly into the form of a UH-60. I let out a whoop and popped my signal flare.

The first thing I saw when they winched me aboard was that it was a civilian chopper, not government Search and Rescue. The crew chief was a big Cajun with a thick goatee and wraparound sunglasses. He asked, "Where de' hell you come from?" Sorry if I butchered the accent. I almost cried and punched him in his thigh-sized bicep. I laughed and said that they work fast. He shot me a look like I didn't know what I was talking about. It turned out later that this wasn't the rescue team but just a routine air shuttle between

Baton Rouge and Lafayette. I didn't know at that moment, and I didn't care. I reported to Mets that I got my pickup, that I was safe. I thanked her for everything she'd done for me, and . . . and so I wouldn't really start bawling, I tried to cover with a joke about finally getting that episode of *The View*. I never got a response.

She sounds like a hell of a Skywatcher.

She was a hell of a woman.

You said you had your "suspicions" by this point.

No civilian, even a veteran Skywatcher, could know so much about what goes into wearing those wings. She was just too savvy, too informed, the kind of baseline knowledge of someone who had to have gone through it herself.

So she was a pilot.

Definitely; not air force—I would have known her—but maybe a squid or a jarhead. They'd lost as many pilots as the air force on resupply hops like mine, and eight out of ten were never accounted for. I'm sure that she must have run into a situation like mine, had to ditch, lost her crew, maybe even blamed herself for it like me. Somehow she managed to find that cabin and spent the rest of the war as one kick-ass Skywatcher.

That makes sense.

Doesn't it?

[There is an awkward pause. I search her face, waiting for more.]

What?

They never found her.

No.

Or the cabin.

No.

And Honolulu never had any record of a Skywatcher with the call sign Mets Fan.

You've done your homework.

I . . .

You probably also read my after-action report, right?

Yes.

And the psych evaluation they tacked on after my official debriefing.

Well . . .

Well, it's bullshit, okay? So what if everything she told me was information I'd already been briefed on, so what if the psych team "claim" my radio was knocked out before I hit the mud, and so the fuck what if Mets is short for Metis, the mother of Athena, the Greek goddess with the stormy gray eyes. Oh, the shrinks had a ball with that one, especially when they "discovered" that my mother grew up in the Bronx.

And that remark she made about your mother?

Who the hell doesn't have mother issues? If Mets was a pilot, she was a natural gambler. She knew she had a good chance of scoring a hit with "mom." She knew the risk, took her shot . . . Look, if they thought I'd cracked up, why didn't I lose my flight status? Why did they let me have this job? Maybe she wasn't a pilot herself, maybe she was married to one, maybe she'd wanted to be one but never made it as far as I did. Maybe she was just a scared, lonely voice that did what she could to help another scared lonely voice from ending up like her. Who cares who she was, or is? She was there when I needed her, and for the rest of my life, she'll always be with me.

AROUND THE WORLD, AND ABOVE

PROVINCE OF BOHEMIA, THE EUROPEAN UNION

[It is called Kost, "the Bone," and what it lacks in beauty it more than makes up for in strength. Appearing to grow out of its solid rock foundation, this fourteenth-century Gothic "Hrad" casts an intimidating shadow over the Plakanek Valley, an image David Allen Forbes is keen to capture with his pencil and paper. This will be his second book, *Castles of the Zombie War: The Continent.* The Englishman sits under a tree, his patchwork clothing and long Scottish sword already adding to this Arthurian setting. He abruptly switches gears as I arrive, from serene artist to painfully nervous storyteller.]

When I say that the New World doesn't have our history of fixed fortifications, I'm only referring to North America. There are the Spanish coastal fortresses, naturally, along the Caribbean, and the ones we and the French built in the Lesser Antilles. Then there are the Inca ruins in the

Andes, although they never experienced direct sieges.[1] Also, when I say "North America," that does not include the Mayan and Aztec ruins in Mexico—that business with the Battle of Kukulcan, although I suppose that's Toltec, now, isn't it, when those chaps held off so many Zed Heads on the steps of that bloody great pyramid. So when I say "New World," I'm really referring to the United States and Canada.

This isn't an insult, you understand, please don't take it as such. You're both young countries, you don't have the history of institutional anarchy we Europeans suffered after the fall of Rome. You've always had standing, national governments with the forces capable of enforcing law and order.

I know that wasn't true during your westward expansion or your civil war, and please, I'm not discounting those pre–Civil War fortresses or the experiences of those defending them. I'd one day like to visit Fort Jefferson. I hear those who survived there had quite a time of it. All I'm saying is, in Europe's history, we had almost a millennia of chaos where sometimes the concept of physical safety stopped at the battlements of your lord's castle. Does that make sense? I'm not making sense; can we start again?

No, no, this is fine. Please, continue.

You'll edit out all the daft bits.

You got it.

Right then. Castles. Well . . . I don't want for a moment to overstate their importance for the general war effort. In fact, when you compare them to any other type of fixed fortification, modern, modified, and so forth, their contribution does seem quite negligible, unless you're like me, and that contribution was what saved your life.

---

1. Although Machu Picchu was quiet throughout the war, the survivors at Vilcabamba did see a minor, internal outbreak.

This doesn't mean that a mighty fortress was naturally our God. For starters, you must understand the inherent difference between a castle and a palace. A lot of so-called castles were really nothing more than just great impressive homes, or else had been converted to such after their defensive value had become obsolete. These once impregnable bastions now had so many windows cut into the ground floor that it would have taken forever to brick them all up again. You'd be better off in a modern block of flats with the staircase removed. And as far as those palaces that were built as nothing more than status symbols, places like Chateau Ussé or Prague "Castle," they were little more than death traps.

Just look at Versailles. That was a first-rate cock-up. Small wonder the French government chose to build their national memorial on its ashes. Did you ever read that poem by Renard, about the wild roses that now grow in the memorial garden, their petals stained red with the blood of the damned?

Not that a high wall was all you needed for long-term survival. Like any static defense, castles had as many internal as external dangers. Just look at Muiderslot in Holland. One case of pneumonia, that's all it took. Throw in a wet, cold autumn, poor nutrition, and lack of any genuine medications . . . Imagine what that must have been like, trapped behind those high stone walls, those around you fatally ill, knowing your time was coming, knowing the only slim hope you had was to escape. The journals written by some of the dying tell of people going mad with desperation, leaping into that moat choked with Zed Heads.

And then there were fires like the ones at Braubach and Pierrefonds; hundreds trapped with nowhere to run, just waiting to be charred by the flames or asphyxiated by the smoke. There were also accidental explosions, civilians who somehow found themselves in possession of bombs but had no idea how to handle or even store them. At Miskolc Diosgyor in Hungary, as I understand it, someone got their hands on a cache of military-grade, sodium-based explosives. Don't ask me what exactly it was or why they had it, but nobody seemed to know that water, not fire, was the catalytic agent. The story goes that someone was smoking in the armory, caused some small fire or whatnot. The stupid sods thought they were preventing an explosion by dousing the crates in water. It blew a hole right through the wall and the dead surged in like water through a breached dam.

At least that was a mistake based on ignorance. I can't even begin to forgive what happened at Chateau de Fougeres. They were running low on supplies, thought that they could dig a tunnel under their undead attackers. What did they think this was, *The Great Escape?* Did they have any professional surveyors with them? Did they even understand the basics of trigonometry? The bloody tunnel exit fell short by over half a kilometer, came up right in a nest of the damn things. Stupid wankers hadn't even thought to equip their tunnel with demolition charges.

Yes, there were cock-ups aplenty, but there were also some noteworthy triumphs. Many were subjected to only short-term sieges, the good fortune of being on the right side of the line. Some in Spain, Bavaria, or Scotland above the Antonine[2] only had to hold out for weeks, or even days. For some, like Kisimul, it was only a question of getting through one rather dodgy night. But then there were the true tales of victory, like Chenonceau in France, a bizarre little Disneyesque castle built on a bridge over the Cher River. With both connections to land severed, and the right amount of strategic forethought, they managed to hold their position for years.

They had enough supplies for years?

Oh good lord, no. They simply waited for first snowfall, then raided the surrounding countryside. This was, I should imagine, standard procedure for almost anyone under siege, castle or not. I'm sure those in your strategic "Blue Zones," at least those above the snowline, operated in much the same manner. In that way we were fortunate that most of Europe freezes in winter. Many of the defenders I've spoken to have agreed that the inevitable onset of winter, long and brutal as it was, became a lifesaving reprieve. As long as they didn't freeze to death, many survivors took the opportunity of frozen Zed Heads to raid the surrounding countryside for everything they'd need for the warmer months.

2. The main British line of defense was fixed along the site of the old Roman Antonine Wall.

It's not surprising how many defenders chose to remain in their strongholds even with the opportunity to flee, be it Bouillon in Belgium or Spis in Slovakia or even back home like Beaumaris in Wales. Before the war, the place had been nothing but a museum piece, a hollow shell of roofless chambers and high concentric walls. The town council should be given the VC for their accomplishments, pooling resources, organizing citizens, restoring this ruin to its former glory. They had just a few months before the crisis engulfed their part of Britain. Even more dramatic is the story of Conwy, both a castle and medieval wall that protected the entire town. The inhabitants not only lived in safety and relative comfort during the stalemate years, their access to the sea allowed Conwy to become a springboard for our forces once we began to retake our country. Have you ever read *Camelot Mine?*

[I shake my head.]

You must find yourself a copy. It's a cracking good novel, based on the author's own experiences as one of the defenders of Caerphilly. He began the crisis on the second floor of his flat in Ludlow, Wales. As his supplies ran out and the first snow fell, he decided to strike out in search of more permanent lodgings. He came upon the abandoned ruin, which had already been the sight of a halfhearted, and ultimately fruitless, defense. He buried the bodies, smashed the frozen Zed Heads, and set about restoring the castle on his own. He worked tirelessly, in the most brutal winter on record. By May, Caerphilly was prepared for the summer siege, and by the following winter, it became a haven for several hundred other survivors.

[He shows me some of his sketches.]

A masterpiece, isn't it, second largest in the British Isles.

What's the first?

[He hesitates.]

Windsor.

Windsor was your castle.

Well, not mine personally.

I mean, you were there.

[Another pause.]

It was, from a defensive standpoint, as close as one could come to per-
fection. Before the war, it was the largest inhabited castle in Europe, almost thirteen acres. It had its own well for water, and enough storage space
to house a decade's worth of rations. The fire of 1992 led to a state-of-the-
art suppression system, and the subsequent terrorist threats upgraded security measures to rival any in the UK. Not even the general public knew
what their tax dollars were paying for: bulletproof glass, reinforced walls,
retractable bars, and steel shutters hidden so cleverly in windowsills and
door frames.

But of all our achievements at Windsor, nothing can rival the siphoning
of crude oil and natural gas from the deposit several kilometers beneath
the castle's foundation. It had been discovered in the 1990s but never exploited for a variety of political and environmental reasons. You can believe we exploited it, though. Our contingent of royal engineers rigged a
scaffolding up and over our wall, and extended it to the drilling site. It was
quite an achievement, and you can see how it became the precursor to our
fortified motorways. On a personal level, I was just grateful for the warm
rooms, hot food, and, in a pinch . . . the Molotovs and flaming ditch. It's
not the most efficient way to stop a Zed Head, I know, but as long as you've
got them stuck and can keep them in the fire . . . and besides, what else
could we do when the bullets ran out and we were left with nothing else
but an odd lot of medieval hand weapons?

There were quite a bit of those about, in museums, personal collections . . .
and not a decorative dud among them. These were real, tough and tested.

They became part of British life again, ordinary citizens traipsing about with a mace or halberd or double-bladed battle-axe. I myself became rather adept with this claymore, although you wouldn't think of it to look at me.

[He gestures, slightly embarrassed, to the weapon almost as long as himself.]

It's not really ideal, takes a lot of skill, but eventually you learn what you can do, what you never thought you were capable of, what others around you are capable of.

[David hesitates before speaking. He is clearly uncomfortable. I hold out my hand.]

Thank you so much for taking the time . . .

There's . . . more.

If you're not comfortable . . .

No, please, it's quite all right.
[Takes a breath.] She . . . she wouldn't leave, you see. She insisted, over the objections of Parliament, to remain at Windsor, as she put it, "for the duration." I thought maybe it was misguided nobility, or maybe fear-based paralysis. I tried to make her see reason, begged her almost on my knees. Hadn't she done enough with the Balmoral Decree, turning all her estates into protected zones for any who could reach and defend them? Why not join her family in Ireland or the Isle of Man, or, at least, if she was insisting on remaining in Britain, supreme command HQ north above the Antonine.

What did she say?

"The highest of distinctions is service to others." [He clears his throat, his upper lip quivers for a second.] Her father had said that; it was the reason he had refused to run to Canada during the Second World War, the reason her mother had spent the blitz visiting civilians huddled in the tube stations beneath London, the same reason, to this day, we remain a United *Kingdom*. Their task, their mandate, is to personify all that is great in our national spirit. They must forever be an example to the rest of us, the strongest, and bravest, and absolute best of us. In a sense, it is they who are ruled by us, instead of the other way around, and they must sacrifice everything, *everything*, to shoulder the weight of this godlike burden. Otherwise what's the flipping point? Just scrap the whole damn tradition, roll out the bloody guillotine, and be done with it altogether. They were viewed very much like castles, I suppose: as crumbling, obsolete relics, with no real modern function other than as tourist attractions. But when the skies darkened and the nation called, both reawoke to the meaning of their existence. One shielded our bodies, the other, our souls.

❦

ULITHI ATOLL, FEDERATED STATES OF MICRONESIA

[During World War II, this vast coral atoll served as the main forward base for the United States Pacific Fleet. During World War Z, it sheltered not only American naval vessels, but hundreds of civilian ships as well. One of those ships was the UNS *Ural*, the first broadcast hub of Radio Free Earth. Now a museum to the achievements of the project, she is the focus of the British documentary *Words at War*. One of the subjects interviewed for this documentary is Barati Palshigar.]

Ignorance was the enemy. Lies and superstition, misinformation, disinformation. Sometimes, no information at all. Ignorance killed billions of people. Ignorance caused the Zombie War. Imagine if we had known then what we know now. Imagine if the undead virus had been as understood as, say, tuberculosis was. Imagine if the world's citizens, or at least those charged with protecting those citizens, had known exactly what they were facing. Ignorance was the real enemy, and cold, hard facts were the weapons.

When I first joined Radio Free Earth, it was still called the International Program for Health and Safety Information. The title "Radio Free Earth" came from the individuals and communities who monitored our broadcasts.

It was the first real international venture, barely a few months after the South African Plan, and years before the conference at Honolulu. Just like the rest of the world based their survival strategies on Redeker, our genesis was routed in Radio Ubunye.[1]

What was Radio Ubunye?

South Africa's broadcasts to its isolated citizens. Because they didn't have the resources for material aid, the only assistance the government could render was information. They were the first, at least, to my knowledge, to begin these regular, multilingual broadcasts. Not only did they offer practical survival skills, they went so far as to collect and address each and every falsehood circulating among their citizens. What we did was take the template of Radio Ubunye and adapt it for the global community.

I came aboard, literally, at the very beginning, as the *Ural*'s reactors were just being put back online. The *Ural* was a former vessel of the Soviet, then the Russian, Federal Navy. Back then the SSV-33 had been many things: a command and control ship, a missile tracking platform, an electronic surveillance vessel. Unfortunately, she was also a white elephant, because her systems, they tell me, were too complicated even for her own crew. She had spent the majority of her career tied to a pier at the Vladivostok naval base, providing additional electrical power for the facility. I am not an engineer, so I don't how they managed to replace her spent fuel rods or convert her massive communication facilities to interface with the global satellite network. I specialize in languages, specifically those of the

---

1. Ubunye: a word of Zulu origin for Unity.

Indian Subcontinent. Myself and Mister Verma, just the two of us to cover a billion people . . . well . . . at that point it was still a billion.

Mister Verma had found me in the refugee camp in Sri Lanka. He was a translator, I was an interpreter. We had worked together several years before at our country's embassy in London. We thought it had been hard work then; we had no idea. It was a maddening grind, eighteen, sometimes twenty hours a day. I don't know when we slept. There was so much raw data, so many dispatches arriving every minute. Much of it had to do with basic survival: how to purify water, create an indoor greenhouse, culture and process mold spore for penicillin. This mind-numbing copy would often be punctuated with facts and terms that I had never heard of before. I'd never heard the term "quisling" or "feral"; I didn't know what a "Lobo" was or the false miracle cure of Phalanx. All I knew was that suddenly there was a uniformed man shoving a collection of words before my eyes and telling me "We need this in Marathi, and ready to record in fifteen minutes."

What kind of misinformation were you combating?

Where do you want me to begin? Medical? Scientific? Military? Spiritual? Psychological? The psychological aspect I found the most maddening. People wanted so badly to anthropomorphize the walking blight. In war, in a conventional war that is, we spend so much time trying to dehumanize the enemy, to create an emotional distance. We would make up stories or derogatory titles . . . when I think about what my father used to call Muslims . . . and now in this war it seemed that everyone was trying desperately to find some shred of a connection to their enemy, to put a human face on something that was so unmistakably inhuman.

Can you give me some examples?

There were so many misconceptions: zombies were somehow intelligent; they could feel and adapt, use tools and even some human weapons; they carried memories of their former existence; or they could be communicated with and trained like some kind of pet. It was heartbreaking, having to debunk one misguided myth after another. The civilian survival guide helped, but was still severely limited.

Oh really?

Oh yes. You could see it was clearly written by an American, the references to SUVs and personal firearms. There was no taking into account the cultural differences . . . the various indigenous solutions people believed would save them from the undead.

Such as?

I'd rather not give too many details, not without tacitly condemning the entire people group from which this "solution" originated. As an Indian, I had to deal with many aspects of my own culture that had turned self-destructive. There was Varanasi, one of the oldest cities on Earth, near the place where Buddha supposedly preached his first sermon and where thousands of Hindu pilgrims came each year to die. In normal, prewar conditions, the road would be littered with corpses. Now these corpses were rising to attack. Varanasi was one of the hottest White Zones, a nexus of living death. This nexus covered almost the entire length of the Ganges. Its healing powers had been scientifically assessed decades before the war, something to do with the high oxygenation rate of the waters.[2] Tragic. Millions flocked to its shores, serving only to feed the flames. Even after the government's withdrawal to the Himalayas, when over 90 percent of the country was officially overrun, the pilgrimages continued. Every country had a similar story. Every one of our international crew had at least one moment when they were forced to confront an example of suicidal ignorance. An American told us about how the religious sect known as "God's Lambs" believed that

2. Although opinion is divided on the subject, many prewar scientific studies have proven that the high oxygenation retention of the Ganges has been the source of its long-revered "miracle" cures.

the rapture had finally come and the quicker they were infected, the quicker they would go to heaven. Another woman—I won't say what country she belonged to—tried her best to dispel the notion that sexual intercourse with a virgin could "cleanse" the "curse." I don't know how many women, or little girls, were raped as a result of this "cleansing." Everyone was furious with his own people. Everyone was ashamed. Our one Belgian crewmember compared it to the darkening skies. He used to call it "the evil of our collective soul."

I guess I have no right to complain. My life was never in danger, my belly was always full. I might not have slept often but at least I could sleep without fear. Most importantly, I never had had to work in the *Ural*'s IR department.

IR?

Information Reception. The data we were broadcasting did not originate aboard the *Ural*. It came from all around the world, from experts and think tanks in various government safe zones. They would transmit their findings to our IR operators who, in turn, would pass it along to us. Much of this data was transmitted to us over conventional, open, civilian bands, and many of these bands were crammed with ordinary people's cries for help. There were millions of wretched souls scattered throughout our planet, all screaming into their private radio sets as their children starved or their temporary fortress burned, or the living dead overran their defenses. Even if you didn't understand the language, as many of the operators didn't, there was no mistaking the human voice of anguish. They weren't allowed to answer back, either; there wasn't time. All transmissions had to be devoted to official business. I don't want to know what that was like for the IR operators.

When the last broadcast came from Buenos Aires, when that famous Latin singer played that Spanish lullaby, it was too much for one of our operators. He wasn't from Buenos Aires, he wasn't even from South America. He was just an eighteen-year-old Russian sailor who blew his brains out all over his instruments. He was the first, and since the end of the war, the rest of the IR operators have followed suit. Not one of them is alive today. The last was my Belgian friend. "You carry those voices with you," he told me one morning. We were standing on the deck, looking into that brown haze, waiting for a sunrise we knew we'd never see. "Those cries will be with me the rest of my life, never resting, never fading, never ceasing their call to join them."

❧

THE DEMILITARIZED ZONE: SOUTH KOREA

[Hyungchol Choi, deputy director of the Korean Central Intelligence Agency, gestures to the dry, hilly, unremarkable landscape to our north. One might mistake it for Southern California, if not for the deserted pillboxes, fading banners, and rusting, barbed wire fence that runs to either horizon.]

What happened? No one knows. No country was better prepared to repel the infestation than North Korea. Rivers to the north, oceans to the east and west, and to the south [he gestures to the Demilitarized Zone], the most heavily fortified border on Earth. You can see how mountainous the terrain is, how easily defensible, but what you can't see is that those mountains are honeycombed with a titanic military-industrial infrastructure. The North Korean government learned some very hard lessons from your bombing campaign of the 1950s and had been laboring ever since to create a subterranean system that would allow their people to wage another war from a secure location.

Their population was heavily militarized, marshaled to a degree of readiness that made Israel look like Iceland. Over a million men and women were actively under arms with a further five in reserve. That is over a quarter of the entire population, not to mention the fact that almost everyone in the country had, at some point in their lives, undergone basic military training. More important than this training, though, and most important for this kind of warfare was an almost superhuman degree of national discipline. North Koreans were indoctrinated from birth to believe that their lives were meaningless, that they existed only to serve the State, the Revolution, and the Great Leader.

This is almost the polar opposite of what we experienced in the South. We were an open society. We had to be. International trade was our lifeblood. We were individualists, maybe not as much as you Americans, but we had more than our share of protests and public disturbances. We were such a free and fractured society that we barely managed to implement the Chang Doctrine[1] during the Great Panic. That kind of internal crisis would have been inconceivable in the North. They were a people who, even when their government caused a near genocidal famine, would rather resort to eating children[2] than raise even a whisper of defiance. This was the kind of subservience Adolf Hitler could have only dreamed of. If you had given each citizen a gun, a rock, or even their bare hands, pointed them at approaching zombies and said "Fight!" they would have done so down to the oldest woman and smallest tot. This was a country bred for war, planned, prepared, and poised for it since July 27, 1953. If you were going to invent a country to not only survive but triumph over the apocalypse we faced, it would have been the Democratic People's Republic of Korea.

So what happened? About a month before our troubles started, before the first outbreaks were reported in Pusan, the North suddenly, and inexplicably, severed all diplomatic relations. We weren't told why the rail line, the only overland link between our two sides, was suddenly closed, or why some of our citizens who'd been waiting decades to see long lost relatives in the North had their dreams abruptly shattered by a rubber stamp. No explanation of any kind was given. All we got was their standard "matter of state security" brush-off.

---

1. The Chang Doctrine: South Korea's version of the Redeker Plan.
2. There have been reports of alleged cannibalism during the famine of 1992 and that some of the victims were children.

Unlike many others, I wasn't convinced that this was a prelude to war. Whenever the North had threatened violence, they always rang the same bells. No satellite data, ours or the Americans, showed any hostile intent. There were no troop movements, no aircraft fueling, no ship or submarine deployment. If anything, our forces along the Demilitarized Zone began noticing their opposite numbers disappearing. We knew them all, the border troops. We'd photographed each one over the years, given them nicknames like Snake Eyes or Bulldog, even compiled dossiers on their supposed ages, backgrounds, and personal lives. Now they were gone, vanished behind shielded trenches and dugouts.

Our seismic indicators were similarly silent. If the North had begun tunneling operations or even massed vehicles on the other side of "Z," we would have heard it like the National Opera Company.

Panmunjom is the only area along the DMZ where opposing sides can meet for face-to-face negotiations. We share joint custody of the conference rooms, and our troops posture for each other over several meters of open courtyard. The guards were changed on a rotating basis. One night, as the North Korean detachment marched into their barracks, no replacement unit marched out. The doors were shut. The lights were extinguished. And we never saw them again.

We also saw a complete halt to human intelligence infiltration. Spies from the North were almost as regular and predictable as the seasons. Most of the time they were easy to spot, wearing out-of-date clothes or asking the price of goods that they should have already known. We used to pick them up all the time, but since the outbreaks began, their numbers had dwindled to zero.

What about your spies in the North?

Vanished, all of them, right about the same time all our electronic surveillance assets went dark. I don't mean there was no disturbing radio traffic, I mean there was no traffic at all. One by one, all the civilian and military channels began shutting down. Satellite images showed fewer farmers in their fields, less foot traffic in city streets, even fewer "volunteer" laborers on many public works projects, which is something that has *never* happened before. Before we knew it, there wasn't a living soul left from the Yalu to the DMZ. From a purely intelligence standpoint, it appeared as if the entire country, every man, woman, and child in North Korea, had simply vanished.

This mystery only stoked our growing anxiety, given what we had to deal with at home. By now there were outbreaks in Seoul, P'ohang, Taejon. There was the evacuation of Mokpo, the isolation of Kangnung, and, of course, our version of Yonkers at Inchon, and all of it compounded by the need to keep at least half our active divisions along our northern border. Too many in the Ministry of National Defense were convinced that the Pyongyang was just aching for war, waiting eagerly for our darkest moment to come thundering across the 38th Parallel. We in the intelligence community couldn't disagree more. We kept telling them that if they were waiting for our darkest hour, then that hour had most certainly arrived.

Tae Han Min'guk was on the brink of national collapse. Plans were being secretly drafted for a Japanese-style resettlement. Covert teams were already scouting locations in Kamchatka. If the Chang Doctrine hadn't worked . . . if just a few more units had broken, if a few more safe zones had collapsed . . .

Maybe we owe our survival to the North, or at least to the fear of it. My generation never really saw the North as a threat. I'm speaking of the civilians, you understand, those of my age who saw them as a backward, starving, failed nation. My generation had grown up their entire lives in peace and prosperity. The only thing they feared was a German-style reunification that would bring millions of homeless ex-communists looking for a handout.

That wasn't the case with those who came before us . . . our parents and grandparents . . . those who lived with the very real specter of invasion hanging over them, the knowledge that at any moment the alarms might sound, the lights might dim, and the bankers, schoolteachers, and taxi drivers might be called to pick up arms and fight to defend their homeland. Their hearts and minds were ever vigilant, and in the end, it was them, not us, who rallied the national spirit.

I'm still pushing for an expedition to the North. I'm still blocked at every turn. There's too much work to do, they tell me. The country is still in shambles. We also have our international commitments, most importantly the repatriation of our refugees to Kyushu. . . . [Snorts.] Those Japs are gonna owe us big-time.

I'm not asking for a recon in force. Just give me one helicopter, one fishing boat; just open the gates at Panmunjom and let me walk through on foot. What if you trigger some booby trap? they counter. What if it's nuclear? What if you open the door to some underground city and twenty-three million zombies come spewing out? Their arguments aren't without merit. We know the DMZ is heavily mined. Last month a cargo plane nearing their airspace was fired on by a surface-to-air missile. The launcher was an automated model, the type they'd designed as a revenge weapon in case the population had already been obliterated.

Conventional wisdom is that they must have evacuated to their subterranean complexes. If that is true, then our estimates of the size and depth of those complexes were grossly inaccurate. Maybe the entire population is underground, tooling away on endless war projects, while their "Great Leader" continues to anesthetize himself with Western liquor and American pornography. Do they even know the war is over? Have their leaders lied to them, again, and told them that the world as they know it has ceased to be? Maybe the rise of the dead was a "good" thing in their eyes, an excuse to tighten the yoke even further in a society built on blind subjugation. The Great Leader always wanted to be a living God, and now, as master not only of the food his people eat, the air they breathe, but the very light of their artificial suns, maybe his twisted fantasy has finally become a reality. Maybe that was the original plan, but something went disastrously wrong. Look what happened to the "mole city" underneath Paris. What if that occurred in the North on a national level? Maybe those caverns are teeming with twenty-three million zombies, emaciated automatons howling in the darkness and just waiting to be unleashed.

❦

KYOTO, JAPAN

[The old photo of Kondo Tatsumi shows a skinny, acne-faced teenager with dull red eyes and bleached blond highlights streaking his unkempt hair. The man I am speaking to has no hair at all. Clean-shaven, tanned and toned, his clear, sharp gaze never leaves mine. Although his manner is cordial and his mood light, this warrior monk retains the composure of a predatory animal at rest.]

I was an "otaku." I know that term has come to mean a great many things to a great many people, but for me it simply meant "outsider." I know Americans, especially young ones, must feel trapped by societal pressure. All humans do. However, if I understand your culture correctly, individualism is something to be encouraged. You revere the "rebel," the "rogue," those who stand proudly apart from the masses. For you, individuality is a badge of honor. For us, it is a ribbon of shame. We lived, particularly before the war, in a complex and seemingly infinite labyrinth of external judgments. Your appearance, your speech, everything from the career you held to the way you sneezed had to be planned and orchestrated to follow rigid Confucian doctrine. Some either have the strength, or lack thereof, to accept this doctrine. Others, like myself, chose exile in a better world. That world was cyber space, and it was tailor-made for Japanese otaku.

I can't speak for your educational system, or, indeed, for that of any other country, but ours was based almost entirely on fact retention. From the day we first set foot in a classroom, prewar Japanese children were injected with volumes upon volumes of facts and figures that had no practical application in our lives. These facts had no moral component, no social context, no human connection to the outside world. They had no reason for existence other than that their mastery allows ascension. Prewar Japanese children were not taught to think, we were taught to memorize.

You can understand how this education would easily lend itself to an existence in cyberspace. In a world of information without context, where status was determined on its acquisition and possession, those of my generation could rule like gods. I was a sensei, master over all I surveyed, be it discovering the blood type of the prime minister's cabinet, or the tax receipts of Matsumoto and Hamada,[1] or the location and condition of all shin-gunto swords of the Pacific War. I didn't have to worry about my appearance, or my social etiquette, my grades, or my prospects for the future. No one could judge me, no one could hurt me. In this world I was powerful, and more importantly, I was safe!

When the crisis reached Japan, my clique, as with all the others, forgot our previous obsessions and devoted our energies entirely to the living dead. We studied their physiology, behavior, weaknesses, and the global response to their attack upon humanity. The last subject was my clique's specialty, the possibility of containment within the Japanese home islands. I collected population statistics, transport networks, police doctrine. I memorized everything from the size of the Japanese merchant fleet, to how many rounds the army's Type 89 assault rifle held. No fact was too small or obscure. We were on a mission, we barely slept. When school was eventually cancelled, it gave us the ability to be wired in almost twenty-four hours a day. I was the first to hack into Doctor Komatsu's personal hard drive and read the raw data a full week before he presented his findings to the Diet. This was a coup. It further elevated my status among those who already worshipped me.

Doctor Komatsu first recommended the evacuation?

He did. Like us, he'd been compiling the same facts. But whereas we'd been memorizing them, he'd been analyzing them. Japan was an overcrowded

---

1. Hitoshi Matsumoto and Masatoshi Hamada were Japan's most successful prewar improvisational comedians.

nation: one hundred and twenty-eight million people jammed into less than three hundred and seventy thousand square kilometers of either mountainous or overurbanized islands. Japan's low crime rate gave it one of the relatively smallest and most lightly armed police forces in the industrialized world. Japan was pretty much also a demilitarized state. Because of American "protection," our self-defense forces had not seen actual combat since 1945. Even those token troops who were deployed to the Gulf almost never saw any serious action and spent most of their occupation duty within the protected walls of their isolated compound. We had access to all these bits of information, but not the wherewithal to see where they were pointing. So it took us all by complete surprise when Doctor Komatsu publicly declared that the situation was hopeless and that Japan had to be immediately evacuated.

That must have been terrifying.

Not at all! It set off an explosion of frenzied activity, a race to discover where our population might resettle. Would it be the South, the coral atolls of the Central and South Pacific, or would we head north, colonizing the Kuriles, Sakhalin, or maybe somewhere in Siberia? Whoever could uncover the answer would be the greatest otaku in cyber history.

And there was no concern for your personal safety?

Of course not. Japan was doomed, but I didn't live in Japan. I lived in a world of free-floating information. The siafu,[2] that's what we were calling the infected now, weren't something to be feared, they were something to be studied. You have no idea the kind of disconnect I was suffering. My culture, my upbringing, and now my otaku lifestyle all combined to completely insulate me. Japan might be evacuated, Japan might

2. "Siafu" is the nickname for the African driver ant. The term was first used by Doctor Komatsu Yukio in his address to the Diet.

be destroyed, and I would watch it all happen from the safety of my digital mountaintop.

What about your parents?

What about them? We lived in the same apartment, but I never really conversed with them. I'm sure they thought I was studying. Even when school closed I told them I still had to prepare for exams. They never questioned it. My father and I rarely spoke. In the mornings my mother would leave a breakfast tray at my door, at night she would leave dinner. The first time she didn't leave a tray, I thought nothing of it. I woke up that morning, as I always did; gratified myself, as I always did; logged on, as I always did. It was midday before I started to feel hungry. I hated those feelings, hunger or fatigue or, the worst, sexual desire. Those were physical distractions. They annoyed me. I reluctantly turned away from my computer and opened my bedroom door. No food. I called for my mother. No answer. I went into the kitchen area, grabbed some raw ramen, and ran back to my desk. I did it again, that night, and again the next morning.

You never questioned where your parents were?

The only reason I cared was because of the precious minutes I was wasting having to feed myself. In my world too many exciting things were happening.

What about the other otaku? Didn't they discuss their fears?

We shared facts not feelings, even when they started to disappear. I'd notice that someone had stopped returning e-mail or else hadn't posted for a while. I'd see that they hadn't logged on in a day or that their servers were no longer active.

And that didn't scare you?

It annoyed me. Not only was I losing a source of information, I was losing potential praise for my own. To post some new factoid about Japanese evacuation ports and to have fifty, instead of sixty, responses was upsetting, then to have those fifty drop to forty-five, then to thirty . . .

How long did this go on for?

About three days. The last post, from another otaku in Sendai, stated that the dead were now flowing out of Tohoku University Hospital, in the same *cho* as his apartment.

And that didn't worry you?

Why should it? I was too busy trying to learn all I could about the evacuation process. How was it going to be executed, what government organizations were involved? Would the camps be in Kamchatka or Sakhalin, or both? And what was this I was reading about the rash of suicides that was sweeping the country?[3] So many questions, so much data to mine. I cursed myself for having to go to sleep that night.

When I woke up, the screen was blank. I tried to sign on. Nothing. I tried rebooting. Nothing. I noticed that I was on backup battery. Not a problem. I had enough reserve power for ten hours at full use. I also noticed that my signal strength was zero. I couldn't believe it. Kokura, like all Japan, had a state-of-the-art wireless network that was supposed to be failsafe. One server might go down, maybe even a few, but the whole net? I realized it must be my computer. It had to be. I got out my laptop and tried to sign on. No signal. I cursed and got up to tell my parents that I had to use their desktop. They still weren't home. Frustrated, I tried to pick up the phone to call my mother's cell. It was cordless, dependent on wall power. I tried my cell. I got no reception.

Do you know what happened to them?

No, even to this day, I have no idea. I know they didn't abandon me, I'm sure of it. Maybe my father was caught out at work, my mother trapped

---

3. It has been established that Japan suffered the largest percentage of suicides during the Great Panic.

while trying to go grocery shopping. They could have been lost together, going to or coming back from the relocation office. Anything could have happened. There was no note, nothing. I've been trying to find out ever since.

I went back into my parents' room, just to make sure they weren't there. I tried the phones again. It wasn't bad yet. I was still in control. I tried to go back online. Isn't that funny? All I could think about was trying to escape again, getting back to my world, being safe. Nothing. I started to panic. "Now," I started to say, trying to command my computer by force of will. "Now, now, NOW! NOW! NOW!" I started beating the monitor. My knuckles split, the sight of my own blood terrified me. I'd never played sports as a child, never been injured, it was all too much. I picked up the monitor and threw it against the wall. I was crying like a baby, shouting, hyperventilating. I started to wretch and vomited all over the floor. I got up and staggered to the front door. I don't know what I was looking for, just that I had to get out. I opened the door and stared into darkness.

Did you try knocking at the neighbor's door?

No. Isn't that odd? Even at the height of my breakdown, my social anxiety was so great that actually risking personal contact was still taboo. I took a few steps, slipped, and fell into something soft. It was cold and slimy, all over my hands, my clothes. It stank. The whole hallway stank. I suddenly became aware of a low, steady scraping noise, like something was dragging itself across the hallway toward me.

I called out, "Hello?" I heard a soft, gurgling groan. My eyes were just beginning to adjust to the darkness. I began to make out a shape, large, humanoid, crawling on its belly. I sat there paralyzed, wanting to run but at the same time wanting to . . . to know for sure. My doorway was casting a narrow rectangle of dim gray light against the far wall. As the thing moved into that light, I finally saw its face, perfectly intact, perfectly human, except for the right eye that hung by the stem. The left eye was locked on mine and its gurgling moan became a choked rasp. I jumped to my feet, sprang back inside my apartment, and slammed the door behind me.

My mind was finally clear, maybe for the first time in years, and I suddenly realized that I could smell smoke and hear faint screams. I went over to the window and threw the curtains open.

Kokura was engulfed in hell. The fires, the wreckage . . . the siafu were everywhere. I watched them crash through doors, invade apartments, devour people cowering in corners or on balconies. I watched people leap to their deaths or break their legs and spines. They lay on the pavement, unable to move, wailing in agony as the dead closed in around them. One man in the apartment directly across from me tried to fight them off with a golf club. It bent harmlessly around a zombie's head before five others pulled him to the floor.

Then . . . a pounding at the door. My door. This . . . [shakes his fist] bom-bombom-bom . . . from the bottom, near the floor. I heard the thing groaning outside. I heard other noises, too, from the other apartments. These were my neighbors, the people I'd always tried to avoid, whose faces and names I could barely remember. They were screaming, pleading, struggling, and sobbing. I heard one voice, either a young woman or a child on the floor above me, calling someone by name, begging them to stop. But the voice was swallowed in a chorus of moans. The banging at my door became louder. More siafu had shown up. I tried to move the living room furniture against the door. It was a waste of effort. Our apartment was, by your standards, pretty bare. The door began to crack. I could see its hinges straining. I figured I had maybe a few minutes to escape.

Escape? But if the door was jammed . . .

Out the window, onto the balcony of the apartment below. I thought I could tie bedsheets into a rope . . . [smiles sheepishly] . . . I'd heard about it from an otaku who studied American prison breaks. It would be the first time I ever applied any of my archived knowledge.

Fortunately the linen held. I climbed out of my apartment and started to lower myself down to the apartment below. Immediately my muscles started cramping. I'd never paid much attention to them and now they were reaping their revenge. I struggled to control my motions, and to not think about the fact that I was nineteen floors up. The wind was terrible, hot and dry from all the fires. A gust picked me up and slammed me against the side of the building. I bounced off the concrete and almost lost my grip. I could feel the bottom of my feet bumping against the balcony's railing and it took all the courage I had to relax enough to climb down just those few extra feet. I landed on my ass, panting and coughing from the smoke. I could hear sounds from my apartment above, the dead that had broken through the front door. I looked up at my balcony and saw a head, the one-eyed siafu was squeezing himself through the opening between the rail and the balcony floor. It hung there for a moment, half out, half in, then gave another lurch toward me and slid over the side. I'll never forget that it was still reaching for me as it fell, this nightmare flash of it suspended in midair, arms out, hanging eyeball now flying upward against its forehead.

I could hear the other siafu groaning on the balcony above and turned to see if there were any in this apartment with me. Fortunately, I saw that the front door had been barricaded like mine. However, unlike mine, there weren't any sounds of attackers outside. I was also comforted by the layer of ash on the carpet. It was deep and unbroken, telling me that no one or nothing had walked across this floor for a couple days. For a moment I thought I might be alone, and then I noticed the smell.

I slid the bathroom door open and was blown back by this invisible, putrid cloud. The woman was in her tub. She had slit her wrists, long, vertical slices along the arteries to make sure the job was done right. Her name was Reiko. She was the only neighbor I'd made any effort to know. She was a high-priced hostess at a club for foreign businessmen. I'd always fantasized about what she'd look like naked. Now I knew.

Strangely enough, what bothered me most was that I didn't know any prayers for the dead. I'd forgotten what my grandparents had tried to teach me as a little kid, rejected it as obsolete data. It was a shame, how out of touch I was with my heritage. All I could do was stand there like an idiot and whisper an awkward apology for taking some of her sheets.

Her sheets?

For more rope. I knew I couldn't stay there for very long. Besides the health hazard of a dead body, there was no telling when the siafu on that floor would sense my presence and attack the barricade. I had to get out of this building, get out of the city, and hopefully try to find a way to get out of Japan. I didn't have a fully thought-out plan yet. I just knew I had to keep going, one floor at a time, until I reached the street. I figured stopping at a few of the apartments would give me a chance to gather supplies, and as dangerous as my sheet-rope method was, it couldn't be any worse than the siafu that would almost certainly be lurking in the building's hallways and stairwells.

Wouldn't it be more dangerous once you reached the streets?

No, safer. [Catches my expression.] No, honestly. That was one of the things I'd learned online. The living dead were slow and easy to outrun or even outwalk. Indoors, I might run the risk of being trapped in some narrow choke point, but out in the open, I had infinite options. Better still, I'd learned from online survivor reports that the chaos of a full-blown outbreak could actually work to one's advantage. With so many other frightened, disorganized humans to distract the siafu, why would they even notice me? As long as I watched my step, kept up a brisk pace, and didn't have the misfortune to be hit by a fleeing motorist or stray bullet, I figured I had a pretty good chance of navigating my way through the chaos on the streets below. The real problem was getting there.

It took me three days to make it all the way down to the ground floor. This was partially due to my disgraceful physical stamina. A trained athlete would have found my makeshift rope antics a challenge so you can imagine what they were for me. In retrospect it's a miracle I didn't plunge to my death or succumb to infection with all the scrapes and scratches I endured. My body was held together with adrenaline and pain medication. I was exhausted, nervous, horribly sleep deprived. I couldn't rest in the conventional sense. Once it got dark I would move everything I could against the door, then sit in a corner, crying, nursing my wounds, and cursing my frailty until the sky began to lighten. I did manage to close my eyes one night, even drift off to sleep for a few minutes, but then the banging of a siafu against the front door sent me scurrying out the window. I spent the remainder of that night huddled on the balcony of the next apartment. Its sliding glass door was locked and I just didn't have the strength to kick it in.

My second delay was mental, not physical, specifically my otaku's obsessive-compulsive drive to find just the right survival gear, no matter how long it took. My online searches had taught me all about the right weapons, clothing, food, and medicine. The problem was finding them in an apartment complex of urban salarymen.

[Laughs.]

I made quite a sight, shimmying down that sheet-rope in a business-man's raincoat and Reiko's bright, pink, vintage "Hello Kitty" schoolbag. It had taken a long time, but by the third day I had almost everything I needed, everything except a reliable weapon.

There wasn't anything?

[Smiles.] This was not America, where there used to be more firearms than people. True fact—an otaku in Kobe hacked this information directly from your National Rifle Association.

I meant a hand tool, a hammer, a crowbar . . .

What salaryman does his own home maintenance? I thought of a golf club—there were many of those—but I saw what the man across the way had tried to do. I did find an aluminum baseball bat, but it had seen so much action that it was too bent out of shape to be effective. I looked everywhere, believe me, but there was nothing hard or strong or sharp enough I could use to defend myself. I also reasoned that once I made it to the street, I might have better luck—a truncheon from a dead policeman or even a soldier's firearm.

Those were the thoughts that almost got me killed. I was four floors from the ground, almost, literally, at the end of my rope. Each section I made extended for several floors, just enough length to allow me to gather more sheets. This time I knew would be the last. By now I had my entire escape plan worked out: land on the fourth-floor balcony, break into the apartment for a new set of sheets (I'd given up looking for a weapon by then), slide down to the sidewalk, steal the most convenient motorcycle (even though I had no idea how to ride one), streaking off like some old-timey *bosozoku*,[4] and maybe even grab a girl or two along the way. [Laughs.] My mind was barely functional by that point. If even the first part of the plan had worked and I did manage to make it to the ground in that state . . . well, what matters is that I didn't.

I landed on the fourth-floor balcony, reached for the sliding door, and looked up right into the face of a siafu. It was a young man, midtwenties, wearing a torn suit. His nose had been bitten off, and he dragged his bloody face across the glass. I jumped back, grabbed on to my rope, and tried to climb back up. My arms wouldn't respond, no pain, no burning—I mean they had just reached their limit. The siafu began howling and beating his fists against the glass. In desperation, I tried to swing myself from side to side, hoping to maybe rappel against the side of the building and land on the balcony next to me. The glass shattered and the siafu charged for my legs. I pushed off from the building, letting go of the rope and launching myself with all my might . . . and I missed.

The only reason we are speaking now is that my diagonal fall carried me onto the balcony below my target. I landed on my feet, stumbled forward, and almost went toppling off the other side. I stumbled into the apartment and immediately looked around for any siafu. The living room was empty, the only piece of furniture a small traditional table propped up against the door. The occupant must have committed suicide like the others. I didn't

4. *Bosozoku:* Japanese youth-oriented motorcycle gangs that reached their popular peak in the 1980s and 1990s.

smell anything foul so I guessed he must have thrown himself out of the window. I reasoned that I was alone, and just this small measure of relief was enough to cause my legs to give out from under me. I slumped against the living room wall, almost delirious with fatigue. I found myself looking at a collection of photographs decorating the opposite wall. The apartment's owner had been an old man, and the photographs told of a very rich life. He'd had a large family, many friends, and had traveled to what seemed every exciting and exotic locale around the world. I'd never even imagined leaving my bedroom, let alone even leading that kind of life. I promised myself that if I ever made it out of this nightmare, I wouldn't just survive, I would *live!*

My eyes fell on the only other item in the room, a Kami Dana, or traditional Shinto shrine. Something was on the floor beneath it, I guessed a suicide note. The wind must have blown it off when I entered. I didn't feel right just leaving it there. I hobbled across the room and stooped to pick it up. Many Kami Dana have a small mirror in the center. My eye caught a reflection in that mirror of something shambling out of the bedroom.

The adrenaline kicked in just as I wheeled around. The old man was still there, the bandage on his face telling me that he must have reanimated not too long ago. He came at me; I ducked. My legs were still shaky and he managed to catch me by the hair. I twisted, trying to free myself. He pulled my face toward his. He was surprisingly fit for his age, muscle equal to, if not superior to, mine. His bones were brittle though, and I heard them crack as I grabbed the arm that caught me. I kicked him in the chest, he flew back, his broken arm was still clutching a tuft of my hair. He knocked against the wall, photographs falling and showering him with glass. He snarled and came at me again. I backed up, tensed, then grabbed him by his one good arm. I jammed it into his back, clamped my other hand around the back of his neck, and with a roaring sound I didn't even know I could make, I shoved him, ran him, right onto the balcony and over the side. He landed face up on the pavement, his head still hissing up at me from his otherwise broken body.

Suddenly there was a pounding on the front door, more siafu that'd heard our scuffle. I was operating on full instinct now. I raced into the old man's bedroom and began ripping the sheets off his bed. I figured it wouldn't take too many, just three more stories and then . . . then I stopped, frozen, as motionless as a photograph. That's what had caught my attention, one last photograph that was on the bare wall in his bedroom. It was black and white, grainy, and showed a traditional family. There was a mother, father, a little boy, and what I guessed had to be the old man as a teenager in uniform. Something was in his hand, something that almost stopped my heart. I bowed to the man in the photograph and said an almost tearful "Arigato."

What was in his hand?

I found it at the bottom of a chest in his bedroom, underneath a collection of bound papers and the ragged remains of the uniform from the photo. The scabbard was green, chipped, army-issue aluminum and an improvised, leather grip had replaced the original sharkskin, but the steel . . . bright like silver, and folded, not machine stamped . . . a shallow, tori curvature with a long, straight point. Flat, wide ridge lines decorated with the kiku-sui, the Imperial chrysanthemum, and an authentic, not acid-stained, river bordering the tempered edge. Exquisite workmanship, and clearly forged for battle.

[I motioned to the sword at his side. Tatsumi smiles.]

KYOTO, JAPAN

[Sensei Tomonaga Ijiro knows exactly who I am seconds before I enter the room. Apparently I walk, smell, and even breathe like an American. The founder of Japan's Tatenokai, or "Shield Society," greets me with both a bow and handshake, then invites me

to sit before him like a student. Kondo Tatsumi, Tomonaga's second in command, serves us tea then sits beside the old master.
Tomonaga begins our interview with an apology for any discomfort I might feel about his appearance. The sensei's lifeless eyes
have not functioned since his adolescence.]

I am "hibakusha." I lost my sight at 11:02 A.M., August 9, 1945, by your
calendar. I was standing on Mount Kompira, manning the air-raid warning
station with several other boys from my class. It was overcast that day, so I
heard, rather than saw, the B-29 passing close overhead. It was only a
single B-san, probably a reconnaissance flight, and not even worth reporting. I almost laughed when my classmates jumped into our slit trench. I
kept my eyes fixed above the Urakami Valley, hoping to maybe catch a
glimpse of the American bomber. Instead, all I saw was the flash, the last
thing I would ever see.

In Japan, hibakusha, "survivors of the bomb," occupied a unique rung in
our nation's social ladder. We were treated with sympathy and sorrow: victims and heroes and symbols for every political agenda. And yet, as human
beings, we were little more than social outcasts. No family would allow
their child to marry us. Hibakusha were unclean, blood in Japan's otherwise pristine genetic onsen.[1] I felt this shame on a deeply personal level.
Not only was I hibakusha, but my blindness also made me a burden.

Out the sanatorium's windows I could hear the sounds of our nation
struggling to rebuild itself. And what was my contribution to this effort,
nothing!

So many times I tried inquiring about some manner of employment,
some work no matter how small or demeaning. No one would have me. I
was still hibakusha, and I learned so many polite ways to be rejected. My
brother begged me to come and stay with him, insisting that he and his
wife would take care of me and even find some "useful" task around the
house. For me that was even worse than the sanatorium. He had just gotten back from the army and they were trying to have another baby. To

1. Onsen: A natural hot spring often used as a communal bath.

impose on them at such a time was unthinkable. Of course, I considered ending my own life. I even attempted it on many occasions. Something prevented me, staying my hand each time I groped for the pills or broken glass. I reasoned it was weakness, what else could it be? A hibakusha, a parasite, and now a dishonorable coward. There was no end to my shame in those days. As the emperor had said in his surrender speech to our people, I was truly "enduring the unendurable."

I left the sanatorium without informing my brother. I didn't know where I was heading, only that I had to get as far from my life, my memories, myself, as possible. I traveled, begged mostly . . . I had no more honor to lose . . . until I settled in Sapporo on the island of Hokkaido. This cold, northern wilderness has always been Japan's least populated prefecture, and with the loss of Sakhalin and the Kuriles, it became, as the Western saying goes, "the end of the line."

In Sapporo, I met an Ainu gardener, Ota Hideki. The Ainu are Japan's oldest indigenous group, and even lower on our social ladder than the Koreans.

Maybe that is why he took pity on me, another pariah cast out by the tribe of Yamato. Maybe it was because he had no one to pass his skills along to. His own son had never returned from Manchuria. Ota-san worked at the Akakaze, a former luxury hotel that now served as a repatriation center for Japanese settlers from China. At first the administration complained that they had no more funds to hire another gardener. Ota-san paid me out of his own pocket. He was my teacher and only friend, and when he died, I considered following him. But, coward that I was, I could not bring myself to do it. Instead I simply continued to exist, working silently in the earth as the Akakaze went from a repatriation center to a luxury hotel and Japan went from conquered rubble to economic superpower.

I was still working at the Akakaze when I heard of the first domestic outbreak. I was trimming the Western-style hedges near the restaurant, when I overheard several of the guests discussing the Nagumo murders. According to their conversation, a man had slain his wife, then set upon the corpse like some kind of wild dog. This was the first time I had heard the term "African rabies." I tried to ignore it and get on with my work, but the next day there were more conversations, more hushed voices across the lawn and beside the pool. Nagumo was old news compared to the much more serious outbreak at Sumitomo Hospital in Osaka. And the next day there was Nagoya, then Sendai, then Kyoto. I tried to push their conversations from my mind. I had come to Hokkaido to escape from the world, to live out my days in shame and ignominy.

The voice that finally convinced me of danger came from the hotel's manager, a stiff, no-nonsense salaryman with a very formal manner of speech. After the outbreak in Hirosaki, he held a staff meeting to try to debunk, once and for all, these wild rumors about dead bodies coming back to life. I had only his voice to rely on, and you can tell everything about a person by what happens when he opens his mouth. Mister Sugawara was pronouncing his words far too carefully, particularly his hard, sharp consonants. He was overcompensating for a previously conquered speech impediment, a condition that only threatened to rise in the presence of great anxiety. I had listened to this verbal defense mechanism before from the seemingly unflappable Sugawara-san, first during the '95 quake, and again in '98 when North Korea had sent a long-range, nuclear-capable "test missile" streaking over our homeland. Sugawara-san's articulation had been almost imperceptible then, now it shrieked louder than the air-raid sirens of my youth.

And so, for the second time in my life, I fled. I considered warning my brother, but so much time had passed, I had no idea how to reach him or even if he was still alive. That was the last, and probably the greatest of all my dishonorable acts, the heaviest weight I will carry to my grave.

Why did you run? Were you afraid for your life?

Of course not! If anything I welcomed it! To die, to finally be put out of my lifelong misery was almost too good to be true . . . What I feared was, once again, becoming a burden to those around me. To slow someone down, to take up valuable space, to put other lives in danger if they tried to save an old blind man who wasn't worth saving . . . and what if those rumors about the dead returning to life were true? What if I were to find myself infected and awake from death to threaten the lives of my fellow countrymen? No, that was not going to be the fate of this disgraced hibakusha. If I was to meet my death, it should be in the same manner as I had lived my life. Forgotten, isolated, and alone.

I left at night and began hitchhiking south down Hokkaido's DOO Expressway. All I had with me was a water bottle, a change of clothes, and my ikupasuy,[2] a long, flat shovel similar to a Shaolin spade but which also served for many years as my walking stick. There was still a sizable amount of road traffic in those days—our oil from Indonesia and the Gulf was still flowing—and many truck drivers and private motorists were kind enough to give me a "ride." With each and every one, our conversation turned to the crisis: "Did you hear that the Self Defense Force has been mobilized?"; "The government's going to have to declare a state of emergency"; "Did you hear there was an outbreak last night, right here in Sapporo?" No one was sure what the next day would bring, how far the calamity would spread, or who would be its next victim, and yet, no matter whom I spoke to or how terrified they sounded, each conversation would inevitably end with "But I'm sure the authorities will tell us what to do." One truck driver said, "Any day now, you'll see, if you just wait patiently and don't make a public fuss." That was the last human voice I heard, the day before I left civilization and trekked into the Hiddaka Mountains.

I was very familiar with this national park. Ota-san had taken me here every year to collect sansai, the wild vegetables that attract botanists, hikers, and gourmet chefs from all over the home islands. As a man who often rises in the middle of the night knows the exact location of every item in his darkened bedroom, I knew every river and every rock, every

---

2. Ikupasuy: The technical term for a small, Ainu prayer stick. When later questioned about this discrepancy, Mister Tomonaga answered that the name was given to him by his teacher, Mister Ota. Whether Ota intended to bestow some spiritual connection to this gardening implement or was simply so out of touch with his own culture (as many Ainu of his generation were), we will never know.

tree and patch of moss. I even knew every onsen that bubbled to the surface, and therefore never wanted for a naturally hot and cleansing mineral bath. Every day I told myself "This is the perfect place to die, soon I will have an accident, a fall of some kind, or perhaps I will become ill, contract some sickness or eat a poisoned root, or maybe I will finally do the honorable thing and just stop eating altogether." And yet, every day, I foraged and bathed, dressed warmly and minded my steps. As much as I longed for death, I continued to take whatever measures necessary to prevent it.

I had no way of knowing what was happening to the rest of my country. I could hear distant sounds, helicopters, fighter planes, the steady, high-altitude whine of civilian jetliners. Perhaps I was wrong, I thought, perhaps the crisis was over. For all I knew, the "authorities" had been victorious, and the danger was rapidly fading into memory. Perhaps my alarmist departure had done nothing more than create a welcome job opening back at the Akakaze and perhaps, one morning, I would be roused by the barking voices of angry park rangers, or the giggles and whispers of schoolchildren on a nature hike. Something did arouse me from my sleep one morning, but not a collection of giggling students, and no, it wasn't one of *them* either.

It was a bear, one of the many large, brown higuma roaming the Hokkaido wilderness. The higuma had originally migrated from the Kamchatka Peninsula and bore the same ferocity and raw power of their Siberian cousins. This one was enormous, I could tell by the pitch and resonance of his breathing. I judged him to be no more than four or five meters from me. I rose slowly, and without fear. Next to me lay my ikupasuy. It was the closest thing I had to a weapon, and, I suppose, if I had thought to use it as such, it might have made a formidable defense.

You didn't use it.

Nor did I want it. This animal was much more than just a random, hungry predator. This was fate, I believed. This encounter could only be the will of the kami.

Who is Kami?

What is kami. The kami are the spirits that inhabit each and every facet of our existence. We pray to them, honor them, hope to please them and curry their favor. They are the same spirits that drive Japanese corporations to bless the site of a soon-to-be constructed factory, and the Japanese of my generation to worship the emperor as a god. The kami are the foundation of Shinto, literally "The Way of the Gods," and worship of nature is one of its oldest, and most sacred principles.

That is why I believed their will was at work that day. By exiling myself into the wilderness, I had polluted nature's purity. After dishonoring myself, my family, my country, I had at last taken that final step and dishonored the gods. Now they had sent an assassin to do what I had been unable to for so long, to erase my stink. I thanked the gods for their mercy. I wept as I prepared myself for the blow.

It never came. The bear stopped panting then released a high, almost childlike whimper. "What is wrong with you?" I actually said to a three-hundred-kilogram carnivore. "Go on and finish me!" The bear continued to whine like a frightened dog, then tore away from me with the speed of hunted prey. It was then that I heard the moan. I spun, tried to focus my ears. From the height of his mouth, I could tell he was taller than me. I heard one foot dragging across the soft, moist earth and air bubbling from a gaping wound in its chest.

I could hear it reaching out to me, groaning and swiping at empty air. I managed to dodge its clumsy attempt and snatched up my ikupasuy. I centered my attack on the source of the creature's moan. I struck quickly, and the crack vibrated up through my arms. The creature fell back upon the earth as I released a triumphant shout of "Ten Thousand Years!"

It is difficult for me to describe my feelings at this moment. Fury had exploded within my heart, a strength and courage that drove away my shame as the sun drives the night from heaven. I suddenly knew the gods had favored me. The bear hadn't been sent to kill me, it had been sent to warn me. I didn't understand the reason right then, but I knew I had to survive until the day when that reason was finally revealed.

And that is what I did for the next few months: I survived. I mentally divided the Hiddaka range into a series of several hundred chi-tai.[3] Each chi-tai contained some object of physical security—a tree or tall, flat rock—some place I could sleep in peace without the danger of immediate attack. I slept always during the day, and only traveled, foraged, or hunted at night. I did not know if the beasts depended on their sight as much as human beings, but I wasn't going to give them even the most infinitesimal advantage.[4]

Losing my vision had also prepared me for the act of ever-vigilant mobility. Those with sight have a tendency to take walking for granted; how else could they trip over something they've clearly seen? The fault lies not in the eyes, but in the mind, a lazy thought process spoiled by a lifetime of optic nerve dependency. Not so for those like me. I already had to be on guard for potential danger, to be focused, alert, and "watching my step," so to speak. Simply adding one more threat was no bother at all. Every time I walked, it was for no longer than several hundred paces. I would halt, listen to and smell the wind, perhaps even press my ear to the ground. This method never failed me. I was never surprised, never caught off guard.

Was there ever a problem with long-range detection, not being able to see an attacker several miles away?

My nocturnal activity would have prevented the use of healthy eyesight, and any beast several kilometers away was no more a threat to me than I was to it. There was no need to be on my guard until they entered what you might call my "circle of sensory security," the maximum range of my ears, nose, fingertips, and feet. On the best of days, when the conditions were right and Haya-ji[5] was in a helpful mood, that circle extended as far as half a kilometer. On the worst of days, that range might drop to no more than thirty, possibly fifteen paces. These incidents were infrequent at best,

3. Chi-tai: Zone.
4. To this day, it is unknown how much the living dead depend on sight.
5. Haya-ji: God of the wind.

occurring if I had done something to truly anger the kami, although I can't possibly imagine what that would be. The beasts were a great help as well, always being courteous enough to warn me before attacking.

That howling alarm that ignites the moment they detect prey would not only alert me to the presence of an attacking creature, but even to the direction, range, and exact position of the attack. I would hear that moan wafting across the hills and fields and know that, in perhaps half an hour or so, one of the living dead would be paying me a visit. In instances such as these I would halt, then patiently prepare myself for the attack. I would unclasp my pack, stretch my limbs, sometimes just find a place to sit quietly and meditate. I always knew when they were getting close enough to strike. I always took the time to bow and thank them for being so courteous to warn me. I almost felt sorry for the poor mindless filth, to come all this way, slowly and methodically, only to end their journey with a split skull or severed neck.

Did you always kill your enemy on the first strike?

Always.

[He gestures with an imaginary ikupasuy.]

Thrust forward, never swing. At first I would aim for the base of the neck. Later, as my skills grew with time and experience, I learned to strike here . . .

[He places his hand horizontally against the indentation between the forehead and nose.]

It was a little harder than simple decapitation, all that thick tough bone, but it did serve to destroy the brain, as opposed to decapitation where the living head would always require a secondary blow.

What about multiple attackers? Was that more of a problem?

Yes, in the beginning. As their numbers swelled, I began to find myself increasingly surrounded. Those early battles were . . . "untidy." I must admit, I allowed my emotions to rule my hand. I was the typhoon, not the lightning bolt. During one melee at "Tokachi-dake," I dispatched forty-one in as many minutes. I was washing bodily fluids from my clothes for a fortnight. Later, as I began to exercise more tactical creativity, I allowed the gods to join me on the battlefield. I would lead groups of beasts to the base of a tall rock, where I would crush their skulls from above. I might even find a rock that allowed them to climb up after me, not all at once, you understand, one by one, so I could knock them back into the jagged outcroppings below. I was sure to thank the spirit of each rock, or cliff, or waterfall that carried them over thousand-meter drops. This last incident was not something I cared to make a habit of. It was a long and arduous climb to retrieve the body.

You went after the corpse?

To bury it. I couldn't just leave it there, desecrating the stream. It would not have been . . . "proper."

Did you retrieve all the bodies?

Every last one. That time, after Tokachi-dake, I dug for three days. The heads I always separated; most of the time I just burned them, but at Tokachi-dake, I threw them into the volcanic crater where Oyamatsumi's[6] rage could purge their stench. I did not completely understand why I committed these acts. It just felt correct, to separate the source of the evil.

The answer came to me on the eve of my second winter in exile. This would be my last night in the branches of a tall tree. Once the snow fell, I would return to the cave where I had spent the previous winter. I had just

6. Oyamatsumi: Ruler of mountains and volcanoes.

settled in comfortably, waiting for dawn's warmth to lull me to sleep, when I heard the sound of footsteps, too quick and energetic to be a beast. Haya-ji had decided to be favorable that night. He brought the smell of what could only be a human being. I had come to realize that the living dead were surprisingly bereft of odor. Yes, there was the subtle hint of decomposition, stronger, perhaps, if the body had been turned for some time, or if chewed flesh had pushed through its bowels and collected in a rotting heap in its undergarments. Other than this, though, the living dead possessed what I refer to as a "scentless stink." They produced no sweat, no urine, or conventional feces. They did not even carry the bacteria within their stomach or teeth that, in living humans, would have fouled their breath. None of this was true of the two-legged animal rapidly approaching my position. His breath, his body, his clothes, all had clearly not been washed for some time.

It was still dark so he did not notice me. I could tell that his path would take him directly underneath the limbs of my tree. I crouched slowly, quietly. I wasn't sure if he was hostile, insane, or even recently bitten. I was taking no chances.

[At this point, Kondo chimes in.]

KONDO: He was on me before I knew it. My sword went flying, my feet collapsed from under me.

TOMONAGA: I landed between his shoulder blades, not hard enough to do any permanent damage, but enough to knock the wind out of his slight, malnourished frame.

KONDO: He had me on my stomach, my face in the dirt, the blade of his shovel-thing pressed tightly against the back of my neck.

TOMONAGA: I told him to lie still, that I would kill him if he moved.

KONDO: I tried to speak, gasping between coughs that I was friendly, that I didn't even know he was there, that all I wanted to do was pass along and be on my way.

TOMONAGA: I asked him where he was going.

KONDO: I told him Nemuro, the main Hokkaido port of evacuation, where there might still be one last transport, or fishing boat, or . . . something that might still be left to get me to Kamchatka.

TOMONAGA: I did not understand. I ordered him to explain.

KONDO: I described everything, about the plague, the evacuation. I cried when I told him that Japan had been completely abandoned, that Japan was nai.

TOMONAGA: And suddenly I knew. I knew why the gods had taken my sight, why they sent me to Hokkaido to learn how to care for the land, and why they had sent the bear to warn me.

KONDO: He began to laugh as he let me up and helped to brush the dirt from my clothing.

TOMONAGA: I told him that Japan had not been abandoned, not by those whom the gods had chosen to be its gardeners.

KONDO: At first I didn't understand . . .

TOMONAGA : So I explained that, like any garden, Japan could not be allowed to wither and die. We would care for her, we would preserve her, we would annihilate the walking blight that infested and defiled her and we would restore her beauty and purity for the day when her children would return to her.

KONDO: I thought he was insane, and told him so right to his face. The two of us against millions of siafu?

TOMONAGA: I handed his sword back to him; its weight and balance felt familiar to the touch. I told him that we might be facing fifty million monsters, but those monsters would be facing the gods.

CIENFUEGOS, CUBA

[Seryosha Garcia Alvarez suggests I meet him at his office. "The view is breathtaking," he promises. "You will not be disappointed." On the sixty-ninth floor of the Malpica Savings and

Loans building, the second-tallest building in Cuba after Havana's
José Martí Towers, Señor Alvarez's corner office overlooks both
the glittering metropolis and bustling harbor below. It is the
"magic hour" for energy-independent buildings like the Malpica,
that time of the day when it's photovoltaic windows capture the
setting sun with their almost imperceptible magenta hue. Señor
Alvarez was right. I am not disappointed.]

Cuba won the Zombie War; maybe that's not the most humble of state-
ments, given what happened to so many other countries, but just look at
where we were twenty years ago as opposed to where we are now.

Before the war, we lived in a state of quasi-isolation, worse than during
the height of the cold war. At least in my father's day you could count on
what amounted to economic welfare from the Soviet Union and their
ComEcon puppets. Since the fall of the communist bloc, though, our existence was one of constant deprivation. Rationed food, rationed fuel . . .
the closest comparison I can make is that of Great Britain during the Blitz,
and like that other besieged island, we too lived under the dark cloud of an
ever-present enemy.

The U.S. blockade, while not as constricting as during the cold war,
nonetheless sought to suffocate our economic lifeblood by punishing any
nation that attempted free and open trade. As successful as the U.S. strategy was, its most resounding triumph was allowing Fidel to use our northern oppressor as an excuse to remain in power. "You see how hard your life
is," he would say. "The blockade has done this to you, the Yankees have
done this to you, and without me, they would be storming our beaches
even now!" He was brilliant, Machiavelli's most favored son. He knew we
would never remove him while the enemy was at the gates. And so we endured the hardships and the oppression, the long lines and the hushed
voices. This was the Cuba I grew up in, the only Cuba I could ever imagine. That is, until the dead began to rise.

Cases were small and immediately contained, mostly Chinese refugees
and a few European businessmen. Travel from the United States was still
largely prohibited, so we were spared the initial blow of first-wave mass mi-

gration. The repressive nature of our fortress society allowed the government to take steps to ensure that the infection was never allowed to
spread. All internal travel was suspended, and both the regular army and
territorial militias were mobilized. Because Cuba had such a high percentage of doctors per capita, our leader knew the true nature of the infection
weeks after the first outbreak was reported.

By the time of the Great Panic, when the world finally woke up to the
nightmare breaking down their doors, Cuba had already prepared itself
for war.

The simple fact of geography spared us the danger of large-scale, overland swarms. Our invaders came from the sea, specifically from an armada
of boat people. Not only did they bring the contagion, as we have seen
throughout the world, there were also those who believed in ruling their
new homes as modern-day conquistadors.

Look at what happened in Iceland, a prewar paradise, so safe and secure
they never found the need to maintain a standing army. What could they
do when the American military withdrew? How could they stop the torrent of refugees from Europe and western Russia? Is it no mystery how that
once idyllic arctic haven became a cauldron of frozen blood, and why, to
this day, it is still the most heavily infested White Zone on the planet?
That could have been us, easily, had it not been for the example set by our
brothers in the smaller Windward and Leeward Islands.

Those men and women, from Anguilla to Trinidad, can proudly take
their place as some of the greatest heroes of the war. They first eradicated
multiple outbreaks along their archipelago, then, with barely a moment to
catch their collective breaths, repelled not only seaborne zombies, but an
endless flood of human invaders, too. They spilled their blood so that we
did not have to. They forced our would-be latifundista to reconsider their
plans for conquest, and realize that if a few civilians armed with nothing
but small arms and machetes could defend their homelands so tenaciously,
what would they find on the shores of a country armed with everything
from main battle tanks to radar-guided antiship missiles?

Naturally, the inhabitants of the Lesser Antilles were not fighting for
the best interests of the Cuban people, but their sacrifices did allow us the

luxury of setting our own terms. Any seeking sanctuary would find themselves greeted with the saying so common among Norteamericano parents,
"While under my roof, you will obey my rules."

Not all of the refugees were Yankees; we had our share from mainland
Latin America, from Africa, and western Europe, Spain especially—many
Spaniards and Canadians had visited Cuba either on business or holiday. I
had gotten to know a few of them before the war, nice people, polite, so
different from the East Germans of my youth who used to toss handfuls of
candy in the air and laugh while we children scrambled for it like rats.

The majority of our boat people, however, originated from the United
States. Every day more would arrive, by large ship or private craft, even on
homemade rafts that brought an ironic smile to our faces. So many of
them, a total of five million, equal to almost half of our indigenous population, and along with all the other nationalities, they were placed under the
jurisdiction of the government's "Quarantine Resettlement Program."

I would not go so far as to call the Resettlement Centers prison camps.
They could not compare to the lives suffered by our political dissidents;
the writers and teachers . . . I had a "friend" who was accused of being a
homosexual. His stories from prison cannot compare to even the harshest
Resettlement Center.

It was not easy living, however. These people, no matter what their prewar occupation or status, were initially put to work as field hands, twelve
to fourteen hours a day, growing vegetables in what had once been our
state-run sugar plantations. At least the climate was on their side. The
temperature was dropping, the skies were darkening. Mother Nature was
kind to them. The guards, however, were not. "Be glad you're alive," they'd
shout after each slap or kick. "Keep complaining and we'll throw you to
the zombies!"

Every camp had a rumor about the dreaded "zombie pits," the hole in
which they'd throw the "troublemakers." The DGI [the General Intelligence
Directorate] had even planted prisoners in the general population to spread
stories about how they personally witnessed men being lowered, headfirst,
into the boiling lake of ghouls. This was all just to keep everyone in line,
you see, none of it was actually true . . . though . . . there were stories about

the "Miami whites." The majority of American Cubanos were welcomed home with open arms. I myself had several relatives living in Daytona who just barely escaped with their lives. The tears of so many reunions in those early, frantic days could have filled the Caribbean Sea. But that first wave of postrevolution immigrants—the affluent elite who had flourished under the old regime and who spent the rest of their lives trying to topple everything we'd worked so hard to build—as far as those aristos were concerned . . . I am not saying there is any proof that they were thrown to the ghouls by their fat, reactionary, Bacardi blanka drinking asses . . . But if they were, they can suck Batista's balls in hell.

[A thin, satisfied smile crosses his lips.]

Of course, we couldn't have actually attempted this kind of punishment with your people. Rumors and threats were one thing, but physical action . . . push a people, any people too far, and you risk the possibility of revolt. Five million Yankees, all rising in open revolution? Unthinkable. It already took too many troops to maintain the camps, and that was the initial success of the Yankee invasion of Cuba.

We simply didn't have the manpower to guard five million detainees and almost four thousand kilometers of coastline. We couldn't fight a war on two fronts. And so the decision was made to dissolve the centers and allow 10 percent of the Yankee detainees to work outside the wire on a specialized parole program. These detainees would do the jobs Cubanos no longer wanted—day laborers, dish washers, and street cleaners—and while their wages would be next to nothing, their labor hours would go to a point system that allowed them to buy the freedom of other detainees.

It was an ingenious idea—some Florida Cubano came up with it—and the camps were drained in six months. At first the government tried to keep track of all of them, but that soon proved impossible. Within a year they had almost fully integrated, the "Nortecubanos," insinuating themselves into every facet of our society.

Officially the camps had been created to contain the spread of "infection," but that wasn't the kind spread by the dead.

You couldn't see this infection at first, not when we were still under siege. It was still behind closed doors, still spoken in whispers. Over the next several years what occurred was not so much a revolution as an evolution, an economic reform here, a legalized, privately owned newspaper there. People began to think more boldly, talk more boldly. Slowly, quietly, the seeds began to take root. I'm sure Fidel would have loved to bring his iron fist crashing down on our fledgling freedoms. Perhaps he might have, if world events had not shifted in our favor. It was when the world governments decided to go on the attack that everything changed forever.

Suddenly we became "the Arsenal of Victory." We were the breadbasket, the manufacturing center, the training ground, and the springboard. We became the air hub for both North and South America, the great dry dock for ten thousand ships.[1] We had money, lots of it, money that created an overnight middle class, and a thriving, capitalist economy that needed the refined skills and practical experience of the Nortecubanos.

We shared a bond I don't think can ever be broken. We helped them reclaim their nation, and they helped us reclaim ours. They showed us the meaning of democracy . . . freedom, not just in vague, abstract terms, but on a very real, individually human level. Freedom isn't just something you have for the sake of having, you have to want something else first and then want the freedom to fight for it. That was the lesson we learned from the Nortecubanos. They all had such grand dreams, and they'd lay down their lives for the freedom to make those dreams come true. Why else would El Jefe be so damned afraid of them?

I'm not surprised that Fidel knew the tides of freedom were coming to sweep him out of power. I am surprised at how well he rode the wave.

[He laughs, gesturing to a photo on the wall of an aged Castro speaking in the Parque Central.]

1. The exact number of allied and neutral ships that anchored in Cuban ports during the war is still unknown.

Can you believe the cojones of that son of a bitch, to not only embrace the country's new democracy, but to actually take credit for it? Genius. To personally preside over the first free elections of Cuba where his last official act was to vote himself out of power. That is why his legacy is a statue and not a bloodstain against a wall. Of course our new Latin superpower is anything but idyllic. We have hundreds of political parties and more special-interest groups than sands on our beaches. We have strikes, we have riots, we have protests, it seems, almost every day. You can see why Che ducked out right after the revolution. It's a lot easier to blow up trains than to make them run on time. What is it that Mister Churchill used to say? "Democracy is the worst form of government, except for all the others." [He laughs.]

PATRIOT'S MEMORIAL, THE FORBIDDEN CITY, BEIJING, CHINA

[I suspect Admiral Xu Zhicai has chosen this particular spot on the off chance that a photographer would be present. Although no one since the war has ever remotely questioned either his or his crew's patriotism, he is taking no chances for the eyes of "foreign readers." Initially defensive, he consents to this interview only on the condition that I listen objectively to "his" side of the story, a demand he clings to even after I explain that there is no other.]

[Note: For the sake of clarity, Western naval designations have replaced the authentic Chinese.]

We were not traitors—I say this before I'll say anything else. We loved our country, we loved our people, and while we may not have loved those who ruled both, we were unwaveringly loyal to our leadership.

We never would have imagined doing what we did had not the situation become so desperate. By the time Captain Chen first voiced his proposal, we were already on the brink. They were in every city, every village. In the nine and a half million square kilometers that made up our country, you couldn't find one centimeter of peace.

The army, arrogant bastards that they were, kept insisting that they had the problem under control, that every day was the turning point and before the next snow fell upon the earth they would have the entire country pacified. Typical army thinking: overaggressive, overconfident. All you need is a group of men, or women, give them matching clothes, a few hours training, something that passes for a weapon, and you have an army, not the best army, but still an army nonetheless.

That can't happen with the navy, any navy. Any ship, no matter how crude, requires considerable energy and materials to create. The army can replace its cannon fodder in hours; for us, it might take years. This tends to make us more pragmatic than our compatriots in green. We tend to look at a situation with a bit more . . . I don't want to say caution, but perhaps more strategic conservatism. Withdraw, consolidate, husband your resources. That was the same philosophy as the Redeker Plan, but of course, the army wouldn't listen.

They rejected Redeker?

Without the slightest consideration or internal debate. How could the army ever lose? With their vast stockpiles of conventional armaments, with their "bottomless well" of manpower . . . "bottomless well," unforgivable. Do you know why we had such a population explosion during the 1950s? Because Mao believed it was the only way to win a nuclear war. This is truth, not propaganda. It was common knowledge that when the atomic dust eventually settled, only a few thousand American or Soviet survivors would be overwhelmed by tens of millions of Chinese. Numbers, that was the philosophy of my grandparents' generation, and it was the strategy the army was quick to adopt once our experienced, professional troops were devoured in the outbreak's early stages. Those generals, sick, twisted old criminals sitting safely in their bunker and ordering wave after wave of conscripted teenagers into battle. Did they even think that every dead soldier was now a live zombie? Did they ever realize that, instead of drowning them in our bottomless well, we were the ones drowning, choking to death as the most populous nation on Earth found itself, for the first time in history, in danger of becoming fatally outnumbered?

That was what pushed Captain Chen over the edge. He knew what would happen if the war continued along its course, and what our chances for survival would be. If he thought that there was any hope, he would have grabbed a rifle and hurled himself at the living dead. He was convinced that soon there would be no more Chinese people, and perhaps, eventually, no more people anywhere. That was why he made his intentions known to his senior officers, declaring that we might be the only chance of preserving something of our civilization.

Did you agree with his proposal?

I didn't even believe it at first. Escape in our boat, our nuclear submarine? This wasn't just desertion, slinking out in the middle of a war to save our own pathetic skins. This was stealing one of the motherland's most valuable national assets. The *Admiral Zheng He* was only one of three ballistic missiles subs and the newest of what the West referred to as the Type 94. She was the child of four parents: Russian assistance, black-market technology, the fruits of anti-American espionage, and, let us not forget, the culmination of nearly five thousand years of continuous Chinese history. She was the most expensive, the most advanced, the most powerful machine our nation had ever constructed. To simply steal her, like a lifeboat from the sinking ship of China, was inconceivable. It was only Captain Chen's force of personality, his deep, fanatical patriotism that convinced me of our only alternative.

How long did it take to prepare?

Three months. It was hell. Qingdao, our home port, was in a constant state of siege. More and more army units were called in to maintain order, and each was just a little less trained, a little less equipped, a little younger, or older, than the one that came before it. Some of the surface ship captains had to donate "expendable" crew to shore up base defenses. Our perimeter was under attack almost every day. And through all of this we had to prepare and provision the boat for sea. It was supposed to be a routinely scheduled patrol; we had to smuggle on board both emergency supplies and family members.

Family members?

Oh yes, that was the cornerstone of the plan. Captain Chen knew the crew wouldn't leave port unless their families could come with them.

How was that possible?

To find them or to smuggle them aboard?

Both.

Finding them was difficult. Most of us had family scattered throughout the country. We did our best to communicate with them, get a phone line working or send word with an army unit headed in that direction. The message was always the same: we'd be heading back out on patrol soon and their presence was required at the ceremony. Sometimes we'd try to make it more urgent, as if someone was dying and needed to see them. That was the best we could do. No one was allowed to go out and physically get them: too risky. We didn't have multiple crews like you do on your missile boats. Every rating would be missed at sea. I pitied my shipmates, the agony of their waiting. I was lucky that my wife and children . . .

Children? I thought . . .

That we were only allowed one child? That law was modified years before the war, a practical solution to the problem of an imbalanced nation of only-child sons. I had twin daughters. I was lucky. My wife and children were already on base when the trouble started.

What about the captain? Did he have family?

His wife had left him in the early eighties. It was a devastating scandal, especially in those days. It still astounds me how he managed to both salvage his career and raise his son.

He had a son? Did he come with you?

[Xu evades the question.]

The worst part for many others was the waiting, knowing that even if they managed to make it to Qingdao, there was a very good chance that we might have already sailed. Imagine the guilt. You ask your family to come to you, perhaps leave the relative safety of their preexisting hideout, and arrive only to be abandoned at the dock.

Did many of them show up?

More than one would have guessed. We smuggled them aboard at night, wearing uniforms. Some—children and the elderly—were carried in supply crates.

Did the families know what was happening? What you were intending to do?

I don't believe so. Every member of our crew had strict orders to keep silent. Had the MSS even had a whiff of what we were up to, the living dead would have been the least of our fears. Our secrecy also forced us to depart according to our routine patrol schedule. Captain Chen wanted so badly to wait for stragglers, family members who might be perhaps only a few days, a few hours, away! He knew it might have jeopardized everything, however, and reluctantly gave the order to cast off. He tried to hide his feelings and I think, in front of most, he might have gotten away with it. I could see it in his eyes though, reflecting the receding fires of Qingdao.

Where were you headed?

First to our assigned patrol sector, just so everything would initially seem normal. After that, no one knew.

A new home, at least for the time being, was out of the question. By this point the blight had spread to every corner of the planet. No neutral country, no matter how remote, could guarantee our safety.

What about coming over to our side, America, or another Western country?

[He flashes a cold, hard stare.]

Would you? The *Zheng* carried sixteen JL-2 ballistic missiles; all but one carried four multiple reentry warheads, with a ninety-kiloton yield. That made her equivalent to one of the strongest nations in the world, enough power to murder entire cities with just the turn of a key. Would you turn that power over to another country, the one country up until that point that had used nuclear weapons in anger? Again, and for the last time, we were *not* traitors. No matter how criminally insane our leadership might have been, we were still Chinese sailors.

So you were alone.

All alone. No home, no friends, no safe harbor no matter how harsh the storm. The *Admiral Zheng He* was our entire universe: heaven, earth, sun, and moon.

That must have been very difficult.

The first few months passed as though it was merely a regular patrol. Missile subs are designed to hide, and that's what we did. Deep and silent. We weren't sure if our own attack subs were out looking for us. In all probability our government had other worries. Still, regular battle drills were conducted and the civilians trained in the art of noise discipline. The chief of the boat even rigged special soundproofing for the mess hall so it could be both a schoolroom and play area for the children. The children, especially the younger ones, had no idea what was happening. Many of them had even traveled with their families across infested areas, some barely escaping with their lives. All they knew was that the monsters were gone, banished to their occasional nightmares. They were safe now, and that's all that mattered. I guess that is how we all felt those first few months. We were alive, we were together, we were safe. Given what was happening to the rest of the planet, what more could we want?

Did you have some way of monitoring the crisis?

Not immediately. Our goal was stealth, avoiding both commercial shipping lanes and submarine patrol sectors . . . ours, and yours. We speculated, though. How fast was it spreading? Which countries were the most affected? Was anyone using the nuclear option? If so, that would be the end for all of us. In a radiated planet, the walking dead might be the only creatures left "alive." We weren't sure what high doses of radiation would do to a zombie's brain. Would it eventually kill them, riddling their gray matter with multiple, expanding tumors? That would be the case for a regular human brain, but since the living dead contradicted every other law of nature, why should this reaction be any different? Some nights in the wardroom, speaking in low voices over our off-duty tea, we conjured images of zombies as fast as cheetahs, as agile as apes, zombies with mutated brains that grew and throbbed and burst from the confines of their skulls. Lieutenant Commander Song, our reactor officer, had brought aboard his watercolors and had painted the scene of a city in ruins. He tried to say that it wasn't any city in particular but we all recognized the twisted remains of the Pudong skyline. Song had grown up in Shanghai. The broken horizon glowed a dull magenta against the pitch-black sky of nuclear winter. A rain of ash peppered the islands of debris that rose from lakes of melted glass. Snaking through the center of this apocalyptic backdrop was a river, a greenish-brown snake that rose up into a head of a thousand interconnected bodies: cracked skin, exposed brain, flesh dripping from bony arms that reached out from openmouthed faces with red, glowing eyes. I don't know when Commander Song began his project, only that he secretly unveiled it to a few of us after our third month at sea. He never intended to show it to Captain Chen. He knew better. But someone must have talked and the Old Man soon put a stop to it.

Song was ordered to paint over his work with something cheerful, a summer sunset over Lake Dian. He then followed up with several more "positive" murals on any space of exposed bulkhead. Captain Chen also ordered a halt to all off-duty speculation. "Detrimental to the morale of the crew." I think it pushed him, though, to reestablish some semblance of contact with the outside world.

Semblance as in active communication, or passive surveillance?

The latter. He knew Song's painting and our apocalyptic discussions were the result of our long-term isolation. The only way to quell any further "dangerous thought" was to replace speculation with hard facts. We'd been in total blackout for almost a hundred days and nights. We needed to know what was happening, even if it was as dark and hopeless as Song's painting.

Up until this point, our sonar officer and his team were the only ones with any knowledge of the world beyond our hull. These men listened to the sea: the currents, the "biologics" such as fish and whales, and the distant thrashing of nearby propellers. I said before that our course had taken us to the most remote recesses of the world's oceans. We had intentionally chosen areas where no ship would normally be detected. Over the previous months, however, Liu's team had been collecting an increasing number of random contacts. Thousands of ships were now crowding the surface, many of them with signatures that did not match our computer archive.

The captain ordered the boat to periscope depth. The ESM mast went up and was flooded with hundreds of radar signatures; the radio mast suffered a similar deluge. Finally the scopes, both the search and main attack periscopes, broke the surface. It's not like you see in the movies, a man flipping down the handles and staring through a telescopic eyepiece. These scopes don't penetrate the inner hull. Each one is a video camera with its signal relayed to monitors throughout the boat. We couldn't believe what we were seeing. It was as if humanity was putting everything they had to sea. We spotted tankers, freighters, cruise ships. We saw tugboats towing barges, we saw hydrofoils, garbage scows, bottom dredgers, and all of this within the first hour.

Over the next few weeks, we observed dozens of military vessels, too, any of which could have probably detected us, but none of which seemed to care. You know the USS *Saratoga?* We saw her, being towed across the South Atlantic, her flight deck now a tent city. We saw a ship that had to be HMS *Victory*, plying the waves under a forest of improvised sails. We saw the *Aurora*, the actual World War I–era heavy cruiser whose mutiny had sparked the Bolshevik Revolution. I don't know how they got her out of Saint Petersburg, or how they found enough coal to keep her boilers lit.

There were so many beat-up hulks that should have been retired years ago: skiffs, ferries, and lighters that had spent their careers on quiet lakes or inland rivers, coastal crafts that should have never left the harbor for which they'd been designed. We saw a floating dry dock the size of an overturned skyscraper, her deck now stuffed with construction scaffolding that served as makeshift apartments. She was drifting aimlessly, no tug or support vessel in sight. I don't know how those people survived, or even if they survived. There were a lot of drifting ships, their fuel bunkers dry, no way to generate power.

We saw many small private boats, yachts, and cabin cruisers that had lashed themselves together to form giant directionless rafts. We saw many purpose-built rafts as well, made from logs or tires.

We even came across a nautical shantytown constructed atop hundreds of garbage bags filled with Styrofoam packing peanuts. It reminded us all of the "Ping-Pong Navy," the refugees who, during the Cultural Revolution, had tried to float to Hong Kong on sacks filled with Ping-Pong balls.

We pitied these people, pitied what could only be their hopeless fate. To be adrift in the middle of the ocean, and prey to hunger, thirst, sunstroke, or the sea herself . . . Commander Song called it "humanity's great regression." "We came from the sea," he would say, "and now we're running back." Running was an accurate term. These people clearly hadn't put any thought into what they would do once they reached the "safety" of the waves. They just figured it was better than being torn apart back on land. In their panic they probably didn't realize they were just prolonging the inevitable.

Did you ever try to help them? Give them food or water, maybe tow them . . .

To where? Even if we had some idea where the safe ports might have been, the captain wouldn't dare take the risk of detection. We didn't know who had a radio, who might be listening to that signal. We still didn't know if we were a hunted boat. And there was another danger: the immediate threat of the undead. We saw a lot of infested ships, some where the crews were still fighting for their lives, some where the dead were the only crew left. One time off Dakar, Senegal, we came across a forty-five-thousand-ton luxury liner called the *Nordic Empress*. Our search scope's optics were powerful enough to see every bloody handprint smeared on the ballroom's windows, every fly that settled on the deck's bones and flesh. Zombies were falling into the ocean, one every couple of minutes. They would see something in the distance, a low-flying aircraft, I think, or even the feather of our scope, and try to reach for it. It gave me an idea. If we surfaced a few hundred meters away, and did everything we could to lure them over the side, we might be able to clear the ship without firing a shot. Who knows what the refugees might have brought aboard with them? The *Nordic Empress* might turn out to be a floating replenishment depot. I presented my proposal to the master at arms and together we approached the captain.

What did he say?

"Absolutely not." There was no way of knowing how many zombies were onboard the dead liner. Even worse, he motioned to the video screen and pointed to some of the zombies falling overboard. "Look," he said, "not all of them are sinking." He was right. Some had reanimated wearing life jackets, while others were beginning to bloat up with decomposition gases. That was the first time I had ever seen a floating ghoul. I should have realized then that they would become a common occurrence. Even if 10 percent of the refugee ships were infested, that was still 10 percent of several hundred thousand vessels. There were millions of zombies falling randomly into the sea, or else pouring in by the hundreds when one of those old hulks capsized in rough weather. After a storm, they would blanket the surface to the horizon, rising waves of bobbing heads and flailing arms. Once we raised the search scope and were confronted with this distorted, greenish-gray haze. At first we thought it was an optical malfunction, as if we'd hit some floating debris, but then the attack scope confirmed that we'd speared one of them right under the rib cage. And it was still struggling, probably even after we lowered the scope. If ever something brought the threat home . . .

But you were underwater? How could they . . .

If we surfaced and one was caught on deck, or on the bridge. The first time I cracked the hatch, a fetid, waterlogged claw darted in and had me by the sleeve. I lost my footing, fell onto the lookout below me, and landed on the deck with the severed arm still clamped to my uniform. Above me, silhouetted in the bright disc of the open hatch, I could see the arm's owner. I reached for my sidearm, fired straight up without thinking. We were showered in bone and bits of brain. We were lucky . . . if any of us had had any kind of open wound . . . I deserved the reprimand I got, although I deserved worse. From that point on, we always did a thorough scope sweep after surfacing. I would say that, at least one in every three instances, a few of them were crawling about on the hull.

Those were the observation days, when all we did was look and listen to the world around us. Besides the scopes we could monitor both civilian radio traffic and even some satellite television broadcasts. It wasn't a pretty picture. Cities were dying, whole countries. We listened to the last report from Buenos Aires, the evacuation of the Japanese home islands, too. We heard sketchy information about mutinies in the Russian military. We heard after reports of the "limited nuclear exchange" between Iran and Pakistan, and we marveled, morbidly, at how we had been so sure that either you, or the Russians, would be the ones to turn the key. There were no reports from China, no illegal or even official government broadcasts. We were still detecting naval transmissions, but all the codes had been shifted since our departure. While this presented something of a personal threat—we didn't know if our fleet had orders to hunt down and sink us—at least it proved our whole nation hadn't disappeared into the stomachs of the undead. At this point in our exile any news was welcome.

Food was becoming an issue, not immediately, but soon enough to begin considering options. Medicine was a bigger problem; both our Western-style drugs and various traditional herb remedies were beginning to run low because of the civilians. Many of them had special medical needs.

Mrs. Pei, the mother of one of our torpedo men, was suffering from chronic bronchial problems, an allergic reaction to something on the boat, the paint or perhaps machine oil, something you couldn't simply remove from the environment. She was consuming our decongestants at an alarming rate. Lieutenant Chin, the boat's weapons officer suggested, matter-of-factly, that the old woman be euthanized. The captain responded by confining him to quarters, for a week, on half-rations, with all but the most life-threatening sickness to go untreated by the boat's pharmacist. Chin was a coldhearted bastard, but at least his suggestion brought our options into the light. We had to prolong our supply of consumables, if not find a way of recycling them altogether.

Raiding derelicts was still strictly forbidden. Even when we spotted what looked like a deserted vessel, at least a few zombies could be heard banging belowdecks. Fishing was a possibility, but we had neither the material to rig any kind of net, nor were we willing to spend hours on the sur-face dropping hooks and lines over the side.

The solution came from the civilians, not the crew. Some of them had been farmers or herbalists before the crisis, and a few had brought little bags of seeds. If we could provide them with the necessary equipment, they might be able to start raising enough food to stretch our existing provisions for years. It was an audacious plan, but not completely without merit. The missile room was certainly large enough for a garden. Pots and troughs could be hammered out of existing materials, and the ultraviolet lamps we used for the crew's vitamin D treatment could serve as artificial sunlight.

The only problem was soil. None of us knew anything about hydropon-ics, aeroponics, or any other alternate agricultural method. We needed earth, and there was only one way to get it. The captain had to consider this carefully. Trying to deploy a shore party was as dangerous as, if not more than, attempting to board an infested ship. Before the war, more than half of all human civilization lived at or near the world's coastlines. The infestation only increased this number as refugees sought to flee by water.

We began our search off the mid-Atlantic coast of South America, from Georgetown, Guyana, then down the coasts of Surinam, and French Guyana. We found several stretches of uninhabited jungle, and at least by periscope observation, the coast appeared to be clear. We surfaced and made a second, visual sweep from the bridge. Again, nothing. I requested permis-sion to take a landing party ashore. The captain was not yet convinced. He ordered the foghorn blown . . . loud and long . . . and then they came.

Just a few at first, tattered, wide-eyed, stumbling out of the jungle. They didn't seem to notice the shoreline, the waves knocking them over, push-ing them back up on the beach or pulling them out to sea. One was dashed against a rock, his chest crushed, broken ribs stabbing through the flesh. Black foam shot from his mouth as he howled at us, still trying to walk, to crawl, in our direction. More came, a dozen at a time; within minutes we had over a hundred plunging into the surf. This was the case everywhere we sur-faced. All those refugees who'd been too unlucky to make it to the open ocean now formed a lethal barrier along every stretch of coastline we visited.

Did you ever try to land a shore party?

[Shakes his head.] Too dangerous, even worse than the infested ships. We decided that our only choice was to find soil on an offshore island.

But you must have known what was happening on the world's islands.

You would be surprised. After leaving our Pacific patrol station, we restricted our movements to either the Atlantic or the Indian Ocean. We'd heard transmissions or made visual observations of many of those specks of land. We learned about the overcrowding, the violence . . . we saw the gun flashes from the Windward Islands. That night, on the surface, we could smell the smoke as it drifted east from the Caribbean. We could also hear islands that weren't so lucky. The Cape Verdes, off the coast of Senegal, we didn't even see them before we heard the wails. Too many refugees, too little discipline; it only takes one infected soul. How many islands remained quarantined after the war? How many frozen, northern rocks are still deeply and dangerously in the white?

Returning to the Pacific was our most likely option, but that would also bring us right back up to our country's front door.

Again, we still did not know if the Chinese navy was hunting us or even if there was still a Chinese navy. All we knew was that we needed stores and that we craved direct contact with other human beings. It took some time to convince the captain. The last thing he wanted was a confrontation with our navy.

He was still loyal to the government?

Yes. And then there was . . . a personal matter.

Personal? Why?

[He skirts the question.]

Have you ever been to Manihi?

[I shake my head.]

You couldn't ask for a more ideal image of a prewar tropical paradise. Flat, palm-covered islands or "motus" form a ring around a shallow, crystal-clear lagoon. It used to be one of the few places on Earth where they cultured authentic black pearls. I had bought a pair for my wife when we visited Tuamotus for our honeymoon, so my firsthand knowledge made this atoll the most likely destination.

Manihi had changed utterly since I was a newly married ensign. The pearls were gone, the oysters were eaten, and the lagoon was crowded with hundreds of small, private boats. The motus themselves were paved with either tents or ramshackle huts. Dozens of improvised canoes either sailed or rowed back and forth between the outer reef and the dozen or so large ships that were anchored in deeper water. The whole scene was typical of what, I guess, postwar historians are now calling "the Pacific Continent," the refugee island culture that stretched from Palau to French Polynesia. It was a new society, a new nation, refugees from all over the world uniting under the common flag of survival.

How did you integrate yourself into that society?

Through trade. Trade was the central pillar of the Pacific Continent. If your boat had a large distillery, you sold fresh water. If it had a machine shop, you became a mechanic. The *Madrid Spirit*, a liquefied natural gas carrier, sold its cargo off for cooking fuel. That was what gave Mister Song his idea for our "market niche." He was Commander Song's father, a hedge-fund broker from Shenzhen. He came up with the idea of running floating power lines into the lagoon and leasing the electricity from our reactor.

[He smiles.]

We became millionaires, or . . . at least the barter equivalent: food, medicine, any spare part we needed or the raw materials to manufacture them. We got our greenhouse, along with a miniature waste recovery plant to turn our own night soil into valuable fertilizer. We "bought" equipment for a gymnasium, a full wet bar, and home entertainment systems for both the enlisted mess and wardroom. The children were lavished with toys and candy, whatever was left, and most importantly, continuing education from several of the barges that had been converted into international schools. We were welcomed into any home, onto any boat. Our enlisted men, and even some of the officers, were given free credit on any one of the five "comfort" boats anchored in the lagoon. And why not? We lit up their nights, we powered their machinery. We brought back long forgotten luxuries like air conditioners and refrigerators. We brought computers back online and gave most of them the first hot shower they'd had in months. We were so successful that the island council even allowed us a reprieve, although we politely refused, from taking part in the island's perimeter security.

Against seaborne zombies?

They were always a danger. Every night they would wander up onto the motus or try to drag themselves up the anchor line of a low-lying boat. Part of the "citizenship dues" for staying at Manihi was to help patrol the beaches and boats for zombies.

You mentioned anchor lines. Aren't zombies poor climbers?

Not when water counteracts gravity. Most of them only have to follow an anchor chain up to the surface. If that chain leads to a boat whose deck is only centimeters above the water line . . . there were at least as many lagoon as beach attacks. Nights were always worse. That was another reason we were so welcome. We could take back the darkness, both above and below the surface. It is a chilling sight to point a flashlight at the water and see the bluish-green outline of a zombie crawling up an anchor line.

Wouldn't the light tend to attract even more of them?

Yes, definitely. Night attacks almost doubled once mariners began leaving their lights on. The civilians never complained though, and neither did the island's council. I think that most people would rather face the light of a real enemy than the darkness of their imagined fears.

How long did you stay in Manihi?

Several months. I don't know if you would call them the best months of our lives, but at the time it certainly felt that way. We began to let our guard down, to stop thinking of ourselves as fugitives. There were even some Chinese families, not Diaspora or Taiwanese, but real citizens of the People's Republic. They told us that the situation had gotten so bad that the government was barely keeping the country together. They couldn't see how, when over half the population was infected and the army's reserves were continuing to evaporate, they had the time or assets to devote any energy to find one lost sub. For a little while, it looked as if we could make this small island community our home, reside here until the end of the crisis or, perhaps, the end of the world.

[He looks up at the monument above us, built on the very spot where, supposedly, the last zombie in Beijing had been destroyed.]

Song and I had shore patrol duty, the night it happened. We'd stopped by a campfire to listen to the islanders' radio. There was some broadcast about a mysterious natural disaster in China. No one knew what it was yet, and there were more than enough rumors to keep us guessing. I was looking at the radio, my back to the lagoon, when the sea in front of me suddenly began to glow. I turned just in time to see the *Madrid Spirit* explode. I don't know how much natural gas she still carried, but the fireball skyrocketed high into the night, expanding and incinerating all life on the two closest motus. My first thought was "accident," a corroded valve, a careless deckhand. Commander Song had been looking right at it though, and he'd seen the streak of the missile. A half second later, the *Admiral Zheng*'s foghorn sounded.

As we raced back to the boat, my wall of calm, my sense of security, came crashing down around me. I knew that missile had come from one of our subs. The only reason it had hit the *Madrid* was because she sat much higher in water, presenting a larger radar outline. How many had been aboard? How many were on those motus? I suddenly realized that every second we stayed put the civilian islanders in danger of another attack. Captain Chen must have been thinking the same thing. As we reached the deck, the orders to cast off were sounded from the bridge. Power lines were cut, heads counted, hatches dogged. We set course for open water and dived at battle stations.

At ninety meters we deployed our towed array sonar and immediately detected hull popping noises of another sub changing depth. Not the flexible "pop-groooaaan-pop" of steel but the quick "pop-pop-pop" of brittle titanium. Only two countries in the world used titanium hulls in their attack boats: the Russian Federation and us. The blade count confirmed it was ours, a new Type 95 hunter-killers. Two were in service by the time we left port. We couldn't tell which one.

Was that important?

[Again, he does not answer.]

At first, the captain wouldn't fight. He chose to bottom the boat, set her down on a sandy plateau at the bare limit of our crush depth. The Type 95 began banging away with its active sonar array. The sound pulses echoed through the water, but couldn't get a fix on us because of the ocean floor. The 95 switched to a passive search, listening with its powerful hydrophone array for any noise we made. We reduced the reactor to a marginal output, shut down all unnecessary machinery, and ceased all crew movement within the boat. Because passive sonar doesn't send out any signals, there was no way of knowing where the 95 was, or even if it was still around. We tried to listen for her propeller, but she'd gone as silent as us. We waited for half an hour, not moving, barely breathing.

I was standing by the sonar shack, my eyes on the overhead, when Lieutenant Liu tapped me on the shoulder. He had something on our hull-mounted array, not the other sub, something closer, all around us. I plugged in a pair of headphones and heard a scraping noise, like scratching rats. I silently motioned for the captain to listen. We couldn't make it out. It wasn't bottom flow, the current was too mild for that. If it was sea life, crabs or some other biologic contact, there would have to be thousands of them. I began to suspect something . . . I requested a scope observation, knowing the transient noise might alert our hunter. The captain agreed. We gritted our teeth as the tube slid upward. Then, the image.

Zombies, hundreds of them, were swarming over the hull. More were arriving each second, stumbling across the barren sand, climbing over each other to claw, scrape, actually bite the *Zheng*'s steel.

Could they have gotten in? Opened a hatch or . . .

No, all hatches are sealed from the inside and torpedo tubes are protected by external bow caps. What concerned us, however, was the reactor. It was cooled by circulating seawater. The intakes, although not large enough for a man to fit through, can easily be blocked by one. Sure enough, one of our warning lights began to silently flash over the number four intake. One of them had ripped the guard off and was now thoroughly lodged in the conduit. The reactor's core temperature began to rise. To shut it down would leave us powerless. Captain Chen decided that we had to move.

We lifted off the bottom, trying to be as slow and quiet as possible. It wasn't enough. We began to detect the sound of the 95's propeller. She'd heard us and was moving in to attack. We heard her torpedo tubes being flooded, and the click of her outer doors opening. Captain Chen ordered our own sonar to "go active," pinging our exact location but giving us a perfect firing solution on the 95.

We fired at the same time. Our torpedoes passed each other, as both subs tried to get away. The 95 was a little bit faster, a little more maneuverable, but the one thing they didn't have was our captain. He knew exactly how to avoid the oncoming "fish," and we ducked them easily right about the time our own found their targets.

We heard the 95's hull screech like a dying whale, bulkheads collapsing as compartments imploded one after the other. They tell you it happens too fast for the crew to know; either the shock of the pressure change renders them unconscious or the explosion can actually cause the air to ignite. The crew dies quickly, painlessly, at least, that's what we hoped. One thing that wasn't painless was to watch the light behind my captain's eyes die with the sounds of the doomed sub.

[He anticipates my next question, clenching his fist and exhaling hard through his nose.]

Captain Chen raised his son alone, raised him to be a good sailor, to love and serve the state, to never question orders, and to be the finest officer the Chinese navy had ever seen. The happiest day of his life was when Commander Chen Zhi Xiao received his first command, a brand-new Type 95 hunter-killer.

The kind that attacked you?

[Nods.] That was why Captain Chen would have done anything to avoid our fleet. That was why it was so important to know which sub had attacked us. To know is always better, no matter what the answer might be. He had already betrayed his oath, betrayed his homeland, and now to believe that that betrayal *might* have led him to murder his own son . . .

The next morning when Captain Chen did not appear for first watch, I went to his cabin to check on him. The lights were dim, I called his name. To my relief, he answered, but when he stepped into the light . . . his hair had lost its color, as white as prewar snow. His skin was sallow, his eyes sunken. He was truly an old man now, broken, withered. The monsters that rose from the dead, they are nothing compared to the ones we carry in our hearts.

From that day on, we ceased all contact with the outside world. We headed for the arctic ice, the farthest, darkest, most desolate void we could find. We tried to continue with our day-to-day life: maintaining the boat; growing food; schooling, raising, and comforting our children as best we could. With the captain's spirit gone, so went the spirit of the *Admiral Zheng*'s crew. I was the only one who ever saw him during those days. I delivered his meals, collected his laundry, briefed him daily on the condition of the boat, then relayed his orders to the rest of the crew. It was routine, day in, day out.

Our monotony was only broken one day when sonar detected the approaching signature of another 95-class attack sub. We went to battle stations, and for the first time we saw Captain Chen leave his cabin. He took his place in the attack center, ordered a firing solution plotted, and tubes one and two loaded. Sonar reported that the enemy sub had not responded in kind. Captain Chen saw this as our advantage. There was no questioning in his mind this time. This enemy would die before it fired. Just before he gave the order, we detected a signal on the "gertrude," the American term for an underwater telephone. It was Commander Chen, the captain's son, proclaiming peaceful intentions and requesting that we stand down from GQ. He told us about the Three Gorges Dam, the source of all the "natural disaster" rumors we'd heard about in Manihi. He explained that our battle with the other 95 had been part of a civil war that the dam's destruction had sparked. The sub that attacked us had been part of the loyalist forces. Commander Chen had sided with the rebels. His mission was to find us and escort us home. I thought the cheer was going to carry us right to the surface. As we broke through the ice and the two crews ran to each other under the arctic twilight, I thought, finally, we can go home, we can reclaim our country and drive out the living dead. Finally, it's over.

But it wasn't.

There was still one last duty to perform. The Politburo, those hated old men who had caused so much misery already, were still holed up in their leadership bunker in Xilinhot, still controlling at least half of our country's dwindling ground forces. They would never surrender, everyone knew this; they would keep their mad hold on power, squandering what was left of our military. If the civil war dragged on any longer, the only beings left in China would be the living dead.

And you decided to end the fighting.

We were the only ones who could. Our land-based silos were overrun, our air force was grounded, our two other missile boats had been caught still tied to the piers, waiting for orders like good sailors as the dead swarmed through their hatches. Commander Chen informed us that we were the only nuclear asset left in the rebellion's arsenal. Every second we delayed wasted a hundred more lives, a hundred more bullets that could be thrown against the undead.

So you fired on your homeland, in order to save it.

One last burden to shoulder. The captain must have noticed me shaking the moment before we launched. "My order," he declared, "my responsibility." The missile carried a single, massive, multi-megaton warhead. It was a prototype warhead, designed to penetrate the hardened surface of your NORAD facility in Cheyenne Mountain, Colorado. Ironically, the Politburo's bunker had been designed to emulate Cheyenne Mountain in almost every detail. As we prepared to get under way, Commander Chen informed us that Xilinhot had taken a direct hit. As we slid beneath the surface, we heard that the loyalist forces had surrendered and reunified with the rebels to fight the real enemy.

Did you know they had begun instituting their own version of the South African Plan?

We heard the day we emerged from under the ice pack. That morning I came on watch and found Captain Chen already in the attack center. He was in his command chair, a cup of tea next to his hand. He looked so tired, silently watching the crew around him, smiling as a father smiles at the happiness of his children. I noticed his tea had grown cold and asked if he would like another cup. He looked up at me, still smiling, and shook his head slowly. "Very good, sir," I said, and prepared to resume my station. He reached out and took my hand, looked up into, but did not recognize, my face. His whisper was so soft I could barely hear it.

What?

"Nice boy, Zhi Xiao, such a good boy." He was still holding my hand when he closed his eyes forever.

❦

SYDNEY, AUSTRALIA

[Clearwater Memorial is the newest hospital to be constructed in Australia and the largest one built since the end of the war. Terry Knox's room is on the seventeenth floor, the "Presidential Suite." His luxurious surroundings and expensive, almost unobtainable medication are the least his government can do for the first and, to date, only Australian commander of the International Space Station. In his words, "Not bad for the son of an Andamooka opal miner."

His withered body seems to liven during our conversation. His face regains some of its color.]

I wish some of the stories they tell about us were true. Makes us sound all the more heroic. [Smiles.] Truth is, we weren't "stranded," not in terms of being suddenly or unexpectedly trapped up there. Nobody had a better view of what was happening than us. No one was surprised when the replacement crew from Baikonur failed to launch, or when Houston ordered us to pile into the X-38[1] for evacuation. I wish I could say that we violated orders or physically fought with one another over who should stay. What really happened was much more mundane and reasonable. I ordered the scientific team, and any other nonessential personnel, back to Earth, then gave the rest of the crew the choice to remain behind. With the X-38 reentry "lifeboat" gone, we would be technically stranded, but when you think of what was at stake then, I can't imagine any of us wanting to leave.

The ISS is one of the greatest marvels of human engineering. We're talking about an orbital platform so large it could be seen from Earth with the naked eye. It'd taken sixteen countries over ten years, a couple hundred space walks, and more money than anyone without job security would admit to finally complete her. What would it take to build another one, if another one could ever be built?

Even more important than the station was the incalculable, and equally irreplaceable, value of our planet's satellite network. Back then there were over three thousand in orbit, and humanity depended on them for everything from communications to navigation, from surveillance to something even as mundane yet vital as regular and reliable weather prediction. This network was as important to the modern world as roads had been in ancient times, or rail lines during the industrial age. What would happen to humanity if these all-important links just started dropping out of the sky?

Our plan was never to save them all. That was unrealistic and unnecessary. All we had to do was concentrate on the systems most vital to the war effort, just a few dozen birds that had to remain aloft. That alone was worth the risk of staying.

Were you ever promised a rescue?

No, and we didn't expect it. The issue wasn't how we were going to get back to Earth, it was how we could manage to stay alive up there. Even

---

1. The station's reentry "lifeboat."

with all our tanked O2 and emergency perchlorate candles,[2] even with our water recycling system[3] operating at peak capacity, we only had enough food for roughly twenty-seven months, and that was including the test animals in the lab modules. None of them were being used to test any kind of vaccines so their flesh was still edible. I can still hear their little shrieks, still see the spots of blood floating in micro gravity. Even up there, you couldn't escape the blood. I tried to be scientific about it, calculating the nutritional value of every floating red globule I sucked out of the air. I kept insisting that it was all for the good of the mission and not my own ravenous hunger.

Tell me more about the mission. If you were trapped on the station, how did you manage to keep the satellites in orbit?

We used the "Jules Verne Three" ATV,[4] the last supply pod launched before French Guyana was overrun. It was originally designed as a one-way vehicle, to be filled with trash after depositing its cargo, then sent back to Earth to burn up in the atmosphere.[5] We modified it with manual flight controls and a pilot's couch. I wish we could have fixed it with a proper viewport. Navigating by video wasn't fun; neither was having to do my Extra Vehicular Activities, my space walks, in a reentry suit because there wasn't room for a proper EVA kit.

Most of my excursions were to the ASTRO,[6] which was basically just a petrol station in space. Satellites, the military, surveillance type, sometimes have to change orbit in order to acquire new targets. They do that by firing their maneuvering thrusters and using up their small amount of hydrazine fuel. Before the war, the American military realized it was more cost-effective to have a refueling station already in orbit rather than

2. The ISS ceased using electrolysis to generate oxygen as a way of conserving water.
3. Prewar specs put the ISS water recycling capability at 95 percent.
4. ATV: Automated Transfer Vehicle.
5. A secondary task of the disposable ATV was to use its booster to maintain the station's orbit.
6. ASTRO: Autonomous Space Transfer and Robotic Orbiter.

sending up a lot of manned missions. That's where ASTRO came in. We modified it to refuel some of the other satellites as well, the civilian models that need just the occasional top-off to boost back up from a decaying orbit. It was a marvelous machine: a real time-saver. We had a lot of technology like that. There was the "Canadarm," the fifty-foot robotic inchworm that performed necessary maintenance tasks along the station's outer skin. There was "Boba," the VR-operated robonaut we fitted with a thruster pack so he could work both around the station and away from it on a satellite. We also had a little squadron of PSAs,[7] these free-floating robots, about the shape and size of a grapefruit. All of this wondrous technology was designed to make our jobs easier. I wish they hadn't worked so well.

We had maybe an hour a day, maybe even two, where there was nothing to do. You could sleep, you could exercise, you could reread the same books, you could listen to Radio Free Earth or to the music we'd brought with us (over and over and over again). I don't know how many times I listened to that Redgum song: "God help me, I was only nineteen." It was my father's favorite, reminded him of his time in Vietnam. I prayed that all that army training was helping to keep him and my mum alive now. I hadn't heard anything from him, or anyone else in Oz since the government had relocated to Tasmania. I wanted to believe they were all right, but watching what was happening on Earth, as most of us did during our off-duty hours, made it almost impossible to have hope.

They say that during the cold war, American spy birds could read the copy of *Pravda* in a Soviet citizen's hands. I'm not sure if that's entirely true. I don't know the tech specs of that generation of hardware. But I can tell you that these modern ones whose signals we pirated from their relay birds—these could show muscles tear and bones snap. You could read the lips of victims crying out for mercy, or the color of their eyes when they bulged with their last breath. You could see at what point red blood began to turn brown, and how it looked on gray London cement as opposed to white, Cape Cod sand.

7. PSA: Personal Satellite Assistance.

We had no control over what the spy birds chose to observe. Their targets were determined by the U.S. military. We saw a lot of battles—Chongqing, Yonkers; we watched a company of Indian troops try to rescue civilians trapped in Ambedkar Stadium in Delhi, then become trapped themselves and retreat to Gandhi Park. I watched their commander form his men into a square, the kind the Limeys used in colonial days. It worked, at least for a little while. That was the only frustrating part about satellite surveillance; you could only watch, not listen. We didn't know that the Indians were running out of ammunition, only that the Zed Heads were starting to close in. We saw a helo hover overhead and watched as the commander argued with his subordinates. We didn't know it was General Raj-Singh, we didn't even know who he was. Don't listen to what the critics say about that man, about how he buggered off when things got too hot. We saw it all. He *did* try to put up a fight, and one of his blokes *did* smash him in the face with a rifle butt. He was out cold when they hauled him into that waiting chopper. It was a horrible feeling, seeing it all so close and yet unable to do anything.

We had our own observation gear, both the civilian research birds and the equipment right there on the station. The images they gave us weren't half as powerful as the military versions, but they were still frighteningly clear. They gave us our first look at the mega swarms over central Asia and the American Great Plains. Those were truly massive, miles across, like the American buffalo must have once been.

We watched the evacuation of Japan and couldn't help but marvel at the scale. Hundreds of ships, thousands of small boats. We lost count of how many helicopters buzzed back and forth from the rooftops to the armada, or how many jetliners made their final run north to Kamchatka.

We were the first ones to discover zombie holes, the pits that the undead dig when they're going after burrowing animals. At first we thought they were just isolated incidents until we noticed that they were spreading all over the world; sometimes more than one would appear in close proximity to the next. There was a field in southern England—I guess there must have been a high concentration of rabbits—that was just riddled with holes, all different depths and sizes. Many of them had large, dark stains around them. Although we couldn't zoom in close enough, we were pretty sure it was blood. For me that was the most terrifying example of our enemy's drive. They displayed no conscious thought, just sheer biological instinct. I once watched a Zed Head go after something, probably a golden mole, in the Namib Desert. The mole had burrowed deep in the slope of a dune. As the ghoul tried to go after it, the sand kept pouring down and filling the hole. The ghoul didn't stop, didn't react in any way, it just kept going. I watched it for five days, the fuzzy image of this G digging, and digging, and digging, then suddenly one morning just stopping, getting up, and shuffling away as if nothing had happened. It must have lost the scent. Good on the mole.

For all our enhanced optics, nothing had quite the same impact as the naked eye. To just look through the view port down on our fragile little biosphere. To see the massive ecological devastation makes one understand how the modern environmental movement began with the American space program. There were so many fires, and I don't just mean the buildings, or the forests, or even the oil rigs blazing out of control—bleeding Saudis actually went ahead and did it[8]—I mean the campfires as well, what had to be at least a billion of them, tiny orange specks covering the Earth where electric lights had once been. Every day, every night, it seemed like the whole planet was burning. We couldn't even begin to calculate the ash count but we guesstimated it was equivalent to a low-grade nuclear exchange between the United States and former Soviet Union, and that's not including the actual nuclear exchange between Iran and Pakistan. We watched and recorded those as well, the flashes and fires that gave me eye spots for days. Nuclear autumn was already beginning to set in, the gray-brown shroud thickening each day.

It was like looking down on an alien planet, or on Earth during the last great mass extinction. Eventually conventional optics became useless in the shroud, leaving us with only thermal or radar sensors. Earth's natural face vanished behind a caricature of primary colors. It was through one of

8. To this day, no one knows why the Saudi royal family ordered the ignition of their kingdom's oil fields.

these systems, the Aster sensor aboard the Terra Satellite, that we saw the Three Gorges Dam collapse.

Roughly ten *trillion* gallons of water, carrying debris, silt, rocks, trees, cars, houses, and house-sized pieces of the dam itself! It was alive, a brown and white dragon racing to the East China Sea. When I think of the people in its path . . . trapped in barricaded buildings, unable to escape the tidal wave because of the Zed Heads right outside their doors. No one knows how many people died that night. Even today, they're still finding bodies.

[One of his skeletal hands balls into a fist, the other presses the "self-medicate" button.]

When I think about how the Chinese leadership tried to explain it all away . . . Have you ever read a transcript of the Chinese president's speech? We actually watched the broadcast from a pirated signal off their Sinosat II. He called it an "unforeseen tragedy." Really? Unforeseen? Was it unforeseen that the dam had been built on an active fault line? Was it unforeseen that the increased weight of a giant reservoir had induced earthquakes in the past[9] and that cracks had already been detected in the foundation months before the dam was completed?

He called it an "unavoidable accident." Bastard. They had enough troops to wage open warfare in almost every major city, but they couldn't spare a couple of traffic cops to protect against a catastrophe waiting to happen? No one could imagine the repercussions of abandoning both the seismic warning stations and the emergency spillway controls? And then to try to change their story halfway through, to say that they'd actually done everything they could to protect the dam, that, at the time of the disaster, valiant troops of the PLA had given their lives to defend it. Well, I'd been personally observing Three Gorges for over a year leading up to the disaster and the only PLA soldiers I ever saw had given their lives a long,

9. The reservoir of Lesotho's Katse Dam was confirmed to cause numerous seismic disturbances since its completion in 1995.

long time ago. Did they really expect their own people to buy such a blatant lie? Did they really expect anything less than all-out rebellion?

Two weeks after the start of the revolution, we received our first and only signal from the Chinese space station, Yang Liwei. It was the only other manned facility in orbit, but couldn't compare to such an exquisite masterpiece as ours. It was more of a slapdash job, Shenzhou modules and Long March fuel tanks cobbled together like a giant version of the old American Skylab.

We'd been trying to contact them for months. We weren't even sure if there was a crew. All we got was a recorded message in perfect Hong Kong English to keep our distance lest we invite a response of "deadly force." What an insane waste! We could have worked together, traded supplies, technical expertise. Who knows what we could have accomplished if we had only chucked the politics and come together as human bloody beings.

We'd convinced ourselves that the station had never been inhabited at all, that their deadly force warning was just a ruse. We couldn't have been more surprised when the signal came over our ham radio.[10] It was a live human voice, tired, frightened, and cutting out after only a few seconds. It was all I needed to board the Verne and head over to the Yang.

As soon as it came over the horizon I could tell that its orbit had shifted radically. As I closed the distance, I could see why. Their escape pod had blown its hatch, and because it was still docked to the primary airlock, the entire station had depressurized in seconds. As a precaution, I requested docking clearance. I got nothing. As I came aboard, I could see that even though the station was clearly large enough for a crew of seven or eight, it only had the bunk space and personal kits for two. I found the Yang packed with emergency supplies, enough food, water, and O2 candles for at least five years. What I couldn't figure out at first was why. There was no scientific equipment aboard, no intelligence-gathering assets. It was almost like the Chinese government had sent these two men into space for no other purpose than to exist. Fifteen minutes into my floatabout, I found

10. The International Space Station is equipped with a civilian ham radio, originally, to allow the crew to talk to schoolchildren.

the first of several scuttling charges. This space station was little more than a giant Orbital Denial Vehicle. If those charges were to detonate, the debris from a four-hundred-metric-ton space station would not only be enough to damage or destroy any other orbiting platform, but any future space launch would be grounded for years. It was a "Scorched Space" policy, "if we can't have it, neither can anyone else."

All the station's systems were still operational. There had been no fire, no structural damage, no reason I could see to cause the accident of the escape pod's hatch. I found the body of a lone taikonaut with his hand still clinging to the hatch release. He was wearing one of their pressurized escape suits, but the faceplate had been shattered by a bullet. I'm guessing the shooter was blown out into space. I'd like to believe that the Chinese revolution wasn't just restricted to Earth, that the man who'd blown the hatch was also the one who had attempted to signal us. His mate must have stuck by the old guard. Maybe Mister Loyalist had been ordered to set off the scuttling charges. Zhai—that was the name on his personal effects—Zhai had tried to blast his mate into space and had caught a round in the process. Makes for a good tale, I think. That's how I'm going to remember it.

Is that how you were able to extend your endurance? By using the supplies aboard the Yang?

[He gives me a thumbs-up.] We cannibalized every inch of it for spares and materials. We would have liked to have merged the two platforms together but we didn't have the tools or manpower for such an undertaking. We might been able to use the escape pod to return to Earth. It had a heat shield and room for three. It was very tempting. But the station's orbit was decaying rapidly, and we had to make a choice then and there, escape to Earth or resupply the ISS. You know which choice we made.

Before we finally abandoned her, we laid our friend Zhai to rest. We strapped his body into its bunk, brought his personal kit back to the ISS, and said a few words in his honor as the Yang burned up in the Earth's atmosphere. For all we knew he might have been the loyalist, not the rebel, but either way, his actions allowed us to stay alive. Three more years we remained in orbit, three more years that wouldn't have been possible without the Chinese consumables.

I still think it's one of the war's great ironies that our replacement crew ended up arriving in a privately owned civilian vehicle. *Spacecraft Three*, the ship originally designed for prewar orbital tourism. The pilot, with his cowboy hat and big, confident Yankee grin. [He tries his best Texas accent.] "Anyone order takeout?" [He laughs, then winces and self-medicates again.]

Sometimes I'm asked if we regretted our decision to stay aboard. I can't speak for my mates. On their deathbeds they both said they'd do it all over again. How can I disagree? I don't regret the physical therapy that followed, getting to know my bones again and remembering why the good Lord gave us legs in the first place. I don't regret being exposed to so much cosmic radiation, all those unprotected EVAs, all that time with inadequate shielding in the ISS. I don't regret this. [He motions to the hospital room and machinery attached to his body.] We made our choice, and, I'd like to think, we made a difference in the end. Not bad for the son of an Andamooka opal miner.

[Terry Knox died three days after this interview.]

❦

ANCUD, ISLA GRANDE DE CHILOE, CHILE

[While the official capital has returned to Santiago, this one-time refugee base now remains the economic and cultural center of the country. Ernesto Olguin calls the beach house on the island's Peninsula de Lacuy home, although his duties as a merchant ship's master keep him at sea for most of the year.]

The history books call it "The Honolulu Conference," but really it should have been called the "Saratoga Conference" because that's all any

of us had a chance to see. We spent fourteen days in those cramped compartments and dank stuffy passageways. USS *Saratoga:* from aircraft carrier,
to decommissioned hulk, to evacuee transport barge, to floating United
Nations HQ.

It also shouldn't have been called a conference. If anything, it was
more like an ambush. We were supposed to be exchanging warfighting
tactics and technology. Everyone was anxious to see the British method
of fortified motorways, which was almost as exciting as that live demonstration of Mkunga Lalem.[1] We were also supposed to be attempting to
reintroduce some measure of international trade. That was my task, specifically, to integrate the remnants of our navy into the new international
convoy structure. I wasn't really sure what to expect from my time aboard
Super Sara. I don't think anyone could have expected what actually
happened.

On the first day of the conference, we'd assembled for the introductions.
I was hot and tired and wishing to God we could just get on without all the
tiresome speeches. And then the American ambassador rose, and the
whole world came to a screeching halt.

It was time to go on the attack, he said, to all get out from behind our
established defenses and begin retaking infested territory. At first I thought
he simply meant isolated operations: securing more inhabitable islands or,
perhaps, even reopening the Suez/Panama canal zones. My supposition
didn't last very long. He made it very clear that this was not going to be a
series of minor tactical incursions. The United States intended to go permanently on the offensive, marching forward every day, until, as he put it,
"every trace was sponged, and purged, and, if need be, blasted from the surface of the Earth." Maybe he thought ripping off Churchill would give it
some kind of emotional punch. It didn't. Instead, the room spontaneously
combusted into argument.

One side asked why in hell should we risk even more lives, suffer even
one more unnecessary casualties when all we had to do was remain safe
and sedentary while our enemy simply rotted away. Wasn't it happening

1. Mkunga Lalem: (The Eel and the Sword), the world's premier antizombie martial art.

already? Weren't the earliest cases starting to show signs of advanced decomposition? Time was on our side, not theirs. Why not let nature do all the work for us?

The other side countered that not all the living dead were rotting away. What about the later cases, the ones still strong and healthy? Couldn't just one restart the plague all over again? And what about those who prowled countries above the snowline? How long would we have to wait for them? Decades? Centuries? Would refugees from these countries ever have a chance of returning home?

And that's when it got ugly. Many of the colder countries were what you used to call "First World." One of the delegates from a prewar "developing" country suggested, rather hotly, that maybe this was their punishment for raping and pillaging the "victim nations of the south." Maybe, he said, by keeping the "white hegemony" distracted with their own problems, the undead invasion might allow the rest of the world to develop "without imperialist intervention." Maybe the living dead had brought more than just devastation to the world. Maybe in the end, they had brought justice for the future. Now, my people have little love for the northern gringos, and my family suffered enough under Pinochet to make that animosity personal, but there comes a point where private emotions must give way to objective facts. How could there be a "white hegemony" when the most dynamic prewar economies were China and India, and the largest wartime economy was unquestionably Cuba? How could you call the colder countries a northern issue when so many people were just barely surviving in the Himalayas, or the Andes of my own Chile? No, this man, and those who agreed with him, weren't talking about justice for the future. They just wanted revenge for the past.

[Sighs.] After all we'd been through, we still couldn't take our heads from out of our asses or our hands from around each other's throats.

I was standing next to the Russian delegate, trying to prevent her from climbing over her seat, when I heard another American voice. It was their president. The man didn't shout, didn't try to restore order. He just kept going in that calm, firm tone that I don't think any world leader has since been able to duplicate. He even thanked his "fellow delegates" for their "valued opinions" and admitted that, from a purely military perspective, there was no reason to "push our luck." We'd fought the living dead to a stalemate and, eventually, future generations might be able to reinhabit the planet with little or no physical danger. Yes, our defensive strategies had saved the human race, but what about the human spirit?

The living dead had taken more from us than land and loved ones. They'd robbed us of our confidence as the planet's dominant life-form. We were a shaken, broken species, driven to the edge of extinction and grateful only for a tomorrow with perhaps a little less suffering than today. Was this the legacy we would leave to our children, a level of anxiety and self-doubt not seen since our simian ancestors cowered in the tallest trees? What kind of world would they rebuild? Would they rebuild at all? Could they continue to progress, knowing that they had been powerless to reclaim their future? And what if that future saw another rise of the living dead? Would our descendants rise to meet them in battle, or simply crumple in meek surrender and accept what they believe to be their inevitable extinction? For this reason alone, we had to reclaim our planet. We had to prove to ourselves that we *could* do it, and leave that proof as this war's greatest monument. The long, hard road back to humanity, or the regressive ennui of Earth's once-proud primates. That was the choice, and it had to be made now.

So typically Norteamericano, reaching for the stars with their asses still stuck in the mud. I guess, if this was a gringo movie, you'd see some idiot get up and start clapping slowly, then the others would join in and then we'd see a tear roll down someone's cheek or some other contrived bullshit like that. Everyone was silent. No one moved. The president announced that we would recess for the afternoon to consider his proposal, then reconvene at dusk for a general vote.

As naval attaché, I wasn't allowed to participate in that vote. While the ambassador decided the fate of our beloved Chile, I had nothing to do but enjoy the Pacific sunset. I sat on the flight deck, wedged in between the windmills and solar cells, killing time with my opposite numbers from France and South Africa. We tried not to talk shop, searching for any common subject as far from the war as we could get. We thought we were safe with wine. As luck might have it, each of us had either lived near, worked on, or had family connected with a vineyard: Aconcagua, Stellenboch, and Bordeaux. Those were our bonding points and, as with everything else, they led right back to the war.

Aconcagua had been destroyed, burned to the ground during our country's disastrous experiments with napalm. Stellenboch was now growing subsistence crops. Grapes were considered a luxury when the population was close to starvation. Bordeaux was overrun, the dead crushing its soil underfoot like almost all of continental France. Commander Emile Renard was morbidly optimistic. Who knows, he said, what the nutrients of their corpses would do for the soil? Maybe it would even improve on the overall taste once Bordeaux was retaken, if it was retaken. As the sun began to dip, Renard took something from his kit bag, a bottle of Chateau Latour, 1964. We couldn't believe our eyes. The '64 was an extremely rare prewar vintage. By sheer chance, the vineyard had had a bumper crop that season and had chosen to harvest its grapes in late August as opposed to the traditional early September. That September was marked by early, devastating rains, which inundated the other vineyards and elevated Chateau Latour to almost Holy Grail status. The bottle in Renard's hand might be the last of its kind, the perfect symbol of a world we might never see again. It was the only personal item he'd managed to save during the evacuation. He carried it with him everywhere, and was planning to save it for . . . ever, possibly, seeing as it looked like none of any vintage would ever be made again. But now, after the Yankee president's speech . . .

[He involuntarily licks his lips, tasting the memory.]

It hadn't traveled that well, and the plastic mugs didn't help. We didn't care. We savored every sip.

You were pretty confident about the vote?

Not that it would be unanimous, and I was damn right. Seventeen "No" votes and thirty-one "Abstain." At least the no voters were willing to suffer the long-term consequences of their decision . . . and they did. When you think that the new UN only consisted of seventy-two delegates, the showing of support was pretty poor. Not that it mattered for me or my other two amateur "sommeliers." For us, our countries, our children, the choice had been made: attack.

TOTAL WAR

[I stand next to General D'Ambrosia in the CIC, the Combat Information Center, of Europe's answer to the massive U.S. D-29 command and control dirigible. The crew work silently at their glowing monitors. Occasionally, one of them speaks into a headset, a quick, whispered acknowledgment in French, German, Spanish, or Italian. The general leans over the video chart table, watching the entire operation from the closest thing to a God's-eye view.]

"Attack"—when I first heard that word, my gut reaction was "oh shit." Does that surprise you?

[Before I can answer . . .]

Sure it does. You probably expected "the brass" to be just champing at the bit, all that blood and guts, "hold 'em by the nose while we kick 'em in the ass" crap.

[Shakes his head.] I don't know who created the stereotype of the hard-charging, dim-witted, high school football coach of a general officer. Maybe it was Hollywood, or the civilian press, or maybe we did it to ourselves by allowing those insipid, egocentric clowns—the MacArthurs and Halseys and Curtis E. LeMays—to define our image to the rest of the country. Point is, that's the image of those in uniform, and it couldn't be further from the truth. I was scared to death of taking our armed forces on the offensive, more so because it wouldn't be my ass hanging out in the fire. I'd only be sending others out to die, and here's what I'd be sending them up against.

[He turns to another screen on the far wall, nodding to an operator, and the image dissolves into a wartime map of the continental United States.]

Two hundred million zombies[1]. Who can even visualize that type of number, let alone combat it? At least this time around we knew what we were combating, but when you added up all the experience, all the data we'd compiled on their origin, their physiology, their strengths, their weaknesses, their motives, and their mentality, it still presented us with a very gloomy prospect for victory.

The book of war, the one we've been writing since one ape slapped another, was completely useless in this situation. We had to write a new one from scratch.

All armies, be they mechanized or mountain guerilla, have to abide by three basic restrictions: they have to be bred, fed, and led. Bred: you need warm bodies, or else you don't have an army; fed: once you've got that army, they've got to be supplied; and led: no matter how decentralized that fighting force is, there has to be someone among them with the authority

---

1. It has been confirmed at least twenty-five million of this number include reanimated refugees from Latin America who were killed attempting to reach the Canadian north.

to say "follow me." Bred, fed, and led; and none of these restrictions applied to the living dead.

Did you ever read *All Quiet on the Western Front?* Remarque paints a vivid picture of Germany becoming "empty," meaning that toward the end of the war, they were simply running out of soldiers. You can fudge the numbers, send the old men and little boys, but eventually you're going to hit the ceiling . . . unless every time you killed an enemy, he came back to life on your side. That's how Zack operated, swelling his ranks by thinning ours! And it only worked one way. Infect a human, he becomes a zombie. Kill a zombie, he becomes a corpse. We could only get weaker, while they might actually get stronger.

All human armies need supplies, this army didn't. No food, no ammo, no fuel, not even water to drink or air to breathe! There were no logistics lines to sever, no depots to destroy. You couldn't just surround and starve them out, or let them "wither on the vine." Lock a hundred of them in a room and three years later they'll come out just as deadly.

It's ironic that the only way to kill a zombie is to destroy its brain, because, as a group, they have no collective brain to speak of. There was no leadership, no chain of command, no communication or cooperation on any level. There was no president to assassinate, no HQ bunker to surgically strike. Each zombie is its own, self-contained, automated unit, and this last advantage is what truly encapsulates the entire conflict.

You've heard the expression "total war"; it's pretty common throughout human history. Every generation or so, some gasbag likes to spout about how his people have declared "total war" against an enemy, meaning that every man, woman, and child within his nation was committing every second of their lives to victory. That is bullshit on two basic levels. First of all, no country or group is ever 100 percent committed to war; it's just not physically possible. You can have a high percentage, so many people working so hard for so long, but all of the people, all of the time? What about the malingerers, or the conscientious objectors? What about the sick, the injured, the very old, the very young? What about when you're sleeping, eating, taking a shower, or taking a dump? Is that a "dump for victory"?

That's the first reason total war is impossible for humans. The second is that all nations have their limits. There might be individuals within that group who are willing to sacrifice their lives; it might even be a relatively high number for the population, but that population as a whole will eventually reach its maximum emotional and physiological breaking point. The Japanese reached theirs with a couple of American atomic bombs. The Vietnamese might have reached theirs if we'd dropped a couple more,[2] but, thank all holy Christ, our will broke before it came to that. That is the nature of human warfare, two sides trying to push the other past its limit of endurance, and no matter how much we like to talk about total war, that limit is always there . . . unless you're the living dead.

For the first time in history, we faced an enemy that was actively waging total war. They had no limits of endurance. They would never negotiate, never surrender. They would fight until the very end because, unlike us, every single one of them, every second of every day, was devoted to consuming all life on Earth. That's the kind of enemy that was waiting for us beyond the Rockies. That's the kind of war we had to fight.

DENVER, COLORADO, USA

[We have just finished dinner at the Wainios. Allison, Todd's wife, is upstairs helping their son, Addison, with his homework. Todd and I are downstairs in the kitchen, doing the dishes.]

It was kinda like stepping back in time, the new army, I mean. It couldn't have been any more different from the one I'd fought, and almost died with, at Yonkers. We weren't mechanized anymore—no tanks, no

2. It has been alleged that several members of the American military establishment openly supported the use of thermonuclear weapons during the Vietnam conflict.

arty, no tread jobs[1] at all, not even the Bradleys. Those were still in reserve, being modified for when we'd have to take back the cities. No, the only wheeled vehicles we had, the Humvees and a few M-trip-Seven ASVs,[2] were used to carry ammo and stuff. We hoofed it, all the way, marching in column like you see in Civil War paintings. There was a lot of references to "the Blue" versus "the Gray," mainly because of Zack's skin color and the shade of our new BDUs. They didn't bother with camo schemes anymore; in any case, what was the point? And, I guess, navy blue was the cheapest dye they had back then. The BDU itself looked more like a SWAT team's coverall. It was light and comfortable and interwoven with Kevlar, I think it was Kevlar,[3] bite-proof threads. It had the option of gloves and a hood that would cover your whole face. Later, in urban hand-to-hand, that option saved a lot of lives.

Everything had kind of a retro feel about it. Our Lobos looked like something out of, I don't know, *Lord of the Rings*? Standard orders were to use it only when necessary, but, trust me, we made it necessary a *lot*. It just felt good, you know, swingin' that solid hunk a' steel. It made it personal, empowering. You could feel the skull split. A real rush, like you were taking back your life, you know? Not that I minded pulling the trigger.

Our primary weapon was the SIR, standard infantry rifle. The wood furniture made it look like a World War II gun; I guess composite materials were too hard to mass-produce. I'm not sure where the SIR supposedly came from. I've heard it was a modcop of the AK. I've also heard that it was a stripped-down version of the XM 8, which the army was already planning as its next-gen assault weapon. I've even heard that it was invented, tested, and first produced during the siege of the Hero City, and the plans were transmitted to Honolulu. Honestly, I don't know, and I so don't care. It might have kicked hard, and it only fired on semi, but it was super accurate and it never, ever jammed! You could drag it through the mud, leave it in the sand, you could drop it in saltwater and let it sit there for days. No matter what you did to this baby, it just wouldn't let you down.

1. Tread jobs: wartime slang for vehicles that traveled on treads.
2. M-trip-Seven: The Cadillac Gauge M1117 Armored Security Vehicle.
3. The chemical composition of the army's battle dress uniform (BDU) is still classified.

The only bells and whistles it had was a conversion kit of extra parts, furniture, and additional barrels of different lengths. You could go long-range sniper, midrange rifle, or close-combat carbine, all in the same hour, and without reaching farther than your ruck. It also had a spike, this little flip-out job, about eight inches long, that you could use in a pinch if your Lobo wasn't handy. We used to joke "careful, you'll poke somebody's eye out," which, of course, we did plenty. The SIR made a pretty good close combat weapon, even without the spike, and when you add all the other things that made it so awesome, you can see why we always referred to it, respectfully, as "Sir."

Our staple ammo was the NATO 5.56 "Cherry PIE." PIE stands for pyrotechnically initiated explosive. Outstanding design. It would shatter on entry into Zack's skull and fragments would fry its brain. No risk of spreading infected gray matter, and no need for wasteful bonfires. On BS[4] duty, you didn't even have to decap before you buried them. Just dig the trench and roll the whole body in.

Yeah, it was a new army, as much the people as anything else. Recruitment had changed, and being a grunt meant something very different now. You still had the old requirements—physical stamina, mental competence, the motivation and discipline to master difficult challenges in extreme conditions—but all that was mouse farts if you couldn't hack long-term Z-shock. I saw a lot of good friends just lose it under the strain. Some of them collapsed, some turned their weapons on themselves, some on their buddies. It didn't have anything to do with being brave or anything like that. I once read this British SAS survival guide that talked all about the "warrior" personality, how your family's supposed to be emotionally and financially stable, and how you're not even supposed to be attracted to girls when you're real young. [Grunts.] Survival guides . . . [Jerks his hand in a masturbatory movement.]

But the new faces, they could have been from anywhere: your neighbor, your aunt, that geeky substitute teacher, or that fat, lazy slob at the DMV. From former insurance salesmen to a guy who I'm damn sure was Michael

4. BS: Battlefield Sanitization.

Stipe, although I never got him to admit it. I guess it all made sense; any-one who couldn't roll wouldn't have made it this far in the first place. Everyone was already a veteran in some sense. My battle buddy, Sister Montoya, fifty-two years old, she'd been a nun, still was I guess. Five three and a buck even, she'd protected her whole Sunday school class for nine days with nothing but a six-foot iron candlestick. I don't know how she managed to hump that ruck, but she did, without complaining, from our assembly area in Needles, all the way to our contact site just outside of Hope, New Mexico.

Hope. I'm not kidding, the town was actually named Hope.

They say the brass chose it because of the terrain, clear and open with the desert in front and the mountains in back. Perfect, they said, for an opening engagement, and that the name had nothing to do with it. Right.

The brass really wanted this test-op to go smoothly. It'd be the first major ground engagement we'd fought since Yonkers. It was that moment, you know, like, when a lot of different things all come together.

Watershed?

Yeah, I think. All the new people, the new stuff, the new training, the new plan—everything was supposed to sort of mix together for this one first big kickoff.

We'd encountered a couple dozen Gs en route. Sniffer dogs would find them, and handlers with silenced weapons would drop them. We didn't want to attract too many till we were set. We wanted this to be on our terms.

We started planting our "garden": shelter stakes with orange Day-Glo tape in rows every ten meters. They were our range markers, showing us exactly where to zero our sights. For some of us there was also some light duty like clearing the brush or arranging the ammo crates.

For the rest of us, there was nothing to do except wait, just grab some chow, recharge our camel packs, or even snag some bag time, if it was pos-sible to sleep. We'd learned a lot since Yonkers. The brass wanted us rested. The problem was, it gave us all too much time to think.

Did you see the movie, the one Elliot made about us? That scene with the campfire and the grunts all jawing in this witty dialogue, the stories and the dreams for the future, and even that guy with the harmonica. Dude, it was so not like that. First of all, it was the middle of the day, no campfires, no harmonica under the stars, and also everyone was really quiet. You knew what everyone was thinking though, "What the hell are we doing here?" This was Zack's house now, and as far as we were concerned, he could have it. We'd all had plenty of pep talks about "The Future of the Human Spirit." We'd seen the president's speech God knows how many times, but the prez wasn't out here on Zack's front lawn. We had a good thing going behind the Rockies. What the hell were we doing out here?

Around 1300 hours, the radios started squawking, it was the K-handlers whose dogs had made contact. We locked and loaded and took our place on the firing line.

That was the centerpiece of our whole new battle doctrine, back into the past like everything else. We massed in a straight line, two ranks: one active, one reserve. The reserve was so when anyone in the front rank needed a weapon recharge, their fire wouldn't be missed on the line. Theoretically, with everyone either firing or reloading, we could keep Zack falling as long as the ammo held out.

We could hear the barking, the Ks were bringing them in. We started seeing Gs on the horizon, hundreds. I started shaking even though it wasn't the first time I'd had to face Zack since Yonkers. I'd been in the clean and sweep operations in LA. I'd done my time in the Rockies when the summer thawed the passes. Each time I got major shakes.

The dogs were recalled, racing behind our lines. We switched over to our Primary Enticement Mechanism. Every army had one by now. The Brits would use bagpipes, the Chinese used bugles, the Sou'fricans used to smack their rifles with their assegais[5] and belt out these Zulu war chants. For us, it was hard-core Iron Maiden. Now, personally, I've never been a metal fan. Straight classic rock's my thing, and Hendrix's "Driving South"

---

5. The assegai: An all-steel, multipurpose implement named after the traditional Zulu short spear.

is about as heavy as I get. But I had to admit, standing there in that desert wind, with "The Trooper" thumping in my chest, I got it. The PEM wasn't really for Zack's benefit. It was to psych us up, take away some of Zack's mojo, you know, "take the piss out," as the Brits say. Right about the time Dickinson was belting "As you plunge into a certain death" I was pumped, SIR charged and ready, eyes fixed on this growing, closing horde. I was, like, "C'mon, Zack, let's fuckin' do this!"

Just before they reached the front range marker, the music began to fade. The squad leaders shouted, "Front rank, ready!" and the first line knelt. Then came the order to "take aim!" and then, as we all held our breath, as the music clicked off, we heard "FIRE!"

The front rank just rippled, cracking like a SAW on full auto and dropping every G that crossed the first markers. We had strict orders, only the ones crossing the line. Wait for the others. We'd trained this way for months. By now it was pure instinct. Sister Montoya raised her weapon above her head, the signal for an empty mag. We switched positions, I flipped off my safety, and sighted my first target. She was a noob,[6] couldn't have been dead more than a year or so. Her dirty blond hair hung in patches from her tight, leathery skin. Her swollen belly puffed through a faded black T-shirt that read G IS FOR GANGSTA. I centered my sight between her shrunken, milky blue eyes . . . you know it's not really the eyes that make them look all cloudy, it's actually tiny dust scratches on the surface, thousands of them, because Zack doesn't make any tears. Those scratched-up baby blues were looking right at me when I pulled the trigger. The round knocked her on her back, steam coming from the hole in her forehead. I took a breath, sighted my next target, and that was that, I was locked in.

Doctrine calls for one shot every full second. Slow, steady, mechanical-like.

[He begins snapping his fingers.]

6. Noob: Short for "newbies," zombies that have reanimated after the Great Panic.

On the range we practiced with metronomes, all the time the instructors saying "they ain't in no hurry, why are you?" It was a way of keeping calm, pacing yourself. We had to be as slow and robotic as them. "Out G the G," they used to say.

[His fingers snap in perfect rhythm.]

Shooting, switching, reloading, grabbing sips from your camel pack, grabbing clips from the "Sandlers."

Sandlers?

Yeah, the Recharge Teams, this special reserve unit that did nothing but make sure we never ran dry. You only had a certain number of clips on you and it would take a lot more time to reload each individual clip. The Sandlers ran up and down the line collecting empty clips, recharging them from crated ammo, and then passing them out to anyone who signaled. The story is that when the army started training with RTs, one of the guys started doin' an Adam Sandler impression, you know, "Water Boy"—"Ammo Boy." The officers weren't too jazzed with the tag, but the Recharge Teams loved it. Sandlers were lifesavers, drilled like a fuckin' ballet. I don't think anyone that day or night ever found themselves one round short.

That night?

They just kept coming, full on Chain Swarm.

That's a large-scale attack?

More than that. One G sees you, comes after you, and moans. A click away, another G hears that moan, comes after it, and moans himself, then another one another click away, then another. Dude, if the area's thick enough, if the chain's unbroken, who knows how far you can pull them in from. And we're just talking one after the other here. Try ten every click, a hundred, a thousand.

They started piling up, forming this artificial palisade at the first range marker, this ridge of corpses that got higher and higher each minute. We were actually building an undead fortification, creating a situation where all we had to do was pop every head that popped over the top. The brass had planned for this. They had a periscope tower thingy[7] that let officers see right over the wall. They also had real-time downlinks from satellites and recon drones, although we, the grunts, had no idea what they were seeing. Land Warrior was gone for now so all we had to do was concentrate on what was in front of our faces.

We started getting contacts from all sides, either coming around the wall or else being drawn in from our flanks and even rear. Again, the brass was waiting for this and ordered us to form an RS.

A Reinforced Square.

Or a "Raj-Singh," I guess after the guy who reinvented it. We formed a tight square, still two ranks, with our vehicles and whatnot in the center. That was a dangerous gamble, cutting us off like that. I mean, yeah, it didn't work that first time in India only 'cause the ammo ran out. But there was no guarantee it wouldn't happen again to us. What if the brass had goofed, hadn't packed enough rounds or underestimated how strong Zack would be that day? It could have been Yonkers all over again; worse, because no one would be getting out of there alive.

But you did have enough ammunition.

More than enough. The vehicles were packed to their roofs. We had water, we had replacements. If you needed a fiver, you just raised your weapon and one of the Sandlers would jump in and take our place on the firing line. You'd grab a bite of I-Rations,[8] soak your face, stretch, drain the weasel. No one would ever volunteer for a fiver, but they had these KO[9] teams,

---

7. M43 Combat Observation Aid.
8. I-Rations: short for Intelligent Rations, they were designed for maximum nutritional efficiency.
9. KO: short for "Knock Out."

combat shrinks who were observing everyone's performance. They'd been with us since our early days on the range, knew us each by name and face, and knew, don't ask me how, when the stress of battle was starting to degrade our performance. We didn't know, I certainly didn't. There were a couple times I'd miss a shot or maybe take a half second instead of a full. Then suddenly I'd get this tap on my shoulder and I knew I was out of it for five. It really worked. Before I knew it, I was back on the line, bladder empty, stomach quiet, a few less kinks and muscle cramps. It made a world of difference, and anyone who thinks we could have lasted without it should try hitting a moving bull's-eye every second for fifteen hours.

What about at night?

We used searchlights from the vehicles, powerful, red-coated beams so it didn't mess with your night vision. The only creepy thing about night fighting, other than the redness from the lights, is the glow a round makes when it enters the head. That's why we called them "Cherry PIES," because if the bullet's chemcomp wasn't mixed right, it would burn so bright it made their eyes glow red. That was a cure for constipation, especially later on, on nights when you pulled guard duty, and one would come at you out of the dark. Those glowing red eyes, frozen in time the second before it falls. [Shivers.]

How did you know the battle was over?

When we stopped shooting? [Laughs.] No, that's actually a good question. Around, I don't know, 0400, it started to taper off. Heads weren't poking out as much. The moan was dying down. The officers didn't tell us that the attack was almost over, but you could see them looking through their scopes, talking on their radios. You could see the relief in their faces. I think the last shot was fired just before dawn. After that, we just waited for first light.

It was kinda eerie, the sun rising over this mountainous ring of corpses. We were totally walled in, all sides were piled at least twenty feet high and over a hundred feet deep. I'm not sure how many we killed that day, stats always vary depending on who you get it from.

The dozer-blade Humvees had to push a path through the corpse ring just to let us get out. There were still living Gs, some slow ones who were late to the party or who had tried to climb up and over their dead friends and had slid back down into the mound. When we started burying the bodies they came tumbling out. That was the only time Señor Lobo saw any action.

At least we didn't have to stick around for BS duty. They had another unit waiting in reserve to clean up. I guess the brass figured we'd done enough for one day. We marched ten miles to the east, set up a bivouac with watchtowers and concertainer[10] walls. I was so damn beat. I don't remember the chem shower, turning in my gear to be disinfected, turning in my weapon for inspection: not one jam, not the whole unit. I don't even remember slipping into my bag.

They let us sleep as late as we wanted the next day. That was pretty sweet. Eventually the voices woke me up; everyone jawing, laughing, telling stories. It was a different vibe, one-eighty from two days ago. I couldn't really put a finger on what I was feeling, maybe it was what the president said about "reclaiming our future." I just knew I felt good, better than I had the entire war. I knew it was gonna be a real, long-ass road. I knew our campaign across America was just beginning, but, hey, as the prez said later that first night, it was finally the beginning of the end.

❦

AINSWORTH, NEBRASKA, USA

[Darnell Hackworth is a shy, soft-spoken man. He and his wife run a retirement farm for the four-legged veterans of the army's

---

10.Concertainer: A prefabricated, hollow barrier constructed of Kevlar and filled with earth and/or debris.

K-9 Corps. Ten years ago farms like these could be found in almost every state in the union. Now, this is the only one left.]

They never get enough credit, I think. There is that story *Dax*, nice
little children's book, but it's pretty simplistic, and it's only about one Dal-
matian that helped an orphan kid find his way to safety. "Dax" wasn't even
in the military, and helping lost children was a tiny fraction of dogs' overall contribution to the fight.

The first thing they used dogs for was triage, letting them sniff for who
was infected. Most countries were just copying the Israeli method of sending people past dogs in cages. You always had to keep them in cages, otherwise they might attack the person, or each other, or even their handler.
There was a lot of that, early in the war, dogs just going ballistic. It didn't
matter if they were police or military. It's that instinct, that involuntary, almost genetic terror. Fight or flight, and those dogs were bred to fight. A lot
of handlers lost hands, arms, a lot of throats got torn out. Can't blame the
dogs for it. In fact, that instinct was what the Israelis were counting on,
and it probably saved millions of lives.

It was a great program, but, again, just a fraction of what dogs were truly
capable of. Whereas the Israelis and, after them, a lot of other countries
only tried to exploit that terror instinct, we thought we could integrate it
into their regular training. And why not, we learned to do it for ourselves,
and are we really that much more evolved?

It all came down to training. You had to start young; even the most dis-
ciplined, prewar veterans were hardwired berserkers. The pups born after
the crisis came out of the womb literally smelling the dead. It was in the
air, not enough for us to detect, but just a few molecules, an introduction
on a subconscious level. That's not to say it made all of them automatic
warriors. The initial induction was the first and most important phase. You
took a group of pups, a random group, or even a whole litter, put them in a
room divided by a wire mesh. They're on one side, Zack's on the other. You
didn't have to wait long for a reaction. The first group we called Bs. They'd
start whimpering or howling. They'd lost it. They were nothing like the
As. Those pups would lock eyes with Zack, that was the key. They'd stand

their ground, bare their teeth, and let out this low growl that said, "Back the fuck off!" They could control themselves, and that was the foundation of our program.

Now, just because they could control themselves didn't mean that we could control them. Basic training was pretty much like the standard, prewar program. Could they handle PT?[1] Could they follow orders? Did they have the intelligence, and the discipline, to make soldiers? It was hard going, and we had a 60 percent washout rate. It wasn't uncommon for a recruit to be badly injured, perhaps even killed. A lot of people nowadays call that inhumane, though they don't seem to have the same sympathy for the handlers. Yeah, we had to do it, too, right alongside the dogs, right from day one of Basic, through ten more weeks of AIT.[2] It was hard training, especially the Live Enemy Exercises. You know we were the first ones to use Zack in our field training, before the infantry, before the Special Forces, even before the Zoomies at Willow Creek? It was the only way to really know if you could hack it, both as an individual and as a team.

How else could you have sent them on so many different missions? There were Lures, the kind that the Battle of Hope made famous. Pretty simple stuff; your partner hunts for Zack, then leads him into our firing line. Ks on early missions used to be fast, run in, bark, then jam it for the kill zone. Later, they got more comfortable. They learned to stay just a few feet ahead, backing away slowly, making sure they herded the maximum amount of targets. In that way, they actually called the shots.

There were also Decoys. Let's say you were setting up a firing line but you didn't want Zack to show up too early. Your partner would circle around the infested zone and only start barking on the far side. That worked with a lot of engagements, and it opened the door for the "Lemming" tactic.

During the Denver push, there was a tall building where a couple hundred refugees had accidentally been locked in with the infection and were now completely reanimated. Before our guys could storm the entrance, one

1. PT: Physical Training.
2. AIT: Advanced Individual Training.

of the Ks had his own idea to run up to the roof of a building across the street and start barking to draw Zack up onto the higher floors. It worked like a dream. The Gs made it up to the roof, saw their prey, made for him, and went spilling over the side. After Denver, Lemming went right into the playbook. Even the infantry started using it when Ks weren't available. It wasn't uncommon to see a grunt standing on the roof of a building, calling out to an infested building close by.

But the primary and most common mission of any K team was scouting, both SC and LRP. SC is Sweep and Clear, just attached to a regular unit, like conventional warfare. That's where training really paid off. Not only could they sniff Zack out miles before us, but the sounds they made always told you exactly what to expect. You could tell everything you needed to know by the pitch of the growl, and the frequency of the bark. Sometimes, when silence was required, body language worked just as well. The arch of the K's back, the raising of dander was all you needed to see. After a few missions, any competent handler, and we had no other kind, could read his partner's every signal. Scouts finding a ghoul half submerged in mud or legless among tall grass saved a lot of lives. I can't tell you how many times a grunt would thank us personally for spotting a concealed G that might have taken his foot off.

LRP was Long Range Patrol, when your partner would scout far beyond your lines, sometimes even traveling for days, to recon an infested area. They wore a special harness with a video uplink and GPS tracker that gave you real-time intel on the exact number and position of your targets. You could overlay Zack's position on a preexisting map, coordinating what your partner saw with his position on the GPS. I guess, from a technical side, it was pretty amazing, real-time hard intel like we used to have before the war. The brass loved it. I didn't; I was always too concerned with my partner. I can't tell you how stressful that was, to be standing in some computer-filled, air-conditioned room—safe, comfortable, and totally helpless. Later harness models had radio uplinks, so a handler could relay orders or, at least, abort the mission. I never worked with them. Teams had to be trained on those from the beginning. You couldn't go back and retrain a seasoned K. You couldn't teach an old dog new tricks. Sorry, bad joke. I heard a lot of those from the intel pukes; standing behind them as they watched the damn monitor, mentally stroking it to the wonders of their new "Data Orientation Asset." They thought they were so witty. Real fun for us to have DOA as an acronym.

[He shakes his head.]

I just had to stand there, thumb up my ass, watching my partner's POV as she crept through some forest, or marsh, or town. Towns and cities, that was the hardest. That was my team's specialty. Hound Town. You ever heard of that?

The K-9 Urban Warfare School?

That's it, a real town: Mitchell, Oregon. Sealed off, abandoned, and still filled with active Gs. Hound Town. It actually should have been called Terrytown, because most of the breeds at Mitchell were small terriers. Little cairns and Norwiches and JRs, good for rubble and narrow choke points. Personally, the hound in Hound Town suited me just fine. I worked with a dachle. They were, by far, the ultimate urban war fighters. Tough, smart, and, especially the minis, completely at home in confined spaces. In fact, that's what they were originally bred for; "badger dog," that's what dachshund means in German. That's why they had that hot dog look, so they could hunt in low, narrow badger burrows. You see how that kind of breeding already made them suited to the ducts and crawl spaces of an urban battleground. The ability to go through a pipe, an airshaft, in between walls, whatever, without losing their cool, was a major survival asset.

[We are interrupted. As if on cue, a dog limps over to Darnell's side. She is old. Her muzzle is white, the fur on her ears and tail is worn to leather.]

[To the dog.] Hey, little miss.

[Darnell gingerly lifts her to his lap. She is small, no more than eight or nine pounds. Although she bears some resemblance to a smooth-haired, miniature dachshund, her back is shorter than the standard breed.]

[To the dog.] You doin' okay, Maze? You feel all right? [To me.] Her full name's Maisey, but we never used it. "Maze" was pretty fitting, don't you think?

[With one hand he massages her back legs while with the other he rubs under her neck. She looks up at him with milky eyes. She licks his palm.]

Pure bloods were a total washout. Too neurotic, too many health problems, everything you'd expect from breeding an animal for just its aesthetic qualities. The new generation [he gestures to the mutt on his lap] was always a mix, whatever would increase both physical constitution and mental stability.

[The dog has gone to sleep. Darnell lowers his voice.]

They were tough, took a lot of training, not just individually but for working in groups on LRP missions. Long range, especially over wild terrain, was always risky. Not just from Zack, but also from feral Ks. Remember how bad they were? All those pets and strays that degenerated into killer packs. They were always a concern, usually in transition through low-infestation zones, always looking for something to eat. A lot of LRP missions were aborted in the beginning before we deployed escort dogs.

[He refers to the sleeping dog.]

She had two escorts. Pongo, who was a pit-rot mix, and Perdy . . . I don't really know what Perdy was, part shepherd, part stegosaurus. I wouldn't have let her anywhere near them if I hadn't gone through basic with their handlers. They turned out to be first-rate escorts. Fourteen times they chased off feral packs, twice they really got into it. I watched Perdy go after this two-hundred-pound mastiff, grab its skull in her jaws, you could actually hear the crack over the harness's surveillance mic.

The toughest part for me was making sure Maze stuck to the mission. She always wanted to fight. [Smiles down at the sleeping dachshund.] They were good escorts, always made sure she got to her target objective, waited for her, and always got her home safely. You know they even took down a few Gs in transit.

But isn't Z flesh toxic?

Oh yeah . . . no, no, no, they never bit. That would have been fatal. You'd see a lot of dead Ks in the beginning of the war, just lying there, no wounds, and you knew they'd bitten infected flesh. That's one of the reasons training was so important. They had to know how to defend themselves. Zack's got a lot of physical advantages, but balance isn't one of them. The bigger Ks could always hit between the shoulder blades or the small of the back, just knock them on their faces. The minis had the option of tripping, getting underfoot, or launching themselves at the knee-pit. Maze always preferred that, dropped 'em right on their backs!

[The dog stirs.]

[To Maze.] Oh, sorry, little miss. [Strokes the back of her neck.]

[To me.] By the time Zack got back up, you'd bought yourself five, maybe ten, fifteen seconds.

We had our share of casualties. Some Ks would have a fall, break a bone . . . If they were close to friendly forces, their handler could pick them up pretty easily, get them to safety. Most of the time they even returned to active duty.

What about the other times?

If they were too far, a Lure or an LRP . . . too far for rescue and too close to Zack . . . we petitioned for Mercy Charges, little explosive packs strapped to the harness so we could detonate them if it looked like there wasn't any chance of rescue. We never got them. "A waste of valuable resources." Cocksuckers. Putting a wounded soldier out of his misery was a waste but turning them into Fragmuts, now, that they'd consider!

Excuse me?

"Fragmuts." That was the unofficial name for the program that almost, *almost* got the green light. Some staff asshole'd read that the Russians had used "mine dogs" during World War II, strapped explosives to their backs and trained them to run under Nazi tanks. The only reason Ivan ended his program was the same reason we never began ours: the situation was no longer desperate enough. How fucking desperate do you have to be?

They'll never say it, but I think what stopped them was the threat of another Eckhart incident. That really woke 'em up. You know about that, right? Sergeant Eckhart, God bless her. She was a senior handler, operated up with AGN.[3] I never met her. Her partner was pulling a Lure mission outside Little Rock, fell in a ditch, broke his leg. The swarm was only a few steps away. Eckhart grabbed a rifle, tried to go out after him. Some officer got in her face, started spouting regs and half-assed justifications. She emptied half a clip in his mouth. MPs tackled her ass, held her on the ground. She could hear everything as the dead surrounded her partner.

What happened?

They hung her, public execution, real high profile. I understand, no, I really do. Discipline was everything, rule of law, that's all we had. But you better

3. AGN: Army Group North.

fucking believe there were some changes. Handlers were allowed to go after their partners, even if it meant risking their own lives. We weren't considered assets anymore, we were half-assets. For the first time the army saw us as teams, that a dog wasn't just a piece of machinery you could replace when "broken." They started looking at statistics of handlers who offed themselves after losing a partner. You know we had the highest rate of suicide among any branch of the service. More than Special Forces, more than Graves Registration, even more than those sick fucks at China Lake.[4] At Hound Town I met handlers from thirteen other countries. They all said the same thing. It didn't matter where you were from, what your culture or background, the feelings were still the same. Who could suffer that kind of loss and come out in one piece? Anyone who could wouldn't have made a handler in the first place. That's what made us our own breed, that ability to bond so strongly with something that's not even our own species. The very thing that made so many of my friends take the bullet's way out was what made us one of the most successful outfits in the whole fucking U.S. military.

The army saw it in me that day on a stretch of deserted road somewhere in the Colorado Rockies. I'd been on foot since escaping my apartment in Atlanta, three months of running, hiding, scavenging. I had rickets, fever, I was down to ninety-six pounds. I found these two guys under a tree. They were making a fire. Behind them was this little mutt. His paws and snout were bound with shoelaces. Dried blood was caked on his face. He was just lying there, glassy-eyed, whimpering softly.

What happened?

You know, I honestly don't remember. I must have hit one of them with my bat. They found it cracked over his shoulder. They found me on the other guy, just pounding his face in. Ninety-six pounds, half dead myself, and I beat this guy to within an inch of his life. The Guardsmen had to pull me off, cuff me to a car hulk, smack me a couple times to get me to refocus. That, I remember. One of the guys I attacked was holding his arm, the

4. China Lake weapons research facility.

other one was just lying there bleeding. "Calm the fuck down," the LT said, trying to question me, "What's wrong with you? Why'd you do that to your friends?" "He's not our friend!" the one with the broken arm yelled, "he's fuckin' crazy!" And all I kept saying was "Don't hurt the dog! Don't hurt the dog!" I remember the Guardsmen just laughed. "Jesus Christ," one of them said looking down at the two guys. The LT nodded, then looked at me. "Buddy," he said, "I think we got a job for you." And that's how I got recruited. Sometimes you find your path, sometimes it finds you.

[Darnell pets Maze. She cracks one eyelid. Her leathery tail wags.]

What happened to the dog?

I wish I could give you a Disney ending, like he became my partner or ended up saving a whole orphanage from a fire or something. They'd hit him with a rock to knock him out. Fluid built up in his ear canals. He lost all hearing in one and partial hearing in the other. But his nose still worked and he did make a pretty good ratter once I found him a home. He hunted enough vermin to keep that family fed all winter. That's kind of a Disney ending, I guess, Disney with Mickey stew. [Laughs softly.] You wanna know something crazy? I used to hate dogs.

Really?

Despised them; dirty, smelly, slobbering germ bags that humped your leg and made the carpet smell like piss. God, I hated them. I was that guy who'd come over to your house and refuse to pet the dog. I was the guy at work who always made fun of people with dog pictures on their desk. You know that guy who'd always threaten to call Animal Control when your pooch barked at night?

[Motions to himself.]

I lived a block away from a pet store. I used to drive by it every day on my way to work, confounded by how these sentimental, socially incompetent losers could shell out so much money on oversized, barking hamsters. During the Panic, the dead started to collect around that pet shop. I don't know where the owner was. He'd pulled down the gates but left the animals inside. I could hear them from my bedroom window. All day, all night. Just puppies, you know, a couple of weeks old. Scared little babies screaming for their mommies, for anyone, to please come and save them.

I heard them die, one by one as their water bottles ran out. The dead never got in. They were still massed outside the gate when I escaped, ran right past without stopping to look. What could I have done? I was unarmed, untrained. I couldn't have taken care of them. I could barely take care of myself. What could I have done? . . . Something.

[Maze sighs in her sleep. Darnell pats her gently.]

I could have done something.

※

SIBERIA, THE HOLY RUSSIAN EMPIRE

[The people who exist in this shantytown do so under the most primitive conditions. There is no electricity, no running water. The huts are grouped together behind a wall cut from the surrounding trees. The smallest hovel belongs to Father Sergei Ryzhkov. It is a miracle to see how the old cleric is still able to function. His walk reveals the numerous wartime and postwar injuries. The handshake reveals that all his fingers have been broken. His attempt at a smile reveals that those teeth not black with decay have been knocked out a long time ago.]

In order to understand how we became a "religious state," and how that state began with a man like me, you have to understand the nature of our war against the undead.

As with so many other conflicts, our greatest ally was General Winter. The biting cold, lengthened and strengthened by the planet's darkened skies, gave us the time we needed to prepare our homeland for liberation. Unlike the United States, we were fighting a war on two fronts. We had the Ural barrier in the west, and the Asian swarms from the southeast. Siberia had been stabilized, finally, but was by no means completely secure. We had so many refugees from India and China, so many frozen ghouls that thawed, and continue to thaw, each spring. We needed those winter months to reorganize our forces, marshal our population, inventory and distribute our vast stocks of military hardware.

We didn't have the war production of other countries. There was no Department of Strategic Resources in Russia: no industry other than finding enough food to keep our people alive. What we did have was our legacy of a military industrial state. I know you in the West have always laughed at us for this "folly." "Paranoid Ivan"—that's what you called us— "building tanks and guns while his people cry out for cars and butter." Yes, the Soviet Union was backward and inefficient and yes, it did bankrupt our economy on mountains of military might, but when the motherland needed them, those mountains were what saved her children.

[He refers to the faded poster on the wall behind him. It shows the ghostly image of an old Soviet soldier reaching down from heaven to hand a crude submachine gun to a grateful young Russian. The caption underneath reads "Dyedooshka, Spaciba" (Thank you, Grandfather).]

I was a chaplain with the Thirty-second Motor Rifle division. We were a Category D unit; fourth-class equipment, the oldest in our arsenal. We looked like extras in an old Great Patriotic War movie with our PPSH submachine guns and our bolt-action Mosin-Nagant rifles. We didn't have your fancy, new battle dress uniform. We wore the tunics of our grand-fathers: rough, moldy, moth-eaten wool that could barely keep the cold out, and did nothing to protect against bites.

We had a very high casualty rate, most of it in urban combat, and most of that due to faulty ammunition. Those rounds were older than us; some of them had been sitting in crates, open to the elements, since before Stalin breathed his last. You never knew when a "Cugov" would happen, when your weapon would "click" at the moment a ghoul was upon you. That happened a lot in the Thirty-second Motor Rifle division.

We weren't as neat and organized as your army. We didn't have your tight, light little Raj-Singh squares or your frugal "one shot, one kill" combat doctrine. Our battles were sloppy and brutal. We plastered the enemy in DShK heavy machine-gun fire, drowned them with flamethrowers and Katyusha rockets, and crushed them under the treads of our prehistoric T-34 tanks. It was inefficient and wasteful and resulted in too many needless deaths.

Ufa was the first major battle of our offensive. It became the reason we stopped going into the cities and started walling them up during winter. We learned a lot of lessons those first months, charging headlong into the rubble after hours of merciless artillery, fighting block by block, house by house, room by room. There were always too many zombies, too many mis-fires, and always too many bitten boys.

We didn't have L pills[1] like in your army. The only way to deal with in-fection was a bullet. But who was going to pull the trigger? Certainly not the other soldiers. To kill your comrade, even in cases as merciful as infec-tion, was too reminiscent of the decimations. That was the irony of it all. The decimations had given our armed forces the strength and discipline to do anything we asked of them, anything but that. To ask, or even order, one soldier to kill another was crossing a line that might have sparked an-other mutiny.

For a while the responsibility rested with the leadership, the officers and

1. L (Lethal) pill: A term to describe any poison capsule and one of the options available to infected U.S. military combatants during World War Z.

senior sergeants. We couldn't have made a more damaging decision. To have to look into the faces of these men, these boys whom you were responsible for, whom you fought with side by side, shared bread and blankets, saved his life or have him save yours. Who can focus on the monumental burden of leadership after having to commit such an act?

We began to see a noticeable degradation among our field commanders. Dereliction of duty, alcoholism, suicide—suicide became almost epidemic among the officer corps. Our division lost four experienced leaders, three junior lieutenants, and a major, all during the first week of our first campaign. Two of the lieutenants shot themselves, one right after committing the deed, and the other later that night. The third platoon leader chose a more passive method, what we began to call "suicide by combat." He volunteered for increasingly dangerous missions, acting more like a reckless enlisted man than a responsible leader. He died trying to take on a dozen ghouls with nothing but a bayonet.

Major Kovpak just vanished. No one knows exactly when. We knew he couldn't have been taken. The area was thoroughly swept and no one, absolutely no one left the perimeter without an escort. We all knew what probably happened. Colonel Savichev put out an official statement that the major had been sent on a long-range recon mission and had never returned. He even went so far as to recommend him for a first-class Order of the Rodina. You can't stop the rumors, and nothing is worse for a unit's morale than to know that one of their officers had deserted. I could not blame the man, I still cannot. Kovpak was a good man, a strong leader. Before the crisis he had done three tours in Chechnya and one in Dagestan. When the dead began to rise, he not only prevented his company from revolting, but led them all, on foot, carrying both supplies and wounded from Curta in the Salib Mountains all the way to Manaskent on the Caspian Sea. Sixty-five days, thirty-seven major engagements. Thirty-seven! He could have become an instructor—he'd more than earned the right—and had even been asked by STAVKA because of his extensive combat experience. But no, he volunteered for an immediate return to action. And now he was a deserter. They used to call this "the Second Decimation," the fact

that almost one in every ten officers killed themselves in those days, a decimation that almost brought our war effort to a crushing halt.

The logical alternative, the only one, was to therefore let the boys commit the act themselves. I can still remember their faces, dirty and pimply,
their red-rimmed eyes wide as they closed their mouths around their rifles.
What else could be done? It wasn't long before they began to kill themselves in groups, all those who'd been bitten in a battle gathering at the
field hospital to synchronize the moment when they would all pull the
trigger. I guess it was comforting, knowing that they weren't dying alone. It
was probably the only comfort they could expect. They certainly didn't get
it from me.

I was a religious man in a country that had long since lost its faith.
Decades of communism followed by materialistic democracy had left this
generation of Russians with little knowledge of, or need for, "the opium of
the masses." As a chaplain, my duties were mainly to collect letters from
the condemned boys to their families, and to distribute any vodka I managed to find. It was a next-to-useless existence, I knew, and the way our
country was headed, I doubted anything would occur to change that.

It was right after the battle for Kostroma, just a few weeks before the official assault on Moscow. I had come to the field hospital to give last rights
to the infected. They had been set apart, some badly mauled, some still
healthy and lucid. The first boy couldn't have been older than seventeen.
He wasn't bitten, that would have been merciful. The zombie had had its
forearms ripped off by the treads of an SU-152 self-propelled gun. All that
remained was hanging flesh and broken humerus bones, jagged at the
edges, sharp like spears. They stabbed right through the boy's tunic where
whole hands would have just grabbed him. He was lying on a cot, bleeding
from his belly, ashen-faced, rifle quivering in his hand. Next to him was a
row of five other infected soldiers. I went through the motions of telling
them I would pray for their souls. They either shrugged or nodded politely.
I took their letters, as I'd always done, gave them a drink, and even passed
out a couple cigarettes from their commanding officer. Even though I'd
done this many times, somehow I felt strangely different. Something was
stirring within me, a tense, tingling sensation that began to work its way

up through my heart and lungs. I began to feel my whole body tremble as the soldiers all placed the muzzles of their weapons underneath their chins. "On three," the oldest of them said. "One . . . two . . ." That was as far as they got. The seventeen-year-old flew backward and hit the ground. The others stared dumbfounded at the bullet hole in his forehead, then up to the smoking pistol in my hand, in God's hand.

God was speaking to me, I could feel his words ringing in my head. "No more sinning," he told me, "no more souls resigned to hell." It was so clear, so simple. Officers killing soldiers had cost us too many good officers, and soldiers killing themselves had cost the Lord too many good souls. Suicide was a sin, and we, his servants—those who had chosen to be his shepherds upon the earth—were the *only* ones who should bear the cross of releasing trapped souls from infected bodies! That is what I told division commander after he discovered what I'd done, and that is the message that spread first to every chaplain in the field and then to every civilian priest throughout Mother Russia.

What later became known as the act of "Final Purification" was only the first step of a religious fervor that would surpass even the Iranian revolution of the 1980s. God knew his children had been denied his love for too long. They needed direction, courage, hope! You could say that it is the reason we emerged from that war as a nation of faith, and have continued to rebuild our state, on the basis of that faith.

Is there any truth to the stories of that philosophy being perverted for political reasons?

[Pause.] I don't understand.

The president declared himself head of the Church . . .

Can't a national leader feel God's love?

But what about organizing priests into "death squads," and assassinating people under the premise of "purifying infected victims"?

[Pause.] I don't know what you're talking about.

Isn't that why you eventually fell out with Moscow? Isn't that why you're here?

[There is a long pause. We hear the sounds of footsteps approaching. Someone knocks at the door. Father Sergei opens it to find a small, ragged child. Mud stains his pale, frightened face. He speaks in a frantic, local dialect, shouting and pointing up the road. The old priest nods solemnly, pats the boy on the shoulder, then turns to me.]

Thank you for coming. Will you excuse me, please?

[As I rise to leave, he opens a large wooden chest at the foot of his bed, removing both a bible and a World War II–era pistol.]

ABOARD USS *HOLO KAI,*
OFF THE COAST OF THE HAWAIIAN ISLANDS

[*Deep Glider 7* looks more like a twin fuselage aircraft than a minisub. I lie on my stomach in the starboard hull, looking out through a thick, transparent nose cone. My pilot, Master Chief Petty Officer Michael Choi, waves at me from the port hull. Choi is one of the "old-timers," possibly the most experienced diver in the U.S. Navy's Deep Submergence Combat Corps (DSCC). His gray temples and weathered crow's-feet clash violently with his almost adolescent enthusiasm. As the mother ship lowers us into the choppy Pacific, I detect a trace of "surfer dude" bleeding through Choi's otherwise neutral accent.]

My war never ended. If anything, you could say it's still escalating. Every month we expand our operations and improve our material and human assets. They say there are still somewhere between twenty and thirty million of them, still washing up on beaches, or getting snagged in fishermen's nets. You can't work an offshore oil rig or repair a transatlantic cable without running into a swarm. That's what this dive is about: trying to find them, track them, and predict their movements so maybe we can have some advance warning.

[We hit the whitecaps with a jarring thud. Choi grins, checks his instruments, and shifts the channels on his radio from me to the mother ship. The water before my observation dome froths white for a second, then gives way to light blue as we submerge.]

You're not going to ask me about scuba gear or titanium shark suits, are you, because that crap's got nothing to do with my war? Spear guns and bang sticks and zombie river nets . . . I can't help you with any of that. If you want civilians, talk to civilians.

But the military did use those methods.

Only for brown water ops, and almost exclusively by army pukes. Personally, I've never worn a mesh suit or a scuba rig . . . well . . . at least not in combat. My war was strictly ADS. Atmospheric Diving Suit. Kind of like a space suit and a suit of armor all rolled into one. The technology actually goes back a couple hundred years, when some guy[1] invented a barrel with a faceplate and arm holes. After that you had stuff like the Tritonia and the Neufeldt-Kuhnke. They looked like something out of an old 1950s sci-fi movie, "Robby the Robot" and shit. It all kinda fell by the wayside when . . . do you really care about all this?

Yes, please . . .

1. John Lethbridge, circa 1715.

Well, that sort of technology fell by the wayside when scuba was invented. It only made a comeback when divers had to go deep, real deep, to work on offshore oil rigs. You see . . . the deeper you go, the greater the pressure; the greater the pressure, the more dangerous it is for scuba or similar mixed-gas rigs. You've got to spend days, sometimes weeks, in a decompression chamber, and if, for some reason, you have to shoot up to the surface . . . you get the bends, gas bubbles in the blood, in the brain . . . and we're not even talking about long-term health hazards like bone necrosis, soaking your body with shit nature never intended to be there.

[He pauses to check his instruments.]

The safest way to dive, to go deeper, to stay down longer, was to enclose your whole body in a bubble of surface pressure.

[He gestures to the compartments around us.]

Just like we are now—safe, protected, still on the surface as far as our bodies' concerned. That's what an ADS does, its depth and duration only limited by armor and life support.

So it's like a personal submarine?

"Submersible." A submarine can stay down for years, maintaining its own power, making its own air. A submersible can only make short duration dives, like World War II subs or what we're in now.

[The water begins to darken, deepening to a purplish ink.]

The very nature of an ADS, the fact that it's really just a suit of armor, makes it ideal for blue and black water combat. I'm not knocking soft suits, you know, shark or other mesh rigs. They've got ten times the maneuverability, the speed, the agility, but they're strictly shallow water at best, and if for some reason a couple of those fuckers get ahold of you . . . I've seen mesh divers with broken arms, broken ribs, three with broken necks. Drowning . . . if your air line was punctured or the regulator's ripped out of your mouth. Even in a hard helmet on a mesh-lined dry suit, all they'd have to do is hold you down, let your air run out. I've seen too many guys go out that way, or else try to race for the surface and let an embolism finish what Zack started.

Did that happen a lot to mesh suit divers?

Sometimes, especially in the beginning, but it *never* happened to us. There was no risk of physical danger. Both your body and your life support are encased in a cast-aluminum or high-strength composite shell. Most models' joints are steel or titanium. No matter which way Zack turned your arms, even if he managed to get a solid grip, which is hard considering how smooth and round everything is, it was physically impossible to break off a limb. If for some reason you need to jet up to the surface, just jettison your ballast or your thruster pack, if you had one . . . all suits are positively buoyant. They pop right up like a cork. The only risk might be if Zack were clinging to you during the ascent. A couple times I've had buddies surface with uninvited passengers hanging on for dear life . . . or undeath. [Chuckles.]

Balloon ascents almost never happened in combat. Most ADS models have forty-eight hours emergency life support. No matter how many Gs dog-piled you, no matter if a hunk of debris came crumbling down or your leg got snagged in an underwater cable, you could sit tight, snug and safe, and just wait for the cavalry. No one ever dives alone, and I think the longest any ADS diver has ever had to cool his heels was six hours. There were times, more than I can count on my fingers, where one of us would get snagged, report it, then follow up by saying that there was no immediate danger, and that the rest of the team should assist only *after* accomplishing their mission.

You say ADS models. Was there more than one type?

We had a bunch: civilian, military, old, new . . . well . . . relatively new. We couldn't build any wartime models, so we had to work with what was already available. Some of the older ones dated back to the seventies, the JIMs and SAMs. I'm really glad I never had to operate any of those. They only had universal joints and portholes instead of a face bowl, at least on the early JIMs. I knew one guy, from the British Special Boat Service. He had these mondo blood blisters all along his inner thighs from where the JIM's leg joints pinched his skin. Kick-ass divers, the SBS, but I'd never swap jobs with them.

We had three basic U.S. Navy models: the Hardsuit 1200, the 2000, and the Mark 1 Exosuit. That was my baby, the exo. You wanna talk about sci-fi, this thing looked like it was made to fight giant space termites. It was much slimmer than either of the two hardsuits, and light enough that you could even swim. That was the major advantage over the hardsuit, actually over all other ADS systems. To be able to operate above your enemy, even without a power sled or thruster packs, that more than made up for the fact that you couldn't scratch your itches. The hardsuits were big enough to allow your arms to be pulled into the central cavity to allow you to operate secondary equipment.

What kind of equipment?

Lights, video, side scanning sonar. The hardsuits were full-service units, exos were the bargain basement. You didn't have to worry about a lot of readouts and machinery. You didn't have any of the distractions or the multitasking of the hardsuits. The exo was sleek and simple, allowing you to focus on your weapon and the field in front of you.

What kind of weapons did you use?

At first we had the M-9, kind of a cheap, modified, knockoff of the Russian APS. I say "modified" because no ADS had anything close to resembling hands. You either had four-pronged claws or simple, industrial pincers. Both worked as hand-to-hand weapons—just grab a G's head and squeeze—but they made it impossible to fire a gun. The M-9 was fixed to your forearm and could be fired electrically. It had a laser pointer for accuracy and air-encased cartridges that fired these four-inch-long steel rods. The major problem was that they were basically designed for shallow water operations. At the depth we needed, they imploded like eggshells. About a year in we got a much more efficient model, the M-11, actually invented by the same guy who invented both the hardsuit and exo. I hope that crazy Canuck got an assload of medals for what he's done for us. The only problem with it was that DeStRes thought production was too expensive. They kept telling us that between our claws and preexisting construction tools, we had more than enough to handle Zack.

What changed their minds?

Troll. We were in the North Sea, repairing that Norwegian natural gas platform, and suddenly there they were . . . We'd expected some kind of attack—the noise and light of the construction site always attracted at least a handful of them. We didn't know a swarm was nearby. One of our sentries sounded off, we headed for his beacon, and we were suddenly inundated. Horrible thing to fight hand-to-hand underwater. The bottom churns up, your visibility is shot, like fighting inside a glass of milk. Zombies don't just die when you hit them, most of the time they disintegrate, fragments of muscle, organ, brain matter, mixed up with the silt and swirling around you. Kids today . . . fuckin' A, I sound like my pops, but it's true, the kids today, the new ADS divers in the Mark 3s and 4s, they have this "ZeVDeK"—Zero Visibility Detection Kit—with color-imaging sonar and low-light optics. The picture is relayed through a heads-up display right on your face bowl like a fighter plane. Throw in a pair of stereo hydrophones and you've got a real sensory advantage over Zack. That was *not* the case when I first went exo. We couldn't see, we couldn't hear—we couldn't even feel if a G was trying to grab us from behind.

Why was that?

Because the one fundamental flaw of an ADS is complete tactile blackout. The simple fact that the suit is hard means you can't feel anything from the outside world, even if a G has his hands right on you. Unless Zack is actively tugging, trying to pull you back or flip you around, you may not know he's there until his face is right up against yours. That night at Troll . . . our helmet lights only made the problem worse by throwing up a glare that was only broken by an undead hand or face. That was the only time I was ever spooked . . . not scared, you understand, just spooked, swinging in this liquid chalk and suddenly a rotting face is jammed against my face bowl.

The civilian oil workers, they wouldn't go back to work, even under threat of reprisals, until we, their escorts, were better armed. They'd lost enough of their people already, ambushed out of the darkness. Can't imagine what that must have been like. You're in this dry suit, working in near pitch-black, eyes stinging from the light of the welding torch, body numb from the cold or else burning from the hot water pumped through the system. Suddenly you feel these hands, or teeth. You struggle, call for help, try to fight or swim as they pull you up. Maybe a few body parts will rise to the surface, maybe they'll just pull up a severed lifeline. That was how the DSCC came into being as an official outfit. Our first mission was to protect the rig divers, keep the oil flowing. Later we expanded to beachhead sanitation and harbor clearing.

What is beachhead sanitation?

Basically, helping the jarheads get ashore. What we learned during Bermuda, our first amphibious landing, was that the beachhead was coming under constant attack by Gs walking out of the surf. We had to establish a perimeter, a semicircular net around the proposed landing area that was deep enough for ships to pass over, but high enough to keep out Zack.

That's where we came in. Two weeks before the landings took place, a ship would anchor several miles offshore and start banging away with their active sonar. That was to draw Zack away from the beach.

Wouldn't that sonar also lure in zombies from deeper water?

The brass told us that was an "acceptable risk." I think they didn't have anything better. That's why it was an ADS op, too risky for mesh divers. You knew that masses were gathering under that pinging ship, and that once they went silent, you'd be the brightest target out there. It actually turned out to be the closest thing we ever had to a cakewalk. The attack frequency was the lowest by far, and when the nets were up, they had an almost perfect success rate. All you needed was a skeleton force to keep a constant vigil, maybe snipe the occasional G that tried to climb the fence. They didn't really need us for this kind of op. After the first three landings, they went back to using mesh divers.

And harbor clearing?

That was *not* a cakewalk. That was in the final stages of the war, when it wasn't just about opening a beachhead, but reopening harbors for deep-water shipping. That was a massive, combined operation: mesh divers, ADS units, even civilian volunteers with nothing but a scuba rig and a spear gun. I helped clear Charleston, Norfolk, Boston, freakin' Boston, and the mother of all subsurface nightmares, the Hero City. I know grunts like to bitch about fighting to clear a city, but imagine a city underwater, a city of sunken ships and cars and planes and every kind of debris imaginable. During the evacuation, when a lot of container ships were trying to make as much room as they could, a lot of them dumped their cargo overboard. Couches, toaster ovens, mountains and mountains of clothes. Plasma TVs always crunched when you walked over them. I always imagined it was bone. I also imagined I could see Zack behind each washer and dryer, climbing over each pile of smashed air conditioners. Sometimes it was just my imagination, but sometimes . . . The worst . . . the worst was having to clear a sunken ship. There were always a few that had gone down within the harbor boundaries. A couple, like the *Frank Cable*, big sub tender turned refugee ship, had gone down right at the mouth of the harbor. Before she could be raised, we had to do a compartment-by-compartment sweep. That was the only time the exo ever felt bulky, unwieldy. I didn't smack my head in *every* passageway, but it sure as hell felt like it. A lot of the hatches were blocked by debris. We either had to cut our way through them, or through the decks and bulkheads. Sometimes the deck had been weakened by damage or corrosion. I was cutting through a bulkhead above the *Cable*'s engine room when suddenly the deck just collapsed under me. Before I could swim, before I could think . . . there were hundreds of them in the engine room. I was engulfed, drowning in legs and arms and hunks of meat. If I ever had a recurring nightmare, and I'm not saying I do, because I don't, but if I did, I'd be right back in there, only this time I'm completely naked . . . I mean I *would* be.

[I am surprised at how quickly we reach the bottom. It looks like a desert wasteland, glowing white against the permanent darkness. I see the stumps of wire coral, broken and trampled by the living dead.]

There they are.

[I look up to see the swarm, roughly sixty of them, walking out of the desert night.]

And here we go.

[Choi maneuvers us above them. They reach up for our searchlights, eyes wide and jaws slack. I can see the dim red beam of the laser as it settles on the first target. A second later, a small dart is fired into its chest.]

And one . . .

[He centers his beam on a second subject.]

And two . . .

[He moves down the swarm, tagging each one with a nonlethal shot.]

Kills me not to kill them. I mean, I know the whole point is to study their movements, set up an early warning network. I know that if we had the resources to clear them all we would. Still . . .

[He darts a sixth target. Like all the others, this one is oblivious to the small hole in its sternum.]

How do they do it? How are they still around? Nothing in the world corrodes like saltwater. These Gs should have gone way before the ones on land. Their clothes sure did, anything organic like cloth or leather.

[The figures below us are practically naked.]

So why not the rest of them? Is it the temperature at these depths, is it the pressure? And why do they have such a resistance to pressure anyway? At this depth the human nervous system should be completely Jell-O-ized. They shouldn't even be able to stand, let alone walk and "think" or whatever their version of thinking is. How do they do it? I'm sure someone real high up has all the answers and I'm sure the only reason they don't tell me is . . .

[He is suddenly distracted by a flashing light on his instrument panel.]

Hey, hey, hey. Check this out.

[I look down at my own panel. The readouts are incomprehensible.]

We got a hot one, pretty healthy rad count. Must be from the Indian Ocean, Iranian or Paki, or maybe that ChiCom attack boat that went down off Manihi. How about that?

[He fires another dart.]

You're lucky. This is one of the last manned recon dives. Next month it's all ROV, 100 percent Remotely Operated Vehicles.

There's been a lot of controversy over the use of ROVs for combat.

Never happen. The Sturge's[2] got way too much star power. She'd never let Congress go 'droid on us.

Is there any validity to their argument?

What, you mean if robots are more efficient fighters than ADS divers? Hell no. All that talk about "limiting human casualties" is bullshit. We never lost a man in combat, not one! That guy they keep talking about, Chernov, he was killed after the war, on land, when he got wasted and passed out on a tram line. Fuckin' politicians.

Maybe ROVs are more cost-effective, but one thing they're not is *better*. I'm not just talking about artificial intelligence; I'm talking heart, instinct, initiative, everything that makes us us. That's why I'm still here, same with the Sturge, and almost all the other vets who took the plunge during the war. Most of us are still involved because we have to be, because they still haven't yet come up with a collection of chips and bits to replace us. Believe me, once they do, I'll not only never look at an exosuit again, I'll quit the navy and pull a full-on Alpha November Alpha.

2. "The Sturgeon General": The old civilian nickname for the present commander of the DSCC.

What's that?

Action in the North Atlantic, this old, black-and-white war flick. There's a guy in it, you know the "Skipper" from *Gilligan's Island*, his old man.[3] He had a line . . . "I'm putting an oar on my shoulder and I'm starting inland. And the first time a guy says to me 'What's that on your shoulder?' that's where I'm settling for the rest of my life."

❦

QUEBEC, CANADA

[The small farmhouse has no wall, no bars on the windows, and no lock on the door. When I ask the owner about his vulnerability he simply chuckles and resumes his lunch. Andre Renard, brother of the legendary war hero Emil Renard, has requested that I keep his exact location secret. "I don't care if the dead find me," he says without feeling, "but I care very little for the living." The former French national immigrated to this place after the official end of hostilities in western Europe. Despite numerous invitations from the French government, he has not returned.]

Everyone else is a liar, everyone who claims that their campaign was "the hardest of the entire war." All those ignorant peacocks who beat their chests and brag about "mountain warfare" or "jungle warfare" or "urban warfare." Cities, oh how they love to brag about cities! "Nothing more terrifying than fighting in a city!" Oh really? Try underneath one.

3. Alan Hale, Senior.

Do you know why the Paris skyline was devoid of skyscrapers, I mean the prewar, proper Paris skyline? Do you know why they stuck all those glass and steel monstrosities out in La Defense, so far from the city center? Yes, there's aesthetics, a sense of continuity and civic pride . . . not like that architectural mongrel called London. But the truth, the logical, practical, reason for keeping Paris free from American-style monoliths, is that the earth beneath their feet is simply too tunneled to support it.

There are Roman tombs, quarries that supplied limestone for much of the city, even World War II bunkers used by the Resistance and *yes*, there *was* a Resistance! Then there is the modern Metro, the telephone lines, the gas mains, the water pipes . . . and through it all, you have the catacombs. Roughly six million bodies were buried there, taken from the pre-revolution cemeteries, where corpses were just tossed in like rubbish. The catacombs contained entire walls of skulls and bones arranged in macabre patterns. It was even functional in places where interlocking bones held back mounds of loose remains behind them. The skulls always seemed to be laughing at me.

I don't think I can blame the civilians who tried to survive in that subterranean world. They didn't have the civilian survival manual back then, they didn't have Radio Free Earth. It was the Great Panic. Maybe a few souls who thought they knew those tunnels decided to make a go of it, a few more followed them, then a few more. The word spread, "it's safe underground." A quarter million in all, that's what the bone counters have determined, two hundred and fifty thousand refugees. Maybe if they had been organized, thought to bring food and tools, even had enough sense to seal the entrances behind them and make damn sure those coming in weren't infected . . .

How can anyone claim that their experience can compare to what we endured? The darkness and the stink . . . we had almost no night vision goggles, just one pair per platoon, and that's if you were lucky. Spare batteries were in short supply for our electric torches, too. Sometimes there was only one working unit for an entire squad, just for the point man, cutting the darkness with a red-coated beam.

The air was toxic with sewage, chemicals, rotting flesh . . . the gas masks were a joke, most of the filters had long expired. We wore anything we could find, old military models, or firefighting hoods that covered your entire head, made you sweat like a pig, made you deaf as well as blind. You never knew where you were, staring through that misty visor, hearing the muffled voices of your squad mates, the crackle of your radioman.

We had to use hardwired sets, you see, because airwave transmissions were too unreliable. We used old telephone wire, copper, not fiber optic. We would just rip it off the conduits and keep massive rolls with us to extend our range. It was the only way to keep in contact, and, most of the time, the only way to keep from becoming lost.

It was so easy to become lost. All the maps were prewar and didn't take into account the modifications the survivors had made, all the interconnecting tunnels and alcoves, the holes in the floor that would suddenly open up in front of you. You would lose your way, at least once a day, sometimes more, and then have to trace your way back down the communications wire, check your location on the map, and try to figure out what had gone wrong. Sometimes it was only a few minutes, sometimes hours, or even days.

When another squad was being attacked, you would hear their cries over the radio or echoing through the tunnels. The acoustics were evil; they taunted you. Screams and moans came from every direction. You never knew where they were coming from. At least with the radio, you could try, maybe, to get a fix on your comrades' position. If they weren't panicked, if they knew where they were, if you knew where you were . . .

The running: you dash through the passageways, bash your head on the ceiling, crawl on your hands and knees, praying to the Virgin with all your might for them to hold for just a little longer. You get to their position, find it is the wrong one, an empty chamber, and the screams for help are still a long way off.

And when you arrive, maybe to find nothing but bones and blood. Maybe you are lucky to find the zombies still there, a chance for vengeance . . . if it has taken a long time to reach them, that vengeance must now include your reanimated friends. Close combat. Close like so . . .

[He leans across the table, pressing his face inches away from mine.]

No standard equipment; whatever one believed would suit him. There were no firearms, you understand. The air, the gas, it was too flammable. The fire from a gun . . .

[He makes the sound of an explosion.]

We had the Beretta-Grechio, the Italian air carbine. It was a wartime model of a child's carbon dioxide pellet gun. You got maybe five shots, six or seven if it was pressed right up to their heads. Good weapon, but always not enough of them. And you had to be careful! If you missed, if the ball struck the stone, if the stone was dry, if you got a spark . . . entire tunnels would catch, explosions that buried men alive, or fireballs that melted their masks right to their faces. Hand to hand is always better. Here . . .

[He rises from the table to show me something on his mantel-piece. The weapon's handle is encased in a semicircular steel ball. Protruding from this ball are two 8-inch steel spikes at right angles from each other.]

You see why, eh? No room to swing a blade. Quick, through the eye, or over the top of the head.

[He demonstrates with a quick punch and stab combination.]

My own design, a modern version of my great-grandfather's at Verdun, eh? You know Verdun—"On ne passé pas"—They shall not pass!

[He resumes his lunch.]

No room, no warning, suddenly they are upon you, perhaps right in front of your eyes, or grabbing from a side passage you didn't know was there. Everyone was armored in some way . . . chain mail or heavy leather . . . almost always it was too heavy, too suffocating, wet leather jackets and trousers, heavy metal chain-link shirts. You try to fight, you are already exhausted, men would tear off their masks, gasping for air, inhaling the stink. Many died before you could get them to the surface.

I used greaves, protection here (gestures to his forearms) and gloves, chain-covered leather, easy to remove when not in combat. They were my own design. We didn't have the American battle uniforms, but we did have your marsh covers, the long, high waterproof boots with the bite-proof fiber sewn into the lining. We needed those.

The water was high that summer; the rains were coming hard and the Seine was a raging torrent. It was always wet. There was rot between your fingers, your toes, in your crotch. The water was up to your ankles almost all the time, sometimes up to your knees or waist. You would be on point, walking, or crawling—sometimes we had to crawl in the stinking fluid up to our elbows. And suddenly the ground would just fall away. You would splash, headfirst, into one of those unmapped holes. You only had a few seconds to right yourself before your gas mask flooded. You kicked and thrashed, your comrades would grab you and haul fast. Drowning was the least of your worries. Men would be splashing, struggling to stay afloat with all that heavy gear, and suddenly their eyes would bulge, and you'd hear their muffled cries. You might feel the moment they attacked: the snap or tear and suddenly you fall over with the poor bastard on top of you. If he wasn't wearing the marsh covers . . . a foot is gone, the whole leg; if he had been crawling and went in face-first . . . sometimes that face would be gone.

Those were times when we called a full retreat to a defensive position and waited for the Cousteaus, the scuba divers trained to work and fight specifically in those flooded tunnels. With only a searchlight and a shark suit, if they were lucky to get one, and, at most, two hours of air. They were supposed to wear a safety line, but most of them refused to do so. The lines tended to get tangled and slow up the diver's progress. Those men, and women, had a one in twenty chance of survival, the lowest ratio of any branch of any army, I don't care what *anyone* says.[1] Is it any wonder they received an automatic Legion of Honor?

And what was it all for? Fifteen thousand dead or missing. Not just the Cousteaus, all of us, the entire core. Fifteen thousand souls in just three months. Fifteen thousand at a time when the war was winding down all over the world. "Go! Go! Fight! Fight!" It didn't have to be that way. How long did it take the English to clear all of London? Five years, three years after the war was officially over? They went slow and safe, one section at a time, low speed, low intensity, low casualty rate. Slow and safe, like most major cities. Why us? That English general, what he said about "Enough dead heroes for the end of time . . ."

"Heroes," that's what we were, that's what our leaders wanted, that's what our people felt they needed. After all that has happened, not just in this war, but in so many wars before: Algeria, Indochina, the Nazis . . . you understand what I am saying . . . you see the sorrow and pity? We understood what the American president said about "reclaiming our confidence"; we understood it more than most. We needed heroes, new names and places to restore our pride.

The Ossuary, Port-Mahon Quarry, the Hospital . . . that was our shining moment . . . the Hospital. The Nazis had built it to house mental patients, so the legend goes, letting them starve to death behind the concrete walls. During our war it had been an infirmary for the recently bitten. Later, as more began to reanimate and the survivors' humanity faded like their electric lamps, they began throwing the infected, and who knows who else, into that undead vault. An advance team broke through without realizing what was on the other side. They could have withdrawn, blown the tunnel, sealed them in again . . . One squad against three hundred zombies. One squad led by my baby brother. His voice was the last thing we heard before their radio went silent. His last words: *"On ne passé pas!"*

---

1. The highest fatality ratio of all allied forces is still hotly debated.

❧

DENVER, COLORADO

[The weather is perfect for the neighborhood picnic in Victory
Park. The fact that not one sighting has been recorded this
spring gives everyone even more reason to celebrate. Todd
Wainio stands in the outfield, waiting for a high fly ball that he
claims "will never come." Perhaps he's right, as no one seems to
mind me standing next to him.]

They called it "the road to New York" and it was a long, long road. We
had three main Army Groups: North, Center, and South. The grand strategy was to advance as one across the Great Plains, across the Midwest,
then break off at the Appalachians, the wings sweeping north and south,
shoot for Maine and Florida, then grind across the coast and link up with
AG Center as they slogged it over the mountains. It took three years.

Why so slow?

Dude, take your pick: foot transport, terrain, weather, enemies, battle doctrine . . . Doctrine was to advance as two solid lines, one behind the other,
stretching from Canada to Aztlan . . . No, Mexico, it wasn't Aztlan yet.
You know when a plane goes down, how all these firemen or whoever
would check a field for pieces of wreckage? They'd all go in a line, real slow,
making sure not one inch of ground was missed. That was us. We didn't
skip one damn inch between the Rockies and the Atlantic. Whenever you
spotted Zack, either in a group or just on his own, a FAR unit would halt . . .

FAR?

Force Appropriate Response. You couldn't stop, like, the whole Army
Group, for one or two zombies. A lot of the older Gs, the ones infected

early in the war, they were starting to get pretty grody, all deflated, parts of their skulls starting to show, some bone poking through the flesh. Some of them couldn't even stand anymore, and those are the ones you really had to watch for. They'd be crawling on their bellies toward you, or just thrashing facedown in the mud. You'd halt a section, a platoon, maybe even a company depending on how many you encountered, just enough to take 'em down and sanitize the battlefield. The hole your FAR unit left in the battle line was replaced by an equal force from the secondary line a click and a half behind you. That way the front was never broken. We leapfrogged this way all the way across the country. It worked, no doubt, but man, it took its time. Night also put the brakes on. Once the sun dipped, no matter how confident you felt or how safe the area seemed, the show was over till dawn the next morning.

And there was fog. I didn't know fog could be so thick that far inland. I always wanted to ask a climatologist or someone about that. The whole front might get slammed, sometimes for days. Just sitting there in zero visibility, occasionally one of your Ks would start barking or a man down the line would shout "Contact!" You'd hear the moan and then the shapes would appear. Hard enough just standing still and waiting for them. I saw a movie once,[1] this BBC documentary about how because the UK was so foggy, the British army would never stop. There was a scene, where the cameras caught a real firefight, just sparks from their weapons and hazy silhouettes going down. They didn't need that extra creepy soundtrack.[2] It freaked me out just to watch.

It also slowed us down to have to keep pace with the other countries, the Mexicans and Canucks. Neither army had the manpower to liberate their entire country. The deal was that they'd keep our borders clear while we get our house in order. Once the U.S. was secure, we'd give them everything they need. That was the start of the UN multinational force, but I was discharged long before those days. For me, it always felt like hurry up

---

1. *Lion's Roar*, produced by Foreman Films for the BBC.
2. Instrumental cover of "How Soon Is Now," originally written by Morrissey and Johnny Marr and recorded by the Smiths.

and wait, creeping along through rough terrain or built-up areas. Oh, and you wanna talk about speed bumps, try urban combat.

The strategy was always to surround the target area. We'd set up semi-permanent defenses, recon with everything from satellites to sniffer Ks, do whatever we could to call Zack out, and go in only after we were *sure* no more of them were coming. Smart and safe and relatively easy. Yeah, right!

As far as surrounding the "area," someone wanna tell me where that area actually begins? Cities weren't cities anymore, you know, they just grew out into this suburban sprawl. Mrs. Ruiz, one of our medics, called it "in-fill." She was in real estate before the war and explained that the hottest properties were always the land between two existing cities. Freakin' "in-fill," we all learned to hate that term. For us, it meant clearing block after block of burbland before we could even think of establishing a quarantine perimeter. Fast-food joints, shopping centers, endless miles of cheap, cookie-cutter housing.

Even in winter, it's not like everything was safe and snuggly. I was in Army Group North. At first I thought we were golden, you know. Six months out of the year, I wouldn't have to see a live G, eight months actually, given what wartime weather was like. I thought, hey, once the temp drops, we're little more than garbage men: find 'em, Lobo 'em, mark 'em for burial once the ground begins to thaw, no problem. But I should be Lobo'd for thinking that Zack was the only bad guy out there.

We had quislings, just like the real thing, but winterized. We had these Human Reclamation units, pretty much just glorified animal control. They'd do their best to dart any quislings we came across, tie 'em down, ship 'em to rehabilitation clinics, back when we thought we could rehabilitate them.

Ferals were a much more dangerous threat. A lot of them weren't kids anymore, some were teenagers, some full grown. They were fast, smart, and if they chose fight instead of flight, they could really mess up your day. Of course, HR would always try and dart them, and, of course, that didn't always work. When a two-hundred-pound feral bull is charging balls out for your ass, a couple CCs of tranq ain't gonna drop him before he hits home. A lot of HRs got pretty badly smashed up, a few had to be tagged and bagged. The brass had to step in and assign a squad of grunts for escort. If a dart didn't stop a feral, we sure as hell did. Nothing screams as high as a feral with a PIE round burning in his gut. The HR pukes had a real problem with that. They were all volunteers, all sticking to this code that human life, any human's life, was worth trying to save. I guess history sorta backed them up now, you know, seeing all those people that they managed to rehabilitate, all the ones we just woulda shot on sight. If they had had the resources, they might have been able to do the same for animals.

Man, feral packs, that freaked me out more than anything else. I'm not just talking dogs. Dogs you knew how to deal with. Dogs always telegraphed their attacks. I'm talking "Flies"[3]: F-Lions, cats, like part mountain lion, part ice age saberfuck. Maybe they were mountain lions, some sure looked like them, or maybe just the spawn of house cats that had to be super badass just to make it. I've heard that they grew bigger up north, some law of nature or evolution.[4] I don't really get the whole ecology thing, not past a few prewar nature shows. I hear it's because rats were, like, the new cows; fast and smart enough to get away from Zack, livin' on corpses, breeding by the millions in trees and ruins. They'd gotten pretty badass themselves, so anything tough enough to hunt them has to be a whole lot badder. That's an F-lion for you, about twice the size of a prewar puffball, teeth, claws, and a real, real jonesing for warm blood.

That must have been a hazard for the sniffer dogs.

Are you kidding? They loved it, even the little dachmutts, made 'em feel like dogs again. I'm talking about us, getting jumped from a tree limb, or a roof. They didn't charge you like F-hounds, they just waited, took their sweet time until you were too close to raise a weapon.

---

3. Pronounced "flies" mainly because their pouncing attacks gave the illusion of flight.
4. At present, no scientific data exist to substantiate the application of Bergmann's Rule during the war.

Outside of Minneapolis, my squad was clearing a strip mall. I was step-ping through the window of a Starbucks and suddenly three of them leap at me from behind the counter. They knock me over, start tearing at my arms, my face. How do you think I got this?

[He refers to the scar on his cheek.]

I guess the only real casualty that day was my shorts. Between the bite-proof BDUs and body armor we'd started wearing, the vest, the helmet . . . I hadn't worn a hard cover in so long, you forget how uncomfortable it is when you're used to going soft top.

Did ferals, feral people that is, know how to use firearms?

They didn't know how to do anything human, that's why they were ferals. No, the body armor was for protection against some of the regular people we found. I'm not talking organized rebels, just the odd LaMOE,[5] Last Man on Earth. There was always one or two in every town, some dude, or chick, who managed to survive. I read somewhere that the United States had the highest number of them in the world, something about our individualistic nature or something. They hadn't seen real people in so long, a lot of the initial shooting was just accidental or reflex. Most of the time we managed to talk them down. Those we actually called RCs, Robinson Crusoes—that was the polite term for the ones who were cool.

The ones we called LaMOEs, those were the ones who were a little too used to being king. King of what, I don't know, Gs and quislings and crazy F-critters, but I guess in their mind they were living the good life, and here we were to take it all away. That's how I got nailed.

We were closing on the Sears Tower in Chicago. Chicago, that was enough nightmares for three lifetimes. It was the middle of winter, wind whipping off the lake so hard you could barely stand, and suddenly I felt

5. LaMOE: pronounced *Lay-moh* with a silent *e*.

Thor's hammer smash me in the head. Slug from a high-powered hunting rifle. I never complained about our hard covers anymore after that. The gang in the tower, they had their little kingdom, and they weren't giving it up for anyone. That was one of the few times we went full convent; SAWs, nades, that's when the Bradleys started making a comeback.

After Chicago, the brass knew we were now in a full, multithreat environment. It was back to hard covers and body armor, even in summer. Thanks, Windy City. Each squad was issued pamphlets with the "Threat Pyramid."

It was ranked according to probability, not lethality. Zack at the bottom, then F-critters, ferals, quislings, and finally LaMOEs. I know a lot of guys from AG South like to bitch about how they always had it tougher on their end, 'cause, for us, winter took care of Zack's whole threat level. Yeah, sure, and replaced it with another one: winter!

What do they say the average temperature's dropped, ten degrees, fifteen in some areas?[6] Yeah, we had it real easy, up to our ass in gray snow, knowing that for every five Zacksicles you cracked there'd be at least as many up and at 'em at first thaw. At least the guys down south knew that once they swept an area, it stayed swept. They didn't have to worry about rear area attacks like us. We swept every area at least three times. We used everything from ramrods and sniffer Ks to high-tech ground radar. Over and over again, and all of this in the dead of winter. We lost more guys to frostbite than to anything else. And still, every spring, you knew, you just knew . . . it'd be like, "oh shit, here we go again." I mean, even today, with all the sweeps and civilian volunteer groups, spring's like winter used to be, nature letting us know the good life's over for now.

Tell me about liberating the isolated zones.

Always a hard fight, every single one. Remember these zones were still under siege, hundreds, maybe even thousands. The people holed up in the

---

6. Figures on wartime weather patterns have yet to be officially determined.

twin forts of Comerica Park/Ford Field, they must have had a combined moat—that's what we called them, moats—of at least a million Gs. That was a three-day slugfest, made Hope look like a minor skirmish. That was the only time I ever really thought we were gonna be overrun. They piled up so high I thought we'd be buried, literally, in a landslide of corpses. Battles like that, they'd leave you so fried, just wasted, body and mind. You'd want to sleep, nothing more, not eat or bathe or even fuck. You'd just want to find someplace warm and dry, close your eyes, forget everything.

What were the reactions of the people who you liberated?

Kind of a mix. The military zones, that was pretty low-key. A lot of formal ceremonies, raising and lowering of flags, "I relieve you, sir—I stand relieved," shit like that. There was also a little bit of wienie wagging. You know "we didn't need any rescuing" and all. I understand. Every grunt wants to be the one riding over the hill, no one likes to be the one in the fort. Sure you didn't need rescuing, buddy.

Sometimes it was true. Like the zoomies outside of Omaha. They were a strategic hub for airdrops, regular flights almost on the hour. They were actually living better than us, fresh chow, hot showers, soft beds. It almost felt like *we* were being rescued. On the other hand, you had the jarheads at Rock Island. They wouldn't let on how rough they had it, and that was cool with us. For what they went through, bragging rights was the least we could give them. Never met any of them personally, but I've heard the stories.

What about the civilian zones?

Different story entirely. We were so the shit! They'd be cheering and shouting. It was like what you'd think war was supposed to be, those old black-and-whites of GIs marching into Paris or wherever. We were rock stars. I got more . . . well . . . if there's a bunch of little dudes between here and the Hero City that happen to look like me . . . [Laughs.]

But there were exceptions.

Yeah, I guess. Maybe not all the time but there'd be this one person, this angry face in the crowd screaming shit at you. "What the fuck took you so long?" "My husband died two weeks ago!" "My mother died waiting for you!" "We lost half our people last summer!" "Where were you when we needed you?" People holding up photos, faces. When we marched into Janesville, Wisconsin, someone was holding up a sign with a picture of a smiling little girl. The words above it read "Better late than never?" He got beat down by his own people; they shouldn't have done that. That's the kind of shit we saw, shit that keeps you awake when you haven't slept in five nights.

Rarely, like, blue-moon rarely, we'd enter a zone where we were totally not welcome. In Valley City, North Dakota, they were like, "Fuck you, army! You ran out on us, we don't need you!"

Was that a secessionist zone?

Oh no, at least these people let us in. The Rebs only welcomed you with gunshots. I never got close to any of those zones. The brass had special units for Rebs. I saw them on the road once, heading toward the Black Hills. That was the first time since crossing the Rockies that I ever saw tanks. Bad feeling; you knew how that was gonna end.

There's been a lot of stories about questionable survival methods used by certain isolated zones.

Yeah, so? Ask them about it.

Did you see any?

Nope, and I didn't want to. People tried to tell me about it, people we liberated. They were so wound up inside, they just wanted to get it off their chests. You know what I used to say to them, "Keep it on your chest, your war's over." I didn't need any more rocks in my ruck, you know?

What about afterward? Did you talk to any of those people?

Yeah, and I read a lot about the trials.

How did they make you feel?

Shit, I don't know. Who am I to judge those people? I wasn't there, I didn't have to deal with that. This conversation we're having now, this question of "what if," I didn't have time for that back then. I still had a job to do.

I know historians like to talk about how the U.S. Army had such a low casualty rate during the advance. Low, as in compared to other countries, China or maybe the Russkies. Low, as in only counting the casualties caused by Zack. There were a million ways to get it on that road and over two-thirds weren't on that pyramid.

Sickness was a big one, the kinds of diseases that were supposed to be gone, like, in the Dark Ages or something. Yeah, we took our pills, had our shots, ate well, and had regular checkups, but there was just so much shit everywhere, in the dirt, the water, in the rain, and the air we breathed. Every time we entered a city, or liberated a zone, at least one guy would be gone, if not dead then removed for quarantine. In Detroit, we lost a whole platoon to Spanish flu. The brass really freaked on that one, quarantined the whole battalion for two weeks.

Then there were mines and booby traps, some civilian, some laid during our bugout west. Made a lot of sense back then. Just seed mile after mile and wait for Zack to blow himself up. Only problem is, mines don't work that way. They don't blow up a human body, they take off a leg or ankle or the family jewels. That's what they're designed for, not to kill people, but to wound 'em so the army will spend valuable resources keeping them alive, and then send 'em home in a wheelchair so Ma and Pa Civilian can be reminded every time they see 'em that maybe supporting this war isn't such a good idea. But Zack has no home, no Ma and Pa Civilian. All conventional mines do is create a bunch of crippled ghouls that, if anything, just makes your job that much harder because you *want* them upright and easy to spot, not crawling around the weeds waiting to be stepped on like land mines themselves. You couldn't know where most mines were; a lot of the units that set them during the retreat hadn't marked them correctly or had lost their coordinates or simply weren't alive anymore to tell you. And then you had all those stupid fuckin' LaMOE jobs, the punji stakes and trip-wired shotgun shells.

I lost a buddy of mine that way, in a Wal-Mart in Rochester, New York. He was born in El Salvador but grew up in Cali. You ever heard of the Boyle Heights Boyz? They were these hard-core LA bangers who were deported back to El Salvador because they were technically illegal. My buddy was plopped there right before the war. He fought his way back up through Mexico, all during the worst days of the Panic, all on foot with nothing but a machete. He didn't have any family left, no friends, just his adopted home. He loved this country so much. Reminded me of my grandpa, you know, the whole immigrant thing. And then to catch a twelve-gauge in the face, probably set by a LaMOE who'd stopped breathing years before. Fuckin' mines and booby traps.

And then you just had accidents. So many buildings had been weakened from the fighting. Throw in years of neglect, and foot after foot of snow. Whole roofs collapsed, no warning, whole structures just tumbling down. I lost someone else like that. She had a contact, a feral running at her across an abandoned auto garage. She fired her weapon, that's all it took. I don't know how many pounds of snow and ice brought that roof down. She was . . . we were . . . close, you know. We never did anything about it. I guess we thought that would make it "official." I guess we thought it would make it easier in case something happened to one of us.

[He looks over at the bleachers, smiling at his wife.]

Didn't work.

[He takes a moment, a long breath.]

And then there were psych casualties. More than anything else combined. Sometimes we'd march into barricaded zones and find nothing but rat-gnawed skeletons. I'm talking about the zones that weren't overrun, the ones that fell to starvation or disease, or just a feeling that tomorrow wasn't worth seeing. We once broke into a church in Kansas where it was clear the adults killed all the kids first. One guy in our platoon, an Amish guy, used to read all their suicide notes, commit them to memory, then give himself this little cut, this tiny half-inch nick somewhere on his body so he would "never forget." Crazy bastard was sliced from his neck to the bottom of his toes. When the LT found out about it . . . sectioned eight his ass right outa there.

Most of the Eight Balls were later in the war. Not from the stress, though, you understand, but from the lack of it. We all knew it would be over soon, and I think a lot of people who'd been holding it together for so long must've had that little voice that said, "Hey, buddy, it's cool now, you can let go."

I knew this one guy, massive 'roidasaurus, he'd been a professional wrestler before the war. We were walking up the freeway near Pulaski, New York, when the wind picked up the scent of a jackknifed big rig. It'd been loaded with bottles of perfume, nothing fancy, just cheap, strip mall scent. He froze and started bawlin' like a kid. Couldn't stop. He was a monster with a two grand body count, an ogre who'd once picked up a G and used it as a club for hand-to-hand combat. Four of us had to carry him out on a stretcher. We figured the perfume must have reminded him of someone. We never found out who.

Another guy, nothing special about him, late forties, balding, bit of a paunch, as much as anyone could have back then, the kinda face you'd see in a prewar heartburn commercial. We were in Hammond, Indiana, scouting defenses for the siege of Chicago. He spied a house at the end of a deserted street, completely intact except for boarded-up windows and a crashed-in front door. He got a look on his face, a grin. We should have known way before he dropped out of formation, before we heard the shot. He was sitting in the living room, in this worn, old easy chair, SIR between his knees, that smile still on his face. I looked up at the pictures on the mantelpiece. It was his home.

Those were extreme examples, ones that even I could have guessed. A lot of the others, you just never knew. For me, it wasn't just who was cracking up, but who wasn't. Does that make sense?

One night in Portland, Maine, we were in Deering Oaks Park, policing piles of bleached bones that had been there since the Panic. Two grunts pick up these skulls and start doing a skit, the one from *Free to Be, You and Me*, the two babies. I only recognized it because my big brother had the record, it was a little before my time. Some of the older Grunts, the Xers, they loved it. A little crowd started gathering, everyone laughing and howling at these two skulls. "Hi-Hi-I'm a baby.—Well what do you think I am, a loaf'a bread?" And when it was over, everyone spontaneously burst into song, "There's a land that I see . . ." playing femurs like goddamn banjos. I looked across the crowd to one of our company shrinks. I could never pronounce his real name, Doctor Chandra-something.[7] I made eye contact and gave him this look, like "Hey, Doc, they're all nut jobs, right?" He must have known what my eyes were asking because he just smiled back and shook his head. That really spooked me; I mean, if the ones who were acting loopy weren't, then how did you know who'd really lost it?

Our squad leader, you'd probably recognize her. She was in *The Battle of the Five Colleges*. Remember the tall, amazon chick with the ditch blade, the one who'd sung that song? She didn't look like she used to in the movie. She'd burned off her curves and a crew cut replaced all that long, thick, shiny black hair. She was a good squad leader, "Sergeant Avalon." One day we found a turtle in a field. Turtles were like unicorns back then, you hardly saw them anymore. Avalon got this look, I don't know, like a kid. She smiled. She never smiled. I heard her whisper something to the turtle, I thought it was gibberish: "Mitakuye Oyasin." I found out later that it was Lakota for "all my relations." I didn't even know she was part Sioux. She never talked about it, about anything about her. And suddenly, like a ghost, there was Doctor Chandra, with that arm he always put around their shoulders and that soft, no-big-deal offer of "C'mon, Sarge, let's grab a cup of coffee."

7. Major Ted Chandrasekhar.

That was the same day the president died. He must have also heard that little voice. "Hey, buddy, it's cool now, you can let go." I know a lot of people weren't so into the VP, like there was no way he could replace the Big Guy. I really felt for him, mainly 'cause I was now in the same position. With Avalon gone, I was squad leader.

It didn't matter that the war was almost over. There were still so many battles along the way, so many good people to say good-bye to. By the time we reached Yonkers, I was the last of the old gang from Hope. I don't know how I felt, passing all that rusting wreckage: the abandoned tanks, the crushed news vans, the human remains. I don't think I felt much of anything. Too much to do when you're squad leader, too many new faces to take care of. I could feel Doctor Chandra's eyes boring into me. He never came over though, never let on that there was anything wrong. When we boarded the barges on the banks of the Hudson, we managed to lock eyes. He just smiled and shook his head. I'd made it.

GOOD-BYES

[Snow has begun falling. Reluctantly, "the Whacko" turns back for the house.]

You ever heard of Clement Attlee? Of course not, why should you? Man was a loser, a third-rate mediocrity who only slipped into the history books because he unseated Winston Churchill before World War II officially ended. The war in Europe was over, and to the British people, there was this feeling that they'd suffered enough, but Churchill kept pushing to help the United States against Japan, saying the fight wasn't finished until it was finished everywhere. And look what happened to the Old Lion. That's what we didn't want to happen to our administration. That's exactly why we decided to declare victory once the continental U.S. had been secured.

Everyone knew the war wasn't really over. We still had to help out our allies and clear whole parts of the world that were entirely ruled by the dead. There was still so much work to do, but since our own house was in order, we had to give people the option to go home. That's when the UN multinational force was created, and we were pleasantly surprised how many volunteers signed up in the first week. We actually had to turn some of them away, put them on the reserve list or assign them to train all the young bucks who missed the drive across America. I know I caught a lot of flak for going UN instead of making it an all-American crusade, and to be totally honest, I really couldn't give a damn. America's a fair country, her people expect a fair deal, and when that deal ends with the last boots on Atlantic beaches, you shake their hands, pay them off, and let anyone who wants to reclaim their private lives do so.

Maybe it's made the overseas campaigns a little slower. Our allies are on their feet again, but we still have a few White Zones to clear: mountain ranges, snowline islands, the ocean floor, and then there's Iceland . . . Iceland's gonna be tough. I wish Ivan would let us help out in Siberia, but, hey, Ivan's Ivan. And we still have attacks right here at home as well, every spring, or every so often near a lake or beach. The numbers are declining, thank heavens, but it doesn't mean people should let down their guard. We're still at war, and until every trace is sponged, and purged, and, if need be, blasted from the surface of the Earth, everybody's still gotta pitch in and do their job. Be nice if that was the lesson people took from all this misery. We're all in this together, so pitch in and do your job.

[We stop by an old oak tree. My companion looks it up and down, taps it lightly with his cane. Then, to the tree . . .]

You're doin' a good job.

❦

KHUZHIR, OLKHON ISLAND, LAKE BAIKAL, THE HOLY RUSSIAN EMPIRE

[A nurse interrupts our interview to make sure Maria Zhuganova takes her prenatal vitamins. Maria is four months pregnant. This will be her eighth child.]

My only regret was that I couldn't remain in the army for the "liberation" of our former republics. We'd purged the motherland of the undead filth, and now it was time to carry the war beyond our borders. I wish I could have been there, the day we formally reabsorbed Belarus back into the empire. They say it will be the Ukraine soon, and after that, who knows. I wish I could still have been a participant, but I had "other duties" . . .

[Gently, she pats her womb.]

I don't know how many clinics like this there are throughout the Rodina. Not enough, I'm sure. So few of us, young, fertile women who didn't succumb to drugs, or AIDS, or the stink of the living dead. Our leader says that the greatest weapon a Russian woman can wield now is her uterus. If that means not knowing my children's fathers, or . . .

[Her eyes momentarily hit the floor.]

. . . my children, so be it. I serve the motherland, and I serve with all my heart.

[She catches my eye.]

You're wondering how this "existence" can be reconciled with our new fundamentalist state? Well, stop wondering, it can't. All that religious dogma, that's for the masses. Give them their opium and keep them pacified. I don't think anyone in the leadership, or even the Church, really believes what they're preaching, maybe one man, old Father Ryzhkov before they chucked him out into the wilderness. He had nothing left to offer, unlike me. I've got at least a few more children to give the motherland. That's why I'm treated so well, allowed to speak so freely.

[Maria glances at the one-way glass behind me.]

What are they going to do to me? By the time I've exhausted my usefulness, I will have already outlived the average woman.

[She presents the glass with an extremely rude finger gesture.]

And besides, they *want* you to hear this. That is why they've let you into our country, to hear our stories, to ask your questions. You're being used, too, you know. Your mission is to tell your world of ours, to make them see what will happen if anyone ever tries to fuck with us. The war drove us back to our roots, made us remember what it means to be Russian. We are strong again, we are feared again, and to Russians, that only means one thing, we are finally *safe* again! For the first time in almost a hundred years, we can finally warm ourselves in the protective fist of a Caesar, and I'm sure you know the word for Caesar in Russian.

BRIDGETOWN, BARBADOS, WEST INDIES FEDERATION

[The bar is almost empty. Most of the patrons have either left by their own power, or been carried out by the police. The last of the night staff clean the broken chairs, broken glass, and pools of blood off the floor. In the corner, the last of the South Africans sings an emotional, inebriated version of Johnny Clegg's wartime rendition of "Asimbonaga." T. Sean Collins absentmindedly hums a few bars, then downs his shot of rum, and hurriedly signals for another.]

I'm addicted to murder, and that's about the nicest way I can put it. You might say that's not technically true, that since they're already dead I'm not really killing. Horseshit; it's murder, and it's a rush like nothing else. Sure, I can dis those prewar mercenaries all I want, the 'Nam vets and Hell's Angels, but at this point I'm no different from them, no different from those jungle humpers who never came home, even when they did, or those World War II fighter jocks who traded in their Mustangs for hogs.

You're living on such a high, so keyed up all the time, that anything else seems like death.

I tried to fit in, settle down, make some friends, get a job and do my part to help put America back together. But not only was I dead, I couldn't think about anything else but killing. I'd start to study people's necks, their heads. I'd think, "Hmmmm, that dude's probably got a thick frontal lobe, I gotta go in through the eye socket." Or "hard blow to the occipital'd drop that chick pretty fast." It was when the new prez, "the Whacko"—Jesus, who the hell am I to call anybody else that?—when I heard him speak at a rally, I must have thought of at least fifty ways to bring him down. That's when I got out, as much for everyone else's sake as my own. I knew one day I'd hit my limit, get drunk, get in a fight, lose control. I knew once I started, I couldn't stop, so I said good-bye and joined the Impisi, same name as the South African Special Forces. Impisi: Zulu for Hyena, the one who cleans up the dead.

We're a private outfit, no rules, no red tape, which is why I chose them over a regular gig with the UN. We set our own hours, choose our own weapons.

[He motions to what looks like a sharpened steel paddle at his side.]

"Pouwhenua"—got it from a Maori brother who used to play for the All Blacks before the war. Bad motherfuckers, the Maori. That battle at One Tree Hill, five hundred of them versus half of reanimated Auckland. The pouwhenua's a tough weapon to use, even if this one's steel instead of wood. But that's the other perk of being a soldier of fortune. Who can get a rush anymore from pulling a trigger? It's gotta be hard, dangerous, and the more Gs you gotta take on, the better. Of course, sooner or later there's not gonna be any of them left. And when that happens . . .

[At that point the *Imfingo* rings its cast-off bell.]

There's my ride.

[T. Sean signals to the waiter, then flips a few silver rand on the table.]

I still got hope. Sounds crazy, but you never know. That's why I save most of my fees instead of giving back to the host country or blowing it on who knows what. It can happen, finally getting the monkey off your back. A Canadian brother, "Mackee" Macdonald, right after clearing Baffin Island, he just decided he'd had enough. I hear he's in Greece now, some monastery or something. It can happen. Maybe there's still a life out there for me. Hey, a man can dream, right? Of course, if it doesn't work out that way, if one day there's still a monkey but no more Zack . . .

[He rises to leave, shouldering his weapon.]

Then the last skull I crack'll probably be my own.

SAND LAKES PROVINCIAL WILDERNESS PARK, MANITOBA, CANADA

[Jesika Hendricks loads the last of the day's "catch" into the sled, fifteen bodies and a mound of dismembered parts.]

I try not to be angry, bitter at the unfairness of it all. I wish I could make sense of it. I once met an ex-Iranian pilot who was traveling through Canada looking for a place to settle down. He said that Americans are the only people he's ever met who just can't accept that bad things can happen to good people. Maybe he's right. Last week I was listening to the radio and just happened to hear [name withheld for legal reasons]. He was doing his usual thing—fart jokes and insults and adolescent sexuality—and I remember thinking, "This man survived and my parents didn't." No, I try not to be bitter.

❦

TROY, MONTANA, USA

[Mrs. Miller and I stand on the back deck, above the children
playing in the central courtyard.]

You can blame the politicians, the businessmen, the generals, the "machine," but really, if you're looking to blame someone, blame me. I'm the
American system, I'm the machine. That's the price of living in a democracy; we all gotta take the rap. I can see why it took so long for China to
finally embrace it, and why Russia just said "fuck it" and went back to
whatever they call their system now. Nice to be able to say, "Hey, don't
look at me, it's not my fault." Well, it is. It is my fault, and the fault of
everyone of my generation.

[She looks down at the children.]

I wonder what future generations will say about us. My grandparents suffered through the Depression, World War II, then came home to build the
greatest middle class in human history. Lord knows they weren't perfect,
but they sure came closest to the American dream. Then my parents' generation came along and fucked it all up—the baby boomers, the "me" generation. And then you got us. Yeah, we stopped the zombie menace, but
we're the ones who let it become a menace in the first place. At least we're
cleaning up our own mess, and maybe that's the best epitaph to hope for.
"Generation Z, they cleaned up their own mess."

CHONGQING, CHINA

[Kwang Jingshu does his final house call for the day, a little boy with some kind of respiratory illness. The mother fears it's another case of tuberculosis. The color returns to her face when the doctor assures her it's just a chest cold. Her tears and gratitude follow us down the dusty street.]

It's comforting to see children again, I mean those who were born after the war, real children who know nothing but a world that includes the living dead. They know not to play near water, not to go out alone or after dark in the spring or summer. They don't know to be afraid, and that is the greatest gift, the only gift we can leave to them.

Sometimes I think of that old woman at New Dachang, what she lived through, the seemingly unending upheaval that defined her generation. Now that's me, an old man who's seen his country torn to shreds many times over. And yet, every time, we've managed to pull ourselves together, to rebuild and renew our nation. And so we will again—China, and the world. I don't really believe in an afterlife—the old revolutionary to the end—but if there is, I can imagine my old comrade Gu laughing down at me when I say, with all honesty, that everything's going to be all right.

WENATCHEE, WASHINGTON, USA

[Joe Muhammad has just finished his latest masterpiece, a thirteen-inch statuette of a man in midshuffle, wearing a torn Baby Bjorn, staring ahead with lifeless eyes.]

I'm not going to say the war was a good thing. I'm not that much of a sick fuck, but you've got to admit that it did bring people together. My parents never stopped talking about how much they missed the sense of community back in Pakistan. They never talked to their American neighbors, never invited them over, barely knew their names unless it was to complain about loud music or a barking dog. Can't say that's the kind of world we live in now. And it's not just the neighborhood, or even the country. Anywhere around the world, anyone you talk to, all of us have this powerful shared experience. I went on a cruise two years ago, the Pan Pacific Line across the islands. We had people from everywhere, and even though the details might have been different, the stories themselves were all pretty much the same. I know I come off as a little too optimistic, because I'm sure that as soon as things really get back to "normal," once our kids or grandkids grow up in a peaceful and comfortable world, they'll probably go right back to being as selfish and narrow-minded and generally shitty to one another as we were. But then again, can what we all went through really just go away? I once heard an African proverb, "One cannot cross a river without getting wet." I'd like to believe that.

Don't get me wrong, it's not like I don't miss some things about the old world, mainly just stuff, things I used to have or things I used to think I could have one day. Last week we had a bachelor party for one of the young guys on the block. We borrowed the only working DVD player and a few prewar skin flicks. There was one scene where Lusty Canyon was getting reamed by three guys on the hood of this pearl gray BMW Z4 convertible, and all I could think was *Wow, they sure don't make cars like that anymore.*

TAOS, NEW MEXICO, USA

[The steaks are almost done. Arthur Sinclair flips the sizzling slabs, relishing the smoke.]

Of all the jobs I've done, being a money cop was best. When the new president asked me to step back into my role as SEC chairman, I practically kissed her on the spot. I'm sure, just like my days at DeStRes, I only have the job because no one else wants it. There's still so many challenges ahead, still so much of the country on the "turnip standard." Getting people away from barter, and to trust the American dollar again . . . not easy. The Cuban peso is still king, and so many of our more affluent citizens still have their bank accounts in Havana.

Just trying to solve the surplus bill dilemma is enough for any administration. So much cash was scooped up after the war, in abandoned vaults, houses, on dead bodies. How do you tell those looters apart from the people who've actually kept their hard-earned greenbacks hidden, especially when records of ownership are about as rare as petroleum? That's why being a money cop is the most important job I've ever had. We have to nail the bastards who're preventing confidence from returning to the American economy, not just the penny-ante looters but the big fish as well, the sleazebags who're trying to buy up homes before survivors can reclaim them, or lobbying to deregulate food and other essential survival commodities . . . and that bastard Breckinridge Scott, yes, the Phalanx king, still hiding like a rat in his Antarctic Fortress of Scumditude. He doesn't know it yet, but we've been in talks with Ivan not to renew his lease. A lot of people back home are waiting to see him, particularly the IRS.

[He grins and rubs his hands together.]

Confidence, it's the fuel that drives the capitalist machine. Our economy can only run if people believe in it; like FDR said, "The only thing we have to fear is fear itself." My father wrote that for him. Well, he claimed he did.

It's already starting, slowly but surely. Every day we get a few more registered accounts with American banks, a few more private businesses opening up, a few more points on the Dow. Kind of like the weather. Every year the summer's a little longer, the skies a little bluer. It's getting better. Just wait and see.

[He reaches into a cooler of ice, pulling out two brown bottles.]

Root beer?

❦

KYOTO, JAPAN

[It is a historic day for the Shield Society. They have finally been accepted as an independent branch of the Japanese Self-Defense Forces. Their main duty will be to teach Japanese civilians how to protect themselves from the living dead. Their ongoing mission will also involve learning both armed and unarmed techniques from non-Japanese organizations, and helping to foster those techniques around the world. The Society's antifirearm as well as prointernational message have already been hailed as an instant success, drawing journalists and dignitaries from almost all UN nations.

Tomonaga Ijiro stands at the head of the receiving line, smiling and bowing as he greets his parade of guests. Kondo Tatsumi smiles as well, looking at his teacher from across the room.]

You know I don't really believe any of this spiritual "BS," right? As far as I'm concerned, Tomonaga's just a crazy old hibakusha, but he has started something wonderful, something I think is vital for the future of Japan. His generation wanted to rule the world, and mine was content to let the world, and by the world I mean your country, rule us. Both paths led to the near destruction of our homeland. There has to be a better way, a middle path where we take responsibility for our own protection, but not so much that it inspires anxiety and hatred among our fellow nations. I can't tell you if this is the right path; the future is too mountainous to see too far ahead. But I will follow Sensei Tomonaga down this path, myself and the many others who join our ranks every day. Only "the gods" know what awaits us at its end.

❦

ARMAGH, IRELAND

[Philip Adler finishes his drink, and rises to leave.]

We lost a hell of a lot more than just people when we abandoned them to the dead. That's all I'm going to say.

❦

TEL AVIV, ISRAEL

[We finish our lunch as Jurgen aggressively snatches the bill from my hand.]

Please, my choice of food, my treat. I used to hate this stuff, thought it looked like a buffet of vomit. My staff had to drag me here one afternoon, these young Sabras with their exotic tastes. "Just try it, you old yekke," they'd say. That's what they called me, a "yekke." It means tight ass, but the official definition is German Jew. They were right on both counts.

I was in the "Kindertransport," the last chance to get Jewish children out of Germany. That was the last time I saw any of my family alive. There's a little pond, in a small town in Poland, where they used to dump the ashes. The pond is still gray, even half a century later.

I've heard it said that the Holocaust has no survivors, that even those who managed to remain technically alive were so irreparably damaged, that their spirit, their soul, the person that they were supposed to be, was gone forever. I'd like to think that's not true. But if it is, then no one on Earth survived this war.

❧

ABOARD USS *TRACY BOWDEN*

[Michael Choi leans against the fantail's railing, staring at the horizon.]

You wanna know who lost World War Z? Whales. I guess they never really had much of a chance, not with several million hungry boat people and half the world's navies converted to fishing fleets. It doesn't take much, just one helo-dropped torp, not so close as to do any physical damage, but close enough to leave them deaf and dazed. They wouldn't notice the factory ships until it was too late. You could hear it for miles away, the warhead detonations, the shrieks. Nothing conducts sound energy like water.

Hell of a loss, and you don't have to be some patchouli stinking crunchhead to appreciate it. My dad worked at Scripps, not the Claremont girl's school, the oceanographic institute outside of San Diego. That's why I joined the navy in the first place and how I first learned to love the ocean. You couldn't help but see California grays. Majestic animals, they were finally making a comeback after almost being hunted to extinction. They'd stopped being afraid of us and sometimes you could paddle out close enough to touch them. They could have killed us in a heartbeat, one smack of a twelve-foot tail fluke, one lunge of a thirtysomething-ton body. Early whalers used to call them devilfish because of the fierce fights they'd put up when cornered. They knew we didn't mean them any harm, though. They'd even let us pet them, or, maybe if they were feeling protective of a calf, just brush us gently away. So much power, so much potential for destruction. Amazing creatures, the California grays, and now they're all gone, along with the blues, and finbacks, and humpbacks, and rights. I've heard of random sightings of a few belugas and narwhals that survived under the Arctic ice, but there probably aren't enough for a sustainable gene pool. I know there are still a few intact pods of orcas, but with pollution levels the way they are, and less fish than an Arizona swimming pool, I wouldn't be too optimistic about their odds. Even if Mama Nature does give those killers some kind of reprieve, adapt them like she did with some of the dinosaurs, the gentle giants are gone forever. Kinda like that movie *Oh God* where the All Mighty challenges Man to try and make a mackerel from scratch. "You can't," he says, and unless some genetic archivist got in there ahead of the torpedoes, you also can't make a California gray.

[The sun dips below the horizon. Michael sighs.]

So the next time someone tries to tell you about how the true losses of this war are "our innocence" or "part of our humanity" . . .

[He spits into the water.]

Whatever, bro. Tell it to the whales.

❦

DENVER, COLORADO, USA

[Todd Wainio walks me to the train, savoring the 100 percent tobacco Cuban cigarettes I've bought him as a parting gift.]

Yeah, I lose it sometimes, for a few minutes, maybe an hour. Doctor Chandra told me it was cool though. He counsels right here at the VA. He told me once that it's a totally healthy thing, like little earthquakes releasing pressure off of a fault. He says anyone who's not having these "minor tremors" you really gotta watch out for.

It doesn't take much to set me off. Sometimes I'll smell something, or somebody's voice will sound really familiar. Last month at dinner, the radio was playing this song, I don't think it was about my war, I don't even think it was American. The accent and some of the terms were all different, but the chorus . . . "God help me, I was only nineteen."

[The chimes announce my train's departure. People begin boarding around us.]

Funny thing is, my most vivid memory kinda got turned into the national icon of the victory.

[He motions behind us to the giant mural.]

That was us, standing on the Jersey riverbank, watching the dawn over New York. We'd just got the word, it was VA Day. There was no cheering, no celebration. It just didn't seem real. Peace? What the hell did that mean? I'd been afraid for so long, fighting and killing, and waiting to die, that I guess I just accepted it as normal for the rest of my life. I thought it was a dream, sometimes it still feels like one, remembering that day, that sunrise over the Hero City.

ACKNOWLEDGMENTS

A special thank-you to my wife, Michelle, for all her love and support.

To Ed Victor, for starting it all.

To Steve Ross, Luke Dempsey, and the entire Crown Publishers team.

To T. M. for watching my back.

To Brad Graham at the *Washington Post*; Drs. Cohen, Whiteman, and Hayward; Professors Greenberger and Tongun; Rabbi Andy; Father Fraser; STS2SS Bordeaux (USN fmr); "B" and "E"; Jim; Jon; Julie; Jessie; Gregg; Honupo; and Dad, for "the human factor."

And a final thank-you to the three men whose inspiration made this book possible: Studs Terkel, the late General Sir John Hackett, and, of course, the genius and terror of George A. Romero.

I love you, Mom.

ALSO BY MAX BROOKS - AVAILABLE NOW

The Zombie Survival Guide

Complete Protection from the Living Dead
ISBN 9780715653746

THE BESTSELLING ZOMBIE SENSATION

This book is your key to survival against the hordes of the undead stalking you right now. Fully illustrated, it covers everything you need to know, from how to understand zombie behaviour to survival in any territory or terrain. It might just save your life.

'A bloody-minded, straight-laced manual for evading the grasp of the undead' *Time Out*

'A tome you start reading for fun and then at page 50 you go out and buy a machete just to be on the safe side' *New York Post*

Recorded Attacks

With illustrations by Ibraim Roberson

ISBN 9780715643051

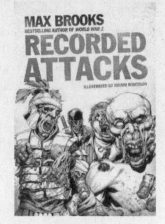

THOSE WHO DON'T LEARN FROM HISTORY ARE CONDEMNED TO REPEAT IT

From the Stone Age to the information age, the undead have threatened to engulf the human race. They're coming again. And they're hungry.

This is the graphic novel the fans demanded: major zombie attacks from the dawn of humanity, complete with eye-popping artwork. By immersing ourselves in past horror we may yet prevail over the coming outbreak... Don't wait for them to come to you!

'An absolute must have... Brooks infuses his writing with such precise detail and authenticity, one wonders if he knows something we don't' Simon Pegg on *World War Z*

'So meticulous and well researched that it's more scary than funny' *Esquire* on *The Zombie Survival Guide*